THE MISTRESS OF STERNWOOD GRANGE

Drawing up her silk panties luxuriously, she lingered at her thighs before snapping them into place. She thumbed the tight material where it snuggled into her cleft, and eased the bite of the amorous silk at her slit. On the bed, the naked man grunted.

'I distinctly said no peeping. No peeping at Nanny in her silk underwear. I know you want to. Every naughty boy does. But I shall spank your bare bottom if I catch you looking at Nanny putting on her suspender belt and stockings. Do you understand?'

'Yes, Nanny,' he said meekly.

THE MISTRESS
OF STERNWOOD
GRANGE

Arabella Knight

This book is a work of fiction.
In real life, make sure you practise safe sex.

First published in 1998 by
Nexus
332 Ladbroke Grove
London W10 5AH

Copyright © Arabella Knight 1998

The right of Arabella Knight to be identified as the Author
of this Work has been asserted by her in accordance with
the Copyright, Designs and Patents Act 1988.

Typeset by TW Typesetting, Plymouth, Devon

Printed and bound by
Cox & Wyman Ltd, Reading, Berks

ISBN 0 352 33241 7

One

Amanda tossed her blonde mane back and surrendered up her nakedness to the shower. Closing her eyes, she relished the sensation of the jet of water raking her breasts. The sluice rinsed the foaming gel she had palmed into her bosom, driving the bubbles down her deep cleavage to her pubis below. The scented foam gathered in the nest of her gold pubic fuzz. Parting her thighs, and crushing her bottom into the black tiles behind, Amanda felt the cascade hammering at her belly, hips and thighs. Soon, the bubbles were swirling at her feet then draining away between her toes. With them went some – but not all – of her anger. Only a week ago, just as the Canadian project had been declared a success, she had been downsized from the consultancy. The process had been brisk and humiliating. Denied access to her desk in the Millbank office block, she had been handed the last eight months of her working life in a bin liner and escorted to the door. The severance cheque had been big, but the lies had been bigger.

'My problem is, Amanda,' the project manager had explained, 'I just don't have the scope here to use your talents to their full potential.'

Blonde, too young, too successful. A threat, Amanda had decoded.

As the anger seeped out of her naked body, new sensations flooded in. Glimpsing the reflection of her breasts in the tiles opposite, Amanda raised her hands and cupped their wet flesh. The trapped nipples, already hardened by the punishing shower, thickened and puckered into pleasure buds. Amanda squeezed her breasts, splaying her thighs wider apart and grinding her buttocks into the tiles behind. Below the dripping pubic fringe, within the velvet curtains of labial flesh, a flame ignited. Her hands worked her breasts more fiercely, ruthlessly seeking to fuel the fire. Closing her eyes tightly, Amanda vowed never to be bullied, cheated or manipulated ever again. She had brains, spirit and a good track record. She had been too naive and trusting – but would be so no more. From now on, she determined, punishing her captive breasts and tormenting her nipples beween finger and thumb pincers, she would play tough. Tough, and dirty, if she had to. The smouldering heat between her thighs blazed, releasing droplets of molten lust. Her labia parted with a hungry smile, the flesh-lips glistening in their eagerness. Amanda guided her right hand down, palming her flat belly and caressing her thighs. The tip of her thumb sought out and found her clitoris. The flesh-thorn rose to salute the touch of her thumb as it stroked – with ever increasing pressure – until Amanda arched up on tiptoe, tensed for her climax.

Snap. The brass letter box rapped loudly against the white door of her Notting Hill flat as the post hit the Macedonian carpet below. In her shower, the water a mere teasing trickle now, Amanda's spinning brain pounced on the sound. Close to orgasm, and surrendering all sensations to it, she struggled to ignore the arrival of her mail and tried to concentrate on coming. But the sound had insinuated itself into her mind. Was it a reprieve? A belated recognition of the vital contribution she had made to the Canadian project? An invitation to return to her desk at Millbank? Thumbing herself mercilessly, the nude blonde pushed

2

these annoying distractions aside – but they remained to haunt her. With a snarl of frustration, she grabbed a towel and scampered out to the hall to pick up the letter. Retracing her damp footprints, she perched her bottom on the edge of a leather sofa, sinking her cheeks into the supple hide. The letter absorbed her for several minutes. She read it quickly then perused it carefully at length, penetrating the thicket of legal jargon. She was, the letter instructed, to contact the senders – a firm of solicitors – who had information to convey to her which could prove to be of considerable material advantage. Pruning the letter of its herewiths and thereunto foliage, she knew she had come into some serious gravy.

'Yippee.' Amanda wiggled her bare bottom into the leather, hugging her breasts excitedly. Aunt Clare had died nine weeks ago. It must be her will. Scanning the letter, Amanda picked up the phone and made an appointment for ten thirty that morning.

Rushing the remains of her cold coffee and toast, Amanda dashed into her bedroom. Picking up the abandoned towel, she patted her breasts, removing stray toast crumbs and sparkling droplets of water. The satin flesh bulged as she rubbed more vigorously, squashing her swollen curves. With the towel between her thighs, she dragged it gently up towards her belly, catching and inflaming her clitoris. The climax denied her in the shower began to well up implacably. Amanda glanced at her Mickey Mouse clock. Nine twenty-three. She just had time.

Kneeling, legs apart, she threaded a single black Fogal stocking between her thighs, clasping it tightly – one hand in front, the other stretched out behind. The sheer nylon caught in her cleft, biting deeply into the shadowed flesh between her heavy buttocks. Amanda dug her toes into the carpet as she guided the stocking expertly, allowing it to ravish the ribbon of velvety flesh between her cheeks. The tremors in her belly arrowed down like forked lightning as the taut nylon skimmed between her sticky labia, teasing her clitoris up into a peak of exquisite agony. The stretched nylon grew stained and glistened darkly as she plied it deftly. Her blue eyes deepened from cornflower to indigo as the Fogal rasped her clitoris with an increasingly savage tenderness. Amanda gasped. Her pumping hands became a blur. At the base of her belly, the inner muscled walls spasmed – she suddenly squealed aloud and tumbled forward, pressing her face into the carpet. Squeezing her thighs together, trapping the skein of black stocking between her labia, she rolled over on to her back. She was coming. As the orgasm surged within her tingling slit, she splayed her legs and arms. Spread-eagled, she surrendered and came, pounding her buttocks into the carpet as the gentle violence of her climax gripped her naked body.

Nine thirty-eight. No time for another shower. Amanda splashed her sticky flesh with cupped handfuls of rose water to mask the pungent tang and stepped into a pair of white cotton panties. Although early June, with all the promise of another hot London day, she knew the treachery of a sudden summer downpour. Skirt and blouse, she decided, playing safe. The white panties stretched across her plump bottom, the elastic hugging her trim waist amorously. Palming them smoothly into place, she plucked at the cleft and fingered the cotton away where it clung to her sticky labia. The brassiere was ice-blue, a lightweight silk half-cupped confection that bound her bosom with surprising firmness, disciplining the ripe breasts and controlling their weight within its strict bondage.

Standing in front of her full-length looking glass, Amanda studied her reflection. The hastily donned scanties of cotton and silk contrived to reveal more than conceal her curved charms. Full frontal: she appraised her slender legs sweeping up to the firm thighs, their

4

flesh honey-hued and satin soft. She patted her flat tummy and allowed her fingers to stray at the cleavage between her thrusting breasts. Through the pale-blue silk, she saw the bold, mulberry nipples. Turning, she glanced into the glass at her profile. The buttocks were pert, slightly heavy and invitingly rounded. The bosom was superb. Amanda twiddled with her left earlobe – a gesture common to her when contemplating. She perused her breasts, scrutinizing them closely – the half-cupped brassiere thrust them up deliciously.

Five to ten. Mickey Mouse looked as if he had just clapped his hands to hurry Amanda out of her narcissistic reverie. Her tangled mane of wet blonde hair was briskly towelled before submitting to twenty punishing strokes of her cherrywood hairbrush. Too hot for tights, and there was no time for the delicacy of stockings and a waspie suspender. Her breasts bulged in their half-cups as she stepped into a cream mini-shirt, and joggled as she struggled into a pale-blue shirt. Gold ear-studs. Cartier watch. One minute past ten. Amanda grabbed her sandals, purse and a cab in Pembridge Road and made it to the solicitors in Bird Cage Walk exactly on time.

The receptionist looked like she should have been in a girl-band. Reluctantly dragging herself away from her nail varnish, Cadbury's Flake and fashion glossy, she showed Amanda into a spacious, yet still cluttered, office. Hogarth prints, deed boxes, files, folders and dusty legal tomes littered the walls, shelves and desk tops in sober chaos. An elderly man looked up, peering quizzically at Amanda over gold-rimmed glasses.

'So good of you to come –' he peered at the letter Amanda had shown him '– Miss Silk.'

Amanda, suppressing her smile at the memory of her black Fogal stocking, merely nodded and looked across the desk expectantly.

Twelve minutes later, Amanda was none the wiser.

The solicitor mumbled and bumbled as he searched for documents, pored through closely typed paragraphs and fiddled endlessly with his glasses. Amanda, quick to think and fast to act, indulged his slow progress. Tuning into his old-fashioned charm and Victorian turn of speed, she settled down and waited patiently – wishing the polished seat of her wooden chair were a little kinder to her numbing buttocks. He rambled, in unconnected snatches of speed, about her late Aunt Clare's sound business sense, but was maddeningly vague on detail. Nothing concrete was forthcoming, but clearly Aunt Clare had been running some sort of lucrative enterprise right up to the end.

'A lady of considerable acumen,' he remarked, flicking open a file which Amanda saw contained the will.

'Am I –' she began.

The door opened abruptly and a stern-faced woman in her thirties walked in. Amanda looked up, noting the grey eyes, dark hair and the supple grace of the athletic figure. Dressed in severely tailored business style, the woman exuded efficiency, authority and a brisk sense of purpose.

'Thank you, Dobson. I will take it from here,' she said crisply. 'Amanda Silk? Celia Flaxstone. I am familiar with your late aunt's affairs. I'm afraid I wasn't available to greet you but I distinctly remember telling that wretched receptionist that I was to deal with you.'

Amanda noted the flash of anger in the grey eyes of Celia Flaxstone, though the thin smile on the lipstick-free mouth was sustained. A woman capable of wrath, Amanda thought. Mr Dobson ambled out as Celia Flaxstone commandeered his vacated chair.

'How much has Dobson told you?'

'Practically nothing.' Amanda shrugged, slightly startled by the ferocity of the tone.

'Practically?' echoed the woman, searching Amanda's face with her grey eyes.

'Only that she was successful in her enterprise.'

'I see.' The tone softened – more from relief than civility. 'To be brief. Your aunt had, in her later years, concentrated all her energies and assets in one enterprise. The details are immaterial –'

'A farm? Racehorses?' Amanda queried, remembering that Aunt Clare lived in the depths of Suffolk.

'She was moderately successful,' Celia Flaxstone continued imperturbably, ignoring Amanda's questions, 'but somewhat eccentric. There is a codicil in her will stipulating that any beneficiaries should refrain from inquiring into the nature of her business or indeed become in any manner whatsoever involved in it. I will add that in my –'

'This business. What is it?'

'I think I have made it clear that the codicil in her will precludes any disclosure of that nature. A little whim of an elderly lady, let us say, but which I, as her executrix, must honour and uphold. I suggest that –'

'How much did it make?'

'Difficult to say,' the solicitor countered suavely. 'I suggest that you leave it all to me. Your aunt was not all that successful. There is no fortune –'

'But Mr Dobson –'

'Dobson was being loyal. Age defending age.'

Amanda tugged at her earlobe, wishing that the gentle if maddeningly slow Mr Dobson were sitting opposite. She trusted him. She did not trust Celia Flaxstone. No, not distrust, exactly. But certainly dislike, Amanda reflected, twiddling with her ear.

'Just leave it to me, Miss Silk. I will tie up all the outstanding loose ends for you and after an initial lump sum, say ten or twelve thousand, I will arrange an annuity for you, possibly amounting to as much as three and a half thousand a year.'

Amanda suddenly resented being managed so efficiently, as if she were a troublesome child. The solicitor was now speaking rapidly, overriding the chance to query or question what seemed to be already settled and decided. Amanda could not recall giving her consent. It was as if Celia Flaxstone were determined to exclude Amanda from getting anywhere near to her late aunt's affairs.

'I will organise death duties and capital gains, of course, as part of my letters of administration.'

She's fobbing me off. She's fobbing me off with ten grand and a yearly handful of chicken feed, Amanda suddenly thought. Her business experience, and the MBA completed last year, had taught her all she needed to know about capital transfer tax. Besides, if her aunt's estate included buildings or land, the legacy would be much greater than any sum Celia Flaxstone had declared.

'Ascot or Epsom?'

Amanda looked blankly across the heap of files.

'The Season. Will you be going? The tennis starts at the Queen's Club tomorrow.'

I'm getting the thank-you-for-coming-in-to-see-me-and-now-it's-time-to-go treatment, Amanda realised, flushing slightly with resentment.

'The will,' she blurted out, not meaning to be so direct. 'May I see –'

'Probably still in the probate office,' Celia lied, closing the folder Mr Dobson had earlier managed to locate and begin to peruse. 'When in due course the document is forthcoming I will of course forward a copy to you.' The grey eyes narrowed, the resolute lips pursed. Celia Flaxstone stood up and held out her hand. The interview was clearly at an end, although Amanda was far from satisfied.

'Nice little windfall, and pocket money to follow. Provided the process is uninterrupted.'

Amanda sensed she was being warned off.

'Best keep these things uncomplicated,' the solicitor purred.

Celia's grey eyes met Amanda's blue gaze over the desk top. They shook hands perfunctorily, though Amanda sensed the strength in the solicitor's firm grip. Amanda knew that the concluding words had been a subtle threat. Accept what I tell you – or else risk delay, perhaps risk everything. With this stern advice ringing in her ears, Amanda was escorted to the front door. It closed behind her and, to her surprise, Amanda heard the latch click and a bolt being drawn.

Blinded by the late-morning sun, Amanda paused, resting her hand on the black iron railings. They were hot. Stung into alertness, she felt her anger rising. She had, she knew, been efficiently managed by Celia Flaxstone, who was even now probably laughing at how she had effectively dealt with the dizzy young blonde who had come in hope of a fortune. Turning, she remembered the sound of the front door being locked and bolted. Amanda felt a blaze of angry resentment surging up within her. She would go straight back in there, she decided, and confront the capable Celia Flaxstone. Undaunted by the stern authority of the dominant woman, Amanda resolved to demand to see the will.

It started to rain. Preoccupied with her resentment of Celia, Amanda had not noticed the dark clouds gather to eclipse the sun over central London. The big spots of summer rain fell sporadically at first, but soon her bosom was damp, the ice-blue material of her blouse clinging to her swollen breasts. She skipped down the five stone steps, along the pavement then around the side of the solicitor's office – a converted Georgian town house. She went down the narrow alley, threaded past a wheely bin and emerged into a postage-stamp-sized rear garden. A pair of French windows, open, would lead her back into the receptionist's office, she calculated. Amanda approached, no real plan of action formed, cowering now in the steady deluge.

'But I forgot –'

'I told you twice. Amanda Silk was not to be seen until I was available,' the harsh voice replied, cutting off the apologetic – almost tearful – receptionist.

Amanda paused, keeping carefully out of sight.

'I'm sorry –'

'You shall be, girl. Forgetfulness can be easily remedied, though. I am going to give you something you'll remember. Bend over. Across the desk. Quickly, girl.'

Amanda's blue eyes widened as she inched closer to the glass, spellbound by what she thought – but could hardly believe – she had just heard. She flinched as the glass doors were suddenly closed shut against the rain, leaving her unable to overhear any more. Pressing her breasts into the wisteria, at which her grazed nipples peaked up in protest, she sidled towards the large pane. Through its spattered glass, she peered in. The receptionist was bending over her desk, the bottle of nail varnish and half-eaten Flake crushed beneath her breasts. Amanda saw the varnished nails of the girl's splayed fingers spangling under the glare of the desk lamp. Celia Flaxstone, her back to the French windows, had already dragged the girl's skirt up over her hips and was now jerking down a pair of tiny black panties. The solicitor had grasped the elastic in her fist and her knuckles dimpled the soft swell of the girl's buttocks as they were bared. The panties were left in a restricting band halfway down the thighs, biting into the flesh that they bound.

Amanda's throat tightened and her pulse raced as she watched the solicitor dominantly palming the bare bottom she was about to punish. Words were being exchanged – stern admonishment from the chastiser, penitent mumbling from the lips of the girl – but Amanda could not make out what was being said. She strained to understand the muffled tones, horrified

10

yet fascinated by the scene that met her gaze. The straightened index finger hovering above the naked buttocks tapped the left cheek imperiously. Amanda knew that the talking was concluded – and that the beating was about to begin.

It was incredible. Here, now, in Bird Cage Walk, where London at noon thronged with taxis, tourists and theatre-ticket touts, a bare-bottomed girl was about to be harshly disciplined.

Amanda felt her slit softening with sticky warmth as, through the glass, she saw Celia Flaxstone stoop, retrieve a wooden hairbrush from the bottom desk drawer, then slide the drawer shut with a thrust of her thigh. Weighing the heavy brush meditatively, she thumbed the soft bristles as the polished pearwood back kissed her open palm. Seconds later, the solicitor planted her feet apart and unbuttoned the cuff of her right sleeve. Loosened, the sleeve was drawn back up to the elbow. The slender fingers gripping the hairbrush tightened around the handle. The brush swept upward, pausing at shoulder height. Across the desk, the bare buttocks clenched, fearful of the impending stroke.

Amanda heard both the sharp sound of hard wood against soft flesh and the yelp of anguish. Twice, in blistering succession, the hairbrush swiped down across the upturned buttocks, reddening their peach tones instantly. The naked cheeks joggled beneath each fierce stroke.

Amanda crushed her rebellious nipples into the wisteria, dragging her bosom against the tangled foliage to fuel the burning delight. Dry mouthed, wide-eyed and with a tingling slit quite wet from her excitement, she stared into the office as though hypnotised. Celia Flaxstone had administered nine slicing swipes of the brush across the scarlet bottom. She now inverted the brush to stroke the bristles across the punished cheeks. Despite the black panties binding her lower thighs, the

11

girl across the desk wriggled and writhed, her white sandals threshing the empty air behind her. Celia, utterly in control, reached down and pinned the squirming receptionist firmly by the nape of her neck. Amanda slipped her hand under her mini-skirt and thumbed her clitoris as she watched the varnished nails scrabbling to grip the desk top. She thumbed more frantically as she watched the dominant chastiser ravish the cleft between the hot cheeks with downward strokes of the bristles. Amanda started to come: she must not, she realised. She winced as she grazed her knees against the wall, desperately trying to deny herself the orgasm she burned for. No, not here, not now. Across the desk, as the bristles licked at her sticky innermost flesh, the receptionist pressed her face on to the polished wood, planting a red lipsticked kiss into the reflection of her own mouth as her clenched fists drummed frantically.

'Pull your panties up, girl, and get back to work. I want that will retyped before it is sent off to the Silk girl,' Celia Flaxstone barked, using the hairbrush fastidiously now to sweep an offending speck from her shoulder.

Retyped. Amanda, her brain a riot of confusion, grasped that single word – and glimpsed the enormous meaning it contained. She turned and scurried away, her heart suddenly hammering as she collided with – but caught and steadied with her trembling hands – a wheely bin.

Cooler, though neither calmer nor more collected, Amanda slipped into the powder room and went straight into a cubicle. Seconds later, with her mini-skirt around her hips, and one outstretched arm against the wall to support her quivering body, she yanked down her damp panties and fingered herself furiously. Crack, crack, crack: summoning up each searing stroke, Amanda relived the delicious display of dominance and

12

discipline she had witnessed minutes before. Crack. At the seventh remembered stroke of polished wood across writhing buttocks, her knees buckled. Crack. At the eighth, her belly dissolved, the muscled walls shuddering as they spasmed. Crack. Behind closed eyes she saw the hot bottom receive the ninth – and came loudly.

Emerging from the cubicle, Amanda was greeted by the wide-eyed stare of three young women. Preening themselves for lunch, they had overheard her orgasm. They stood, open-mouthed, lipsticks frozen in midair. Amanda rinsed her hands, tossed her blonde hair and strode out into the busy restaurant.

London was lunching. The Cypriot manager, a wily old fox, placed the single blonde in the blue blouse on a banquette in the window. A lamb to pull in the expense-account wolves passing by. Amanda ordered lemon chicken and a Sea Breeze. Gazing out of the window as she nibbled at a bread stick, she suddenly realised that she could just see, sixty yards away on the opposite side of the street, the solicitor's office. It had stopped raining. At the next table, the three pretty young lambs from the powder room chain-smoked through their first bottle of Chardonnay as they pretended to ignore the wolves at the window. From time to time they would glance at Amanda. Looking up, she saw the curiosity in their eyes develop into a keen interest. Later, tackling her mango water-ice, Amanda tried to shut out the braying laughter around her. Three wolves had joined the three lambs at their table – the Cypriot knew his stuff – and champagne had been ordered. Amanda needed to concentrate.

Her options were entirely different now, she realised. It was no longer a matter of simply returning to confront Celia Flaxstone about the will. Two significant things had altered all that. The words 'bend over' and 'retyped'. Celia Flaxstone was a force to be reckoned with. That much Amanda fully appreciated. How to do

13

so, she was not at all certain. Admitting her fear of the stern solicitor, Amanda scraped her spoon across her empty dish. Confrontation was completely out of the question. The memory of Celia Flaxstone burned as brightly in her mind as those strokes of the hard wooden hairbrush had burned that girl's bare bottom. No, she decided, remembering some of the tricks her MBA had taught her. Lateral thinking was called for. Subterfuge.

She paid her bill but lingered over coffee. Before it had gone cold, Amanda saw what she had hoped to see: Celia Flaxstone emerging from the doorway, descending the stone steps into Bird Cage Walk and hailing a cab. Three minutes later – Amanda had calculated for five – the receptionist skipped down the pavement, yogurt and Walkman in hand, heading no doubt for St James's Park. The hairbrush had not, Amanda noted, taken the wiggle from her pert walk.

She left the restaurant, detoured to buy a Hermes scarf and a pair of Raybans, and mounted the steps once more. Inside, closing the door carefully, she stood by the receptionist's desk, listening intently. She heard the ragged applause from the Oval as Atherton swiped a six. Mr Dobson was listening to the cricket. But where? Three oak doors were ajar, because of the heat. The middle office was the one where the will awaited her curiosity. Amanda tiptoed to the door on her left. Peering in, she smiled as she saw Mr Dobson sipping his pale sherry. Good. The Hermes scarf and Raybans – together with her cover story of buying a farmhouse in Chiantishire and needing guidance on Italian property laws – would not be necessary if she was quick.

Inside the middle office, her search for the will proved fruitless. Damn. She could not risk staying too long, or making too much noise. At the Oval, the crowd roared as Atherton was dropped at the slips. Amanda froze, relaxing as she heard the cork to the sherry bottle pop softly. Defeated, she sighed and resigned herself to failure. Out by the receptionist's desk, she paused, fingering the desk across which the girl had been punished. Remembering the wood spanking across bare buttocks, Amanda opened the drawer and peeped at the cruel brush. Fingering it slowly, her nostrils caught the unmistakeable tang of excitement and arousal. In the paper bin, she spotted the damp tissues. The receptionist had dried herself after the punishment, tossing the tissues away with the remains of her Cadbury's Flake. Amanda smiled, thrilled to know another's intimate secrets. Then she saw the will. Of course, she realised. Celia Flaxstone's last words were to have the will retyped. As Atherton skied another improbable six, Amanda xeroxed the four-page original and made her exit unobserved.

Two days later, with London sweltering under a pitiless sun, Amanda sat naked in front of a large electric fan. It whipped up strands of her blonde mane, the fine hair lashing her cheeks. It whipped up the corners of the pages set out in two piles before her. Amanda ignored her hair but pinned the rippling pages down with her thumbs. Drawing her knees up to her breasts, her frown of concentration deepened as she studied the contents before her. The pages under her left thumb were from Celia Flaxstone, supposedly a copy of her late aunt's will. The codicil preventing Amanda from making any inquiries into her aunt's affairs was clearly typed before the date and spidery signature. The pages under her right thumb were those she had xeroxed from the original will. They contained several references to her aunt's enterprises – hereafter known as 'the business' – but no codicil.

'Gotcha,' Amanda whispered, peeling her perspiring breasts away from her knees and, splaying her thighs as she swivelled towards the electric fan, surrendered her hot slit to its cool zephyrs. It was already in the eighties, and the fan proved insufficient. Scampering into the kitchen, she raided a bottle of Krug from the fridge. Squatting back down before the fan, she raised a toast to Aunt Clare and then hugged the chilled Krug between her thighs, allowing her labial lips to kiss the dark-green glass.

It was only after she had put the phone down that she was pleased she had decided to use the kiosk. Already, inquisitive fingers at the other end of the line would be jabbing at the 1471 buttons to trace her call. Using the phone in Westbourne Park Road, Amanda had dialled one of the two Suffolk numbers scribbled in the margin of the original will. Not her aunt's home number, which she recognised. The other one.

'Sternwood Grange?' she asked, using the only clue buried in the four pages she had xeroxed.

'Who is calling?' a cautious voice countered, giving nothing away.

Ignoring this, Amanda asked for her aunt by name.

Amanda was in turn ignored. 'Who is calling?' the voice repeated.

Amanda echoed her request to speak with her aunt. A safe gambit, she thought. It was checked.

'One moment please.' Amanda was being redirected.

As she listened to the extension ring, she fed another pound into the box. The line went absolutely dead as the secrecy button was applied. There was a click. She heard breathing.

'Sternwood Grange?' Amanda asked.

'How did you come by this number?' a different voice countered politely.

Amanda pressed on, ducking the challenge and asking for her aunt, carefully avoiding any claim to kinship.

'This number is ex-directory. Who are you, please, and how did you get this –'

Amanda, her hands now wet from the humidity of the phone box, hung up.

The weekend brought the inevitable thunderstorm and, with it, a slim report from the agency Amanda had instructed to investigate Sternwood Grange. The agency had been thorough but the facts were meagre. Confirming the address and ex-directory number, the report set out its findings in two brief paragraphs. Amanda read them over and over again. Sternwood Grange had been acquired by her aunt six years ago. Not listed as either a country club or a private hotel, it operated as something of an exclusive retreat for the very privileged. Special Branch had been known to escort some of the more illustrious visitors. Set in deep isolation in a forgotten pocket of rural Suffolk, it had a heli-pad, but otherwise access was severely restricted and strict privacy maintained. It was still a going concern, Amanda read, but the agency could not estimate its worth or value, drawing a blank after persuing a financial trail that expired in an offshore company.

One detail detained her. The female staff of ten were not recruited locally but were young women rescued from the wrath of Knightsbridge and Mayfair magistrates courts. Aunt Clare, Amanda mused, must have been running some eccentric charitable sideline, saving girls already in jeopardy from ending up on the game.

As the thunder cleared over west London, so did her resolve. The next step was obvious. Contact Celia Flaxstone, accept her terms. Then get down to Sternwood Grange, in disguise. Seek work there, as a maid, perhaps. Just for a week or two, giving Amanda the chance to work out exactly how much this exclusive retreat generated and how much her late aunt's legacy was really worth.

* * *

Amanda settled back into the first-class comfort of the 15.05 as the train pulled out of Liverpool Street and nosed its way out across north-east London. Gazing out at the winking beacon on top of Canary Wharf, she caught a glimpse of her reflection in the carriage window. Her blonde mane was now a brunette bob, the cut severely chic. She grinned at the transformation. She had shopped in the Portobello Road for the most tarty outfit, dumped the Cartier and worked out a plausible cover. Things had got a bit hot at the escort agency, she would say. The police had visited, so had the VAT men. Amanda – Mandy from now on – needed to go to ground for a couple of weeks. She had heard through the other girls about this place. Sternwood Grange, a place where a girl could seek work and refuge.

She dozed, lulled by the rhythm of the wheels. The train journey reminded her of going back to boarding school eight or nine years ago. Sleeping fitfully, she dreamed of those schoolgirl days – and nights.

Days spent on the hockey pitch, serge knickers biting into her buttocks as, below the hem of her short pleated skirt, her naked legs goose-pimpled in the autumn chill. The shrill blast of a whistle, the patter of pumps, the squeals of excitement, the sudden rush of play. Her breasts bouncing loosely beneath her skimpy hockey vest, she would sweep up the wing. Off-side. Pausing to finger the annoying serge knickers from her cleft, she would plant her feet apart, gripping the hockey stick for a bully-off. A furious tackle: two panting, sweating girls. A collision thigh to thigh, buttock to buttock, with a spirited defender. Later, in the steaming showers, naked girls would shriek and giggle as towels were flicked across bare bottoms, bosoms were squeezed and nipples pinched, and old scores settled as new 'crushes' began. Sometimes, the captain of prefects would prowl the changing rooms, cane in hand. The girl who had fouled so blatantly would be called out of the steam and sternly instructed to bend over. Instantly surrounded by a dozen naked, glistening girls who shivered with excitement, the bare-bottomed miscreant would be slowly, searchingly caned.

Then there were the nights. Murmuring contentedly in her dream, Amanda recaptured delicious memories of her boarding-school nights. The scramble for bed to avoid the swish of a slipper or sterner crack of a wooden paddle across upturned, defenceless young bottoms as the dorm senior patrolled between the beds. Lights out. Furtive rustlings as pubescent maidenhood pushed away thoughts of Latin unseens and the French pluperfect and secretly studied more urgent texts: fingers blindly reading the warm flesh between parted thighs. Lights on, abruptly. The dorm senior back to uncover and punish anything untoward. Forbidden literature, smuggled tuck, a trace of lipstick or any infringement of the spartan rules would merit instant chastisement. Amanda recalled spankings as discipline was dispensed. Lights out. Muffled sobbing from the hot-bottomed girl three beds along. Snuggling down into her starched sheets, Amanda would kindle her burning delight, her fingers busy at her hot slit.

The train hurtled through Manningtree. Amanda stirred sleepily and opened one eye. Startled by her silver leather jacket reflected by the tinted glass at her shoulder, she smiled and woke up. She was beginning a little adventure, an adventure in which she would outwit Celia Flaxstone and defend not only her late aunt's wishes but her true inheritance.

Aunt Clare. Amanda resumed her interrupted sleep. Aunt Clare. The rhythm of the train repeated the name, insinuating it into Amanda's dreams. She had not seen Aunt Clare since her eighteenth birthday. What a day to remember. Aunt Clare had taught Amanda at her knee – and across it – passing on her shrewd business acumen. She had sold the shares her aunt had given her for her seventeenth just before her eighteenth, the cash going on an extravagant caprice from Hyper Hyper for just under a thousand pounds. Asked for an explanation, Amanda had lied. Aunt Clare had been cross, very, very, cross. I'm too big to be spanked, thank goodness, and she's too old to do it, Amanda had thought. As the stern sermon had come to a crisp conclusion, her aunt had taken the birthday blonde up from the drawing room to a bedroom above. A surprise, Amanda had thought gleefully. Upstairs, Aunt Clare's hand had pressed the bell.

'I am going to punish you,' Aunt Clare had declared.

Amanda laughed in reply. 'You're too old,' she had mocked, repeating her earlier thoughts. 'And I'm too big –'

'For your boots, young lady. Come in.'

Answering her aunt's command, the new housekeeper stepped into the bedroom. 'Madam?'

A beautiful young woman with large brown eyes. In her early thirties, she proved too strong for the younger girl to resist. Amanda was stretched across the bed, and her bottom was bared and prepared for punishment. Using the belt of the dress that had caused all the problems – crafted from supple pale-yellow leather – the athletic housekeeper had lashed Amanda as instructed.

'Eighteen strokes,' Aunt Clare had ordered. 'One for each vain, foolish year.'

Cracking loudly and snapping harshly, the leather barked down across her reddening bottom. The hide proved painfully pliant, the young housekeeper deceptively strong.

'Again,' Aunt Clare had thundered, stretching out her hand to pin her squealing niece down by her shoulder into the duvet. 'Again.'

'No –' Amanda sat bolt upright.

'Ticket please, miss,' a uniformed man said, shaking

Amanda's shoulder firmly to wake the sleeping blonde. 'Thank you, miss. Change at Ipswich.'

Amanda drew several lingering glances as she waited for the queue at the coffee stall to shorten. The train to Saxmundham rattled in just as she asked for a large unsugared black. She made her train with seconds to spare. The summer countryside had not changed. It was exactly as Amanda remembered it when visiting her aunt. Deeply wooded acres opening out into large grain fields, the pale gold of June splashed with the scarlet of poppies.

She alighted at Saxmundham and almost made the mistake of giving her late aunt's address to the taximan.

'Sternwood Grange,' she remembered, just in time.

'You sure?' he replied, the country vowels slow and almost slurred.

Amanda, conscious of her tarty appearance, flushed.

'Cost you. It's over fifteen miles away.' He eyed her shrewdly. 'Well off the beaten track.' He got out of his taxi to take her bag, his frown showing his reluctance.

She got in, showing him a couple of tenners.

Sternwood Grange was tucked away in the heart of a densely wooded estate. Standing in two acres of neglected grounds, it was an early-Elizabethan pile which successive generations had both added to and improved. It boasted lawns which rabbits had commandeered for themselves, an overgrown terrace, a dilapidated tennis court and an overall air of faded grandeur. No gardener had plied a trowel or pushed a mower here for at least six years, probably from the time my aunt acquired the place, Amanda thought as she walked the last hundred yards from the taxi up the weed-choked drive to the front door.

A neatly uniformed, heavily breasted maid looked surprised to find Amanda on the doorstep. Reluctantly, she showed Amanda into the spacious hall. Amanda noted the lavish furnishings, ranging from gilded baroque to exquisite late Adam. The maid took her downstairs and disappeared into the housekeeper's office, once the preserve of butlers who used it for their pantry.

'Yes?' the housekeeper inquired briskly, dismissing the maid and appraising Amanda's tarty clothes.

Amanda's heart stood still for a few seconds, then pounded rapidly against her ribs. It was Aunt Clare's housekeeper – the new one – the one who had been instructed to lash Amanda's birthday bottom with the supple leather belt.

'Well?' the housekeeper insisted crisply.

She won't remember me. We only met once – memorably – and then she saw more of my bottom than my face, Amanda calculated, grateful for her disguise. Tears, she suddenly thought, might help. She let them flow, managing to sob gently. The housekeeper thawed and took the weeping visitor into her office. Strong tea was supplied from a blue and white pot. Sipping slowly, Amanda allowed herself to recover her poise.

'You are in trouble?' the housekeeper asked gently, her brown eyes softening as they drank in the young girl's beauty.

Amanda took a deep breath and told her prepared tale.

'And who was it you said told you of Sternwood Grange?'

Amanda hadn't. 'Foxie, a girl I know. That was her working name.' Amanda decided to take a risk. She remembered the curious item about staff recruitment mentioned in the agency's report. 'She said some solicitor fixed it up for her.'

The housekeeper repressed a knowing smile. Amanda sensed that the risk had paid off.

After answering a few more questions which she had

carefully anticipated, Amanda knew she was home and dry.

'You may stay here on a trial basis for three weeks. The work is hard and the rules are very strict. And must be obeyed. And we will have to do something about those clothes, of course.'

Miss Partridge, the housekeeper, briefly outlined what Amanda's duties as a maid would entail, warning her that the residents' privacy must be observed at all times. Amanda was forbidden to approach or disturb them, or even go upstairs near their quarters, until given permission.

'Who knows? If you work hard and obey the rules, we might promote you from maid to angel.'

'Angel?'

'They started out, like you, as maids, but progressed. They are devoted to the personal needs of our residents.'

'You do pamper them,' Amanda observed.

'They pay,' was the brief reply.

After an early supper of poached eggs, Amanda was shown to her room up in the rambling attic. They used the back staircase, bypassing the main house entirely.

'Who owns Sternwood Grange? It's beautiful, isn't it?' Amanda added hastily, not wishing to appear too inquisitive.

Miss Partridge said rather vaguely that it was in trust.

'I will see you first thing in the morning, Mandy,' the housekeeper said, drawing the curtains together and switching on the dim light.

'Thank you,' Amanda replied, appalled at her dismal room. 'What –'

'No more questions for tonight, Mandy,' Miss Partridge interrupted. 'I've still got lots to do. The residents can be very demanding and the maids, I fear, are not always up to scratch. I hope you prove to be both willing and obedient.'

'Oh, I will.'

'There are a few simple but absolute rules the maids must observe. The only one you must obey tonight is not to leave your room. Understand?'

Amanda nodded.

'Goodnight.'

The door closed, leaving Amanda feeling forlorn in her drab surroundings. She sat down on her narrow bed and reflected. The food was good, if sparse – she was going to miss raiding her fridge for wine and treats – and she was going to get a pert maid's uniform, a secret fantasy she had never dared to indulge. She giggled naughtily. Most of all, a chance to work out the true worth of her legacy. This place must be worth a fortune, she must get to work at once. How many residents were there? How long did they stay? How much did they pay?

Time for bed. Tomorrow promised to be a busy day. No longer Amanda Silk, sophisticated business consultant, bubbling blonde girl about town – she was Mandy, Mandy the maid.

Naked, she slipped into bed. The late sunset fingered her bedroom with pinkish-gold light. She hugged her breasts happily at both the nightingale in the violet sky outside and at the success of her subterfuge which had launched her campaign.

Spank. Spank. Spank.

Mandy sat up in her narrow bed, propping herself on her elbows.

Spank. Spank. A smothered squeal followed, and was followed in turn by the sound of a bare bottom suffering two more crisp spanks. The punishment was being administered next door. Probably two maids quarrelling. Spank. Spank. Mandy strained to listen. Punishment? Or fierce love play? The squeals of protest suggested punishment. The plaster wall was thin. Through it, she heard the stern tones of the chastiser admonishing the chastised. The words were obscured by

24

the wall between them but Mandy recognised the strictness in the timbre. A pause. A muffled sob. Spank. Spank.

Thrilling to the sounds of flesh upon flesh, the curved palm cracking down across rounded cheeks, Mandy kicked down her top sheet and parted her thighs. In the dying rays of the setting sun which bathed her skin in a lemon light, she prised her sticky labia apart and gently but firmly slid two straightened fingers into her tight slit, using the tip of her thumb to tease out and torment her clitoris. Spank. Spank. The bare buttocks next door were certainly getting it hot and strong. It was, it sounded to the eavesdropping nude, a ferocious punishment. Spank. Spank. The girl's bottom must surely be ablaze by now. Squeezing her buttocks together, Mandy worked her fingers and thumb with cunning expertise. Spank. Spank. Closing her eyes, she imagined the naked bottom deepening from scalding pink to searing crimson. Spank. Spank. Faster and faster, she pleasured her wet flesh until with a suppressed gasp she arched up, her buttocks clear of her bed, and came. Squashing her breasts, punishing her erect nipples with sticky fingers, she orgasmed heavily. Lowering her hips, she ground her bottom into the bed, causing the headboard to rock and bump against the wall.

Her bedroom door opened and swung wide. Mandy jumped and whipped round, horrified at the intrusion. Staring with unfocused eyes, her face flushed, she grunted thickly. Miss Partridge filled the doorway, rolling down the sleeve of her spanking arm and buttoning the cuff deftly.

'I am so glad to find you in bed,' the housekeeper said softly. 'I thought I heard a noise.'

Mandy, appalled at being discovered naked and in orgasm, scrabbled for her sheet and drew it over her belly and breasts.

'Had you disobeyed me, I would have had to give you the same as I gave the girl next door. Understand?'

Mandy nodded meekly.

'The rules here at Sternwood Grange must be strictly obeyed. I see,' the brown-eyed housekeeper said in a softer voice, perusing Mandy candidly, 'that you have just been amusing yourself. An innocent diversion, no doubt but –' her voice hardened '– if the sheet is stained, you will find two pounds deducted from your wages to cover the costs of the laundry bill. Goodnight.'

Two

Two turtle doves murmuring at her window woke
Mandy just as a hand tapped on her door. Stung by the
memory of Miss Partridge's brusque intrusion last night
– and blushing furiously at being discovered naked and
enjoying her climax – Mandy appreciated the courtesy
of the tapping at her door.

'Mandy. Wake up,' a voice whispered urgently.

'Come in.'

It was the maid who had opened the front door on
her arrival at Sternwood Grange, a large cup of coffee
balanced in her hand. 'Better drink this up, then I'll get
you into your uniform. We're late.'

Dropping the sheet from her bosom, Mandy stretched
out to take the large cup. The maid's eyes widened as
she glimpsed Mandy's breasts: as ripely firm, if not as
heavily fleshed, as her own. Mandy perused the maid.
She was dressed in a green silk mini-kimono. Mandy
knew from the clinging silk that the girl was naked
underneath. The maid gave her name and smiled.

'Thanks, Sophie,' Mandy said sleepily. She was still
drowsy from the deep sleep induced by the heavy
country air.

Sophie padded across to the window. Stretching up,
she parted the curtains, scattering the turtle doves.
Sunshine streamed in. Mandy blinked. Focusing in the
sudden light, she saw the reddened buttocks as the hem
of the mini-kimono inched up briefly to reveal the swell

27

of the cheeks. It was Sophie, she realised, who was being spanked last night.

'Finished?' Sophie encouraged.

Mandy drained the cup. It was freshly ground arabica. Dark, delicious and expensive.

'Come on,' Sophie said, taking the cup.

Next door, in Sophie's room, Mandy watched as the maid rinsed the cup out and hid it under her bed. Puzzled, she said nothing as she took her turn at the sink to splash her face. Cupping the cold water up to rinse away her sleep, she shivered as it spilled down on to her breasts. Sophie came to the rescue, patting the nipples gently with a soft towel. At the touch of the towel, Mandy remembered that she was naked. Turning to dry her eyes, she saw the mini-kimono being abandoned. Sophie was naked too.

'Panties, no bra. Regulations,' Sophie said, sheathing her spanked bottom in tight cotton after throwing a pair to Mandy.

Miss Partridge entered the room without knocking. The large brown eyes raked the pantied girls. 'Hurry along, the pair of you. It is already –' She paused, sniffing the air. 'Have you been drinking coffee?' she demanded, looking directly at Sophie.

'No, Miss Partridge.' Sophie blushed, twiddling with her elastic waistband nervously.

'I can distinctly smell coffee. Good coffee. Stolen, no doubt. Give me the cup, girl.'

'There isn't –'

'At once.'

Sophie's bottom bulged within the white panties as she bent down to retrieve the cup. Taking it, the housekeeper sniffed.

'Arabica. You should, if you must, stick to instant, Sophie. I will deduct five pounds from your wages and see you in my office at ten sharp. Four strokes.'

Sophie bowed her head.

28

'Now hurry up and get downstairs. Your duties await you.'

Miss Partridge went. Mandy broke the solemn silence. 'You were spanked last night, weren't you?'

'Orange juice.' Sophie grinned. 'I pinched some orange juice. Mind you,' she giggled, 'I laced it with champagne. A girl's got to have her buck's fizz.'

'Four strokes,' Mandy murmured. 'Does that mean –'

'The cane.'

'But you gave the coffee to me. It doesn't seem fair.' Approaching the mischievous maid, Mandy hugged her affectionately.

'She just likes my bottom,' Sophie laughed. 'Can't leave it alone. Come on, get dressed.' She carefully passed Mandy a blouse. 'Silk.'

Mandy's head jerked up, almost betraying her.

'Silk,' Sophie repeated. 'The blouse.'

Mandy blushed, angry with herself at the slip that could have exposed her.

'Hell to launder,' said Sophie.

Mandy's blush deepened, remembering the wet stain on her sheet last night.

'No bra?'

'Nope,' Sophie affirmed, buttoning down her blouse over her heavy breasts. Mandy was three buttons behind, delayed slightly by the sight of the dark nipples probing Sophie's silk. She sighed as her own breasts kissed the cool silk, her nipples peaking and tightening as she buttoned it firmly over the swell of her bosom. Her brain whirled with urgent questions. How often did the brown-eyed housekeeper punish the maids? How? Spanking, strap or whippy bamboo cane? When would it be Mandy's turn to bare her cheeks, bend over and surrender her bottom to the impending pain?

'She'll get you before sunset,' Sophie said drily.

Mandy looked up, startled by the accuracy of the other maid's mind-reading prowess.

'I wasn't –'

'Yes, you were. When will it be my turn, you were wondering. Don't worry. It can be divine,' Sophie whispered, busy with her cuffs. 'When you go across Miss Partridge's knee, your bottom is hers, utterly and absolutely. Know what I mean?'

Mandy busied herself with her cuffs, avoiding Sophie's searching gaze.

'Cute, eh?' Sophie grinned, offering Mandy a black velvet pleated skirt. 'There's a starched apron to go with it.'

They wrapped their thighs with the dark velvet skirts and zipped them up in unison.

'Quick, come on.'

'No stockings?' Mandy asked.

'White ankle socks and white pumps downstairs in the maids' room. Here, I'll do that.'

Mandy was struggling with her apron. Turning, she offered the linen tabs to Sophie. Feeling the heavy breasts crushing into her, Mandy inched back a deliberate fraction, colliding her buttocks into Sophie's thighs. The light touch of the other girl's fingers around her hips as the apron was deftly tied and expertly adjusted sent tiny spiders of delight scurrying down her spine.

'You'll do for me.' The words came on sweet breath into her ear. Mandy closed her eyes and trembled, almost fainting with sudden delight as Sophie's lips brushed the nape of her neck. Lick me, Mandy thought, her hunger for Sophie's mouth upon her bare flesh growing ravenous. Lick me. Let me feel your wet tongue.

Smack. Mandy opened her big blue eyes wide.

'Time to go,' Sophie said in a husky voice, lowering Mandy's pleated skirt down over the buttock she had just slapped. 'We'll really catch it from Erica if we are late.'

* * *

Erica, the senior maid who deputised for Miss Partridge – and who was permitted to punish the maids beneath her – was a slender thirty-year-old with cropped blonde hair and ever vigilant eyes. She nodded silently to Mandy and grasped the new maid's hands firmly.

'Nails?'

They were clean and passed her close scrutiny.

'And don't let me see you in a soiled uniform, lipstick or make-up.'

Mandy, chastened, stood smartly to attention as Erica detailed her tasks for the morning.

'You know that you must not disturb the residents?'

Mandy nodded.

'Get to work,' Erica ordered, leaving to supervise the two maids busy at the Agas in the other, larger kitchen, cooking the residents' breakfasts.

Sophie and Mandy prepared the trays. Like an undercover auditor, Mandy made a mental note of everything, estimating costs, outgoings and turnover. She was amazed to see solid-silver wine buckets, brimming with ice and bearing vintage champagne, going upstairs. From the box of empty bottles from last night's dinner, she knew that the residents were not claret-shy, the stained labels revealing a penchant for the Bordeaux *grands crus*. The cellar must be cavernous. Nine trays were set, soon to be laden with tempting delicacies. Other maids, mere fleeting shadows in the corner of Mandy's eye, skipped in and out to whisk them upstairs.

'They only go as far as the locked doors,' Sophie explained. 'The angels take over from there.'

The basement kitchens were vast. Apart from the large, low-ceilinged areas, there was a pantry, a cold room, two larders and a still room. Mandy was confused and stuck close to Sophie. In the middle kitchen, where exposed beams spoke of their Eliza-bethan origins, the equipment was hi-tech, state of the

31

art. As good and as expensive as any behind the scenes in a top London restaurant like L'Escargot or Le Pont de la Tour.

'Some of the maids went to finishing school. Cordon bleu trained.'

Mandy had wondered at the provenance of the Bradenham ham in sherry sauce, quenelles of sole, quails eggs and *fois gras blinis* flowing from the inner kitchen.

'We don't fare so well,' Sophie whispered grimly, avoiding Erica's unblinking eye.

Three large cream-coloured American fridgidaires were lined up against the whitewashed wall of the smaller of the three connected kitchens.

'More champagne?' Mandy asked, nodding at them.

'Orchids. Orchids and roses,' Sophie replied. 'Take a look.' Opening the doors, she gave Mandy a glimpse of a perfumed profusion of fresh flowers stacked up neatly inside.

'But the gardens are neglected –'

'All this –' Sophie swept her hands around, encompassing delicious foods, wines and flowers '– comes at night, when we are asleep. The vans bring it all down from London, twice a week. I've heard them unloading and loading.'

'Loading?'

'Laundry, and the rubbish bags. Sternwood Grange has no real contact with the outside world. We don't even get to use the phone. It's locked away.'

Mandy felt a pang – not of fear or dismay – just a sudden pang of doubt. Had she been foolish to rush headlong into this enterprise, like a fly darting into a sticky web? She tugged at the lobe of her left ear.

'Don't daydream, girl. Get busy,' Erica rasped, tapping her open palm with a wooden spoon.

The first of the breakfast trays had started to return. Sophie and Mandy washed up, handling the Sèvres porcelain carefully, arms elbow deep in the prickling suds. Peering closer at what she thought to be a coat of arms as it emerged beneath a smear of sherry sauce, Mandy discerned a crop of sprouting bamboo canes. The pale-gold wands swayed with supple grace, pliant and pliable and ripe for harvest.

'Sugar canes. West Indies? Or a Far Eastern connection. Malaya perhaps?' Mandy asked.

'Not exactly,' was all Sophie said in enigmatic reply. Adding, 'Though many find the bamboo to be the sweetest wood of all.'

As she dried each plate, cup and saucer, and stacked them with a layer of soft tissue in between, Mandy revised her audit, adding a nought to her initial figure of the potential value of Sternwood Grange.

'Breakfast,' one of the maids called.

After the delicacies consumed upstairs, Mandy was disappointed to sit down at the scrubbed pine table to weak tea, an apple and cold buttered toast.

'Stop talking,' Erica snapped at Mandy, who was trying to get acquainted with the other maids. 'Eat up. There's work to be done.'

Two angels came down and collected their breakfasts from the bottom oven of the Aga. Mandy envied their haddock. Her own repast was as meagre as it was brief.

'I want the entire kitchen floor swept, scrubbed and disinfected. An old place like this is bound to have mice. After that,' Erica continued, 'prepare the vegetables. Sophie, peas and asparagus. And you'd better do some broccoli too. You –' she addressed Mandy '– get those flowers into their vases, polish the wine glasses – they're Milan crystal, mind – and then prepare the lunch trays. Eight will suffice. One of the residents is departing by helicopter at eleven.'

'That means we have to keep away from the windows,' Sophie interpreted. 'Don't forget, we maids are not supposed to see the quality until we've been promoted to being angels.'

33

What windows, Mandy thought ruefully, gazing at the expanse of whitewashed walls around her.

Down in the kitchens, the heat grew stiflingly oppressive. Mandy worked hard, losing track of time. Once, her mind wandered back to Notting Hill, her Mickey Mouse clock and her life of pampered ease. The arteries of London would be pumping traffic along less sluggishly now, after the early-morning rush hour. Back in her flat, Amanda Silk would be phoning Daphne's in South Ken, reserving a table for a networking lunch of laptops, lobster and Marlboro Lights. Here in deepest Suffolk, Mandy was drudging – but securing her fortune. A glimpse into the huge wine cellar had added yet another nought to the rapidly revised estimate of Sternwood Grange's assets. Her duties gave her full access to the kitchens and storerooms. There, she had glimpsed the dressed crabs, the entrecôte steaks, the venison, the sea bass and the white truffles in virgin oil. In another room – raided by Sophie for the delicious arabica coffee – she sniffed in the dizzying aromas of vanilla, walnuts, nutmeg, expensive teas and robust coffee.

One item puzzled her. A black chain, the links no bigger than a fifty-pence piece, hung down by the door. Leather cuffs were attached to the chain.

'Jacobean game hooks,' Sophie explained. 'See, the hare was threaded through, there, and hung. All game was served very high then.'

'An old curio, and original piece,' Mandy said, automatically pricing it at two thousand at Christies.

'Not exactly,' Sophie said, lowering her voice to a whisper. 'It is still used, only it's called the Gibbet now.'

'Whatever for?'

'Don't ask –'

'You, girl. Mandy, isn't it?' Erica called.

Mandy looked up.

'Don't just stand there gossiping. If you've finished,

give Sophie a hand. She has an appointment with Miss Partridge at ten.'

Erica stalked off. Mandy turned to Sophie, whose fingers struggled nervously with the pea pods. Neither of them spoke, their thoughts of the punishment to come preoccupying them deeply. Mandy wondered what it would be like, being caned across the bottom by the brown-eyed Miss Partridge. Sophie merely wondered why she liked being caned across the bottom by the brown-eyed Miss Partridge.

'I'm supposed to be hoovering the Long Gallery this morning. I'll never get it done.'

'I'll do it,' Mandy said, remembering that Sophie had earned her coming stripes sneaking a stolen cup of coffee to her earlier that morning. 'Of course I will,' she promised, dismissing Sophie's look of gratitude.

'No, don't do that, Mandy –' Sophie gasped.

Mandy crammed a handful of freshly shelled peas into her mouth.

Swish, swipe. The wooden spoon cracked across her bottom harshly. Mandy squealed, and the stolen peas flew out of her mouth.

'Don't let me catch you stealing ever again,' Erica snarled, appearing out of thin air. 'And I'm going to deduct four pounds out of your wages to cover anything else you've had this morning.'

'That's not fair –'

'Hands on the table, girl,' barked Erica.

Mandy, stubborn and proud, refused.

'Do it,' hissed Sophie.

Mandy turned to face the table, bent down and placed her hands before her on the scrubbed pine. She flinched as, kneeling down behind her, Erica flipped the hem of Mandy's skirt up over her hips. Mandy flinched again as she felt her panties being peeled down and a firm hand cupping her left buttock. Erica placed her hand, palm inwards, just at the crease between the

35

upper thigh and the swell of the captive cheek. She squeezed, the buttock bulged. Crack. Crack. Crack. Mandy's white pumps drummed the fragstone floor as the wooden spoon ravished her naked flesh.

Pulling up the panties and rearranging the pleated skirt, Erica rose and told the girls to get on with their duties. 'You're here to work. Work hard and obey. Understand?'

Mandy was on the brink of an angry response when Sophie, patting a stray wisp of her platinum-blonde hair, smoothly intervened.

'She understands. It's her first day. Mandy will learn.' Sophie placed a protective arm around the new maid. 'Come along.'

Mandy followed Sophie up the flight of stone steps leading from the kitchens into the sunlight above.

'Be careful of Erica. That wooden spoon never sleeps. And she's a vixen with the strap.'

'Strap?' protested Mandy hotly.

'We get it at least once a week. Always some excuse –'

'No way –'

'Oh?' The platinum blonde's violet eyes flashed. 'And what makes you so different?' Sophie challenged, turning to confront Mandy as they reached the top of the stairs. 'You're just another maid. A girl in trouble like the rest of us here. London is too hot for you so you're keeping your head down. And it's a fifteen-mile walk to anywhere,' she warned, adding with perfect logic, 'but like the rest of us you've nowhere else to go or you wouldn't be at Sternwood Grange.'

Mandy made no further protest as Sophie spelt out the rules, the rigours, and the dangers to a maid's bare bottom that governed their life at Sternwood Grange. As Mandy listened, she thought of Aunt Clare and her true purpose here. She must, she knew, continue to play the part of a young woman in hot water, grateful to be given refuge. Drawing Sophie gently to her, she kissed her protectress.

36

'Thank you,' she whispered.

'Mmm,' Sophie murmured, reluctant to peel her lips away from Mandy's warm mouth. 'Just be more careful. Adapt. Adapt and conform, or your poor bottom will suffer.'

They ascended an Adam staircase, drenched in sunlight pouring through a magnificent oval window.

'I'll take you to the Long Gallery.'

It was sixty, perhaps seventy feet long and ten feet wide.

'King Charles spent a Christmas here. The Cavalier troops quartered hereabouts in the worst of the winter. They used to hold races along the Long Gallery. Naked wenches would compete for a prize of Seville oranges, a cup of malmsey . . .'

Or a coveted place in a royalist's bed. Mandy closed her eyes and imagined the flickering candlelight, the bellowing laughter, the flushed faces – and the naked wenches, their tiny feet scampering the length of the polished floor. Bare breasted, eyes sparkling, they would race before their king. Fierce wagers, purses of gold, would be exchanged. Fanny, from the kitchens, fleet of foot, would be put against Susie, the spritely little minx who served the wine. Studded gauntlets would cup and squeeze the ripe breasts of the winner, and a gold sovereign would be thrust between her upper thighs. Lazy Susie, who had stumbled and lost pace, would be spanked by Lord Percy, the guttering candlelight winking on her hot reddened rump.

'The Roundheads were dug in the following Christmas,' Sophie continued. 'No more fun or Yuletide festivities. Grim lot, the Roundheads.'

Mandy pictured the scene. Fanny from the kitchens, now in drab black and grey, kneeling on the flagstones for communal prayers. Susie, now toiling in the dairy, being slowly whipped for dipping her finger into a jug of cream.

37

'Don't disturb the residents and don't go near their doors,' Sophie warned, wheeling out the hoover before returning to the kitchens downstairs.

The Long Gallery divided the East Wing from the West. The dark polished floor was covered with several thousand pounds' worth – Mandy automatically put a price on everything she saw – of six-foot wide purple carpet. Both sides of the Long Gallery were punctuated by large double doors, six to her left and six to her right. Behind the firmly closed doors, massively hewn from oak, the residents were cosseted in expensive splendour. Was Sternwood Grange an idyllic rural retreat? A rest home, providing escape from the pressures and problems of the public glare? Mandy wondered about her late aunt's enterprise as she propelled the whispering hoover along, playing the looped flex out as she ate up the vast stretch of purple. The rubber lead tapped against her thigh below the hem of her pleated skirt like the touch of a crop applied to a pony in dressage. The hoover glided in silence, passing the huge double doors; to her left, the East Wing and, to her right, the West. Suddenly, the machine stopped abruptly. Only the loss of the tiny red light told her that the motor had died. She had trodden on the lead, yanking out the plug thirty feet away. Retracing her steps, she passed the first of the stout double doors. A prolonged moan greeted her ears as she bent down to reinsert the plug. The moan was followed by a sharp shriek.

Fascinated, Mandy inched towards the doors on tiptoe. Silence. Had she been mistaken? She thought that the moan, low and sweet, had held a note of carnal suffering. The shriek had been a protest against sudden pain. Kneeling at the keyhole, she pressed up against the doors. Inside, she glimpsed a sumptuously furnished room. Down on the satin cushions strewn across the richly patterned carpet, a kneeling naked woman was burying her face into the leather of a saddle.

38

'Lick,' a stern voice commanded. 'Faster.'

The naked young woman obeyed. Mandy saw the pink tongue sparkle as it lapped at the polished leather, staining the light tan a darker shade of brown.

'Kiss. Kiss the leather.' Swish, swipe. The instruction was delivered with a searing lash of a riding crop across the upturned buttocks. The whipped woman smothered her moan as, hugging the saddle to her bulging breasts, she crushed her parted lips on to the hide.

Mandy's nipples thickened in response. She squashed her bosom into the ancient oak. In the room, the young woman lay face down, spread-eagled across the satin cushions. No, not exactly spread-eagled. Mandy saw that her ankles were bound together.

'Turn over.'

The rounded cheeks, reddening under the kiss of the crop, sank into the cushion beneath them as the woman obeyed. Mandy raked her avidly from head to toe. The loose tangle of matted chestnut curls sticking to the perspiring face, the delicate, aristocratic features, the small, apple-like breasts, the swell at the hips and the long, tanned legs.

Two black velvet riding hats tumbled to the carpet at her side.

'Put them on,' snapped the voice of the unseen tormentress.

Placing a riding hat over each of her apple breasts, filling the velvet void within with her firm flesh, the nude gripped them, rotating them as she ground them harshly into her bosom.

'Harder, bitch.'

The tip of the crop brushed the woman's lips. She craned her neck up, lunging to snap and bite at it. The crop flicked down, settling under her chin. Slowly, with absolute dominance, the crop forced the nude's head backwards and upwards.

'Up.' Crack, snap. As the naked buttocks swung

around, offering themselves submissively to the crop, the crop greeted them with a withering slice, striping the punished cheeks and adding yet another thin red line. The girl squealed as she struggled up, hampered by her bound feet.

'No, kneel. On all fours.' The tip of the crop pressed the turmoil of chestnut curls down.

Was this a resident? Mandy's tongue felt swollen and too big for her dry mouth. Her aching nipples tormented her. Her hot slit wept.

'I believe you ride hard at hounds, Lady Davinia,' the unseen speaker taunted.

Lady Davinia, the superbly buttocked beauty, nodded. Mandy watched the chestnut curls rippling.

'Speak up, bitch. Louder.'

The naked aristocrat peeled her lips away from the satin cushion. 'Yes,' she confessed, her voice a thickened whisper.

'We're going for a little canter this fine morning –' Crack, snap. The crop whistled down across the bare bottom. '– but I shall be up in the saddle.'

Mandy's slit tingled and burned at the words. She forced her hand between her thighs, palming her pubis to ease the surge of excitement. Through the keyhole, she strained to steal a glimpse of the dominatrix but, as her line of vision swept towards the unseen speaker, she was dazzled by the sunshine. Blinking, she closed her eye, squeezing a tear out and wiping it with her crisp apron. She had been denied, so far, any clue to the tormentress – apart from brief glimpses of the red-sleeved arm swiftly delivering the cutting strokes of the crop.

Crack, snap. Lady Davinia moaned, drawing Mandy back to the keyhole. She spied the dark chestnut-hued pubic fuzz peeping between the splayed thighs as Lady Davinia dipped her tummy and jerked her bottom up eagerly for the crop.

In the room, on an unseen mantelpiece, a carriage clock struck. The Cambridge chimes tinkled the hour. Gazing at the striped bottom, Mandy suddenly remembered Sophie. Sophie was due to be caned at ten. Had the carriage clock struck ten? Or was it only nine? Mandy had lost all sense of time. Swivelling back, and sinking her bottom on to her heels, she peered through the keyhole towards the sound of the clock. Yes. There it was. She could just make it out. It was ten. Sophie's suffering, she knew, was under way behind the frosted-glass door of the housekeeper's office. Mandy smothered her cry of surprise.

Behind the clock, there was a mirrored panel. In the glass, she saw the face of one of the angels who had come down to the kitchens earlier to collect her breakfast. The angel, silhouetted in a haze of golden sunshine, was dressed for the hunt. Almost, but not entirely. A black velvet riding hat perched on her head. An unbuttoned red hunting jacket allowed her breasts to spill out. Shiny black leather boots hugged her lower legs. The angel was, otherwise, quite naked – except for dark leather gloves and the crop quivering in her right hand.

Mandy knew at once what she never could have imagined. She knew the truth of Aunt Clare's enterprise: Sternwood Grange was an erotic playpen for the rich. An exclusive palace of pleasures where the wealthy could indulge their darkest desires.

In the mirrored panel above the mantelpiece, Mandy saw the angel wrapping a thin leather harness around her naked hips and buttocks. The gloved fingers tightened the short straps. Grinding the heels of her polished boots into the carpet, the angel turned and bent down briefly, presenting her buttocks to Mandy's gaze. Mandy licked her lips as the bare bottom bulged, the cheeks seemingly threatening to burst the criss-crossed strapping. The taut leather harness rendered the cleft between the cheeks a severe flesh-crease. Rising up to face Mandy once more, the angel produced an eight-inch ivory dildo, kissed its blunt snout fleetingly, then jammed it into a socket in the harness at her pubis. The gloved fingers slowly twisted the dildo, tightening it, before slowly stroking its gleaming length. Lady Davinia whimpered. Mandy saw the black boot pinion the whipped buttocks imperiously, crushing the swollen cheeks down in a display of utter dominance. The angel's fingers continued to skim along the shaft. As they were withdrawn, the ivory phallus sprang up, alert and erect. Mandy swallowed, and used both hands to steady herself against the oak.

Crack, snap. The crop seared down across the buttocks still flattened by the controlling boot. Lady Davinia screamed softly into her satin cushion.

'Head up,' the angel snarled.

Still writhing after the fierce stroke of crop across flesh, the nude tossed her chestnut curls. A leather glove descended and taloned a fistful of the shining hair. 'I said head up, bitch. I need reins to ride you, don't I?'

Straddling her naked mount, the angel squeezed her polished boots against the hot buttocks. With her left hand still clutching the chestnut mane, and her right hand gripping the crop, the angel guided her splayed thighs down on to the helpless woman below. Thrusting her hips forward, the rider pressed the tip of the dildo into the exposed nape of the aristocratic neck. Lady Davinia shivered. Easing back, her riding boots shuffling carefully, the angel swept her hips and thighs slowly, raking the length of smooth ivory down along Lady Davinia's spine. Mandy heard the satin-smothered moan, and tensed as she watched the bound, naked feet twitching frantically in their strict bondage. The angel paused, the tip of the dildo now dimpling the reddened cheek of the left buttock. Slowly, a heartbeat at a time, the probing snout centimetred towards the rosebud sphincter winking wetly between the parted, whipped buttocks.

The chatter of an approaching helicopter, and the chorus of scattered rooks startled from the elms, broke the spell holding Mandy in its thrall. She blinked. Steadying herself, she put her hand down, accidentally forcing her palm on to the upturned plug on the carpet. The flash of pain cleared her brain.

'What are you doing?' hissed Miss Partridge, treading the purple carpet silently as she approached.

Mandy, kneeling on one knee, looked up, the plug in her hand. She blushed.

'You've been spying, haven't you? Listening at the door.'

In the silence after the roar of the helicopter, Mandy could hear her heart hammering. A squeal came from behind the oak doors – where the angel was riding the nude.

'I trod on the lead. The plug came out.'

'Stand up,' the housekeeper hissed, now towering over Mandy.

Another sound – one of anguished ecstasy – echoed from behind the doors. Mandy tried to ignore the image burning in her brain: the leather boots controlling the imprisoned thighs, the glove-held hair, the red jacket from which perspiring breasts spilled and bounced. The soft whisper of flesh riding flesh.

'Lift up your skirt. Quickly,' Miss Partridge demanded.

Mandy dropped the plug and obeyed. The housekeeper knelt down and inspected Mandy's cotton panties. Mandy tried to suppress the image of the angel astride her naked mount, the length of ivory dildo disappearing a fraction at a time with every hip-thrust as the crop cracked down. Just as Miss Partridge pulled the panties down to examine Mandy's labia, the maid bubbled her wet excitement. Mandy shivered with both fear and shame as she heard Miss Partridge sniffing at the heavy tang of arousal.

'Wet,' the housekeeper pronounced. 'You've been spying. Pull your panties up and get downstairs at once. I'll see you in my office when our resident has departed.'

The helicopter coughed, roared and rose up into the sky above Sternwood Grange. Banking steeply, it veered towards London, its shadow skimming the Suffolk treetops below. Mandy heard its departure from the housekeeper's office. Having seen the resident off, Miss Partridge would be returning any second now. The door opened. Mandy froze – relaxing a little as Sophie looked in.

'What –'

'She caught me. I was listening at the door. I didn't mean –'

'She caught you spying? You'll get six, at least. Come upstairs to my room when it's over –'

Sophie disappeared abruptly at the sound of approaching footsteps. Unlike the silent tread upon the purple carpet nine minutes ago, Mandy heard the housekeeper's measured steps across the flagstone floor.

Miss Partridge closed the frosted-glass door behind her firmly, turning the key in the lock. Mandy wiped her wet palms into the apron at her thighs.

'I'm extremely busy this morning and extremely angry. I have little to say to you other than to express my deep disappointment at your wilful disobedience. I believe that actions speak louder than words. Bend over.'

Mandy's blue eyes widened in alarm. Miss Partridge narrowed hers.

'No, leave your panties alone. Touch your toes, girl,' the housekeeper murmured, selecting a bamboo cane from a choice of seven stacked in the corner by a filing cabinet.

44

'Right over. Feet together for the first three strokes, then apart for the next three, understand?'

Mandy whispered her obedience. She shuddered as she felt the tip of the yellow wood flick the hem of her pleated skirt up over her hips, and clenched her buttocks as Miss Partridge thumbed her panties down. Using the cane tip against the exposed cheeks, Miss Partridge judged the distance. Mandy closed her eyes tightly.

'Your first taste of discipline?' the housekeeper asked, her tone almost politely conversational.

'N–no,' whispered Mandy thickly, dreading yet adoring the dominant tap of the cane against her bare cheeks.

'Nor the last, I'm sure,' Miss Partridge observed.

Swish. Mandy's eyes opened wide as the flash of crimson exploded in her brain. The supple bamboo had sliced down, lashing her bottom harshly. Swish. The second stroke, crisply stinging, seared her defenceless buttocks. Her fingers splayed in a reflex of anguish. Swish. The third cut of the cane sliced down with an evil whistle, leaving a reddening line of pain across the punished cheeks.

'Feet apart. Hands behind your knees,' Miss Partridge instructed.

Mandy almost stumbled forward as she struggled to obey, hampered by the tight stretch of her panties just above her knees. The punisher steadied the bending girl with a tap of the yellow bamboo. Head down, with her bottom presented perfectly for punishment, Mandy hoped that the pungent perfume from her wet slit would go undetected. Both her buttocks and her face burned with shame and pain. The tip of the cane quivered as it lightly grazed the outer cheek of her naked bottom.

'Naughty girl,' the housekeeper murmured, her tone stern but not angry. The bamboo traced the curve of the buttock down to the crease of the thigh. Sweeping inwards, it paused at the glistening fig. Mandy steadied

45

herself against the swoon that threatened to engulf her. The punishment was sweet, the dominance delicious. Sophie's words haunted her. When Miss Partridge dispensed discipline, she owned your bottom utterly. Mandy surrendered to the truth of these words – and, inching up on her toes a fraction, submitted her bare buttocks to the cane.

Swish. Swish. A merciless double swipe of supple wood swept down across the upturned cheeks. Mandy squealed and grasped her legs tightly as if squeezing out the pain. A dreadful pause ensued. Miss Partridge had lost the button from the cuff she had undone in preparation for the punishment. Scanning the flagstone floor, she pounced, retrieved her stray button and pocketed it. A silent scream welled up inside Mandy's throat. Her bare bottom blazed beneath an invisible flame of pain. The housekeeper had accidentally brushed against the bare buttocks with her thigh when scooping up the button, grazing the swell of their hot curves with the fabric of her skirt. Mandy moaned at the fleeting touch: so unexpectedly delicious, so disturbingly delightful. Confused, her mind in sudden chaos, the bending girl struggled to deny the dark joy dictated by the Judas wood. In her tumult of emotions, she forgot about the sixth stroke.

Swish – Miss Partridge hadn't. The thin cane sliced down, planting a kiss of savage affection across the scalded cheeks. Mandy's left leg shook uncontrollably despite her gripping hand.

One. Two. Three. The tip of the cane, now wet and stained with the lust-juice from her slit, tapped her bottom as it counted the six red lines. Satisfied, Miss Partridge took a linen hankie out of her pocket, first drying the tip of the cane and then applying it to the labial lips peeping between Mandy's thighs. Mandy gasped aloud at the intimacy, and the dominance, of the touch of cool linen against her hot, silken flesh. Miss

Partridge pocketed the hankie and replaced the cane in the corner of her office. Pacing back to the bare-bottomed girl she had just chastised, she cupped the ravished cheeks and slowly squeezed. Mandy cried out – a shrill squeal of tormented delight. Shutting her eyes tightly, almost as if unwilling to witness her own actions, she thrust her captive cheeks up into the controlling hands that held them, squeezed them, possessed them. She thrilled to their firm control just as she would when a tight silk brassiere imprisoned her bulging breasts.

Silence filled the room. Mandy sensed that Miss Partridge was savouring her moment of supreme sovereignty. Her punisher would be gazing down at the punished bottom, examining the blushing cheeks intimately. Surrendering completely to these delicious sensations of submission, Mandy wept freely from her slit.

Miss Partridge squeezed harder, then swept her thumbs upwards, widening the captive cleft. Mandy tensed, clenching her cheeks tightly, fearful of what she desired. Miss Partridge spanked the left buttock sharply.

'Back to your duties, girl. I hope I don't have to punish you – too frequently.' Once again, the tone was excitingly ambiguous, a stern warmth blending with the sweet severity.

Mandy stood up, her head spinning. Tugging her panties up, she winced as they hugged her hot bottom, and blushed as they grew damp at her pubis. Her heart was beating wildly and her caned buttocks burned, but deep down inside her a strange sensation blossomed. Tugging her panties up into her flesh, she tried to name the nameless feeling of this new, unexpectedly pleasurable, aching anguish.

'You got six. I said you would,' Sophie murmured, tracing each reddening line across Mandy's bottom with her fingertip. 'I only got four.'

Mandy cuddled into Sophie's embrace. Staring into the mirror, she counted the four scarlet stripes across the other maid's bare bottom. They were upstairs, their uniforms abandoned across Sophie's bed.

'We haven't much time. It's always so busy at lunch. This'll make it better. Give me your bottom.'

Mandy turned, offering her buttocks to Sophie. The naked platinum blonde knelt, her face inches away from the punished buttocks before her.

'Mmm,' Mandy sighed, parting her thighs slightly and pushing her bottom back into the healing touch of cold cream-dripping fingers busy at her flesh. 'That's wonderful.'

Sophie dipped her fingers into the pot of cream once more and applied them to the proffered cheeks. With slow, circular sweeps, she soothed the ravished flesh. 'Nearly done,' she whispered, lightly stroking her fingertip down along the cleft. Mandy moaned, clamping her thighs together.

Sophie kissed the flesh before her. 'More?' she teased, murmuring the word directly into Mandy's warmth.

'Yes,' Mandy gasped. 'Yes,' she added urgently, surrendering completely to her implaccable, inner desires wakened by the cane.

Sophie paused, her cream-anointed finger at the base of Mandy's spine. Slowly, deliberately, she dragged it down, forcing it between the quivering cheeks. The lubricated fingertip slid down along the flesh, sensing no resistance. Mandy planted her feet apart and surrendered her bottom to the devilish delight, her excitement sharpened by the knowledge of her wickedness, her forbidden sins of Sapphic pleasure. The fingertip came to rest against the rosebud of her anal whorl. For a brief moment, her heart ceased beating, the throbbing pulse at her throat stopped still. Gently, then with an increasing touch of dominance, the fingertip probed. Mandy's brain kaleidoscoped with a riot of spinning images: the angel's dildo penetrating Lady Davinia as the rider's black leather boots squeezed the whipped bottom; the touch of the housekeeper's skirt against her own ravished cheeks; the inquisitive touch of the cane tip at her weeping fig; Sophie's face at her bottom, so close, so very close.

'Not now,' Sophie sighed, withdrawing her finger. 'It's late. Erica will be on the prowl.'

'Please . . .' mewed Mandy, inching her bottom back to regain and reclaim the finger.

In seconds, Sophie had dressed and gone, zipping up her pleated black maid's skirt as she vanished through the door.

Mandy stood still, naked in the sunbeams. Her hot slit pulsed as a rush of understanding and self-knowledge swept over her. Alone in the bedroom, she listened to her heartbeat in the silence of the room. Approaching Sophie's bed, she knelt down, pressing her belly into the corner of the mattress. Between her thighs, her fig split wide open, fully ripened by the blaze of her kindled heat. The wet labia kissed the mattress as Mandy crushed them into its soft solidity. Gripping the edges with both fists and thighs, she rode the corner of the mattress with increasing fury, dragging her clitoris and slit repeatedly down against its rough graze.

A renewed riot of images tumbled behind her tightly shut eyes: burning images of submission, punishment, domination and sweet surrender. The voyeuristic glimpses of the angel dominantly mounting the naked aristocrat, Miss Partridge thumbing the cleft between the cheeks she had just striped with the bamboo cane, Sophie's probing fingertip at her anal whorl.

Sophie. Mandy murmured the name slowly, allowing the vowels to fill her mouth like too big a bite of fudge cake. Sophie. The stray wisps of Sophie's platinum blonde hair. The soft glow in Sophie's violet eyes. Mandy thrust her hot wet flesh savagely against the mattress in a frenzy of lust. Sophie's lips kissing her bottom – Mandy started to climax – Sophie's dripping finger – the climax gripped her inner muscles in its fist of velvet steel – Sophie's finger probing, probing – Mandy's knuckles whitened as they gripped the mattress – Sophie's probing finger sliding into her tight warmth – Mandy screamed aloud and came. She came violently, hammering her hips into the mattress and crying out aloud: Sophie's name upon her parted lips.

The sunbeams turned from gold to crimson, and then from crimson into black as Mandy, ravished by her orgasm, trembled on the very brink of consciousness, never before having experienced such violent delights or such savage joy. Buckling under her climax, she shuddered and gasped as it raked her naked body mercilessly.

Both the heat and the silence of the late afternoon bore down oppressively on the four maids as they toiled in the kitchens under the ever vigilant gaze, and hovering wooden spoon, of Erica. High tea was a pleasurable ritual that all the residents took seriously. Eggs were carefully boiled and shelled, cress washed and diced, crabs dressed, six types of cakes sliced and plated and no less than seven blends of tea brewed in pots of Georgian silver. Scones were split, their fluffy crumbs exposed to receive clotted cream and fragrant raspberry jam.

There was a loud crash: the kitchen reverberated to the sound of a stone jar smashing down on the flagstones. Erica pounced, her wooden spoon erect and alert. The guilty maid fingered her apron nervously.

'Big deal,' Sophie said, cutting a large chocolate cake carefully. 'It's only a pot of jam.'

Mandy, catching the delicate aroma of *framboise* from the scarlet ooze treacling from the splintered shards, knew better.

'You stupid girl,' Erica hissed. 'You'll find that a costly mistake.'

'French conserve. Eight pounds a jar,' Mandy whispered.

Sophie whistled and nodded, throwing a sympathetic look at the miserable maid, already down on her knees and scrubbing at the stone floor.

'Five pounds deduction,' Erica snapped, 'from each of your wages. As for you, girl, it's the Gibbet.'

'It's only jam,' the unlucky maid wailed.

'Only jam?' echoed Miss Partridge, entering the kitchen. 'That is a singularly expensive conserve supplied exclusively from France.'

'The Gibbet?' Erica prompted eagerly.

'Yes,' the housekeeper confirmed. 'These wretched maids must be taught a lesson.'

Miss Partridge withdrew to her office and an expectant silence settled over the kitchen.

'Strip,' Erica commanded, tapping the palm of her hand impatiently with her wooden spoon.

The maid, a dark-eyed little minx called Sonia, peeled off her uniform and stood, naked and fearful, her head bowed, her hands cupped inwards to hide her pubic fuzz.

'Arms up,' Erica barked, propelling the naked girl across the flagstones to the Gibbet, the wooden spoon speaking twice across the maid's bare bottom.

Sonia stood beneath the leather cuffs suspended by the chain from the ceiling. Erica threaded Sonia's hands and wrists through the cuffs and, having secured her victim, yanked at the chain above. Sonia's arms arrowed upwards, suspending her naked body. Mandy stole a furtive peep over her shoulder. She saw the naked girl's tiny toes whitening as they scrabbled on the cold flagstones below.

'Sonia will be in the Gibbet for two hours. Each of you will lose money,' Erica informed the rest of the

51

assembled maids, 'due to her stupidity. Two strokes each.'

'What does she mean?' Mandy whispered.

'You'll see,' Sophie replied.

The maids were ordered to line up.

'Quickly,' Erica rasped. 'With one maid short you'll have extra work to do this afternoon. Remember that, and your loss of earnings, as you stripe her.'

Mandy gazed at the suspended maid. Sonia spindled slowly, presenting her breasts, belly and pubis, then turning to reveal her hip, thigh – and, finally, her ripe peach buttocks. Mandy's nipples thickened and peaked as she gazed at the plump swell of the pink cheeks. Sonia's bottom was undoubtedly both spankable and biteable – but now it was to be beaten. Mandy, at the end of the queue, realised she was part of a punishment squad.

The maids stepped up briskly, accepted the wooden spoon from Erica and cracked it down twice across the vulnerable cheeks. The suspended girl's naked bottom was perfectly poised and presented for punishment. Mandy's heart fluttered. She closed her eyes. Swish, swipe. Swish, swipe. The little minx squealed and jerked, rattling the chain above her. Mandy blinked and looked up. The punished maid's fingers splayed out in their cuffed bondage, signalling her suffering. Swish, swipe. Swish, swipe. Sonia squealed again, almost drowning out the dry rattle of the chain. Sophie's turn came. She stepped up, accepted the wooden spoon and gripped the handle tightly. Sonia's toes curled in anguish as her naked feet paddled the flagstones. Up in their leather cuffs, the maid's wrists writhed. Swish, swipe. The spoon swept across the reddening cheeks. Swish, swipe.

It was Mandy's turn. She accepted the spoon with a trembling hand and took the short step forward that brought her within striking distance of the suffering maid's buttocks.

* * *

'Your first time? Never punished before?'

'Yes. No. I mean –'

'Nice?' Sophie teased.

Mandy blushed in her confusion. Yes. It had been nice. It had been wonderful. She remembered how the pliant flesh had absorbed the swishing spoon. Sonia's soft cheeks had flattened under the first stroke, and shuddered beneath the second. The wooden spoon had made a satisfying 'splat' across the cheeks, blazing their pink sheen with a fiery crimson.

Mandy tossed her head back and enjoyed the stream of warm water. They were sharing the shower together. Two naked girls forced into the intimacy of the confined space. Bosoms collided, nipples grazed and peaked. Wet slippery thighs conspired to entwine. They kissed, slowly and deeply, Mandy felt the force of Sophie's pubic mound pressing into her own. They kissed again, flickering the tips of their tongues into each other's open mouths. Mandy took Sophie's lower lip between her teeth, her slit on fire as Sophie's tongue found the roof of her mouth. They embraced, hugging each other's wet nakedness. Sophie's fingers came to rest against Mandy's labia. Palm inwards, she opened the tingling flesh lips as her thumb prised up the clitoris.

'So? Which would you rather be? The spanker, or the spanked?'

'I don't . . .' Mandy hesitated. 'The spanker. No. I mean . . .'

'Both?' Sophie whispered.

'Both,' murmured Mandy huskily, recognising the truth as she spoke it. 'Mmm,' she whispered. 'Both.'

Giggling, Sophie spun round, squashing her face and breasts into the tiles. Jerking her buttocks up as she braced herself on arched feet, she waggled her bottom and pleaded to be soaped. Mandy palmed the soap, conjuring up a luxurious lather, and spread the creaming suds over each rounded cheek. Sophie gurgled her delight and spread her wet thighs wide. Mandy's throat tightened as she saw the cleft yawn invitingly. Emboldened, she skimmed her fingertip along the ribbon of velvet deep between the buttocks. Sophie cried aloud, and begged for more, urging Mandy to be firmer, much firmer, with her bare bottom.

Mandy knelt, the shower drumming down on her face and shoulders, and gripped the hips, drawing the bare wet bottom closer to her parted lips. In the rain of water, her white teeth sparkled.

'Shush. Someone's coming.'

Mandy rose, chastened by Sophie's whispered warning.

They heard the echo of two pairs of approaching footsteps. Shivering, they huddled together. The plastic curtain of the first shower rustled as it was dragged open. The footsteps neared. Another shower curtain scraped the rail as unseen hands flung it wide open. Mandy pressed her body into Sophie's. Who could it be? Two angels, perspiring after pleasuring the residents? Two naughty maids, coming to shower after a long day's toil? Erica and Miss Partridge, prowling for bare bottoms to punish?

'Excellent,' they heard a voice rasp. 'That almost completes my tour of inspection. We'll examine the maids' rooms next.'

'I'm sure you'll find everything in order,' Miss Partridge replied. 'Go ahead, Miss Flaxstone, I'll catch you up. I'll just turn this tap off in here.'

Miss Flaxstone. Mandy's brain froze. She did not hear the curtain of their shower being dragged back. She did not hear the gasp of surprise, or see the flash of jealous anger in the housekeeper's wide eyes. All she heard was her heart hammering furiously as her wet bosom crushed against Sophie's soft breasts.

Three

Mandy, still wet and naked from her interrupted shower, sat on her bed, her buttocks pressed into the duvet, her towel abandoned at her feet. Her hand tugged at her ear as she tried to marshall her thoughts. Celia Flaxstone was here at Sternwood Grange. On a tour of inspection, as if she owned it all. Mandy recalled her encounter in Bird Cage Walk, and how the shrewd, grey-eyed solicitor had successfully managed to deflect all of Mandy's questions. Suspecting her late aunt's legal adviser of nothing more than financial sharp practice, the sudden presence of Celia Flaxstone here at Sternwood Grange threw Mandy's brain into a whirl.

Mechanically, she brushed away a droplet that had gathered into a jewel at her nipple. Her cornflower-blue eyes widened a fraction as her palm grazed the swollen, pink bud. The sensation brought Mandy back from her confused speculations to the present moment. A present moment full of the promise of imminent pain. Straining to catch the sound of approaching footsteps, Mandy shivered as she remembered the housekeeper's fiercely whispered words. 'Go to your rooms, you wicked girls,' Partridge had hissed. 'I will deal with you both when I have seen the mistress back to her room.'

The mistress. Despite the threat of the promised punishment, the words burned brightly in Mandy's brain. Celia Flaxstone, the formidable woman with the athletic body and razor-sharp mind, was mistress of

Sternwood Grange. Mandy sensed that she was no longer in danger of just losing a few thousand pounds – she had probably already lost her entire inheritance.

She would fight, she resolved, gripping the duvet with whitening knuckles. She would fight every inch of the way. Shrugging off the haunting image of the receptionist being competently whipped, Mandy swallowed and closed her eyes. Sternwood Grange was rightfully hers, she vowed, and she would become its mistress.

Footsteps approached along the landing, heralding the approach of Partridge. Suddenly, Mandy was a naked young woman once more. Gone was her bold resolve. She shivered as the door handle rattled at the housekeeper's firm touch.

'You nearly caused me a great deal of trouble, you wicked girl,' Partridge snapped, closing the bedroom door behind her. 'Silence,' she barked, raising her hand to quell Mandy's protest. 'If the mistress had caught you neglecting your tasks she would have thought me incapable of doing my duty. And I am fully capable of doing my duty, which is to supervise and punish the maids. Bend over.'

Mandy peeled her hands away from her breasts and turned to face the bed. She stretched her arms out and bent down.

'No. Right across the bed. Arms out straight.'

Mandy's breasts, then her belly, kissed the silk.

'Feet together, girl,' Partridge ordered, unbuckling the leather belt that hugged her slender waist.

Mandy's toes scrabbled into the floor as she positioned herself in preparation for the punishing strokes. They came in a fierce rain of pain: a swift onslaught of eight lashes, in rapid succession and with startling severity. Eight times the cruel leather belt whipped down to scald her upturned cheeks. Eight times, Mandy's hands clutched the duvet as she smothered her gasps of anguish. Beneath the single lightbulb, which cast a dull, yellow glare, the taut flesh of the naked buttocks blazed after the fury of the leather. Mandy buried her face in the duvet, muffling her squeals.

The punishment ceased; the leather belt dangled limply against the housekeeper's thigh. Planting her feet apart, and leaning over to scrutinise the striped bottom, Partridge shouldered her belt and studied the hot cheeks. After a full two minutes, Mandy felt the outstretched finger of her punisher press down dominantly on her bottom, circling then dimpling the scarlet domes of her buttocks.

'The mistress will be gone by noon tomorrow. Be on your best behaviour, girl –'

Once more, the belt whistled down, snapping across the bare bottom.

'Attend to your duties –'

The leather punctuated the stern warning with a final snapping crack across the punished flesh.

'And do not betray the kindness I have shown you. Understand?'

'Yes,' Mandy whispered thickly, mouthing her words into the silk duvet.

'Make sure you are down and at work early in the morning. And be spick and span. The mistress will want to inspect all the maids.'

Partridge left as abruptly as she had arrived, closing the door firmly and leaving Mandy alone across the bed of pain with a reddened, sore bottom – and fresh anxieties. Celia Flaxstone was departing at noon. That was good. It would at least leave Mandy with the scope to review her position here at Sternwood Grange. Celia Flaxstone was going to inspect the maids in the morning. That was bad, very bad indeed. How close, how intimate, would the inspection of the maids be? And would Mandy be recognised? If so, what would become of her once she was in the thrall of the grey-haired solicitor, here in this isolated corner of forgotten Suffolk.

Mandy sat on the bed, her hot bottom cooled by the silk duvet. Drawing her knees up to her chin in contemplation, she purred with pleasure at her squashed breasts, and at the ooze of wet excitement silvering her slit. After all, she comforted herself, her only meeting with the solicitor had been a brief affair. Ten minutes, no more. Mandy tried to reassure herself. And, in that office, Amanda Silk was a confident blonde: not Mandy the maid with the dark, bobbed hair who Celia Flaxstone would be examining before breakfast. Despite these thoughts, Mandy remained frightened and anxious. Sitting on her bed, naked and still smarting from the leather belt's bite, she felt vulnerable and alone.

Friendless, because she could not share her secret with anyone here in Sternwood Grange. Friendless. Her thoughts quickly turned to Sophie in the next room. Mandy smiled: by now, Partridge would have arranged the platinum blonde across the unmade bed and the unfurled leather belt would be hovering above the bare bottom. Grinning mischievously, Mandy skipped across the room to the wall and pressed her naked body up against it, positioning her ear to the cool plaster. Sophie's violet eyes would be clouding with delicious dread, Mandy thought, as she squirmed beneath the potent length of leather. She pressed her head against the wall. Silence greeted her eager ear.

No, not silence, exactly. Mandy frowned. From the next room, instead of the harsh snapping of supple hide across smooth, pink cheeks, she caught the sweeter sound of Lully's *Les Amants Magnifiques*. The sensual music wove an invisible web in the heavy air of the warm summer night. As Mandy rubbed her sore bottom, delicately palming each scalded cheek, she felt a rush of affection for Partridge. Despite the whipping, and other stern discipline the housekeeper had dispensed, Partridge was a decent type. She had been loyal to Mandy's late aunt, and had taken Mandy in when told the tale of woe. Yes, Partridge was OK. Warm-hearted, generous – and those large, brown eyes. So deliciously dominant and so expertly in control when punishing a young female's bare bottom.

Lulled into this brief reverie, Mandy lost her concentration at the plaster wall. She slipped slightly, but steadied herself by cushioning her breasts into the cool surface. Her nipples rose up in peaked protest as they were crushed beneath her. The old wall had a rough patch where her nipples kissed into it. Her sensitive flesh grazed against the roughness. Mandy smothered her gasp. Blinking away the brief spasm of pleasure-pain from her widened eyes, Mandy stretched up on tiptoe to listen: eager for the expected sounds of punishment. No crisp snap of leather across smooth cheeks greeted her, but she could just detect two voices in muted murmuring, and the sweet notes of the music, beyond the plaster wall. A jealous pang surged up inside her. Partridge was not punishing Sophie, she was pleasuring her. Or being pleasured by the platinum blonde?

Mandy remembered the housekeeper's angry eyes as the shower curtain had been dragged aside. They had, she suddenly thought, blazed with something fiercer than anger when discovering the two naked girls entwined. Sophie, Mandy swallowed with difficulty as the truth dawned, was Partridge's favourite maid. They were together, next door. Naked? Was Partridge feeding greedily from the firm young flesh of the writhing blonde? Her full lips sucking and feasting at Sophie's neck, shoulders and bare bosom. Mandy moaned as she denied the image of the housekeeper's mouth buried in Sophie's quivering breast. Or was Sophie, blonde head bowed, kneeling, her shining face pressed between the

59

housekeeper's splayed thighs? Were those violet eyes flickering up in timid adoration into the housekeeper's stern gaze as, her chin wedged in the fragrant wet warmth, Sophie's lapping tongue busied itself in the parted, sticky fig.

Stumbling back to her bed across which she had been briskly lashed by Partridge some minutes ago, Mandy stretched her nakedness belly down into the duvet. Closing her eyes, she gripped the pillow with clenched fingers. The imagined snapshots of the couple in the next room were replaced by slowly developing images in the red light of her jealous anger. In her fevered imaginings, Mandy saw Partridge palming Sophie's captive breasts, cupping then weighing their swollen warmth, squeezing the bunched flesh with dominant tenderness, before anointing each peaked nipple with her parted lips. Kissing and sucking the hard peaks until Sophie squealed with raw pleasure. Then the dark flesh of the flickering tongue-tip would emerge to ravish and enflame the swollen, subjugated bosom.

Mandy tried to bleach the tormenting image out of her mind – but it grew more powerful, more maddening. She writhed on her bed, crushing her breasts into the duvet, as fresh images flashed across her mind. She saw Sophie's wide mouth stretch wider then form a silent oval of delight as, down at her firm belly, the housekeeper's wet tongue flattened against her flesh. Then, further down below, gently licking the wisps of pubic fuzz. So vivid were her tormenting imaginings, Mandy even heard the soft rustle as the tongue probed the glistening crease. Then the tongue tip flickered once more, stretched and gleaming, to probe the sticky petals of the labia.

Clamping her thighs together and clenching the cheeks of her recently whipped bottom, Mandy softly drummed the duvet with fists of fury. She tasted the sharp tang of envy at the thought of Partridge tonguing and tasting Sophie's secret flesh, and winced at the bitter thought of the brown-eyed housekeeper pleasuring her favourite maid.

Sophie should be punished. She should be suffering sweet pain, Mandy thought. Yes, Partridge should be pinning the naked blonde across her thighs, one firm hand at the maid's neck, the other curled across the swell of the bare bottom. Yes. Mandy squeezed her thighs together tightly, wriggling down into the duvet as she conjured up the imminent spanking. Partridge spanking Sophie's bare bottom searingly and searchingly, the ruthless hand sweeping down to scald the defenceless cheeks. Cheeks ablaze now as they deepened from pink to a burning crimson. Mandy relished the imagined crack of the hard palm against the smoothness of the maid's naked cheeks. Yes. That was better, much better.

Satisfied, and with her wet slit pulsing pleasurably, Mandy curled up and drifted off to sleep. But it was a restless sleep, troubled by unbidden dreams. In her dreams, Mandy watched as the spanking continued, and gloated at Sophie's sore bottom as it bucked and bounced in a vain attempt to escape the fierce chastisement. Then the brown eyes of the housekeeper narrowed. She paused, her hot palm resting silently across the hotter cheeks. In her sleep, Mandy moaned. No. Not that. That should not be happening, she whimpered. Frozen and helpless in her dreamscape, Mandy was forced to witness the housekeeper inching her heavy breasts down on to the bottom of the maid she had just spanked so severely. No, whimpered Mandy, burning with a surge of jealous rage as she saw, but could not stop, Partridge slowly and deliberately dragging her hard nipples across the crimson domes before crushing her bosom with tender dominance into the favourite's hot bottom.

* * *

61

The preparation of tea, coffee and toast were Mandy's allotted tasks the following morning. She was soon engrossed in her duties, buffing up a sheen on the silver Georgian coffee pots and decrusting the perfect triangles of golden toast. Partridge flitted between the kitchens, offering praise and encouragement in her anxious supervision of the scurrying maids. Erica, Mandy noticed, was less flustered, remaining cool and calm as she stalked the flagstone floor, spoon alert and ready to swipe the maids' bottoms. The bustle increased into a frenzy, but still Erica remained serene.

There had been no time to talk. Sophie had, twice, flashed warm smiles across her laden trays to Mandy, but Mandy had ignored them, pretending to be busy with her pots of aromatic Earl Grey tea. She was still angry, angry and jealous of the housekeeper's preference for the platinum-blonde maid.

A sudden hush greeted the arrival of Celia Flaxstone, who swept into the kitchens, mistress of all she surveyed. Partridge stiffened with tension, Mandy thought as she glimpsed the housekeeper's hands fluttering anxiously. Was she afraid? Afraid of Celia Flaxstone. If so, why? Pushing these thoughts aside, Mandy turned strategically away from the kitchen and attended to her steaming kettles ranged across the Aga. Out of the corner of a wary eye, she saw Celia Flaxstone approach Erica and greet the cropped blonde with a warm kiss. For Partridge, Mandy noted, the mistress of Sternwood Grange had only a few curt words. Celia Flaxstone sauntered across the flagstones, pausing to finger the leather harness of the Gibbet.

'I shall inspect the maids now,' she announced.

Putting her plan into action, a plan she had devised in the grey dawn hours, Mandy placed an almost empty kettle on to the hottest part of the Aga.

'Girls –' Partridge cried, her voice shrill with anxiety.

'Erica,' the mistress of Sternwood Grange purred,

silencing the housekeeper with a raised hand. 'Would you line up the maids for inspection?'

Erica smiled fleetingly and triumphantly at Partridge before, with a sharp clap of her hands, ordering the maids to form a line. All five girls present, including Mandy, responded with alacrity. Mandy saw that Celia Flaxstone was impressed. The cropped blonde strode behind the line of maids, tapping their buttocks with the wooden spoon. The maids shuffled into rigid formation. Again, Mandy caught the nod of approval from the solicitor.

'Ready for inspection,' Erica snapped briskly.

'Excellent. I'm so glad to see that someone is managing to keep a firm hand on the tiller down here.'

Partridge, Mandy observed, paled at the jibe. She suddenly felt a pang of anxiety for the brown-eyed housekeeper. Clearly, she sensed, the days of the woman who had served her late aunt so loyally were numbered. Celia Flaxstone favoured the sterner, bullying skills of Erica, and Mandy quickly deduced that, before long, the cruel, cropped blonde would reign supreme.

Mandy tensed expectantly as the grey eyes began their inspection. Passing along the line of maids, they scrutinized hands, fingernails, uniforms, aprons and faces. Sonia, the dark-eyed little minx, surrendered her hands, palms up, for scrutiny. Reversing them, she shivered as Celia Flaxstone bent down to examine the nails.

'This girl needs to learn, and learn quickly, how to scrub her hands,' the mistress of Sternwood Grange murmured. 'Paying particular attention to her nails.'

Even before the offending hands had been released from the strong grip of the examiner, Erica's wooden spoon had spoken harshly across Sonia's plump cheeks. The minx squeaked her anguish.

'So prompt to punish. An excellent management skill,' the solicitor purred.

The inspection continued, pausing then stopping at Sophie.

'There is a smudge of lipstick on your face, girl.'

Sophie's left hand flew up to her face and wiped her lips. Mandy watched as Sophie fingered her lower lip anxiously.

'No, not there, but from your gesture you thought you'd left some lipstick on.'

Mandy shivered at the cunning entrapment. The solicitor could now have Sophie punished twice.

'There, girl, on your cheek. A curious shade of pink. Where have I seen it before?' The grey eyes narrowed.

Partridge, Mandy thought. It's the housekeeper's lipstick, from last night. From her manner, Mandy knew that Celia Flaxstone thought the same.

'She's always such a good girl,' Partridge intervened, defending Sophie. 'I'm sure –'

'And I'm sure she deserves to be punished. Four strokes,' came the stern response, a response which once more rudely cut off the housekeeper.

Erica pounced, dragging Sophie out of the line. Seconds later, the platinum blonde was bending to touch her toes, the hem of her maid's uniform flipped up and her cotton panties dragged down to her knees.

'I think Partridge should administer the punishment,' the solicitor said, smiling maliciously.

She knows. She knows, Mandy realised. But how could she have known that Partridge was fond of Sophie? How cruel this grey-eyed woman is, Mandy thought. Such a sharp mind – it misses nothing. Would it – Mandy's heart skipped a beat then thumped heavily – miss her disguise?

Erica was chuckling as she returned from the office, swishing a bamboo cane which she handed to Partridge.

'Since my arrival at Sternwood Grange, you have seemed eager to demonstrate your competence, Partridge. Now,' whispered Celia Flaxstone softly, 'you have the chance to do so.'

Mandy thrilled to the swishing slice of the supple wood as it thrummed the air and swept down, biting into the bare bottom. Still smarting from her jealous discovery of the previous night, and from the burning torment of her jealous imaginings, Mandy relished the first two strokes of the punishment, delighting at the kiss of the bamboo and the two pink lines bequeathed by the wood, across Sophie's upturned cheeks. Then she softened, relenting, and ashamed at her thrill of response. Poor Sophie, she thought. And poor, dear Partridge.

The sharp whistle of the Judas wood as it sliced down and across Sophie's striped buttocks for the third time caused Mandy to wince, and burn with the slow flames of shame. She felt so sorry for them both. The punisher and the punished. The fourth stroke lashed down, bringing Sophie up on her toes in a squeal of torment.

'Four more,' Celia Flaxstone whispered. 'She was wearing lipstick, after all. Somebody elses, to be sure.' She paused, letting the accusation hang heavily in the air. 'But from the way she wiped her lips, she obviously disobeys the rules as well. Another four.'

The length of supple wood glinted in the harsh neon light, and sparkled as it swept down. More thin red lines joined those already burning across the creamy cheeks. At the final stroke, tears of remorse clouded Mandy's cornflower-blue eyes. She felt so sorry for poor Partridge, ordered to punish the one she favoured. And sorry for Sophie, too. They had both been so kind to her when she had arrived at Sternwood Grange. She regretted her spiteful jealousy and vowed to reward them when the opportunity arose.

When the opportunity arose. The words mocked her. Here she was, standing in line, about to be inspected – punished perhaps – by the clever solicitor. With a ferocity which alarmed her, Mandy knew she hated Celia Flaxstone. Hated her for being a thief and a cheat, of course, but also for being so cruel and ruthless.

Dismissing Partridge with a curt nod, Celia Flaxstone grazed the caned cheeks with her thumb. Mandy saw the striped bottom spasm with fear. Gazing down imperiously at the punished buttocks, the mistress of Sternwood Grange addressed the anxious maids. Her tone was cold.

'Now that I am in control here, things will be different. All fines and penalty deductions from wages will be doubled with immediate effect. Two weeks loss of pay for Sophie. Please make a note of my decision, Erica.'

Erica nodded.

'Discipline will also be doubled. No misdemeanor, breakage or petty theft will go unpunished. There has been too much laxity of late. I intend to operate Sternwood Grange with efficiency and strict discipline. Costs must be kept to an absolute minimum. Profits must grow. This can only be achieved by effective management, and effective management means constant vigilance and harsh punishments.'

Mandy wondered what the regime must have been like when her late aunt ran Sternwood Grange. She was convinced that the maids and angels were encouraged and rewarded. All would have been paid properly, and would have shared the residents' sumptuous meals. Discipline would have been mild, with spankings across the housekeeper's knee for those who had been naughty. It would have been such fun.

Now, under the strict administration of Celia Flaxstone, profit and efficiency were to be driven up by fear, oppression and harsh coditions of service. Tricked out of their savings by punitive fines and penalties, the maids and angels were little more than bondmaidens, doomed to servitude under the cruel gaze of Erica.

How could a poor maid like Sonia, paid a pittance, ever hope to save up enough to escape this wretched bondage? It was a clever, cunning and cruel mistress now running her late aunt's enterprise. Would she, Mandy wondered, be able to bring back those sunnier times?

'You, girl. What is your name?' rasped the solicitor, staring across at Mandy.

Mandy lowered her gaze as she mumbled her name.

'A new maid. How long have you been here?'

As planned for, the kettle on the Aga started to give a shrill whistle. Mandy had timed it perfectly. She pretended to be concerned about her duties, glancing anxiously across at the Aga.

'She's a quick learner,' Erica remarked. Tapping Mandy's bottom with her wooden spoon, she added, 'Go back to your duties, girl.'

Mandy escaped with relief to the whistling kettle.

'Pert little thing,' the solicitor observed, her grey eyes devouring Mandy's bottom.

'Willing, but needs a sharp reminder now and then. Nice bottom,' Erica purred. 'I know, I've punished it.'

Mandy cringed as she heard them both laugh. At the fierce heat of the Aga, the steam from the kettles moistened the blouse at Mandy's breasts. They rose, swelling in angry resentment as she listened to more mocking laughter. Her anger turned to fear as she realised that Erica and the solicitor were discussing her with the purring malice of two cats contemplating a shivering mouse trapped between cruel paws.

The morning had been hectic. Fearful of Erica, everyone had worked hard: harder than usual, despite the sweltering heat. Swollen up into new heights of arrogance by Celia Flaxstone's evident patronage, Erica seemed determined to make her mark in the new regime. She made it, memorably, across the buttocks of two maids caught nibbling at a strip of marzipan. As the spoon cracked down across their bare bottoms, Mandy remembered her visit to the Long Gallery, where she had learnt of the roisterous Cavaliers being ousted by Cromwell's sterner troops – and thought of dark-eyed Susie being whipped in the pantry. Then, as now, days of pleasure had been supplanted by a reign of pain. As the hours dragged slowly towards lunch, Mandy made sure she was busy, keeping out of sight and avoiding any chance encounter with Celia Flaxstone.

After lunch had been prepared and sent upstairs, Mandy had slipped away for a quick bath. With the lukewarm water lapping at her breasts, she relaxed and felt momentarily safe. The grey-eyed solicitor would be returning to London within the hour, leaving Mandy free to complete her audit. Armed with precise knowledge, she would herself return to London and prepare to claim and secure her inheritance.

London. She closed her eyes and pictured her flat in Notting Hill. In a month or so, the Carnival would be throbbing as it snaked through the surrounding streets. She smiled, remembering how, last year, the very air seemed to pulse till well after midnight. Opening her eyes, she sought and found the soap. It was a mean tablet of unscented wax. The maids were allowed few privileges and denied all luxuries. She splashed the tepid bathwater angrily with a sudden fist of frustration. In her Notting Hill flat, she would enjoy the scented comforts of expensive oils and lotions. Here, she was grudged hot water. Yet all of this was hers. Seized by the indignities and privations, Mandy stood up, grabbed a rough towel and rubbed her nakedness vigorously. Hating the mean and petty restrictions endured since her arrival, she resolved to strike a blow against the tyranny. It would be a small, careful blow. She grinned as she struggled into her panties. Not a full-blown rebellion: too much to risk, too much at stake. Just a small gesture: two pieces of forbidden cake, one for herself and one for poor Sophie who had been so harshly caned.

* * *

Down in the kitchens, she tiptoed across the flagstone floor, tense and alert. They should be, she had calculated, deserted. A slight sound behind her caused her to freeze on the spot. Glancing anxiously over her shoulder, she saw that she was still alone. Resuming her stealthy tread towards the forbidden cake, she brushed against the Gibbet. It rattled noisily. Stilling the chains with upstretched arms, Mandy felt the leather collar tapping against her breasts. Silence returned to the kitchens – except for the wild hammering of her heart. She crept into the pantry and secured two huge slices of chocolate cake. Juggling with her stolen loot, she decided to eat her slice on the spot. She finished it with relish, sucking at her chocolate-darkened fingertips to remove any telltale traces of her guilt, and wrapped Sophie's slice in a napkin.

Voices approaching down the corridor beyond the kitchen door sent Mandy scuttling for shelter between two of the large fridges. She cowered between them, her buttocks clenched in fearful expectation. If Erica caught her, it would mean the Gibbet – and the Gibbet would mean a scorched bottom.

The two speakers paused in the doorway, blocking Mandy's escape route. Trapped, she held her breath, wishing her heart would stop beating so loudly.

'Now the old bat is gone, I can really make something of this place,' the voice of Celia Flaxstone said.

'I'm sure you will,' the voice of Erica simpered.

'You will have a very important role to play, my dear,' the solicitor continued. 'I have many proposals for change here at Sternwood Grange in mind. You feature significantly in my plans.'

'And Partridge?' Erica prompted, her Judas whispering quivering with interest.

'Partridge will have to go. How and when, I am not sure, but an opportunity is bound to present itself. Too attached to the old ways, I'm afraid. By the way,' the solicitor added suavely, 'that new maid.'

Mandy stiffened.

'The beautifully bottomed Mandy?' Erica chuckled.

Mandy froze, clutching Sophie's cake so tightly she squeezed the chocolate cream out like toothpaste.

'Yes, the beautifully bottomed Mandy. I think she could have the potential to be an angel. Try her out this afternoon.'

'Upstairs?' Erica murmured, doubtfully.

'No, not yet. Put her to work in the sauna. Ring me tonight at my flat. Let me know how she progresses. On my next visit, I must take a closer look at the girl, and her beautiful bottom.'

Mandy shivered.

'Certainly,' Erica replied obsequiously. 'And are the kitchens to your satisfaction?'

'Perfectly,' came the response. Evidently, the solicitor was conducting a snap inspection before her departure. 'But then you have already proved your suitability for promotion. Come along.'

Mandy heard the retreating footsteps echo along the corridor as the mistress of Sternwood Grange and her eager lieutenant departed.

'I had mine earlier. Go on, it's delicious.'

Sophie grinned naughtily as she accepted the huge slice of stolen chocolate cake. 'Sure you couldn't pinch a bigger piece?' she giggled, her mouth full. 'Anybody'd think you owned the place the way you make free with –'

'Quick, hide it,' Mandy hissed, suddenly remembering that the footsteps mounting the stairs would be those of Erica, coming to escort her to the sauna.

Sophie gulped, her eyes bulging as she swallowed. Panicking, she danced around the bedroom flapping her hands.

'Mandy,' Erica said, entering the room. 'I want you to come with me –' Her suspicious eyes flashed across at

70

Sophie. 'What are you eating, girl?' she demanded sternly. 'Well?'

Sophie swallowed painfully and blinked, her violet eyes widening with fear. 'Just a slice of bread,' she whispered.

'Show me your hands.'

Mandy saw Sophie's fists clench.

'Show me,' Erica purred softly, 'or you'll be showing me your bare bottom.'

Sophie offered her hands up for inspection, palms down. Erica grasped the outstretched wrists and, with a twisting wrench, turned the palms upwards. Lowering her cropped blonde head, she inched her face towards the pinioned hands. Mandy shuddered as she saw Erica's tongue tip flicker and dart, licking and tasting the trembling fingertips.

'Chocolate cake. Twelve strokes.'

Sophie paled as Mandy flushed and blurted out a protest.

'No, please, she didn't –'

'Didn't what?' Erica snapped impatiently. 'You know the rules, Mandy. Did you have chocolate cake? No. Let me see your hands. There. Spotless.'

Mandy rallied for a second attempt to exonerate Sophie, but Erica was implacable.

'I think you had better keep away from this girl, Mandy. We have plans for you, she will always be a troublesome little maid. A sore-bottomed little maid. No,' Erica continued, producing a two-foot bamboo cane. 'After you have caned her bare bottom, stay away from her. I don't want Sophie leading you astray.'

Mandy's face reddened as she felt Sophie's accusing glare burn into her. Out of the corner of her eye, she saw Sophie's violet eyes. They were not widening with fear as they gazed upon the cane, but narrowing with resentment as they examined her own chocolate-smeared fingertips. Mandy saw what Sophie was thinking: she had been framed by Mandy in a deliberate trap, caused by spiteful jealousy of Partridge, or simply to oust Sophie from the chance of being trained to become an angel – leaving the field clear for herself. Mandy did not know which of these ideas had sprung to Sophie's mind. All she saw – and felt – was the burning hatred in the platinum blonde's face.

'Panties down and touch your toes,' Erica ordered. 'Mandy, take this cane and show me your technique. Caning bare bottoms will play a significant part in your duties as an angel. Show me if you are worthy of the privilege to serve.'

Mandy took the cane reluctantly, tightening her trembling fingers around the slender rod of supple wood. Sophie, as instructed, had peeled down her panties to her ankles and was stretching down to touch her toes. Naked and bending, she presented her bottom for the bamboo.

'Twelve,' Erica murmured, sitting down on the bed to appraise the punishment at close quarters. 'No,' she added quickly, as Mandy shouldered the cane. 'You must prepare for the caning much more carefully. Do not worry about any delay. It merely adds to the miscreant's sense of dread and heightens their discomfort. First of all, you must judge the distance.'

Mandy took a half-step back from the bare-bottomed, bending girl, lowered the cane and rested the tip of the yellow bamboo at the top of the cleft between the passive cheeks.

'That's better, though you need to take another half-step back,' Erica commented. 'And come around to the left a little bit more. Remember, each stroke must stripe both buttocks, not just the cheek nearest to you.'

Mandy repositioned herself as advised and levelled the length of cane against the swell of the bare bottom, pressing it firmly into the twin curves of smooth flesh.

'Commence,' Erica whispered softly.

The first stroke sliced down with a venomous swish to stripe the creamy cheeks with a thin line of reddening fire. Mandy hated every moment: hated herself for bringing this doom down upon poor Sophie; hated the cruel, cropped blonde on the bed; hated the supple wand of woe clenched in her right hand.

'No, not yet. Do not hurry the punishment. Both the caner and the caned must savour, in their different ways, each individual stroke.'

Mandy bowed her head in shame, avoiding the scarlet stripe she had just drawn across the pale cheeks with her cane.

'It is often quite useful to touch the buttocks lightly, just a tap of the cane across the cheeks, between each stroke,' Erica observed. 'This both paces the punishment and, while reminding the punished of the impending lash, establishes the dominance that exists between the whipper and the whipped.'

Mandy raised the cane, swept it down to kiss the swell of the soft cheeks sharply, then raised it once more. The second stroke had been planted exactly a quarter of an inch below the burning brand of the first, and had caused Sophie's toes to scrunch into the cotton panties at her feet. Mandy had seen the naked cheeks spasm in anguish – and had heard the yelp of response torn from Sophie's parted lips.

'No, no, no,' Erica snapped impatiently. 'Give me that cane. Watch. I'll show you how to stripe a bare bottom.'

Surrendering the cane, Mandy shuffled across to the end of the bed.

'Come back. I want you to watch. Watch and learn. Kneel down there,' Erica ordered, jabbing her finger at the floor. 'Observe my methods closely. I'll make an angel of you yet. As for you,' she snarled, tapping Sophie's twice-striped buttocks with her cane, 'I'll start again. Twelve strokes, I think we said.'

Mandy smothered her gasp of dismay but Sophie failed to stifle her moan. Mandy knelt and gazed up, burning with shame and remorse at Sophie's suffering. How stupid I have been, she thought. Worse still, Sophie was probably thinking that the cake had been bait for a trap. The trap had snapped shut, and the suffering was about to begin.

Erica was thrumming the empty air above the bending girl with the wood. It whistled a note of eerie venom. Addressing the smooth cheeks with the levelled cane, Erica judged the distance with faultless exactitude. The cane rose up – then swept down with a cruel swish. Mandy blinked as the thin rod whipped down across the helpless cheeks, and closed her eyes tightly as Sophie squealed.

'The punisher must own the bottom of the punished,' Erica remarked briskly. 'Observe.'

From her kneeling position, Mandy gazed up to see Erica lowering the length of glinting wood across the cusp of the proffered buttocks. Depressing the yellow wand firmly, she dimpled the smooth curves of flesh. It was a display of sheer dominance.

'Now I tap the buttocks,' Erica continued, doing so in a gesture of superb control. 'This reminds the whipped one of the stroke just delivered,' Erica whispered, then plied the cane swiftly to lash the bottom with stinging accuracy, 'and of the stroke to come.'

Despite her remorse and sorrow, Mandy could not deny the hypnotic fascination of the dominance and discipline played out before her. Between her clamped thighs, her slit prickled and grew moist.

Four more strokes followed, leaving thin pink lines that slowly turned blue across the creamy flesh of the suffering bottom.

'Be sure to pace the punishment as carefully as you place the stripes. They should be at least twenty seconds apart,' Erica said softly as, breasts bouncing, she

74

delivered the seventh searing swipe, 'and at least a quarter of an inch below the previous cut. See?'

Mandy nodded, mesmerised by the caning. She hated it, but despite her hate she drank in every vivid detail: the long, slender legs sweeping up to the ripe peaches above; the blush of those superb peaches criss-crossed with reddening stripes; the sudden creasing of the cleft as the whipped buttocks spasmed in sweet pain. Dark as it was, Mandy acknowledged that discipline in all its aspects was quite delicious. More delicious than she would ever have dared admit before coming to Sternwood Grange.

Erica was adept: a capable caner and a consummate chastiser. More, she was a cruel controller of bare bottoms with bamboo. Despite herself – and poor Sophie's suffering – Mandy became a keen disciple of stern discipline as the cane swished down again and again, and the plucking sensation in her hot slit throbbed with a galloping pulse.

'Three left. Three more strokes to administer,' Erica said. 'You will have noticed that this girl's bottom is softly fleshed. The cheeks are pliant beneath their taut, satin sheen. When dealing with this type of bottom, I recommend very crisp strokes delivered to the centre and the lower quadrant of the buttocks.'

'Yes,' Mandy mumbled, nodding. She swallowed, her tongue now swollen with thickened lust. The tang of her excitement rose up from her wet slit to stab her nostrils. Kneeling to attention under Erica's stern gaze, she ached to finger her labia further apart, and probe the burning flesh within the sticky flesh-folds.

'Feet apart,' Erica ordered, dragging the tip of the cane down along Sophie's quivering thigh.

The bending girl obeyed, well drilled in the ways of dominance. Parting her thighs a fraction, then a fraction more, she allowed Mandy a delicious glimpse of her dark fig. Mandy's breasts tightened and weighed heavy as she saw how wet and juicy Sophie's forbidden fruit had become.

'Wider,' Erica commanded, tapping the buttocks sharply.

The pink lips greeted Mandy's gaze with a welcoming, wet smile as Sophie parted her thighs. Erica's stern voice was the only sound in the intense silence of the warm afternoon, but Mandy could hardly hear it, so loud was the rushing of hot blood in her ears. She could now see Sophie's wet crease in its entirety, and shuddered with wonder at the oozing sparkle on the pouting lips.

'I will let you dispense her concluding strokes, Mandy. Get up and show me if you have learnt anything this afternoon.'

Mandy rose from her knees, accepted the cane and, as Erica retreated to the bed, swished the bamboo down across the striped cheeks. Sophie squealed her torment but then, to Mandy's surprise, appeared to inch her bottom up in supplication for the next stroke. More in eagerness than in anxiety, the whipped girl submitted her bottom to the bamboo. Mandy frowned. What did this dark ambiguity mean? Was there pleasure for Sophie in her pain? Why was the bare bottom now seemingly eager to embrace rather than escape its sweet sorrow.

Glancing at the spot where the rounded cheeks merged into the soft sweep of the thigh, Mandy saw a silver bubble at the caned girl's labia. Biting her lower lip in concentration, she steadied the cane and tapped it briskly at the winking wetness. The bubble popped silently, and Sophie sighed softly with a shudder of pleasure. The tip of the yellow bamboo darkened slightly, stained with her hot juice. The cane trembled in Mandy's grip, and she felt a flicker of delight forking down from the base of her belly to the tightening muscles within her innermost flesh.

'Again,' intoned Erica.

Mandy raised the wet cane, then plied it with swift

savagery across the bare bottom, bringing Sophie up on her toes in an anguish of ecstasy.

'And again,' instructed the cropped blonde, her voice curdled with lust.

The cane glinted in the sunlight as it bequeathed a final kiss of fire across the crimsoned cheeks.

'That was better, Mandy. Much better. You seem to have an appetite for doing your stern duty. And you seem,' Erica purred, 'to understand the importance of the dominance the caner must exercise over the caned. Punishment,' she continued softly, 'promises much more than mere pain. It is so rich in potential pleasures. Later, I will teach you and you will learn that the time spent examining and inspecting the punished bottom can be as rewarding as the time spent dispensing the discipline. But more of those matters later, perhaps. It is time to take you to the sauna.'

The sauna was for the exclusive use of the residents, Erica told Mandy as they entered the spacious room. Before being converted, Mandy speculated, it must have been a ballroom. The high ceiling was completely covered in pale-blue mirroring glass, the walls gleamed with clinically white Italian tiles. Six large bay windows, once overlooking the neatly arrayed rose beds outside, had been rendered opaque by gold frosting. It was well equipped – better than her Knightsbridge health spa, Mandy concluded as she ran her auditing eye over the silver chrome and dark-leather fixtures and fittings.

'Strip,' Erica ordered, flicking on a panel of lighting controls.

Blinded by the flood of neon, Mandy hesitated.

'Quickly, girl. You will be receiving two residents shortly. I want you to serve them.'

Mandy raised an eyebrow.

'See to their every whim,' Erica translated. 'You must be changed and ready to receive them.'

Mandy wriggled out of her vest and skirt and stood, braless but tightly pantied, before Erica. The cropped blonde's cruel mouth pursed appreciatively as she stared at the proud swell of Mandy's pubis sheathed within the stretch of cotton.

'Panties off.'

Mandy thumbed them down over the swell of her ripe hips and rump and stepped out of them, her face a sullen mask of resentment as she felt Erica's narrowed eyes feasting on her nakedness.

'Hmm. A natural blonde,' Erica murmured.

Mandy flushed, covering her pubic nest with both hands. That was a bit close, she realised. If Celia Flaxstone ever came to notice her blonde curls, she might just possibly recall the blonde Amanda Silk.

'Apron and gloves,' Erica said, handing the clear-plastic uniform over. 'Hurry up.'

Mandy wrapped the plastic apron around her belly and breasts. It was not an easy task: the thin plastic clung to her lovingly. Twice she had to peel it away from her soft nakedness and start anew. Eventually, she had donned the plastic apron and, reaching out behind, was struggling with blind fingers at the tabs.

'Come here,' Erica snapped crossly. 'Turn around.'

Mandy obeyed, presenting her bare bottom to the cropped blonde. Erica drew the tabs together tightly and tied them, causing the plastic apron to squeeze Mandy's bosom, pressing the trapped breasts deliciously. Down at her golden nest, the stretch of plastic crackled the pubic fuzz. Mandy shuddered at the sudden closeness of Erica: the cropped blonde's hot breath on the nape of her bowed neck, the swell of the breasts thrust into her naked back, the brush of Erica's firm hips against her bare bottom.

'Now the gloves.'

The command, and the warm breath that carried it, made Mandy shudder. She took a step forward and struggled with the clear-plastic gloves. Erica took a similar pace, matching Mandy's, bringing her lower belly close against Mandy's naked cheeks once more. Reaching around her captive, the cropped blonde snapped the stretchy gloves into place. Mandy flexed and splayed her fingers, thrilling to the unexpected pleasure of the tight feel.

'Red robes are dominants, yellows are subs. You'll get one of each this afternoon.'

Mandy turned, frowning.

'Red robes. Worn at all times by the dominant-type residents outside their private quarters. Here in the sauna or down in the gym. They are very strict with the angels and have sharp appetites. They take pleasure in others' pain. The yellow-robed residents,' Erica continued, disregarding the mounting look of dismay on Mandy's face, 'are subs. Submissive types. They take pain for their pleasure. Be stern with them, and manage them strictly. They yearn for the humiliation, discipline and bondage you will dispense.'

As these words sent her pulse throbbing, Mandy dragged her gloved palms down across her belly and smoothed the plastic apron over the swell of her upper thighs.

The door opened. 'They're here,' Erica warned. 'Remember, when serving a dom, you are hers entirely. And, when serving a sub, she is utterly yours. I will,' Erica said sternly, 'deal with you most severely should you fail to please.'

Erica withdrew, leaving Mandy to greet and receive a red-robed dominant resident. Mandy gasped. Surely she had seen this beautiful woman's face on late-night intellectual talk shows shredding to pieces the vapid opinions of the good and the televisually great. Yes. It was her, here in the flesh.

The resident gazed impassively ahead of her, ignoring Mandy completely. Only the impatient jerk of her shoulder signalled her readiness to be disrobed. With trembling fingers, Mandy led her client into a cubicle, drawing the curtains together behind her. Turning, she caught the edge of the red towelling robe gingerly, curling her fingers into its softness to steady herself. After pulling at the belt, she peeled it down over the woman's shoulders, exposing her superb breasts. The dominant, a haughty beauty of thirty-six, tossed her raven hair as she stepped out of the robe. Mandy stooped to gather up and fold the discarded robe, shyly glimpsing the arrogant thrust of the proud bosom above. Silently, the raven-haired beauty motioned Mandy to stand before her. For a full minute, Mandy shivered in her client's stern gaze.

'Kneel,' whispered the sensual, cruel lips.

Mandy knelt, her knees kissing the cold tiles.

'You will attend to me in the sauna, then dry me when I emerge. Understand?'

'Yes,' Mandy murmured, her eyes level with the dark, matted pubic nest before her.

'And I shall need to be oiled.'

Mandy raised her face, expectantly.

'Not now, fool. Later.'

Mandy cast her large eyes down and blushed. She attempted to rise, but was immediately quelled by an imperious hand on her shoulder.

'Shave me first, before the sauna,' came the strict command.

The nest of matted pubic curls rustled softly as the thighs before Mandy's face parted an inch, then another half-inch. Stretching out her plastic-gloved hand, she tentatively stroked the dark fuzz with her fingertip. Shave her? Mandy's heart thumped against her rib cage at the very thought of this intimate act of homage and service. But how? With what?

'Over there.' As if reading Mandy's mind, the dominant woman placed three fingers under the kneeling girl's chin and swivelled her face towards the sink. It was, Mandy saw, a small onyx basin with taps of dull gold. Mandy shuffled across the hard tiles on her knees, gathered up the scented foam, petite razor and hand towel. Returning to kneel submissively before the naked dominatrix, she set out her equipment in neat array.

'You'd better lick me first,' came the curt command.

Inching her face closer, Mandy heard her taut plastic apron crackle. Within its crisp embrace, her heavy bosom bunched, the breasts swollen and rounded as they bulged within the sheen of bondage. Maddened by her tingling nipples as they pressed into the clinging plastic, she risked a furtive touch. Instantly, the nude's right hand taloned her hair, forcing her head back.

'You are here to pleasure me, girl. Not yourself. If I catch your fingers where they should not be once more, I shall have you whipped. Do you hear me?'

Mandy nodded, wincing at the controlling hand that punished her hair.

'What will you be if caught once more?' came the stern interrogation.

'Whipped,' Mandy whispered through dry, parched lips.

The fierce fingers in her hair relaxed and Mandy saw the hand return to brush against the swell of the woman's naked thigh.

'Lick me. Wet me thoroughly, then shave me.'

Timorously at first, but with a gathering boldness soon fuelling her tongue, Mandy moistened the nest of dark pubic curls. At last, sniffing the feral tang of the pubis, she flattened her tongue against the rasping fuzz.

'Good,' the dominatrix remarked, nodding her apparent satisfaction as she fingered her delta.

Mandy squeezed out a line of scented foam into the open palm of her left hand. With the first and second fingers of her right hand, she scooped up a smear and worked the white softness into the pubic curls. As the tip of her third finger accidentally caressed the hood of the clitoris with a fleeting touch, she sensed the woman rise up on her toes.

'Careful,' came the stern warning. 'Serve me carefully or your bottom will suffer.'

Mandy, panicking, accidentally parted the thick labial lips. Her cornflower-blue eyes flickered up penitently. The towering nude merely grunted softly, motioning her kneeling slave to continue. Mandy took up the tiny golden razor and, taking a deep breath to steady her excited hand, started to shave the foaming delta. With short, delicate, sweeping strokes she exposed the gleaming skin beneath.

As the foamed coils curled up before the blade, a strange sensation tightened Mandy's breasts and thickened her tongue. Suddenly, the pulse at her throat throbbed uncontrollably. The sensation was confusing, erotic and disturbingly delicious. Kneeling in submission and forced to perform this humiliating act of intimacy, she nevertheless sensed a curious feeling of power and of being in control. This dominant woman with her legs splayed apart was, she realised, utterly at her mercy. The tiny golden razor in her hand was as potent as any cane or crop hovering above bare buttocks. Fired by this electrifying awareness, Mandy grew imperceptibly bolder: she framed the flesh of the delta with two fingers, stretching the skin and exposing it to her blade. Soon, the proud swell of the pubic delta surrounding the glistening fig was shaved clean. Mandy felt a heady mixture of relief and exultation surge up within her. Though kneeling in subjugation before the dominatrix, she still felt the intoxicating thrill of being in control.

'Kiss it,' whispered the raven-haired beauty, cupping her ripe breasts and squeezing them ruthlessly.

The harsh command broke the spell: Mandy was a

slave once more. She strained forward, steadying herself with her plastic-gloved hands delicately upon either hip. Her lips closed on the sweet flesh-folds.

'Suck.'

She sucked, hard.

'Lick me, bitch.'

Mandy's tongue lapped hungrily at the slightly salty flesh.

'And kiss me once more.'

Mandy pressed her mouth firmly into the labia.

'Not with those lips, bitch,' came the dark command. For a brief moment, Mandy was puzzled. The dominatrix raised her right foot and, pressing her toes into Mandy's slit, raked them against the shiny plastic. 'Those lips.'

Mandy blushed as a sudden rush of understanding flooded her brain. Peeling up the clinging sheath of plastic, she exposed her own blonde curls. Crablike, between the splayed legs of the naked dominatrix, she struggled to inch her hips up towards the recently shaved delta. Amused at her awkward, and painful, attempts, the woman gazed down into Mandy's blue eyes. Mandy stared directly up, shuddering as the raven hair tumbled down over the woman's shoulders as her tormentress tossed her head in cruel amusement.

'Do it, bitch, or you'll feel the lash.'

With a supreme effort, Mandy jerked her hips up, fusing her blonde curls into the warm, wet slit above. A hot spasm of shame, and some unknown sensation not unlike forbidden lust, exploded deep down in Mandy's tightened belly. Above, the woman growled softly as she savoured the ultimate gesture of submission and surrender one female can offer another.

'Well done, slave,' she whispered, then abruptly pushed Mandy away. In a cold tone, she ordered Mandy to attend to her needs in the sauna.

Mandy perspired freely in her tight plastic apron and

gloves as the dominatrix luxuriated in her steam bath. Emerging, pink and glowing, her raven tresses matted to her temples, the nude stood alongside a narrow leather couch as Mandy plied a soft towel.

'Not bad,' the dominatrix conceded grudgingly as her slave completed the intimate act of towelling her body dry. 'Bend over.'

Alarm tightened Mandy's throat at these unexpected words. The towel fell from her hands, slithering silently to the cool tiles. After all her efforts, punishment was the last reward she expected.

'Four strokes,' the dominatrix snarled softly, suddenly clapping her hands.

An angel poked her head through the parted curtains.

'Crop,' demanded the raven-haired nude.

Six seconds later, a crop was supplied. The curtains closed, leaving Mandy in seclusion with her tormentress once more.

'Further across the couch. Give me your bottom. No, bigger. I want it big and round,' the dominatrix purred. She continued almost pleasantly, 'I would have given you ten if I was displeased. You have served me reasonably well.'

Mandy squirmed across the soft leather of the couch but froze as the tip of the crop descended to depress the swell of her exposed left buttock.

'Perfectly still while I stripe you, girl.'

The crop withdrew, only to return a fraction of a second later to bite into her bunched cheeks with a searing swipe. A crimson flashbulb popped silently behind Mandy's tightly shut eyes as the leather-sheathed crop sliced her soft cheeks with vicious tenderness. The red light exploded once more as, again, the crop kissed her cheeks with savage affection. The third stroke, slightly delayed, cut across the quivering crown of her bare bottom, rocketing her hips into the leather surface of the couch.

An agonising pause followed, during which the fierce

heat spread down from her whipped cheeks to the shadowed flesh between her clamped thighs. Mandy ground her clitoris into the shining leather, humping herself rhythmically into its dark hide. She tightened her buttocks as she felt the tip of the crop tap-tapping her upturned cheeks to quell her writhing. Steadied and stilled, she stretched across the couch, submissively awaiting the fourth searing swipe. The dominatrix lingered, pressing the length of the crop down into the fleshy cheeks. Mandy shivered and moaned, tonguing the leather in her anguished torment. Suddenly, within three quarters of a second, the crop had been whisked up – only to crack down mercilessly across the ravished bottom.

'Oil me. Gloves off,' the nude commanded, tossing the crop aside and easing her splendid nakedness face down on to the couch.

Mandy shivered after the brief but blistering punishment, and searched about in vain for the oil. Her bottom ablaze, she poked her head out between the curtains and whispered to a nearby angel. Oil was produced by the redhead, Rowena, and handed over with a sympathetic grimace. Mandy grinned and returned to the naked woman stretched out on the leather couch. To her dismay, Mandy watched the raven hair cascade as the nude reached down and picked up the abandoned crop. More? Was there to be more of the fierce discipline? To her puzzlement, the nude slipped the crop down between her thighs, crushing and trapping it between the leather and her pubis.

Oiling the dominatrix was a slow, sensual pleasure for both the mistress and the slave. As Mandy applied the sheen with her palm, she was acutely conscious that the crop which had lashed her bare bottom was now being manipulated by the nude: the thicker end rolling against her dark nipples, the tapered, whipping end worrying the labia below.

The nude's heavy, slightly muscular buttocks were

now raised about three inches up off the leather couch, impatiently spasming for the oiling. Sore bottomed and perspiring, Mandy tasted the bitter fruits of submission and humiliation as she palmed each swollen cheek with the sticky, scented oil. Supremely indifferent to her toiling slave, the dominatrix continued to ravish her slit with the wet tip of the crop. Grunting softly, she approached her climax, squeezing her buttocks and trapping Mandy's oiled finger between their warmth.

'Oil me there,' the nude gasped, tossing her raven hair as she offered up her now gaping, stretched cheeks to reveal the pink rosebud of her sphincter. 'Quickly, bitch.'

Mandy's index finger, dripping with the gleaming unction, hovered above the anal whorl.

'Do it, bitch. Now,' she rasped, almost choking on her own thickening lust.

Probing the tight warmth tentatively, Mandy shuddered as she savoured her burning shame. The strong muscles within the heavy buttocks trapped her finger as the next wave of orgasm rippled and threatened to explode. The snarling dominatrix stiffened as she crushed her breasts into the leather. Mandy saw the right hand guiding and pumping the vicious crop against the clitoris. The oiled hips jerked up, the nude screamed softly. With her finger still buried deep inside the heavy buttocks, Mandy suffered the ultimate humiliation of servicing another's orgasm – not as a pleasure-partner, but as an insignificant slave.

The submissive was easier to manage. Mandy propelled the slender blonde into her sauna with sharp spanks to each soft cheek. The gentle blonde purred with pleasure as Mandy controlled her, ordering her about with stern authority. Even towelling the glistening blonde after the sauna was a strict affair, with Mandy punishing the blonde's bouncing breasts briskly with the brushed cotton, carefully savaging the defenceless nipples until they peaked with delicious pain.

'Hazel twigs. Whip her bottom lightly,' Rowena, the red-haired angel murmured, appearing through the curtains and offering Mandy a small, bound bundle.

Mandy smiled and nodded as she accepted the scourge. Turning to her shivering blonde, she spoke sternly. 'Face down on the couch.'

The blonde straddled the leather with pleasurable anticipation as Mandy studied the hazel twigs, inspecting them closely. The scourge was made up of fourteen supple twigs, each trimmed to a length of eleven inches. They had been bound together at the base with waxed cord. Pliant and springy, they were potent with pleasure and bristled with the promise of pain. Mandy dragged the tips of the quivering twigs down across her bosom. She gasped softly as her nipples stiffened and rose up, peaking and saluting the gentle torment.

'Hands up on the couch. No, by your face. Palms down.'

The blonde obeyed with alacrity, waggling her slender bottom invitingly as if impatient for the stinging caress of the scourge.

'Feet and thighs tightly together,' Mandy ordered crisply, carefully maintaining the waspish note of dominance. She watched with growing satisfaction as the obedient blonde welded her legs and thighs together, forcing her cleft into a fierce crease between the naked cheeks.

'No,' Mandy said. 'Relax your bottom. I want it soft for the whipping. 'Make it rounder,' she whispered, secretly amazed at how easily she found the words of command. 'I am going to whip you slowly with these hazel twigs,' she explained, as if in a schoolroom before an attentive row of adoring students. 'Slowly and gently. Enough to bring you to the boil,' Mandy purred, thrilling to the effect of her dominant voice on the squirming blonde, 'but not enough to make you spill over.'

Sugared sorrow was what the blonde wanted. Sweet torment. The promise of pleasure offered up in a cup – only to be dashed from her eager lips. Mandy suddenly knew with an absolute knowledge her role as dominatrix to this submissive. Just as she had detested pleasure-serving the red-robed dominant, now Mandy anticipated the dark delights of twig-whipping this beautiful blonde's bare bottom.

Mandy savoured every moment of this new-found delight. She paced herself carefully, prolonging the exquisite pleasure. When she was with the red-robed dominant, she had been forced to serve at a tempo dictated by the other's whim. Now, Mandy felt a surge of excitement burning within her. Already her slit was hot and wet. She was in total control of the naked blonde stretched out before her: in absolute command of both the submissive's imminent joy and sweet despair.

With a soft swish, Mandy raked the bare bottom with the bunched hazel twigs. The blonde squealed her delight into the leather, clouding its sheen with her hot excitement. Again, Mandy dominantly swept the supple scourge down across the beautiful cheeks. Hips bucking and jerking up in response, the blonde arched her buttocks up for more. Levelling the bunch of twigs against the smooth thighs, Mandy flicked her wrist, causing the tips of the dancing hazel rods to pepper the curves of the blushing cheeks with stinging kisses. Writhing on the leather, the naked blonde furtively inched her fingers down towards her bosom.

'No,' Mandy warned, tapping the knuckles smartly. 'Hands up where I can see them.'

The blonde tongued the leather in her sweet torment. Ignoring her, Mandy plied the hazel scourge seven more times, leisurely reddening the delicious bottom. As Mandy lightly whipped the bouncing buttocks, the blonde surreptitiously managed to cup and squeeze her naked breasts.

'I warned you.'

The scourge lashed down, eliciting a squeal.

'Hands by your face,' Mandy hissed, now relishing her supreme dominance.

Submissively, the naked girl obeyed, splaying both hands by her tousled blonde mane.

'And if you come before I give you permission,' Mandy continued, astounded at her confidence as dominatrix, 'I will punish you harshly. I will bind your hands and feet together,' she whispered, raking the nude's spine with the hazel twigs, 'and whip you till you beg for mercy.'

The blonde purred her pleasure into the damp leather and inched up her buttocks for the lash she desired. Mandy would not be bidden. She teased the bare bottom, tracing the outline of the curved cheeks with the trembling twig-tips. Slowly, she raised the scourge up, smiling as the buttocks rose up in an arch of anticipation. Mandy lowered the bunched twigs, allowing the hot flesh to kiss its sweet torment.

'More. Harder. Lash me.'

The urgent tone, the note of demand, annoyed Mandy. It reminded her of earlier moments of humiliation and subjugation. A flash of anger arrowed through her brain. The mocking words of Celia Flaxstone – calling her late aunt an old bat – and the brazen attempt to steal Mandy's inheritance. The arrogant red-robed dominant who had forced Mandy to serve her. These, and other, recollections of her recent suffering and humiliation flooded Mandy's consciousness.

For a brief, ungovernable moment, she was no longer Mandy the maid, cunningly seeking to retrieve her fortune, but Amanda Silk: proud, sophisticated and accomplished.

The bare bottom before her was no longer that of a submissive blonde pleading for the pleasures of pain. It represented everything Mandy had been forced to suffer and endure since coming to Sternwood Grange. Discomfort, dismay and distress.

She whipped the hazel twigs down savagely – the blonde squealed her raw delight. Mandy's arm rose and fell again and again. Closing her eyes and shutting out the memory of her own humiliations and privations, Mandy gripped the scourge tightly and lashed it down repeatedly with increasing ferocity. A shrill scream of ecstasy forced her eyes wide open. Her cornflower-blue eyes widened at the unexpected sight before them: whipped into a climax, the blonde bucked and threshed abandonedly, pounding herself into the leather as she screamed her long, loud orgasm, 'My angel, oh my beautiful angel.'

Four

The summer sun blazed down upon Sternwood Grange, its heat silencing the doves sheltering in the wilting elms. Mandy had hardly seen the blue sky stretching wide over Suffolk since her arrival. She had been toiling in the basement kitchens, preparing delicacies for the exotic tastes of the residents up above, and had then been made to labour in order to satisfy their more peculiar appetites for pleasure and pain.

'You were quite a hit in the sauna,' Erica commented, escorting Mandy towards the gym. 'I've had some very good reports from the blonde submissive you attended to after her sauna. Wants to see a lot more of you, my girl. Enjoy yourself?'

Mandy blushed but made no reply.

'You seem to have a flair for dealing with the submissive type. I think we'll focus your activities as an angel on the yellow robes to begin with.'

To begin with. Mandy was momentarily distracted by a sticky warmth oozing at her labial lips, prompted by the memory of whipping the blonde's bare bottom with the hazel scourge yesterday. To begin with. Erica's words echoed in her brain. How long would she be trapped here? Could she really make her escape whenever she chose? With the stiff imposition of fines and penalties, it could take weeks, months perhaps, before she had amassed the means to escape. And then what? How and when would she confront Celia Flaxstone?

'Stop daydreaming, girl, or I'll use my strap,' Erica rasped. 'Come along. This way.'

At the end of the cool corridor they turned left and entered the gym. It was brightly lit, spacious and superbly equipped. Silver mirroring lined three of the four walls. Mandy followed Erica across the polished wooden floor, her mind trying to form pictures to fit the muffled sobs of pleasure and soft gasps of sweet pain that filled the vast echoing space around her.

'All submissives.' Erica nodded to the line of pegged yellow robes. 'Let's see how the angels are entertaining them.'

They approached a prickly mat. Mandy remembered the type from her boarding-school days. It was the type that scratched soft schoolgirl bottoms through their blue serge knickers. The older girls in the Upper Sixth used to giggle and call it 'pussy teaser' – Mandy never knew why until, when she was in the Lower Sixth one chill November morning, she crushed her wet labia down into it during an attempt at five press-ups. She had lingered until the bell rang. 'Pussy teaser.' Mandy smiled at her schoolgirl memories. Smack. Smack. Erica slapped Mandy's bottom harshly, the double spank echoing around the gym.

'Pay attention.'

Mandy donned the mask of alertness. She saw a naked brunette squatting on one of the mats, her bare cheeks pressed painfully down into the tormenting bristles. The brunette was nursing a scuffed medicine ball, cradling the heavy sphere against her bulging breasts. Standing at the edge of the mat, cool and clinical in a simple white sheath dress, stood the brunette's angel.

'Now lift it up above your head and keep it up while I count to twenty,' came the sternly spoken instruction.

The brunette's bosom bobbed delightfully as her slender arms stretched up. Mandy studied the face of the perspiring brunette as she struggled to keep the medicine ball aloft. It was, she considered, probably the pale face of the eldest daughter of some Shires squire, or perhaps that of a neglected niece frequently found haunting vast rectories. Now, under the pitiless gaze of her cruel, brooding angel, the brunette was blossoming: flushed with excitement, apprehension and strenuous effort. The angel counted slowly, the slender arms sagged slightly.

'I shall punish you if you fail. I shall punish your bare bottom with my cane,' promised the angel sweetly, thrumming the air with a short length of bamboo.

Mandy saw the brunette grimace with renewed effort, her bosom heaving and her face set with determination.

'Thirteen, fourteen, fifteen,' counted the angel methodically, tapping the short cane against her thigh.

The left arm spasmed and gave way. The heavy leather ball fell with a thud on to the polished wooden floor and rolled towards the angel. She stopped its progress with a jab of her foot, then kicked it back to the panting brunette who lay slumped on the mat.

'You failed. You know what that means, don't you?' the angel murmured, fingering her cane. 'Don't you?'

'Yes,' mumbled the brunette thickly, cupping her breasts and squeezing hard. 'Yes. I must be punished. I must bend over and have my bare bottom –'

'Must?' challenged the angel, dragging the tip of the cane up along the brunette's throat until it captured her chin and controlled it. 'Must? I say what may and may not happen to your bottom.'

'Sorry. You are right, of course. You own my bottom. Do with it what you will,' the brunette gasped, looking up at her angel with dark, sparkling eyes.

'Pick up the medicine ball.'

Scrambling across the mat, the brunette obeyed. Kneeling in front of the ball, which she steadied with her hands, she eased her breasts, then her belly, across the surface, presenting her naked buttocks for discipline.

93

'No, I don't want you across the ball, yet,' the angel said quietly. 'Pick it up and let's try again, hmm?'

Mandy and Erica watched. This time, the brunette managed to keep the ball aloft until the angel had counted seventeen.

'Again, you have failed. Across the ball,' the angel snapped, her tone crisper.

Crushing her bosom into the soft leather, the naked brunette straddled the medicine ball, presenting her bottom for punishment.

'Discipline and dominance is all about timing,' Erica whispered into Mandy's ear. 'The promise of punishment must be delayed, before it is fulfilled. Always dictate terms, and deny for as long as you can what the submissive most desires.'

Mandy nodded her understanding.

The angel knelt, thighs parted, alongside the bending brunette and fingered the cleft between the upturned cheeks. Thumbing the left buttock, she dimpled its soft satin swell.

'I am disappointed in you,' she whispered, now punishing the captive left cheek in a severe pincer of finger and thumb. 'And when I am disappointed, what do I do?'

'P–p–punish me,' grunted the brunette, squeezing her thighs together against the leather ball.

The cane cracked sharply down across the creamy cheeks, leaving a thin red line of fire across their curved swell. Again, the bamboo sang – a tuneless note of pain. Then again. The brunette squealed her dark response as she ground her splayed labia into the scuffed hide beneath. The angel, supremely indifferent to the brunette's writhing, sliced the cane down three more times in a savage staccato, rocketing the brunette into the ball.

Savouring every delicious moment of the discipline, Mandy gazed at the brunette's mask of frozen ecstasy –

gazed and suddenly understood. This domination and discipline brought the brunette back to some beloved memory of distant years: back to the dusty attic in the rambling rectory, perhaps, when, after tea, an angry aunt would spank her naughty niece for stealing plums from the orchard. Discipline and punishment were delicious, and here, at Sternwood Grange, the brunette's yearning could be met by a discerning angel who could diagnose the need, and dispense the appropriate treatment.

At the ninth stroke of the cane, the brunette cried out softly and hammered her thighs into the medicine ball with renewed fury. Methodically, imperiously, the angel plied her glinting yellow wand. At the thirteenth stroke, Mandy saw the crimson buttocks spasm as the girl tensed for her orgasm. Again, and yet again, the wood viciously caressed the curved cheeks. Peeling her breasts and belly away from the dull hide, the brunette toppled and rolled over on to her back. Pounding her whipped cheeks into the prickly mat, she orgasmed loudly. The angel bent over her, pressing the hot tip of the cane against her parted lips, quelling the brunette's shriek of delight. Mandy's heart thumped wildly within her, then stopped as her eyes fell on the dark wet patch where the whipped girl's pubis had kissed the sphere's scuffed leather.

'Let's see what's going on over there,' Erica suggested, touching Mandy's elbow gently.

As they approached the wall bars, Mandy could not resist the temptation to glimpse over her shoulder. On the mat, the young brunette lay spread-eagled, spent and exhausted after her violent climax. The angel knelt beside her, worrying the nipples of her captive with the tip of the bamboo. Mandy sensed the climactic release of pent-up longing from the brunette. After long winter months in the rectory, in the dimly lit drawing room where the large black grand piano was never played, and only scratchy 78s of Kathleen Ferrier grated against the heavy silence, the spring had come, quickly followed by the full blaze of summer. And under the fierce heat of the Suffolk sunshine, a spell for the brunette at Sternwood Grange. Such delicious memories to store up for the lonely months ahead, once harvest was home, for the girl. Memories of Sternwood Grange, and the angels, to consume furtively like the box of chocolate gingers smuggled up to her bedroom in the rectory on a cold winter night. Mandy remembered the wet patch on the hide of the medicine ball – and felt a surge of admiration for her late aunt and all she had achieved here at Sternwood Grange.

'Bondage can be a difficult art to master,' Erica remarked as they approached the wall bars. 'What qualities do you think an angel needs?'

Mandy remained silent, considering the question.

'Not just for effective bondage, but for discipline and domination?' Erica pressed.

'The ability to create and sustain an aloof intimacy?'

'Good. Yes. I like that. And?' Erica coaxed.

'A savage gentleness and an impatient patience.'

'Excellent,' Erica said, 'you demonstrate a clear understanding of the qualities required in an angel. Our residents expect their angels to be either angels without mercy, or angels for whom mercy is denied.'

Mandy paled at these words, fully aware of their dark meaning.

'The angel must be remote from, yet intensely connected to, her submissive client. And, when dispensing strict discipline, a touch of tenderness should sweeten her savagery. The punisher should have, shall we say, a fierce affection for the punished. Yes,' Erica concluded, 'I think the mistress will be pleased with your progress.'

The mistress. Mandy's heartbeat quickened.

'Is she returning soon?'

'No, but I am in constant touch. I believe she has hopes of you making a significant contribution to the success of Sternwood Grange. Do not disappoint her. Look –' Erica pointed, directing Mandy's gaze to the naked woman roped to the wall bars. 'See how tightly those knots have been tied.'

Mandy's eyes flickered up. On the wall bars, spread-eagled and securely bound, was the submissive blonde she had birched with the hazel twig scourge in the sauna. The naked buttocks still wore the crimson kiss of the rods.

'Your friend and admirer from yesterday,' Erica purred.

A waxed cord, threaded tightly round the captive breasts, was stretched out to bind the splayed arms at each wrist. A second biting cord hugged the hips to the wall bars, rendering the woman completely immobile. A third cord lashed the thighs together, welding the soft flesh into a cruel crease of suffering. Mandy's gaze lingered on the fourth waxed cord of the naked blonde's bondage. It arrowed down from the neck and shoulders, which it effectively haltered, along the sweep of her spine, buried itself in the cleft between the bound cheeks and disappeared up between the shadowed thighs against the pubis.

Mandy plucked furtively at her wet labia, the sight before her had turned her hot and sticky with keen arousal almost instantly.

The attending angel reached up, tugged the fourth tight cord and released it back into the cleft. The nude blonde grunted her pleasure.

'Shouldn't she be gagged?' Mandy whispered thickly.

'Not at this stage,' Erica replied, obviously appreciative of the studious attention Mandy was paying to events.

Taking two steps back from the wall bars, Mandy looked up at the ceiling, then lowered her gaze to the vast sheet of glass. Eight feet from the wooden floor of the gym, the mirrored glass reflected a perfect image of the immobile blonde in her strict bondage. Mandy saw where the fourth waxed cord emerged against the pubis, threading between the splayed labia. She narrowed her blue eyes, noting where the bosom bulged within a fiercely restricting rope. Mandy's gaze came to rest where the bound nude stared hypnotically into her own expression of exquisite anguish. At the point where the parted lips almost kissed the silvery glass, the blonde's heated excitement spread a dull, opaque smudge.

'It is always a difficult decision for the dominatrix to make,' Erica remarked. 'What would you choose to do now?'

'Do?' Mandy echoed, puzzled.

'Whip her while she is still in her bondage or cut her down and release her for the lash, hmm?'

Mandy considered this slowly, replying at length that she thought it all depended.

'On what?' Erica pressed.

'On what she begged for. Whatever she implored me to do, I would do the opposite, to begin with. I would at first deny her desires, only later granting them – but strictly on my terms.'

'Wonderful. You understand the submissive type really rather well, girl. And what about you, yourself?'

'Me?' Mandy blurted out, alarmed.

'Do you prefer to be punished, or to punish?'

Mandy blushed, unprepared for the question – and not willing to respond.

'The whipper or the whipped? Which is it to be?'

Mandy rubbed her foot into the polished wooden floor, her head bowed.

'I'll find out soon enough,' Erica chuckled. 'Half an hour down here in the gym, with you bare bottomed across that vaulting horse. My cane will soon search out your secret desires.'

Mandy reddened, bitterly resenting the casual intimacy of the cruel, cropped blonde.

'Punishing the maids is purely a matter of good governance,' Erica observed, 'but, with the angels, discipline is more of a voyage of mutual discovery. The mistress,' Erica added, 'has asked me to take close control of the angels. To become their tutor and mentor.'

Tormentor, Mandy murmured silently, shrinking slightly from Erica. Anxious at the direction the discussion was taking, Mandy sought refuge in the plight of the naked blonde.

'I'll just see how tight those bonds are,' Mandy said, mounting the bars slowly. Her foot curled over the smooth wood as she came to rest five and a half feet above the floor. Inching closer to the blonde, Mandy tentatively fingered the rope that bisected the rounded buttocks. Inserting her index finger knuckle inwards, Mandy felt the intense pressure of the waxed cord against her flesh. Gliding her knuckle down into and along the velvety ribbon of the cleft, Mandy gasped as the naked blonde shuddered, suddenly tightening the strain of the rope so that Mandy's knuckle was pushed into the wet sphincter. Writhing in the strictures of the waxed cords, the blonde groaned her delight.

Who was she, really? Perhaps not the daughter of the shambling rectory, Mandy thought. No. A high-powered futures dealer from the City? Perhaps. If so, she would be one of that army of Armani-suited executives making million-pound decisions in a minute, shaping future fortunes in an hour. Fingering the roped breasts lingeringly, Mandy formed a picture of the blonde. Driving a gunmetal BMW down to Dulwich under the sodium street lights after a gruelling day in the Square Mile. On the front seat, a winking laptop that never slept. Mandy imagined the crisp blouse, expensive dark tights and a pert but appropriate hemline: the blonde was shrewd enough to know that girls who dare to bare mid-thigh do not make important decisions in the office – they make the tea.

'Ask her,' Erica called up. 'Ask her what she wants. Make her confess to you.'

Mandy nodded down obediently, secretly resenting the intrusion into her thoughts. Deciding that the blonde was indeed a supercharged City high-flyer, Mandy mused upon the path that had brought the girl here to her bondage in Sternwood Grange. It was a chance to shrug off the huge burden of pressure and responsibility, no doubt. An opportunity to taste the delicious torments of surrendering utterly, of submitting completely, to the stern authority and cruel will of another.

Mandy, who had been caressing the tightened cheeks once more, withdrew her finger. The waxed cord snapped back into the dark cleft. Mounting another bar, Mandy levelled her face with that of the blonde. Slowly, carefully, Mandy stretched out her thumb and brought it to the passive lips. The mouth formed a surprised circle and then closed over the thumb, sucking fiercely. Mandy probed the wet warmth of the blonde's mouth, marvelling at the strength of the tugging muscles. Reflected back from the mirrored glass, the blonde's eyes were wide with excitement. Mandy stiffened. The sound was unmistakable: warm golden pee was cascading down between the blonde's thighs. She's wetting herself, Mandy realised. Actually wetting herself in ecstasy.

Back down on the floor, Mandy stared in fascination at the dark stain below the blonde.

'The angel will take her away shortly,' Erica remarked, 'for a bath. Then she'll be dried, powdered and babied. A spanking will follow, then nappies, perhaps, or a bed made up with a rubber sheet. But not yet. The angel has not finished with her submissive blonde.'

Mandy shivered as she saw the angel produce an eight-inch solid-rubber dildo.

'Dominance and discipline, for the female, is not always achieved with a cane, crop or cords,' Erica remarked, reading the wonder in Mandy's widening eyes. 'Come along.'

As they turned and walked away from the wall bars, Mandy stole a backward glance. The cord that had arrowed down into the dark cleft was now bisecting the bulging left buttock. The bulbous tip of the rubber dildo was being firmly stroked down the cleft. Below, the wet, shining thighs – recently soaked by the golden rain of the blonde's delight – were clamped tightly together. A shrill scream echoed around the gym. Mandy quickened her pace to catch up with Erica. As she joined the cropped blonde in the centre of the gym, another piercing scream of raw pleasure split the air. The probing rubber shaft would now be gliding firmly into the blonde, she realised, exactly where her own knuckle had worried and nuzzled the hot, sticky sphincter. Mandy shivered with delight and fingered her own seething slit.

They stopped at the edge of a black rubber mat. Straddled by a strap-wielding angel (Rowena, the redhead who had helped Mandy in the sauna yesterday), a submissive was executing sweaty press-ups face down into the rubber. Mandy recognised the bare buttocks. She had seen them being punished shortly after her arrival at Sternwood Grange. It was Lady Davinia, her matted chestnut curls tumbling down in a riot about her aristocratic features.

'Faster,' instructed Rowena. 'You're not really trying, are you?' The leather barked harshly as it lashed the buttocks.

As Lady Davinia's spilling breasts grazed the rubber mat, they bunched deliciously. Mandy watched, transfixed, as the next press-up was completed: it powered the hips down and forced the pubis to kiss the dark rubber. Another crack of the strap made Mandy blink, and the naked hips of Lady Davinia jerk: pounding the nest of chestnut fuzz into the hard rubber once more. Rowena placed her bare foot dominantly down upon the hot cheeks. Lady Davinia wriggled and writhed, squealing her excitement. The angel's foot lifted, moved up the sweep of the spine, and lowered itself into the chestnut curls, toes curled. Lady Davinia's second squeal of delight was smothered as she mouthed the rubber mat.

'Silence,' snarled the redheaded angel, fingering her length of leather.

'This is a simple exercise, devised by the former owner of Sternwood Grange,' Erica observed. 'Simple but very effective.'

Aunt Clare? Had her late aunt really devised this exercise herself? Mandy was about to follow up this unexpected line of inquiry, but remained silent. Better not raise any suspicions by showing any interest whatsoever, she decided, in the provenance of Sternwood Grange. But, in her silence, Mandy was amazed. The casual remark fired her imagination. Aunt Clare was more suited, she thought, to a mild hand of bridge and a traditional high tea served in the drawing room at three minutes after four. But if this was all her work, what was Mandy's potential? A blood relative, similar talents for dark pleasure probably flowed through her veins, she conceded. Was her inheritance from her late aunt to be more than money and property? Was it also a Sadean propensity for devising delicious torments for naked females?

Mandy brushed these thoughts away and tried to concentrate. Erica was speaking. Mandy listened.

'Simple, but an exercise in which control is exerted absolutely. The subject is brought to the very edge of her ecstasy –' a harsh snap of the belt whipping down across the upturned cheeks punctuated Erica's commentary '– but her climax is denied. Let's just stay and watch. I think you'll find it quite instructive.'

They sat down together at the edge of the rubber mat. Rowena, Mandy noted, was not wearing the clinical white uniform sported by the other angels in the gym. Like Lady Davinia, she was utterly naked. No, not exactly, Mandy realised. Rowena was wearing a pair of light bronze tights. As she turned, Mandy caught their delicious sheen in the glare of the bright neon light. The tights sculpted Rowena's buttocks superbly, moulding and hugging the bottom as the dominatrix bent over to ply the lash. Mandy, her wet slit now almost molten, yearned to lick and tongue the tights, mouth the thighs they sheathed, bite the soft buttocks imprisoned in their taut sheen.

Rowena snapped the leather down once more. Screaming softly, Lady Davinia sprawled across the rubber, dragging her nipples across its dull surface. Mandy knew that, like the erect nipples, the nude's clitoris would be rasping the rubber, hungry for orgasm.

'Bottom up,' Rowena commanded, positioning her foot – which Mandy had supposed naked until she had seen the gleam of the sheer nylon – upon the nude's neck.

The whipped cheeks rose up in submissive obedience, peeling the pubis away from the rubber mat.

'Her climax –' Erica motioned to the prostrate nude '– is now within her angel's gift.'

Mine too, Mandy realised with a sudden rush of self-knowledge. She parted her thighs a fraction to ease the burning torment. Mine too.

'It is for the angel to grant or deny the ultimate pleasure,' Erica added. 'See how absolute the authority of the angel is.'

Pointing her foot as she lifted it up from the nude's neck, Rowena dragged her nylon-sheathed toes down along the spine, bringing her foot to rest on the crown of the left, reddened cheek. Mandy's slit spasmed and tightened as she watched the dominant foot spreading the whipped cheeks apart. Into the yawn of the cleft, the angel dipped the tip of her dangling leather strap. Lady Davinia bucked and jerked – to reject the cruel hide? Or hug it between her hot cheeks? Mandy considered the problem, but could not be sure, could not be certain, of the answer. Slowly, she forced her brain to repeat the question, applying it to herself. She blushed and shivered as she saw the answer unfolding: if she were Lady Davinia, she would want to capture and keep the tormenting strap between the buttocks it had just severely lashed.

Mandy shrugged these thoughts away and watched as the redhead teased her submissive for several spellbinding minutes before eventually allowing the bottom to secure the dangling leather.

'Any moment now,' Erica whispered, recognising the signal.

Mandy's fingers plucked feverishly at the edge of the rubber mat. The polished wooden floor at her slit was clouded with her moist heat. She smothered her mounting excitement as she watched Lady Davinia grind her pubis into the rubber, her thighs and buttocks tightening and spasming rhythmically. Rowena gazed down with knowledgeable eyes and smiled. Reading every little twitch and jerk accurately, she suddenly wrenched the strap aloft. The crimson cheeks rose up as if in pursuit of the sticky dark hide. Rowena inched the strap up higher; tormented and denied, Lady Davinia pummelled the rubber with fists of frustrated fury.

'Now,' hissed Erica excitedly. 'The bitch gets it now.'

Mandy, to her horror and delight, started to come. Rocking slightly, she pressed her labial flesh-folds down into the wooden surface of the gym floor. The feral aroma of her excitement hung like the scent of a Chinese musk-rose in the air. Mandy bit her lip as the tightness within became deliciously unbearable.

Snapping the strap down four times in merciless succession, Rowena flattened the nude down into the rubber and jabbed her stockinged toes into Lady Davinia's wet fig. Tossing the strap aside, the redhead angel scrunched her toes into her victim's open crease, treading the flesh firmly to a strict tempo. Seconds later, the nude threshed in the frenzy of her long, shrill climax.

'Go and look at our equipment,' Erica said, rising from the edge of the rubber mat, utterly indifferent to the paroxysms of the nude orgasming at her feet.

Mandy, her own muted climax still welling rather than spilling inside her, rose a little groggily and sought the dark, cool sanctuary of the storeroom. Fingering the gleaming chrome calmed her, but a brush with the polished leather of a vaulting horse – the harsh tang of the hide stabbing her nostrils – quickly inflamed her. Steadying herself against the horse, she found and fingered herself ruthlessly.

'Caner or caned?' whispered Erica, emerging from the shadows.

Mandy, about to spill her own violent climax, gave a drunken grunt of surprise. She flinched as she felt the cool kiss of a cane pressed against her bottom.

'Or are you not quite sure?' Erica teased, levelling her cane firmly against Mandy's cheeks. 'You may come,' she said, her tone crisply clinical.

The presence of the wood against her bare bottom; the cool authority of the intimate command; indeed, the very fact of her self-pleasuring being scrutinized and sanctioned by the predatory cropped blonde rocketed Mandy into a fierce orgasm. Sinking down on to her knees, she came violently.

'As your tutor and mentor, I am in control of you completely,' Erica whispered, bringing the cane down on to the nape of the kneeling girl's neck. 'The mistress was most insistent on that point.'

Celia Flaxstone. Mandy's bare buttocks tightened in response to the unexpected reference to the solicitor.

'You belong to me, just as we all belong to the mistress of Sternwood Grange,' Erica continued, her voice treacling with excitement.

Mandy felt the tip of the cane dragging down along her spine, pause at the swell of her buttocks, then visit her wet delta, tapping it gently.

'As an angel under my tutelage, it is important that you share all your secrets with me. It will help me make a better angel of you, help you discharge your duties.' The tip of the cane emphasised these words by tapping at the glistening labia. 'And your duties as an angel are?'

'To pleasure the residents,' Mandy whispered. Looking down at the quivering cane, she saw the yellow wood darkened with her lust juice.

'Precisely. Now go and wash yourself thoroughly and go back out into the gym. I will arrange to have a resident brought to you.'

The gym was deserted when Mandy emerged from her shower. The doors flapped softly. She looked across to see Sophie entering. Mandy smiled.

'Bitch,' Sophie hissed. 'You deliberately ditched my chances of being an angel, didn't you?'

Mandy instantly remembered the slice of stolen cake – given with affection – and the hot bottom it had incurred for the platinum blonde. 'I didn't mean –'

'Got your wish, didn't you?' Sophie snarled. 'She's making you an angel.'

'How is Partridge? I haven't seen her –'

'Keep your little claws off Partridge, understand?' Sophie snapped.

Mandy was surprised at the venom of the response. Turning away, she walked towards the vaulting horse. 'Erica said she was sending a resident down to me.'

'She's here,' Sophie snarled.

Mandy smoothed the surface of the horse with both palms. She did not see Sophie usher in the resident, a red-robed dominant. Sophie slipped off the red robe and buried it under a yellow one.

'Your angel,' Sophie announced softly, indicating Mandy at the horse.

Mandy turned. Sophie was holding up a yellow robe and folding it carefully. In silence, Sophie retreated to the doors, pegged the yellow robe and departed. Mandy ignored the resident, merely snapping her fingers and pointing to the vaulting horse.

Raising her eyebrows in surprise, the dominant strode purposefully across the polished wooden floor.

'Up,' ordered Mandy, still ignoring the approaching nude.

It was a disaster. Within a minute and a half, during which Mandy had treated the dominant to a taste of what was usually experienced by the submissive residents, the nude exploded in outrage.

'How dare you? Are you stupid? Stupid, or simply wicked?'

Mandy paled. 'I don't understand –'

'Fetch my robe this instant,' thundered the angry dominatrix. Stunned and uncomprehending, Mandy took down the yellow robe from where Sophie had pegged it.

'No, not that one. My red one.'

A red robe. Mandy suddenly understood. Understood what an enormous error she had made – with Sophie's cunning assistance. Trembling, she found the red robe buried beneath the others and retrieved it.

Putting on her robe, the dominant sat down on a low bench and ordered Mandy across her knee. Arranging the angel across her lap, she sniffed at the musky tang of Mandy's recent arousal. Prising Mandy's thighs apart, she fingered the exposed fig.

'Moist, hmm?' the stern voice remarked. 'We'll see how wet a severe spanking makes you, shall we?'

Mandy shrank at the touch of a firm hand pinning her down by the nape of her neck, and shuddered as a firmer hand palmed her upturned buttocks. The spanking hand stuttered into life, raining down a savage staccato across Mandy's bare bottom. The spanked girl wriggled and squirmed but the spanker's grip was as sure as her unerring aim was certain, allowing no possibility of escape for the sore-bottomed angel.

'What's this?' Erica asked, entering the gym between the flapping doors. 'Not satisfied with the girl?'

'She is either colour blind, or very stupid,' the dominant snapped, vigorously palming the buttocks she had just chastised.

'Then should we not make the punishment fit the crime?' Erica purred solicitously, anxious to assuage the resident. 'Give her to me and allow me to punish her for your pleasure.'

The dominant surrendered Mandy to her fate. Erica gripped a cruel handful of Mandy's dark hair and led the captive angel across to the wall bars.

'Touch your toes, girl,' Erica ordered.

Mandy obeyed, seeing the approaching feet of the curious dominant in her inverted vision.

'I won't be a moment,' Erica remarked, departing. Seconds later, she returned from the storeroom, a table tennis bat in her right hand.

'What colour is a dominant's robe?'

Mandy replied, whispering the word red.

'And what colour is this bat?' Erica murmured.

'Red,' repeated Mandy, peering through her legs at her bottom reflected in the mirror behind the wall bars.

Erica examined the dimpled latex surface of the bat and nodded. 'Red,' she echoed. 'And what colour is your bottom?'

Mandy remained silent.

The bat swept down, splatting against the peach-cheeks. Seven times, in a furious onslaught, the bat whipped down, flattening the swelling curves on impact. The dimpled latex left blazing red blotches of pain on the creamy skin.

'What colour is your bottom, girl?' Erica hissed.

'Red,' gasped Mandy, squeezing a tear from her eye.

'Wrong,' Erica snapped. 'The robe is red. The bat is red. Your bottom is not red. Enough. Not yet.'

Thrilled by the discipline, the dominant nodded vigorously.

'But it will be when I have finished with you. Up. Get up,' Erica ordered. 'I want you across the vaulting horse.'

Mandy stumbled, naked and ashamed, across the polished wooden floor. Erica's pumps squeaked as she followed with a menacing, measured tread. The red-robed dominant, her eyes sparkling excitedly, joined both punisher and punished at the leather horse.

'Up,' Erica commanded, swiping the bat down across the hide.

Hot bottomed and afraid, Mandy straddled the horse then eased her breasts down to kiss the leather. The table tennis bat suddenly appeared before her eyes.

'Kiss it,' Erica demanded.

Mandy pressed her dry lips into the dimpled latex submissively.

'Lick it.'

Licking the latex with her rasping tongue, Mandy shivered at the watching dominant's appreciative grunt.

'I'll hold her down, my dear, while you use the bat on her bottom,' the red-robe volunteered eagerly.

Mandy felt the powerful grip at her shoulders, and, to her misery, felt the warm breath of the dominant against her nakedness. Erica swished the table tennis bat down – again, again and yet again. Pinioned, naked and helpless, Mandy squealed as her bare bottom blazed.

'Harder,' hissed the dominant, her face now pressed into Mandy's flesh. 'Harder.'

Erica needed no such encouragement, but heeded it as the bat swept down repeatedly to explode across the upturned cheeks.

As the cool of the evening bathed the elms surrounding Sternwood Grange with its soothing air, the doves broke their silence and murmured dreamily. In the purple twilight at the edge of the darkening copse, an early owl hooted its mournful reply. Someone, somewhere – a maid in a remote attic dorm – was playing Elvis Costello's 'Watching the Detectives'. It was a short-lived pleasure. Someone, probably Partridge on the prowl, Mandy thought, had quickly seen to that.

Outside the linen room, she paused, her hand resting lightly on the door handle. From inside came the muffled sound of a girl weeping. Mandy entered and found Sonia, the little minx of a maid she had seen, and had been obliged to spank, in the Gibbet. Sonia sniffed, hastily wiping her eyes.

'Whatever's the matter?' Mandy whispered, circling her arm around the minx and cradling her gently.

'Had enough of this place. Not enough to eat and Erica's always punishing me and all my so-called wages go in fines and I'm going to run away tonight and I don't care –'

Mandy stemmed the sobbed outburst with a kiss and a tender caress. Aunt Clare, she knew, would be horrified to see any of her girls in such a state. She felt honour bound to help. Besides, she liked the plucky little minx.

'But you can't possibly get away. Not without proper plans.'

Mandy listened as the minx defiantly said that she had been watching the midnight arrival of vans and thought it was a perfect means of escape and return to London. Mandy made no comment, but filed the information away for her own, undisclosed, purposes.

'But where will you go if you make it to London? What will you do?'

'I'll sort it when I get there,' Sonia sniffled, nuzzling her wet face into Mandy's soft bosom.

'And how much have you actually got?' The question was put gently, without any hint of sarcasm.

Sonia murmured that she had amassed the prodigious sum of seventeen pounds. Struggling not to smile, Mandy hugged the minx, then slipped her hands down to cup and squeeze the girl's firm buttocks.

'You know you can't survive. Not on seventeen pounds. Wouldn't last long on seventy, in London. You can't go. Not yet. Let me look after you, hmm? I'll see you're OK.'

'And what can you do?' the minx snapped petulantly. 'Oh, I'm sorry, I didn't mean . . .'

'Stay here,' Mandy said quickly. 'I'll be back in a minute or two,' she promised, resolving to give the minx a special treat.

The housekeeper's office was empty, the kitchens deserted. With her heart hammering louder than the clock ticking on the wall, Mandy secured biscuits, sweets and fruit by the handful, and, scuttling away with her brazen spoils, rejoined Sonia in the linen room.

'Here, enjoy these. Eat the apple last, it'll mask the smell,' Mandy whispered, showering Sonia with treats.

Wide-eyed, the pert little maid accepted the gifts and was soon gobbling greedily. 'You have some,' she said generously, her mouth full of Belgian pralines.

'No, you enjoy them,' Mandy said. 'And we'll talk about getting you out of here later.'

'You could get the Gibbet for this,' the minx said solemnly, swallowing an inelegant chunk of Mantuan nougat. 'You're just like a prefect I knew in school. She was kind.'

Mandy snapped a chocolate biscuit in half and munched it quietly. 'Better now?' she asked the minx at length.

111

'Mmm.'

They embraced and kissed, the minx's tongue-tip flickering out to wipe the tiny biscuit crumbs from Mandy's lips before Mandy forced her mouth dominantly down on to the upturned face of the younger girl. Again, Sonia's tongue wriggled and probed.

'Is that what your prefect taught you at school?' Mandy asked in a tone of mock severity, squeezing Sonia's bottom.

'Mmm.'

'What else?'

Sonia slid her hand, palm inwards, up inside Mandy's blouse. The inquisitive fingertips paused at the swell of the left breast, then inched up boldly to rub and stroke the nipple. Mandy pulled the minx towards her. The minx was fresh from the bath, scrubbed, and mildly carbolic to the nose. Mandy sniffed the delicious scent of freshly washed, slightly aroused girl. The busy fingers at her nipple brought the pink nub of flesh up into a peak of pleasure. Mandy eased her thighs apart, feeling the stretch of her damp panties across her mons veneris. The minx playfully pinched the nipple, and pulled. Mandy spanked the minx. Sonia's fingers withdrew, sliding sinuously down across Mandy's belly. Mandy felt them scrabbling at the elastic waist of her panties.

'Not now, little one. I will try to come and see you.'

'When?' whispered Sonia urgently.

Mandy cupped the minx by her buttocks, then, dividing them with her thumbs, spread the soft hillocks painfully apart. Sonia squealed, and rose up on tiptoe.

'Soon. Now off you go.' She spanked the bottom firmly. 'And no more wild talk of running away. Not till we plan it properly. Understand?'

Sonia, nibbling her apple, nodded. Looking up, she smiled shyly. 'You're just like that prefect,' Sonia blurted out. 'I loved her so much.' Turning, the minx ran out of the linen room, dropping the apple in her haste.

112

Mandy picked up the apple, wiped and then ate it, carefully disposing of the core. Even a stray pip could merit a whipped bottom in Sternwood Grange.

Remembering the deserted office in the empty kitchens, she returned, opened the door and entered: risking a brief examination of the accounts. The encounter with Sonia had unsettled her, troubling her mind with thoughts, and possible means, of escape. But her work here was not yet completed. She needed more facts and figures. She needed to open and peruse Partridge's carefully kept ledgers.

She was not disappointed, and within ten minutes had gleaned a great deal of new information. A strange sensation of discomfort, almost like the chill of a sudden draught, stilled her hand on the page of the accounts book. What was it? What was her sixth sense telling her? Something was wrong. Something was different, missing. She closed the leather-bound volume and stole out of the housekeeper's office into the shadows of the kitchen. The coast was clear. She relaxed a little, the tightness in her belly easing. All was still and silent. Silent? The clock. Mandy's brain missed the ticking of the clock.

'Looking for something?'

Mandy turned swiftly and saw Erica emerging from the shadows. She was cradling the clock against her breasts.

'I was just –'

'Just?' Erica sneered. 'I rather think that anything you had in mind was far from just. Quite criminal, no doubt.'

Mandy shivered. Had Erica seen her emerging from the housekeeper's office?

'This little chap needs regular attention,' Erica whispered, winding the clock up with a slow, rhythmic motion of her supple wrist. 'If I neglect it, the mechanism becomes irregular.' She paused, then added meaningfully, 'I abhor irregularity.'

Mandy tugged at the cuff of her blouse nervously. 'I only came down to see if there was a bit of spare fruit. Spoiled fruit,' she added earnestly, trying to minimise her crime – and impending punishment. 'Bruised apples that wouldn't be fit for the residents.'

Erica ignored this frank confession and patted the clock at her bosom. 'It is quite simple. If I attend to this clock, it serves me well. Works for me, reliably. And it is the same with both the maids and the angels. To make sure they run reliably, I attend to them. Vigilantly. Sternwood Grange has a delicate mechanism. I strive to maintain the balance. I find that nothing oils the wheels better than punishment. Into the Gibbet, girl. At once.'

'But I was only –'

Dangling in the Gibbet, her panties pulled down to her knees, Mandy clenched her bare buttocks in fearful expectation. Erica checked the leather collar around her captive's wrists, then addressed the ripe swell of the naked buttocks with her wooden spoon.

'Looking for a bruised apple, you say. I think,' she whispered, tracing the curved cheeks menacingly, 'you will not go to bed disappointed. You start with an advantage,' she purred, lowering her face down to slowly lick, then fiercely bite, the fleshy warmth. 'Being apple-buttocked,' she mouthed into the squirming cheeks, 'all you need is the bruising.'

Twisting and writhing, Mandy shuddered in her bondage. Erica went upstairs and returned with a bustle of naked, sleepy maids for the group punishment.

'Pay attention,' the cropped blonde barked.

Mandy, her wrists burning as they hung painfully from the leather collar, jabbed at the empty air with her naked feet.

'I promised you that I would bring order and discipline to Sternwood Grange and, as you will discover, I never break my word. You will all lose one week's pay.'

The assembled maids moaned in dismay.

'Silence. And I want you to bear that in mind while punishing our little thief here. Four strokes apiece. Commence.'

Sophie stepped up, accepted the wooden spoon and swiped Mandy's bare bottom savagely, evidently relishing her chance for revenge. After the four searing swipes, Mandy's buttocks tightened, as if squeezing out the pain from her ravished cheeks. Sonia followed, her strokes softer. The rest of the maids queued impatiently to vent their anger at the loss of yet another week's wages. Mandy's bottom paid a hot and heavy price as they blazed her crimson cheeks with the cruel wooden spoon.

'Excellent,' Erica remarked, stepping up to thumb the hot flesh and inspect it intimately. 'Back to bed with you all. As for you, girl,' she remarked to Mandy, 'you can stay up there for a while. Stay and suffer.'

'It's only me,' Sonia whispered, tiptoeing back across the flagstones eight minutes later. 'Are you all right?'

Mandy nodded silently, smiling down at the minx.

'Ooh, your poor bottom. Let me make it better.'

Mandy closed her eyes, wriggling her wrists in their leather collar to ease the burning ache. She opened her eyes at the soft sound of the fridge door. Sonia giggled as she rattled the ice tray, deftly closed the fridge door with her foot and scampered across to the hot, punished bottom swaying in suspended bondage.

Mandy gasped as the ice cube swept across the swell of her ravished cheeks, and gasped again as the minx traced slow circles on the crimsoned globes.

'There,' Sonia whispered. 'Better?'

'Mmm.'

'I hated it. Spanking you with that awful wooden spoon.'

'I understand.'

The minx drew the ice cube down along the length of Mandy's cleft. Mandy grunted softly.

'Nice?'

'Mmm. Very.'

The cube paused, glistening against the sphincter. Mandy twisted and bucked in her bondage.

'May I kiss you?' Sonia murmured, her lips now inches from Mandy's pubic fuzz.

'Lick me,' Mandy whispered huskily, her words half command, half imprecation.

Sonia wedged the ice cube between the punished buttocks and gently rotated Mandy, bringing the proud pubis three inches from the tip of her tongue. The distance between the two pairs of glistening lips – one darkly fleshed and vertical, the other pink and horizontal – vanished as Sonia brought her mouth up to, then into, Mandy's delta. A lapping sound filled the silent kitchen, almost but not quite drowning out the soft moans of delight. A fiercer sucking sound followed. Mandy squeezed her buttocks together, forcing a trickle of cold ice-water to sparkle as it slivered down her cleft and dripped, dripped slowly on to Sonia's breasts below. Fused, flesh to flesh, mouth to splayed labia, the minx furiously tongued the girl suspended in the Gibbet.

A sound at the door made Sonia spring back, her chin as wet as her gleaming bosom. Released, Mandy swung slowly round in a slow agony of anguish. Had Erica, and her spoon, returned? Mandy twisted to see. The velvet voice of Partridge broke the tense silence.

'Should you not be upstairs and in bed?' she inquired. The tone was not stern, more one of concern. 'You know what will happen if Erica catches you here, Sonia.'

'But Mandy was punished unfairly and she's been so kind to me,' Sonia replied breathlessly, 'and she –'

'Talked you out of any foolish ideas about running away, I hope,' Partridge interrupted gently.

116

Sonia blushed and looked down at the flagstone floor.

'Kiss Mandy goodnight, Sonia. I will take care of her now.'

'Will you?' the minx asked eagerly. 'Promise?'

Mandy, twisting in the Gibbet, turned to face Partridge just in time to see the housekeeper's large, brown eyes devouring her helpless nakedness. Partridge nodded and smiled. Sonia encircled Mandy's thighs with her embracing arms, and kissed the flaming buttocks tenderly. Without another word, the little maid scurried out of the kitchen, nimbly dodging a spank aimed at her retreating bottom.

'We don't need the light,' Partridge said, reaching out and switching it off.

The chain suspending Mandy rattled expectantly.

'It was really very good of you to take care of little Sonia. You stopped her doing something very foolish, tonight. Running away: it would have been a disaster. But then all the maids, and many of the angels, are unhappy here. Things are so different since –'

'Erica took control.'

'The mistress has her reasons,' Partridge said, her voice sad and gentle. 'Fruit, wasn't it?' she inquired brightly.

'Fruit?' Mandy echoed.

'I was informed that you are being punished for attempting to steal fruit.'

Mandy remained silent. In the darkness of the larder, she heard Partridge rustling. The rustling stopped. Footsteps approached her. A hand swept up between her thighs and grazed her pubic mound. Mandy welded her legs together. Partridge laughed gently and, reaching out, cupped and weighed the soft warmth of Mandy's bare bottom. Imperceptibly, she inched the cheeks apart, slowly widening the cleft. Mandy gasped.

'I cannot take you down from the Gibbet. Erica is now in a position of power here since the mistress came down from London to inspect her enterprise.'

117

Mandy quelled her surge of anger at these words.

'But I can reward you, Mandy. Reward and pleasure you for taking care of little Sonia. You are generous and unselfish. Such qualities cannot go unrecognised.'

Mandy felt the hands at the cheeks of her bottom slide down her thighs, following the line of her naked legs to her feet. Stooping, Partridge picked up an unseen object from the flagstone floor.

'Feet together,' the housekeeper whispered.

Mandy's feet pressed together as if joined in silent prayer.

'I could only find this orange, my dear, but I'm sure it will serve.'

Placing the orange just above Mandy's knees, Partridge palmed the fruit slowly upwards, rolling it against the naked flesh. The leathery touch of the peel on her own satin sheen sent a thrill arrowing down from Mandy's belly into the tightening muscles below. She clamped her thighs fiercely as the orange approached her pubic mound.

'Open wide,' Partridge whispered.

Mandy inched her thighs apart, admitting the orange in between them. The palm positioned the fruit, pressing it against the labial lips, and crushing them tenderly, before raking it up across the tiny, erect clitoris. Mandy screamed softly, jerking violently in her bondage.

Partridge deftly shifted her hand to cup and press the fruit up into the pubis. Rolling it gently at first, then with a mounting frenzy, she ravished the clitoris. Mandy squealed as her pink thorn rose up, only to be pressed beneath the soft weight. The hand that held the maddening fruit suddenly squeezed: zest spurted out, invisible in the darkness but filling Mandy's nostrils with its delicious tang. The juice scalded her open sex. Mandy threshed, rattling the taut chain that stretched up above her to the oak-beamed kitchen ceiling. Mandy sensed the hand guiding the fruit down against her

118

splayed labia. They widened into a welcoming smile and kissed the thick peel. Mandy whimpered. With a burst of intimate fury, Partridge skimmed the bound and helpless girl's wet slit mercilessly, stretching up with a warning hand against Mandy's lips to stem her welling screams.

The housekeeper removed her hand. 'Open your mouth,' she commanded.

Mandy parted her dry lips as the legs of an unseen chair scraped the flagstone floor. Mandy sensed, rather than saw, Partridge mount the chair. The haunting tang of the zest flooded Mandy's senses as Partridge held the orange just above her upturned face.

'Wider,' came the command.

Mandy's mouth stretched open, her tongue flattened like that of an exhausted animal. Mandy heard Partridge grunt softly with effort as she squeezed the orange viciously. A cascade of pulpy juice rained down over Mandy's face, splashing her with sweet, sticky wetness. Lowering the split and weeping fruit, Partridge allowed Mandy to bite deeply into it.

'Enjoy,' urged her sweet tormentress, cramming the wet flesh into Mandy's mouth.

Eyes tightly shut, her slit tingling and ablaze, Mandy mouthed the citric pulp, violently sucking its ripe sweetness. Partridge dragged the orange away. Mandy's chain rattled as she jerked in a spasm of ecstasy.

'No noise, my dear, no noise when you come,' Partridge cautioned, her voice warm and tender. 'This must be a silent pleasure.'

The chair squeaked in the darkness as, having dismounted, the housekeeper removed it. Mandy quivered expectantly, the pain in her bound wrists now pleasantly, unexpectedly sweet. Partridge returned the split fruit to Mandy's labia. Grinding the pulp into the flesh-lips, and pleasure-punishing the clitoris, the brown-eyed housekeeper fuelled the flames of Mandy's

119

burning climax. Working the orange adroitly, the controlling hand scrubbed the crease until a suppressed scream filled the darkness as, writhing in her bondage, Mandy came.

Turning slowly, her arms stretched painfully up into the leather collar, Mandy listened to the loud silence that remained after the housekeeper's departure. Nothing broke the stillness except the rushing sound in her ears: the beating pulse of her hot blood quickened by orgasm. No, she realised. She listened intently, and heard the tick of the clock. The clock, she remembered, which Erica had been winding earlier on. Winding with such grim exactitude: each twist of the supple wrist had tightened the spring just as effortlessly as each twist of her supple wrist would tighten the skin of a bottom she was punishing. Clocks suited Erica, Mandy mused.

The cropped blonde was blindly obedient. A clockwork martinet. Slavishly obeying the controlling mechanism: Celia Flaxstone. The grey-eyed solicitor controlled Erica and, through her, Sternwood Grange. The new mistress planned to run her private realm with clockwork precision. Partridge, Mandy smiled as she considered the comparison, was too tender-hearted to survive in the new regime. Partridge, with her big brown eyes and her gentle severity.

Mandy resolved, if and when she gained her rightful inheritance, to keep Partridge on, certain that the housekeeper would serve her as loyally as she had served Aunt Clare. And the minx, Sonia, would have no more reasons to attempt another escape. Harmony, happiness and pleasure would come back to visit – and stay at – Sternwood Grange. When Mandy was mistress of Sternwood Grange, pleasure would come before profit, and all profits would be shared.

The door squeaked. Mandy tensed with pleasurable expectation. It would be Sonia, sweet little Sonia, the ponytail-swishing minx. Sonia, back to show her affection and devotion.

Mandy took a deep breath and wriggled eagerly, twisting in her bondage to catch a glimpse of the little maid. One fingertip, then a second, grazed her pubic fuzz. Mandy mewed like a kitten at its cream.

'Bitch.'

A scarlet flash of light flickered across Mandy's brain as the unseen fingers plucked at her pubic tuft.

'Bitch,' Sophie hissed. 'I saw you seducing her. Leave her alone.' The fingers tweaked the soft curls again. 'Partridge is mine.'

Erica would be on patrol, and would deliberately leave Mandy in the Gibbet for at least another hour. Mandy jerked her wrists as the chair legs scraped the flagstone floor and Sophie mounted. Helpless in her bondage, she squirmed at the hot breath of the jealous maid as it neared her left breast. Where there was hot breath so close to her nipple, Mandy knew, sharp teeth must surely follow.

Five

'Up. No, leave that towel alone. I will dry you then dress you for the part.'

Mandy got out of the bath and surrendered her shining nakedness to Erica's towelling hands. She shuddered as the fabric enfolded her and she felt the thorough palms first at her breasts, then at her buttocks – and, finally, in between her thighs.

Another dawn had broken over Sternwood Grange. The sun was already blazing down, promising a fiercely hot day. Mandy was being bathed and prepared for her training. As an angel, under Erica's tutelage, she was about to encounter the first of her three test residents. A debriefing would follow, at the end of each trial, at which it would be decided if she had won her spurs.

Towelled, talcumed, and in a pair of tight white panties, Mandy was given a pair of sheer, black, nylon stockings.

'That is all you will require,' Erica remarked, appreciating the swell of her pantied cheeks as Mandy stepped into each black nylon and smoothed them up her slender legs.

Fingering the dark band of the stocking-tops, Mandy followed Erica along the length of the Long Gallery. Her heart raced. Would Erica turn to the left, or to the right? Was Mandy going to serve a dominant, or discipline a submissive? Erica strode purposefully ahead, her rippling buttocks giving no hint of which way the cropped blonde was heading. Mandy's concern grew into curiosity as they passed by the last of the double doors. At the far end of the Long Gallery, Erica unpocketed a key and opened a green-baize door.

'The Games Room,' she announced, stepping inside and beckoning Mandy in.

Sunlight streamed in through an oriel window. Through it, Mandy glimpsed the heat haze shimmering above the distant elms. The walls of the room were covered with a dull ochre paper, slightly peeling. A map of Scotland, a sketch of Mozart and a shelf of geological specimens furnished one wall. A bust of Dante, a faded diagram of a Roman amphitheatre and a botanically labelled fern graced another wall. Dusty books on dustier bookshelves lined the third wall. The floor was scrubbed pine. A school desk and a chair, a larger teacher's desk on a raised platform and a blackboard completed the furniture.

I'm to be a schoolgirl and have my naughty bottom caned, Mandy thought, biting her lower lip.

'Your cap and gown are over there.' Erica pointed. 'Your cane, slipper and strap, together with ink, pens and paper are waiting for you in your desk.'

'I'm the teacher?' Mandy squeaked.

Erica nodded briskly. 'Your submissive loves to relive the harsh delights of her schooldays. Her boarding school was notoriously strict.'

I'm to be the teacher, Mandy repeated silently, a surge of relief coming up through her tightening bosom. My resident will be a submissive – a submissive eager for the stern delights of crisp discipline. She strode across to the peg and took down a black gown. Slipping it on, she failed to cover her near nakedness underneath. The gown flapped open, allowing enticing glimpses of her bare breasts, white panties and black-stockinged thighs.

'This is the Schoolroom. Your submissive will be arriving shortly. Rowena –'

123

'Rowena?' Mandy echoed.

'The red-haired angel.'

Mandy nodded.

'Rowena will be in attendance throughout the entire session,' Erica continued, drawing a fastidious fingertip along a dusty bookshelf. 'Photographing your efforts.'

Mandy paused in the process of adjusting a perky mortarboard on her dark, bobbed hair. She looked up. 'Photographing?' she queried.

'Yes. She will take no part whatsoever. Your task is to follow this set of cue cards and entertain your submissive. Rowena will be here merely to record what you achieve.'

'But the photographs? I don't understand –'

'Thirty-five millimetre stills. Sharper than video. We provide each resident with a souvenir of their visit to Sternwood Grange, and the snapshots provide me with evidence of your skills and abilities.'

'I see.' Mandy nodded. Her mortarboard slipped and tumbled to the floor. Bending to retrieve it, she saw Rowena silently enter the classroom. Dressed in a skin-tight bodystocking, Rowena's heavy breasts bounced as she paced over to the oriel window and checked the light source with her meter. A Pentax dangled against her thigh.

'Better take a look at those,' Erica said, handing Mandy the cue cards. 'That's the scenario you must improvise.'

As Mandy studied the cards, Erica took up a duster and wiped out the past historic of the French verb *fouetter*, leaving the blackboard clean and the air thickened with chalkdust in the streaming sunlight.

Mandy read the four white cue cards carefully. Moments later, the classroom door opened and a breathless schoolgirl bounded in. A schoolgirl of twenty-six summers, but a schoolgirl nonetheless, wearing a short, grey, pleated skirt; white ankle socks and black sandals; a starched white shirt buttoned firmly at each sleeve and a blue, red and silver striped tie. The long blonde hair, Mandy noticed, was drawn back into severely plaited pigtails. Under the blouse, the outline of the Playtex bra proudly announced the pubescent swell of the Sixth Former's breasts. The schoolgirl's green eyes sparkled with expectancy. Mandy noted the lipsticked, slightly sullen mouth. Glancing down at her cue card, she read: LATE FOR SCHOOL.

Erica withdrew silently, slipping out through the sunbeams like a shadow, leaving them swirling in her wake. Rowena levelled her Pentax, remaining invisible in the shadows, her bodystockinged buttocks thrust up against the far wall. Mandy took the lapels of her black gown between pincered finger and thumb of both hands and pulled it forward. Her naked bosom spilled out deliciously, wobbling slightly as she planted her nyloned feet apart.

'Late?' she barked.

'Yes,' lisped the uniformed blonde, giggling. 'I stopped to speak with a boy.'

'Come here, you naughty girl. And is that lipstick I see, hmm?'

The blonde pigtails flounced as the girl mounted the platform, fingering her tie nervously.

'Not a good start this morning. Bend over.'

The naughty schoolgirl shrugged the leather strap of her satchel down from her left shoulder, faced the teacher's desk and, bending over, touched the black sandals with splayed fingers. Mandy raised the lid of her oak desk. It squeaked softly. The bending schoolgirl shivered pleasurably. Withdrawing the eighteen-inch cane, Mandy lowered the lid of the desk.

'Panties,' she prompted, tap-tapping the sweep of her thigh.

The Pentax clicked as the blue knickers were peeled away from the peach-cheeks. Rowena snapped another shot of the poignant white socks all but buried in the blue serge of the panties snuggling the ankles.

'We do not speak to common boys,' Mandy said briskly, swishing the cane across the upturned buttocks. Her pupil suppressed a squeal. 'We do not come to school late,' she continued, whipping the cheeks once more with the supple bamboo. 'And we certainly do not wear lipstick.' The cane sliced down across the bare bottom for a third time, bringing the pigtailed schoolgirl up on her toes in anguish. The Pentax snapped the three pink stripes as they darkened into crimson against the creamy cheeks.

'No. Remain bending,' Mandy instructed, pressing the girl's neck down dominantly, and controlling her with the cane. 'Have you done your homework?'

The penitent remained silent.

'Well? Or am I to take your silence as an admission of your guilt?' Mandy whispered suavely, bringing to life once more the almost forgotten sarcastic cadences of her own former history mistress.

The schoolgirl shuffled anxiously, squeezing her thighs together.

'Legs apart. Four strokes.'

The cane caressed the soft swell of the buttocks with intimate severity. Mandy counted out the strokes aloud, swishing the pert bottom accurately and ruthlessly. After dispensing the prescribed punishment, Mandy tapped the sore buttocks with her yellow bamboo cane. 'Panties up. Go back to your desk. And wipe that lipstick off at once.'

Meekly, the whipped schoolgirl obeyed, stealing a shy glance at Mandy, adoration sparkling in her tear-dimmed green eyes.

The morning progressed satisfactorily. Mandy established and sustained a strict authority and a stern atmosphere in the classroom. After attempting some algebra, the schoolgirl's fingertips grew inky as she struggled to construe Juvenal in translation. The Latin irregulars caused her much distress, as did the bark of the leather strap several times across her bare bottom.

Lunch was served, during which Rowena withdrew, leaving Mandy to dine from a schoolmistressy portion of fried plaice served with boiled potatoes and peas. Imprisoned at her desk, her punished pupil silently munched her packed lunch of a cheese roll, salted crisps and a Mars bar.

Mandy daintily wiped her lips with a napkin. From the desk came the loud slurping sound as the schoolgirl sucked Ribena up through a straw. Mandy raised an eyebrow, silencing the sound.

GYM KIT. Mandy read the next cue card with a slightly puzzled frown. What rich possibilities lay within the potential of those two simple words?

Rowena returned, entering the classroom unobtrusively to occupy the shadows once more, her Pentax primed and eagerly poised, the lens erect and alert.

'I have received a complaint from Miss Meadows,' Mandy announced. 'Girls are attending gym in items of kit other than those prescribed. I understand that one girl came in a silver leotard last week, for which she was soundly chastised. I have decided to hold a snap inspection. Stand up and step over to the wall.'

The wooden chair legs scraped the scrubbed boards as the blonde obeyed, rising from behind her desk and stepping across to the wall below the map of Scotland. She trailed her kit bag reluctantly, dragging it by the tightened drawstring.

'Undress quickly and get changed into your gym kit. I will come and inspect you when I have completed marking your miserable history test.'

Minutes later, the chalk squawked across the blackboard as Mandy wrote up the correct answers. Reaching up to underline a date, her naked bosom pressed against the blackboard. Mandy gasped softly as her nipples kissed the dark wood, accidentally erasing the first and last O in Marco Polo.

'Ready?' Mandy rasped, brushing the chalk from her fingertips.

The schoolgirl was still struggling into her gym kit, hopping on one bare foot as she drew her tiny shorts up over her thighs.

'Hurry up, girl,' Mandy ordered, smiling a secret smile at the thought of the black pump she had earlier stolen from the gym bag and hidden in her desk.

'I can't find the other one,' the schoolgirl wailed, her green eyes troubled with sorrow.

'Search your bag properly.'

The bending blonde rummaged in vain, frantically fingering the corners of the kit bag for the missing pump.

'You are not property attired for gym. Miss Meadows, quite correctly, is strict in her requirements. You have failed to meet them. Come here, girl.'

Limping in one pump, the reluctant blonde approached Mandy, who sat at her desk, her black gown wide open.

'Give me that pump,' Mandy ordered, pointing down at the covered foot. 'It is quite useless as it is, but I'm sure I'll find a purpose for it.'

She did, as Rowena's Pentax recorded. Across Mandy's black-stockinged thighs, bare bottomed and whimpering, the schoolgirl felt the blaze of the pump against her punished cheeks. Mandy grew sticky during the chastisement, thrilling to the way the spongelike mounds of naked flesh flattened beneath the sweep of the pump, flattened and wobbled, as if soaking up the pain. Nine strokes later, Mandy dragged the ribbed sole of the pump across the crown of each reddened buttock. Her tongue was thick, her throat dry. She battled against an overwhelming urge to kiss the hot hottom, lick it slowly then bury her face into its swollen warmth.

128

No. Not that. Not yet. It would break the spell that bound the submissive to the dominant, the punished to the punisher. Tossing the pump aside, she suggested tea.

Breaktime brought a cup of strong, brown tea and biscuits for the teacher and a glass of milk for the pupil. Mandy gave the schoolgirl two biscuits from her plate but warned her sternly not to make crumbs. After their break, as the rooks slowly returned from their day to circle above the elms, Mandy set the last lesson of the day.

'I want you to write an essay for me.'

After dictating the title and the length required, Mandy sat at her desk, solemnly filling out the punishment book. The brass nib of her pen flashed orange and gold in the late-afternoon sunshine as she dipped it into the inkwell, tapped the surplus ink off and returned it to the pages of the calfskin-bound volume. The white pages were scored across with thin red lines. Mandy appreciated the sweet irony of the pages echoing the very punishments they recorded: red lines against a pale cream surface. So very much like a whipped bottom. Completing the entry of all the punishments administered that day in the Schoolroom, Mandy signed and dated it. Calling to the schoolgirl, who sat, head bowed at her essay, Mandy instructed her to read and countersign the punishments.

'Aloud,' the teacher interrupted sternly, forcing the silent lips to return to the top of the page and, humiliatingly, announce the sufferings of the day.

'Where do I sign?' lisped the penitent, pressing her uniformed body closely into the teacher she adored. 'Here?'

'No. Leave a space. The day is not yet over.'

Shivering at these words, and at their delicious threat, the pigtailed schoolgirl signed the punishment book, blotted it carefully and padded back across the scrubbed pine floor to her desk.

Mandy peeked at the final cue card. Caught cheating, was all it suggested. Mandy put her mind to the challenge, anxious to make it a memorable session for the submissive. All she had to work with was the folio of erotic prints secreted in the schoolgirl's desk. But how to bring it into play?

Rising from her desk on the podium, she stepped down and trod the pine floor, circling the girl at her desk with quiet menace. Mandy let her loose black gown part and flap open, exposing her delicious bosom to the chalkdust and sunbeams. Her pink nipples stiffened and rose, thickening with pleasure. From her desk, the schoolgirl stole a furtive peep. Her hand trembled, blotting her essay atrociously. Rowena, plucking at her black stretchy bodystocking where it bit into her cleft, studied the map of Scotland, her Pentax pointing down at the floor, the eye of the lens dull with indifference.

The schoolgirl creaked in her chair as she shifted her weight from one punished cheek on to the other.

'I will be deducting marks for poor presentation,' Mandy intoned, 'and indeed for poor punctuation. But I will deal with any spelling mistakes severely. Most severely.'

The schoolgirl's pen continued to scratch busily across her page. Rowena silently calculated the distance from Perth to Oban. The rooks fluttered down from the sky into the elms.

Moments later, the lid of the desk squeaked.

Mandy pounced. 'Cheating? What have we here? A dictionary,' she thundered, confiscating the small book. 'And what else have you in that desk that should not be there?'

The schoolgirl paled. Mandy prised up the lid of the desk and unearthed the folio she knew to be there.

'That's not mine –'

'So, what have we here?' Mandy whispered, ignoring the stammering denials. 'Danish maidens espied bathing,' Mandy read, perusing the gold lettering of the title page. 'A folio of vintage cameos,' she continued in a tone of studied disgust, 'depicting the wicked frolics of three naughty maidens and their subsequent chastisement by the governess who discovers their naked antics.'

Rowena turned from the map of Scotland, her fingers tightening around the Pentax.

'I approve of your appetite for knowledge, girl,' Mandy purred, 'but I certainly do not approve of the diet with which you feed it. Stand up this instant.'

The blonde pigtails bounced, as did her ripe breasts imprisoned within the schoolgirl uniform blouse, as the pupil pushed her chair back with a jerk of her bottom and stood up against her desk.

'Skirt up, knickers down,' Mandy instructed crisply.

In the gathering shadows of dusk, the snoutlike lens of the Pentax flickered up with interest. Rowena checked the lightmeter and steadied the camera, dropping down on one knee to get a low-angle shot of the bared buttocks.

The schoolgirl bowed her head, her pigtails cascading down over her shoulders. With splayed fingers, she steadied herself at her desk – bare bottomed and apprehensive.

'Legs back a little, I think,' Mandy mused. 'Now bend over. No, more. Give me your naughty bottom, you wicked little wretch.'

As her instructions were obeyed, Mandy slipped the folio down on to the desk, beneath the troubled gaze of the wide, green eyes of the schoolgirl.

'You find the contents of this forbidden album fascinating, no doubt. Perhaps you would be good enough to share your keen interest with me, hmm? Tell me exactly what you see as I turn the pages, girl.'

Mandy flipped over the purple vellum binding, opening the album to reveal the first of ten sepia prints.

'Well?' Mandy demanded, tapping the print impatiently with her index finger. 'I'm waiting.'

131

'It is a picture of a young woman. A young woman disrobing. You can see her bottom,' came the lisping reply.

Smack. Mandy spanked the curved, up-thrust cheeks of the bending girl. Flipping over the next page, she ordered the spanked girl to continue.

Almost drowned out by the whirring of the Pentax, the schoolgirl lisped a husky description, explaining how the naked bather was now thigh-deep in the pool, the waters lapping at the swell of her wide, white buttocks.

Again, the spanking hand swept down across the naked bottom, cracking sharply against the peach-cheeks and reddening them instantly with a second stamp of pain. The Pentax clicked its greedy fill, capturing the exact moment when the palm seared the soft cheeks: the knuckled fingers gripping the desktop, the bounce of the schoolgirl's breasts in the bondage of the tight blouse, the flounce of the pigtails as the girl jerked in anguish.

'Next page.'

The inquisition, stammered response and attendant punishment continued slowly and methodically. As the pages of the album were turned, the tearful schoolgirl described each sepia print in detail, her voice growing more excited by the minute. She described the nude bather splashing her breasts with the icy water, the arrival and undressing of a second bather, then a third. Exact details were demanded. How the breasts differed in size and shape. How one bottom was heavily fleshed, the second apple-buttocked, the third a mouthwatering peach. Mandy arrived at the sixth print. The spanked girl, her voice a tense whisper, described how wet breasts were cupped and squeezed, bottoms caressed, parted thighs explored by inquisitive fingers. Mandy scalded the reddening buttocks of the bending schoolgirl with three severe spanks and turned over to page seven. It showed the arrival of an angry governess.

'Continue.'

The girl described the governess, detailing the tall, forbidding beauty buttoned up tightly in shining black bombazine. The severe bun of hair, the cruel mouth, the gloved hands. In the gloved right hand, the schoolgirl whispered – her voice taut with arousal – was a dog whip.

'They are being ordered out of the pool. The whip is pointing to the reedbank.'

'And?' Mandy spanked her again.

'You can see their bottoms.'

'Continue.' Mandy spanked again.

Mandy was told how the first naked young female was already up on the mossy lawn, shivering and shielding her bosom, exposing her exquisite delta below. The second nude, water dripping from her spilling breasts, was scrambling up the bank. The third was staring in fear at the dog whip.

'They are afraid. The governess is so angry.'

Again, the pupil's hot bottom joggled beneath the teacher's spanking palm.

'And here?' Mandy demanded, revealing the tenth and final sepia print.

The spanked schoolgirl gasped. Gazing down, she saw the three naked bathers, arranged thigh to thigh, bending. Their bottoms faced the camera, each pair of cheeks already adorned with the imprint of the dog whip, each pair of cheeks sporting several stripes. Above the whipped buttocks, the gloved hand of the governess gripped the supple lash.

Mandy stepped back a pace as, grunting thickly, her pupil collapsed down over the desk, thrusting her buttocks up and crushing her bosom into the front edge of her desk. Mandy – and Rowena behind her whirring Pentax – saw the schoolgirl's spanked cheeks spasm and dimple as they were clenched in orgasm: mewing softly, the pupil ground her hot slit into the sepia print and came.

Mandy allowed the orgasm to run its violent course to a softly screamed climax, then gathered up both pigtails, wrapped them around her wrist, and peeled the spent blonde pupil away from her desk.

'Just look at what you've done to that print. The print of those three naughty girls being whipped. You've ruined it. You've smeared it with your sticky juices, you wicked little wretch. This,' Mandy whispered fiercely, 'I fear, means a very special punishment. One that I cannot possibly enter into the punishment book but one which –' she tugged at the pigtails, turning the green eyes around to gaze into her stern blue stare '– will be a lesson your bare bottom is never, ever going to forget.'

'Come in.'

Mandy, showered and suppered, entered Erica's lair. It was spartanly furnished with clinical chrome and black leather. No velvet, damask or chintz softened the harsh tone. Austerity was the keynote, severity the achievement.

'Your debriefing. Rowena's first rush of prints are out. Let us examine your first day's work. Together. Closely.'

Erica was eating a late supper of celery stalks and Stilton. She napkined her lips fastidiously and wiped her fingers.

'Not bad, not bad at all,' she murmured, leafing through the glossy blow-ups. 'But look. Here. Your first mistake. Flip the hem of the skirt up with the tip of the cane. It is a more dominant approach. And here,' Erica continued, worrying a stray sliver of celery with her tongue tip, 'another mistake. The panties of the punished should always be drawn down to a restricting band at the knees. It bunches the buttocks beautifully and hobbles the victim, rendering her more helpless. Understand?'

Mandy, mesmerised momentarily by the blow-ups laid out before her, blinked and nodded.

'Now here,' Erica murmured, pausing to suck at a tooth, 'you should have touched the bottom with your hand.'

Mandy gazed down across the cropped blonde's shoulder to see.

'Count the stripes which you have just administered. Count them aloud, and use your fingertip. The touch of flesh upon flesh, at this stage of the domination and discipline, is yearned for by the submissive. But be careful of any display of tenderness. It is too soon for that. A dominant touch to the whipped cheeks will suffice.'

'I understand,' Mandy whispered.

'Now this, this was excellent.'

Mandy preened herself.

'Excellent.' Erica had discovered the gym-kit sequence. The Pentax had captured everything: including a big close-up of the anxious schoolgirl scrabbling for the missing pump, her teeth biting down pensively into her lower lip. 'Quite inspired,' Erica enthused, nodding approvingly. 'We'll make an angel of you yet. Hiding the pump and using the other one for punishment. A neat touch. Yes, I like that.'

Mandy felt a surge of pride welling up inside her. The next shots showed the schoolgirl accepting a biscuit and dipping it into her milk. Erica thoroughly approved, saying it was an authentic gesture between teacher and pupil, but one that sustained the power balance between the dominatrix and her charge.

The inquisition, punishment and subsequent climax over – and into – the album of erotic prints captured by the Pentax were studied carefully. Erica pronounced her verdict.

'Magnificent,' she sighed, lingering over a huge close-up of the spanked cheeks frozen in their spasm of orgasm. 'The mistress will be pleased.'

The mistress. Mandy felt a flash of anger wipe out her

glow of triumphant pride. She detested the very sound of the word.

'Keep them,' Erica said, passing up the snapshots.

Mandy looked at her inquiringly.

'You can have that set as a trophy. You can learn so much from them. Study them closely when you are in bed, tonight. You will find them quite diverting, no doubt,' Erica chuckled darkly, her teeth closing down over a freshly salted stick of erect celery.

The next day, Erica led Mandy once more along the carpeted length of the Long Gallery. Once more, Mandy was ushered into one of the many Games Rooms behind the locked, green-baize door.

She found herself standing in a prison dungeon. The rough sandstone walls loomed up, windowless, to an oppressive granite roof. Flickering torches provided a mean but adequate source of light. Sand had been sprinkled on the floor, rendering all footsteps silent. Mandy, dressed by Erica in a simple white robe, examined the few furnishings: a full-length looking glass fixed to the far wall, steel rings fixed to the wall and suspended from the roof, a pair of wooden stools and a whipping post.

'No cue cards for you today. Your brief is simple.'

Slave or mistress, Mandy wondered, a trickle of sweat glistening on her temples.

'This is the antechamber where captive slaves are prepared for the harem.'

Slave, Mandy shuddered. I'm to be the slave girl, utterly at the whim of some dominant resident. She looked at the whipping post and felt the spiders of alarm scurrying across her buttocks.

'Today, you will be pleasuring another submissive. I think you have a flair for games of dominance and discipline. You will be preparing the captive for the harem. Invest the session with your full imagination.

Deny her nothing and do not spare her the opportunity to taste the bittersweet delights she craves. Rowena will be here to record your achievements.'

Mandy, relieved, simply nodded.

'Keep in mind these three words: humiliation, bondage and punishment. Yearn to see her weep her tears of sugared sorrow just as passionately as she yearns for your strict word, your stern voice and your severe touch.'

Mandy swept her hand down to the base of her belly and thumbed her slit absently as Erica spoke. Her labial lips responded to her touch: parting and pouting, they briefly kissed the cotton of her simple robe.

The door to the dungeon opened, admitting a shaft of light. Breaking the shaft of light, in stepped Rowena, her Pentax swinging from its black leather strap. Prepared for the heat of the dungeon, the redhead was scantily dressed in a pale-blue bikini. The underwired cups gave her a deep, inviting cleavage, bunching the rounded breasts up into delicious flesh-mounds. Mandy felt her hot slit-juice, and silently wished Rowena were hers for the day, hers to slowly strip, examine and bind to the whipping post.

Erica was pulling at the rings in the wall, ensuring that they were securely embedded. 'Surprising how frenzied a whipped nude can become,' she purred, 'when struggling to escape the lash she deeply desires.'

Mandy considered this paradox. Looking up, she shivered as she saw the cropped blonde walk past the whipping post. Turning her body deliberately towards the post, Erica grazed her pubis against the leather-cladding and grunted a soft, animal moan.

'I will bring you your submissive,' Erica whispered, crushing her bosom into the post and fluttering her hands down along its phallic length. 'She will come to you naked. See to it that when she departs she is wearing red stripes of sorrow and is dressed in the pleasures of pain.' She left.

Rowena ran her splayed fingers through her red hair and spoke, breaking the sultry silence after Erica's departure. 'Hot in here,' she observed laconically. 'And you'll be making things even warmer for your submissive.'

Mandy looked up and grinned, but Rowena was engrossed in her Pentax. The submissive entered the room, blinking in the unaccustomed darkness. Mandy noted that she was wide hipped – always the promise of heavily fleshed buttocks – and blessed with a firm, ripe bosom. The naked woman's nipples were already thick and dark. Turning, the nude briefly presented Mandy with a glimpse of her plump bottom: as Mandy had anticipated, the cheeks were superbly swollen. Mandy felt the pulse at her neck quicken. In her dry mouth, her tongue grew heavy and slow. Swallowing silently, Mandy examined the arrival's beauty. It was the bloom of a thirty-three-year-old in the summer of her splendour. The limbs were lithe and supple, the hands daintily small. Mandy paused to take in the glory of the dark, tumbling curls and, set on the pale face, the look of shy eagerness. Mandy's stern gaze came to rest on the dark pubic curls – and then on the darker eyes, already swimming in liquid desire.

'You are here to learn how to serve and please my master,' Mandy said, her tone curt. 'My master has turned his harem into a temple of pleasure.'

Deliberately ignoring the submissive brunette, Mandy turned to examine the contents arranged on a silver tray. She picked up and scrutinized a curled whip – holding the leather up to the flickering torchlight – and then fingered an ivory dildo before sniffing with satisfaction at pots of cream and phials of scented oils.

The woman grew restless, shaking her dark curls impatiently as she plucked at her left nipple.

'But before you have the privilege of surrendering yourself for his delight, and the fierce joys of his crimson couch, you must be thoroughly prepared. Trained and prepared in the arts of pleasure and lust. Be warned, slave. If you fail in any way to please my master, then you fail to please me. And, if you fail me, I will punish you severely. Go before the glass,' Mandy instructed, pointing to the full-length mirror. 'Let us see what fruits of the flesh you bring to the banquet before you.'

The brunette obeyed, shivering with delicious dread as Mandy tapped her bare bottom with the coiled whip. In the glass, the dark eyes widened as they gazed into their own reflection. Mandy, her white cotton grazing the swollen cheeks of the nude's bottom, stood dominantly behind.

'Your eyes,' she instructed. 'Keep them cast down when in the presence of my master. A bold gaze is insolent and will be dealt with harshly. Better to keep your eyes lowered,' Mandy whispered softly, 'than tightly shut against the kiss of the crop.'

Rowena, fingering her bra strap to keep the bikini cups comfortably in place, positioned herself at an angle, pointing her Pentax into the mirroring glass. As Mandy tapped the captive's chin with the stock of the coiled whip, tilting the slave's head back to keep her in thrall, the Pentax snapped twice.

'Your mouth, slave, must remain silent, except to scream your delight. No words must be uttered, no questions asked. But you may moan. However,' Mandy continued, 'you must not keep your mouth closed when in my master's bed.' Using the tip of the whip handle as a lipstick, Mandy dragged the slave's lower lip down. 'My master may wish to use your mouth for pleasures other than discourse.'

Continuing her inspection of the naked slave, Mandy dropped the whip down on to the warm sand. Encircling the brunette from behind, she cupped, weighed and then dominantly squeezed the ripe breasts.

'Melons. You bring melons to my master's banquet.

That is good. When feasting, my master likes all fruits fully ripe.'

The brunette shuddered and clamped her thighs tightly together.

'Fine, broad hips,' Mandy murmured, framing their outline with her palms. 'Again, that is good. My master will ride you like a desert steed. He prefers firm flesh between his thighs when he is asaddle. Your buttocks,' Mandy purred, spinning the brunette around briskly and presenting the bare bottom to the glass, 'are superb. You bring rare fruits to the feast before you. My master cannot pass over the plumpness of peaches.'

The Pentax snapped three times as Mandy palmed and gripped the bare cheeks in her taloned fingers. Placing her hands on the brunette's shoulders, Mandy turned her round again to face the glass.

'What fruit have we overlooked?' she whispered.

In silence, the brunette fingered her dark pubic curls.

'Yes,' whispered Mandy. 'Sticky dates, split figs or dark, oozing plums. My master feeds greedily on such delicacies as these. What do you bring to tempt his fingers and tongue? Is it a sticky date?' Mandy prised the labia apart expertly. The brunette squealed. 'Or is it a split fig?' The labia opened out, the flesh-lips already wet with pleasure. 'Or is it a dark, oozing plum?'

The Pentax devoured the images of submission and subjugation fixed and frozen in the glass.

'Remember, slave, when pleasing and pleasuring my master, no part of you must be denied to him. He has an appetite for all fruits, especially those that are forbidden.'

The nude moaned and buckled slightly at the knees. Mandy scooped up the whip and directed her captive across to the rings on the wall. They were fixed at a height of seven feet above the floor. Mandy arranged the slave so that each wrist threaded through and was then bound to the rings. Mandy dismounted from the wooden stool and stood before her spread-eagled prize.

'My master has a splendid hawk,' she began. 'It gives him endless pleasure. But the hawk has to be blindfold and rendered mute, or else it grows wilful and rebellious. You, slave, will of course taste the lash if you grow wilful, but like my master's prized hawk, perhaps you will benefit from a blindfold and a gag.'

Both were provided by strips of red velvet which proved effective when applied to the dark eyes and red lips. Suddenly denied the power of sight and speech, the bound nude wriggled and writhed. Mandy stilled the dancing feet with a caress of the whip. The terrified toes stiffened and pointed down in obedient submission.

'Sweetmeats will be served when you are on the couch of pleasure,' Mandy explained, crossing the dungeon to collect a silver tray. Returning, she remounted the stool and passed a succession of sticky morsels beneath the quivering nostrils.

'Spiced lamb, aromatic rice, honeycombs cleaved open and almond nougat will be served,' she promised, her voice now warm and urgent, 'but only if you please him.'

The slave craned her neck, eager to taste the delights despite the velvet that sealed her lips tightly.

'Fail to please, slave, and you will dine on dry bread and bitter herbs – bitter as the sorrow you will feel as the scourge stripes your buttocks.'

The brunette tongued her gag in mounting excitement. Mandy returned the tray of sweetmeats and exchanged it for another. Placing it down carefully on the sanded floor, she selected one of many small porcelain pots. Mounting her stool, Mandy opened the pot and placed it under the suspended slave's nose.

'Thickened oil of attar,' she whispered.

Beneath the blindfold, the nostrils flared as they drew in the heady scent.

'To lubricate those orifices my master may choose to probe with his curiosity, with his lust.'

Despite her bondage, which pinned her helplessly against the wall, the nude seemed to shrink back at the touch of the perfumed oil at her gleaming slit. Mandy stroked the lower labia gently, working the unction into the flesh. The nude grunted into her gag. Reaching around the left hip, Mandy fingered and anointed the rosebud sphincter buried between the heavy cheeks. As her oiled fingertip probed the anal whorl, the slave threshed helplessly.

'My master will treat you like a captured city,' Mandy continued suavely, over the whirr of the excited Pentax. 'When a captured city is breached,' she hissed, 'be warned: no gate remains closed to the victor.'

The Pentax snapped three times: freezing the images of the nude twisting and jerking to avoid the oiled finger at her sphincter, of Mandy mastering her slave, and of the finger sliding dominantly between the clenched cheeks.

'When it pleases my master to do so, he will turn your face down into the satin cushions. Crop in hand, he will straddle you and ride you, ride you fiercely as if racing the wind. A small show of modesty is permitted, for it will serve to sharpen his keen desire. But be warned, my master can be cruel in his pleasures. They say that, when out hunting, he enjoys the quivering terror of his quarry, and savours the despair of cornered, helpless prey. And they say that his laughter is demonic when he spears the captive flesh, driving home his shaft to the very hilt to impale and quell the struggling victim.'

The brunette almost swooned. Mandy pinched each nipple swiftly, bringing the slave to alert attention. Perched up on the footstool, Mandy untied the submissive, only to march her halfway across the sanded floor and retie her to the single ring suspended from the ceiling by a chain. Removing the blindfold – but not the gag – Mandy turned the dangling nude to face her.

'I must make you familiar with the prowess of my master. His fame sweeps through the harem before him like the crackling flames of a wheatfield on fire. You should, I think,' Mandy said, as if considering an option and deciding in favour of it, 'be given a taste of his brute manhood.'

She padded softly across the floor, her toes leaving faint footprints impressed in the sand, and scooped up the ivory phallus. The heat in the dungeon made her loose gown stick to the moist warmth of her breasts and buttocks. She plucked at it, peeling it away from her nipples and cleft. Over in the shadows, crouched behind her Pentax, Rowena was taking aim. In the flickering torchlight, Mandy spied a soft gleam of flesh. The redhead had abandoned her bikini top. Her loose breasts glistened beneath their sheen of sweat. Mandy, her hot slip now throbbing, returned to the naked slave in her bondage.

'This,' she explained, raising the dildo aloft, 'is my master's prowess. It is a likeness taken directly from the original.'

The gasp of the slave was audible through the velvet at her lips as the dildo was pressed against her left breast. Mandy teased the nipple, then transferred the ivory shaft to the right breast. Mandy squashed the pliant globe of flesh beneath the hard dildo. The chain rattled as the nude threshed in response. Tracing the snout down across the flat belly, Mandy paused before gliding it down over the clitoris to stroke, and splay, the labia.

The Pentax whirred as Rowena took her shot. Mandy glanced down and saw the redhead's toes scrunching the sand excitedly. Looking back up at her slave, into the widening, dark eyes, Mandy gripped the nude and turned her around, presenting the heavy buttocks for her inspection.

'In a moment I shall whip you.'

The chain rattled as the nude shuddered in anguish.

'I shall whip you to give you a taste of the harsh

143

pleasures of serving my master, of surrendering and submitting yourself to him completely. And,' Mandy said, dropping her voice to a venomous whisper, 'of the sweet agony you shall suffer if you should fail in the harem.'

The slave moaned, her long legs threshed in midair, the thighs welded into one flesh. Mandy glimpsed the nude's toes scrabbling five inches above the sand.

'Open your thighs,' she commanded.

Slowly, reluctantly, the slave obeyed.

'You have the beauty, the flesh-fruits, to both inflame and quench my master's desire. But have you the stamina? Have you the dedication? I shall place this here,' she murmured, inserting the dildo into the cleft between the heavy buttocks. 'Hold it there, hold it there while I whip you. Let it fall, and we shall go back to the beginning and repeat the entire exercise. Many times, if necessary. Here in the desert,' Mandy whispered, 'time is erased like the sand dunes before the winds of eternity.'

A soft sound in the shadows caused Mandy to pause. Looking across into the gloom, she saw Rowena cover the Pentax carefully with her bikini bottom before kneeling down on the sand. Head bowed, her bare bottom burying her heels as she squatted, the red-haired girl thrust her hands between her slightly parted thighs. Mandy smiled and understood, tugging her white robe away from her own sticky labia. A surge of burning pride seared through her veins. Brought here to witness and record Mandy's emerging skills in domination and discipline, Rowena was already kneeling in admiration – in participation – in masturbatory celebration.

Turning, Mandy snapped her short whip before flicking it leisurely across the swell of the heavy cheeks. They spasmed under the lash, trapping the phallic shaft deep inside the hot cleft. A thin red line burned across the creamy gobes where the whip had kissed the naked flesh. Mandy jerked her supple wrist, flicking the whip once more, lick-lashing the bare bottom. Still the dildo remained trapped between the squeezed cheeks of the punished nude. Four more times, Mandy plied the cruel lash, crack-snapping the length of dead hide across the living flesh. The brunette's bottom blazed beneath the strokes, but the dildo remained clenched between the whipped cheeks. Over in the shadows, Rowena buckled forward and came – her groan of ecstasy echoing around the dungeon.

The brunette, stretched out across the sand, was tightly bound with eight lengths of waxed cord. It secured her ankles, burned into her wrists, bit into her thighs and buttocks and bound her swollen bosom. Rendered helpless and utterly motionless in her strict bondage, the slave listened eagerly as Mandy read aloud.

'Should these pitiful pages ever fall into Christian hands, let it be known by all who knew me for a daughter of decency and a child of chastity that I, Leonora of Palermo, did not go willingly to the couch of the Mamaluke lord. It was misfortune upon misfortune that brought me to his bed of burning shame . . .'

Mandy had elected to read from the papers smuggled out of a Zanzibar seraglio. Penned by an unfortunate noblewoman who had fallen into the rapacious clutches of a Mamaluke warlord in 1732, they provided a dire warning to spirited European ladies intent on travelling into uncharted seas and across unmapped lands east of the Bosphorus.

Binding her naked, oiled slave in the strictest ropes of bondage, Mandy was reading the selected extracts as a warning to the brunette of the rigours of the harem – and the painful punishments awaiting anyone contemplating rebellion among the scented, satin cushions. Equally captivated, though free from the bite of searing hemp, Rowena listened enthralled as Mandy read on.

'After the second shipwreck,' Mandy continued, 'and our base betrayal at the hands of hired Janissaries, I was led here in chains, in servitude, to this nest of perfumed vice, this Garden of Excess where even sin is perfumed. The gross Mamaluke toyed with me at first, marvelling at the whiteness of my skin, the firmness of my bosom which he likened to ripened apples, the music of my occidental voice, the swell of my buttocks which recalled to him the moon above the Nile. My bottom, dear reader, provoked much excitement in him. He would stroke me firmly there with his open palm, squeezing and cupping the flesh for his dark delight. I shudder at the memory of his rough hands, strong fingers, sucking lips, leathery tongue and eager teeth. Yes, his mouth did taste me and his teeth did eat me as if my buttocks were cold viands spread out for his supper. The European bottom, I later learnt, when bared, has a less pronounced swell than that of duskier maidens. I swear, dear reader of my tale of woe, that I fought hard for my modesty and struggled for my virtue but he had a short whip to hand and plied it freely across my naked cheeks. It was as if he were breaking in a wild horse taken from the desert beyond the Atlas mountains. After the whip had visited my flesh for the third time, I succumbed. I succumbed, I admit, and surrendered. Once more of my nakedness did he eat, tonguing me in nameless places as if I were a roasted fowl. To my eternal shame, a dark, disturbing sense of pleasure –'

The slave moaned. Placing the papers down, Mandy moved across and examined the bound nude, checking her cords and the tightness of their knots. A thin rope hugged the belly, disappeared between the thighs and tightened as it coursed up the cleft between the buttocks and arrowed up the spine. Bending, Mandy inspected the waxed cord at the labia. With her fingers, she inched it directly over the wet flesh-lips so that it tormented the slit within. The rope pressed down into the clitoris –

Mandy saw to that – causing the slave to whimper. Mandy sternly silenced the nude and resumed her reading beneath the flickering torchlight.

'His tongue drove deep within me, forming strange fancies to haunt my brain. Fancies young virgins admit to when whispering their confessions – and for which they are later scourged by nuns with rods of supple willow. My strongest and most wicked fancy was that I was upon a horse – a muscled beast of Satan – with no cloth or leather betwixt my naked flanks and the steed's hot flesh. I whipped the stallion on and on, until he bolted in a frenzy, rendering the most private and secret parts of my body as hot as a coal plucked from Hell. This, and betimes other dark fancies, clouded my mind and dimmed my proper judgement. I confess to this quite openly. I confess –'

The slave writhed. The cord ravished her clitoris; the slave moaned sweetly. Rigid in her thrall of roped bondage, the merest twitch brought sweet torments to her naked flesh.

'When I came round from my lust-drugged stupor,' Mandy read, her voice a silky whisper, 'I knew from the burning pleasure in my private parts that I had endured the Mamaluke to enact enormous indignities and outrages upon my person. It was not I upon a horse I half-dreamed of, it was he upon me, whip in hand, riding me to the very edge of Heaven through the gates of Hell. Whip in hand, and with the usage of my hair as reins, he rode me on his crimson couch of shame. He lashed my buttocks and then ventured deep inside them with his long sword of manhood. I cried for pity, my tears soon staining the satin cushions as I buried my face in shame. But shame soon ceded to a dark, devilish delight.'

Mandy paused, allowing her closing words to linger and haunt the fevered minds of the listeners. Pitilessly disregarding the wriggling slave stretched out across the sand, she resumed the final part of the reading.

'He deflowered me daily, often more so, spearing me with his extraordinary shaft of flesh both at sunrise and then again at sunset, changing his choice of access to my innermost flesh at whim. My hands, my hair, my very mouth itself were used to satisfy and sate his demonic appetites. But it was, dear reader, under the cold gaze of the Zanzibar moon that he took possession of me in that most forbidden place – that place some speak in whispered tones of as the Jewel of Sodom. Yes, it is true, for it was there that he enjoyed me to the utmost of his heathen carnality. And always, always, I shivered under the shadow of his raised whip.'

In the concluding passage, Mandy recounted how, when whipped, the Mamaluke would prise open the wretched captive to see if she, like the oyster that bore the prized pearl upon the ocean bed, was wet and sparkling. The final sentence was a forlorn sentiment.

'Here I weep in my prison of shame, ready to bear the keen stripes across my bare buttocks as the zebra is fabled to wear the stripes of Nature's rod.'

Mandy closed the pages and set them aside. Kneeling over the bound brunette, she thumbed the slave's nipples slowly, then guided her fingers down to the weeping fig below. The flesh was glistening.

The Pentax clicked hungrily as, bending closer to her squirming victim, Mandy licked at the rope-tormented labia with her thickened tongue.

'This tongue that spoke from those pages,' Mandy murmured, working her lips into the hot slit, 'is now speaking to your flesh.'

Jerking in her bondage, the brunette screamed and came.

Exhausted and utterly spent, the brunette, still bound, slept deeply. Mandy sat on the sand floor in silence, slowly contemplating her submissive charge. Had the session been successful? What would the photos show?

Was she truly skilled enough to be an angel? Would her late aunt have applauded her efforts?

The slave stirred and moaned softly.

'You are awake now,' Mandy said, 'but not entirely free from suffering.'

The brunette's dark eyes flashed up fearfully. Sorrow framed her sensual lips into an anxious pout. Mandy squatted down alongside the bound nude and slowly unpicked the knots securing the searing ropes. Unleashed, the slave rolled over, squashing first her heavy breasts and then her broad buttocks into the sand.

'A message from my master. You are not yet ready for his divan of desire. You have much to learn,' she purred, 'your lesson in pain must continue.'

The brunette shrank back in the sand, scrabbling in retreat from Mandy's tone – and look – of venomed velvet.

'Up,' came the promise of imminent pain. 'You will be pleased to learn that my master has kindly supplied me with the instrument for your punishment. See how he attends to the smallest detail, even in the matter of your continuing sorrow. Look,' she cried, flourishing a silver slipper. 'This is for you. For your bottom. You will bend and I will beat. Feel it,' Mandy enthused, tossing it down. 'Crush the leather to your bosom.'

Snatching at the slipper, the brunette caught it clumsily. Obediently, she brought the supple sole to her nipples.

'The silvered hide is snakeskin, the sole is fashioned from the hide of a Barbary goat. Give me the slipper,' Mandy ordered, her tone strengthening to one of stern command.

The brunette peeled the slipper away from her bosom and surrendered it to the waiting hand above.

'Bend over. Part your legs a little. No, take your hands away. Put them up to your breasts. That's right.

Cup them. Good. Now squeeze them in time to the strokes.'

The bending nude's elbows angled as she cupped her spilling breasts, capturing and containing their weight in her sweating palms. Mandy lightly brushed the sparkle of sand sticking to the swell of the proffered cheeks, briskly dusting the curved buttocks with her knuckles. The soft bottom clenched in a spasm of anguish.

'Kiss the slipper, you miserable wretch,' Mandy instructed.

Tossing her cascade of dark curls, the brunette raised her face to plant her thick lips on to the supple hide.

The punishment was slowly dispensed, each of the fifteen strokes searching out and scalding every inch of the upturned cheeks. Before the twelfth blistering swipe, both punisher and punished bowed before the implaccable surge of an approaching climax: as the slipper kissed the crimson buttocks for the fifteenth time, both punisher and punished buckled into their slit-searing orgasms.

Erica had completed her supper of grilled mushrooms on toast and was sipping a glass of Médoc.

That's my wine, you bitch, Mandy silently seethed, noting the vintage and the provenance of the prized red. You've no right to be here, in Sternwood Grange, drinking –

'I've seen the photos,' Erica began, putting her glass down beside her chair.

Mandy set aside her suppressed rage and listened. A pause ensued. The pause became a silence. Mandy grew anxious. Had she failed? Had she failed to fully pleasure the submissive slave this afternoon, in the hot dungeon?

'Excellent. Quite excellent,' Erica murmured, inspecting the snapshots for a fourth time. 'The weaknesses in your technique are of no importance and can be soon ironed out.'

She listed Mandy's errors and mistakes, illustrating each one with a graphic black and white blow-up.

'When examining the naked subject, especially in front of a mirror, don't omit to rasp your pubis down across their buttocks. It is a supreme gesture of domination and suitably establishes the relationship between a dominatrix and her naked slave. Peculiar to the female, of course, but most effective. And,' Erica continued, 'drag down the lower lip and keep it depressed. It deprives the victim of her power of speech. Humiliating, is it not?'

Mandy nodded.

'Yes, this was good. But with the sweetmeats, in future, I would like you to remove the gag. Not the blindfold,' Erica stipulated, 'just the gag. Allow the tantalised a brief taste – the merest lick – of each morsel.'

Grudgingly, Mandy had to secretly agree that Erica was a superb dominatrix. The cropped blonde sipped her Médoc.

'What about –'

'The reading?' Erica asked, anticipating Mandy's question. 'As for the reading, let the submissive read from the text. Be sure to punish her should she falter or stumble over tricky foreign vowels.'

Again, Mandy bowed – literally – to Erica's judgement.

Erica continued. 'The good points, indeed the excellent aspects of your session today are as follows: the phallus wedged between the cheeks during the whipping, thumbing the victim in her bondage, pacing and delaying her climax – these were superb touches of domination, discipline and humiliation. I particularly recommend your control of her orgasm. And the snake skin slipper . . .' Erica's voice drowned in her own dark laughter. 'A delicious touch. Yes, my girl, I can safely report to the mistress that you brought your submissive

151

down a tortured path signposted towards desire, which twisted slowly through the fields of dread and meadows of despair.'

Mandy sighed her relief. Fearful of Erica, indeed despising the cropped blonde, she held the cruel witch in grudging respect. For Erica was a priestess in the dark arts of domination.

'There is only one thing that puzzles me,' Erica murmured, sipping again from her expensive Médoc. 'There appears to be something of a time-lapse. Look. I have no photos between here –' she held up a snap '– and here.' She held up another.

No, you don't, do you. Mandy smiled secretly in her triumph. You won't find any photos there, bitch, because I was so good down in the dungeon I even made Rowena come right then and there.

'Probably changing her film,' Mandy ventured.

'Probably,' Erica echoed, far from persuaded. 'But it is surprising. Talking of surprises, I have one planned for you tomorrow.'

Six

Early the following morning, Erica led Mandy along the Long Gallery. Mandy, naked, wondered who it could be requiring attention at such an unholy hour. She glimpsed the green-baize door leading to the Games Room. What was the surprise, she wondered apprehensively.

The cropped blonde paused, turned abruptly to her left and entered through a pair of massive double doors. Mandy, disturbed by the lingering fear that Erica's planned surprise might mean a painful encounter with a dominant, relaxed instantly. They had entered the room of a submissive.

Erica strode across to the bay windows and drew back the heavy curtains. Thunderclouds darkened the Suffolk dawn, filling the vast sky with their swollen shadows – and the promise of a summer storm. The submissive stirred sleepily beneath the silken sheets.

'Today, you will be a nanny. Your uniform and equipment are over there.'

Mandy peered across at the crisp nanny's uniform dress, buckled belt and sensible brogues, arranged by a long cheval mirror.

'You will wake the resident up, then see to the usual nursery routine: bed making, breakfast and bathing. Be stern and dispense strict discipline.'

Mandy, edging closer to the bed, looked up and nodded.

'Wake up,' Erica barked, snatching up the silken sheet and dragging it down to the bottom of the bed.

Mandy gasped aloud. The sleeping resident was naked. A naked young man.

That was my surprise, Erica's smile seemed to say as she turned to the double doors and departed.

The naked man stirred and rubbed his eyes. His nakedness sharply reminded Mandy of her own. Like Eve in the moment of carnal knowledge, she blushed and covered her breasts with her hands in a show of modesty. Like Eve before her, Mandy felt their swollen ripeness – as ripe and swollen as the stolen apple plucked from the tree of shame.

He opened his eyes, staring at Mandy's blonde pubic curls. She dropped her hands down to shield her delta. His eyes widened as they devoured her breasts. Mandy's gaze raked the bed, taking in the teddy bear, the Biggles book, the box of Bassett's Liquorice Allsorts. The young man lay back on his pillows. He had dark, curled hair – expensively cut. His face was square, though lined with the burden of some heavy office. His mouth hinted at character, and the patrician nose suggested an easy arrogance: it was the face of a man accustomed to command. Army? A multi-national director? Her eyes met his gaze. She studied their cold blue quartz – but noted how wide they were with both wonder and expectation. Then Mandy recognised him. The young Turk, a political firebrand who had bullied his way to the brink of Cabinet. The Sunday heavies, with glowing editorials, had mapped out his path to Number Ten.

'Who –' he mumbled, his voice thick with sleep.

'Say good morning to Nanny properly,' Mandy ordered, getting into her stride instantly.

'Good morning, Nanny,' he whispered excitedly, a thrill lubricating his Etonian vowels.

'Nanny must get dressed and then she will see to you.'

See to you. His flaccid penis twitched at the delicious

154

threat of her final words. Mandy saw it stir in the mirror as she stretched up to take down the pale-ivory brassiere.

'No peeping at Nanny putting on her scanties or it'll be a smacked bottom before breakfast, young man.'

The shaft stiffened. Mandy, keeping her bottom towards the bed, gazed into the glass of the cheval as she filled the cool silk cups of her brassiere with the warm weight of her breasts. Stretching, she snapped the straps together. In the glass, her bosom bulged within its silk bondage. In the glass, his blue eyes glinted, wide with adoration. Planting her feet apart, causing her soft buttocks to joggle, she fingered the bra cups and adjusted them for comfort. The shaft between his thighs thickened appreciatively, and nodded as it rose.

Bending, at which he gasped with delight at her widening cheeks, she stepped daintily into the stretchy silk panties. Drawing them up luxuriously, she lingered at her thighs before snapping them into place. She thumbed the tight material where it snuggled into her cleft, and eased the bite of the amorous silk at her slit. On the bed, the naked man grunted.

'I distinctly said no peeping. No peeping at Nanny in her silk underwear. I know you want to. Every naughty boy does. But I shall spank your bare bottom if I catch you looking at Nanny putting on her suspender belt and nylon stockings. Do you understand?'

Silence.

'I said, do you understand?' she repeated sternly.

'Yes, Nanny,' he said meekly.

The suspender belt hugged her tightly, framing and pronouncing her hips and buttocks superbly. On the bed, the engorged shaft rose in a stiff salute. Slowly, deliberately, Mandy rolled up the dark-bronze stockings and stepped into them. Smoothing down the sheath of glistening nylon, she palmed her inner thighs and slender legs until the stockings fitted like a second skin.

155

The suspenders snapped into place, tugging up the darker band of bronzed nylon at her thighs.

In the mirror, she saw his left hand inching down towards his erection.

'No. Nanny has spoken to you before about doing that, hasn't she? You must not touch or play with it. What did Nanny say she would do if she ever caught you doing that?'

He swallowed, flushed with excitement.

'Nanny will have to use the hairbrush, won't she?'

'Yes,' he replied eagerly.

'And how does Nanny use the hairbrush when punishing naughty boys?'

He remained silent.

'Well?' she demanded.

'On my bottom. On my bare bottom.'

'Exactly so,' Mandy said, her voice slightly muffled by the uniform dress she was pulling down over her head. 'Nanny will arrange you across her stockinged thighs, pin you down firmly, and then spank your bare bottom with the hairbrush until it is red and sore.'

Her blue and white striped uniform fitted her like a glove. Pleased, she glanced in the cheval mirror and patted her dark bobbed hair into place.

Moments later, replete in a plastic apron, nurse's watch at her left breast and the leather brogues, Mandy the nanny turned to face the bed, meditatively buttoning up her starched cuffs.

'Are the seams of my stockings straight?'

'Don't know, wasn't looking,' he replied sullenly.

'Stop sulking. Now tell me, are my seams straight? Nanny needs to know.' Turning slowly, she inched the hem of her uniform dress up until the dark stocking-tops – and the swell of her lower buttocks – were revealed.

After a long silence, the voice from the bed whispered yes.

'Yes, what?' she demanded primly.

'Yes, Nanny.'

'That's better,' she approved, approaching the bed and sitting down. 'But I think you've been peeping at Nanny.' Reaching across to close the Biggles book and place it on the bedside cabinet, she deliberately brushed the tip of his throbbing erection with her starched cuff. The shaft twitched in response. 'And you've been eating sweets after lights out,' she continued sternly, picking up the box of Liquorice Allsorts. 'I'm very much afraid I'm going to have to punish you after all.'

The erection spasmed. She saw his knuckles whiten as he gripped the bedsheet.

'But first, before I spank your bare bottom, Nanny will wash you.'

Retreating to the hand basin, she wet and soaped a flannel. Returning to the bed, she filled the air with a strong whiff of carbolic. She sat down on the bed and began to wipe his face vigorously. Submissively, he surrendered to the brisk flannelling.

'Hands.'

He offered up each hand in turn, which she dealt with firmly. Having completed the task, she casually draped the warm flannel over his stiffened shaft. He gasped aloud.

'Hands by the pillow, please, while Nanny washes you properly.'

The dark hair sank back on to the white pillow as he lay prone and passive, his naked body tensed with expectation. Closing the fingers of her left hand around the flannel-wrapped flesh-spear, she pumped and slowly squeezed.

'No. No noise,' she said to quell his groaning. 'No noise while Nanny washes you.'

Within the hot flannel, she felt the captive flesh pulse. Gripping and pumping more fiercely, she gazed dominantly down into his eyes. She watched them

157

widen, narrow – and then close. The harder she pumped, the faster his fingers scrabbled at the pillow, digging into its softness in an ecstasy of sweet suffering. Suddenly, his hips jerked up from the bed. The loud groan and the surge of wet warmth between her fingers signalled his release.

'That was very, very naughty,' Mandy whispered, peeling away the flannel and opening it up across the palm of her hand. 'Just look what you've done, you wicked little boy.'

He struggled up on to his elbows. Their hands almost touched as, gazing down together, they inspected the sticky cloth.

'You certainly are heading for a severe spanking this morning, my lad. I've never known such wilfulness. Reading and eating sweets in bed, peeping at Nanny when she was naked, watching her putting on her brassiere and panties, and now this.' She folded the flannel in a talon of fingers. 'I think we'd better have that bottom smacked before breakfast.'

Ordering him out of bed, she spread him across her lap and firmly pinned him down. His bare cheeks were quickly turned pink, then an angrier shade of crimson, beneath her spanking hand. He wriggled and squirmed but her grip was firm. As her hand swept down across the upturned buttocks, she felt his thickening shaft digging into her plastic apron as he propelled himself into her, his toes splayed on the carpet below. The crisp spanks echoed around the nursery as she chastised him severely. As she increased both the frequency and the severity of the discipline, he jerked into her faster and faster, rocking across her clamped thighs and driving his hot erection into the plastic apron. Mandy paused, deliberately fingering the scalded cheeks.

'Nanny has a cane in her cupboard. A cruel little yellow wand of bamboo. You know that, don't you?'

Trembling to contain his orgasm, he whispered his response.

'If you splash Nanny's nice clean apron with your sticky mess, you'll get four strokes of the cane.'

She saw his buttocks spasm as he squeezed his thighs together. But her words had the desired effect. Stiffening briefly, he shuddered. She watched his hot cheeks tighten as he came – emptying himself into her plastic-sheathed lap. As the last twitchings ebbed and died, she fingered his bottom as if tracing where the four slices of the cane would cut. He moaned softly, parted his thighs in submission and slumped across her.

'Did Nanny say four strokes?' Mandy murmured, peeling his wet belly away from her plastic apron. 'Better make it six for being such a bad boy.'

She left him kneeling on the carpet, head bowed penitently, as she stood up and removed her apron.

'Just look at that,' she chided, holding the apron aloft.

He looked up, his blue eyes meeting her stern gaze through the clear plastic. The centre of the apron was clouded with a wide opaque smear.

'Stand up.'

He staggered to his feet.

'Bend over. Touch your toes,' she instructed, tossing the spoiled apron aside as she strode across to the cupboard, her menacing brogues silent despite her measured tread. The cupboard door squeaked as it opened. Removing a black and green railway engine and another teddy bear, she unearthed a thin bamboo cane. Swishing it twice as she returned, she saw his toes curl into the carpet.

'Head down,' she said crisply, levelling the wood against his recently spanked cheeks.

He drew his thighs together, the cleft between his buttocks becoming a thin flesh-crease.

'No, legs apart. You know how Nanny wants you when she's going to cane your bottom.' She tapped the upturned buttocks dominantly. 'Legs apart. Give me your bottom.'

Whimpering softly, he obeyed.

The six strokes of the cane across the buttocks were delivered slowly, each measured swipe leaving a thin red line of suffering. Between the fourth and the fifth, she tapped the tip of his penis with the cane, saying, 'When Nanny gives you an order, she expects you to obey it.'

His muted moan of delight was drowned by the harsh swish-slash of the concluding strokes.

'Breakfast,' Nanny said brightly, after returning the cane with a dry rattle to the top shelf of the cupboard, 'and Nanny wants you to eat it all up.' She pressed a bell.

Four minutes later, the double doors opened and Sonia appeared, bearing the breakfast tray. Lowering it carefully on to a small, walnut table, the pert minx looked across at Mandy and then at the caned man. Sonia's eyes were wide – her grin wider. Mandy's finger flew up warningly to her lips. Sonia nodded, turned and withdrew.

'Eggie soldiers. Come along.'

He ate the fingers of toast dipped in a softly boiled egg. Mandy busied herself at the unmade bed, gathering up the teddy bear and smoothing back its ears with her thumbs. Outside, the morning was growing darker beneath a scowl of storm clouds. Soon, Mandy thought, the storm would break.

What next? How was she going to entertain this submissive? What did Nannies do, she wondered. What possible opportunities for sustained dominance and discipline were there in a nursery?

Lunchtime would be different, she decided. She'd order horrid food – braised liver or boiled cod in parsley sauce – and put him in a high chair and spoon feed him. Yes. And make him swallow every awful mouthful. He would rebel and she would punish him. Good, she thought. Then there was the school desk, she mused, picking up a Liquorice Allsort and popping it into her

160

mouth. Yes, there was the school desk – but above all, she suddenly realised, planting teddy in a chair by the darkening window, there must be strict, stern discipline, and Nanny's buckled belt.

She tidied up the bedclothes. 'What is this?' she inquired, holding up a fluttering nylon stocking which she had just pretended to discover under the pillow.

Don't know, the shrugged reply implied. He swallowed the last of his toast and squirmed uneasily.

'Stealing Nanny's stocking? What a wicked thing to do. Come here this instant, you naughty little boy.'

He approached, his hands folded at the base of his taut belly.

'Hands behind your back and stand up straight. No slouching.'

Obeying, he revealed his gathering excitement.

'So, my lad, you steal Nanny's nylon stockings, do you? We'll see about that. Kneel.'

He dropped to his knees, almost as if genuflecting in adoration.

Bending down, Mandy quickly bound his penis with the soft, shining stocking, sensing the throb of the thickening shaft against her palm. She threaded the loose nylon between his thighs and let it trail between his ankles. He tensed, his body rigid with delicious anguish.

'Nanny's nylons are forbidden to naughty boys,' she purred, standing in front of him, her brogues planted apart.

Below his belly, the nylon-sheathed erection nodded as it rose.

'Nanny's nylons,' she whispered, 'must not be touched.' She inched the hem of her striped uniform dress up slowly. 'But you want to touch, don't you?'

He nodded eagerly.

'Answer me properly.'

'Yes, Nanny. I want to touch.'

'But Nanny says you mustn't. And Nanny's word is law. You can look,' she said softly, inching her thighs towards him, 'and you can smell.' She pushed her pubis against his face, feeling the aquiline nose probing. 'And you can taste.'

He buried his face between her warm thighs, his hot tongue flattened against the darker bands of nylon at the stocking-tops.

'Smell and taste Nanny's forbidden stockings, you naughty boy.'

Already, the head of his throbbing, nyloned shaft was tapping at his hard belly. Mandy closed her eyes as the tongue lapped at her stockings, and fought to deny the hot pulse tormenting her slit. This, she fully understood, was the sweet taste of utter dominance. The dark delight of having a naked man in absolute submission, in supreme thralldom.

No. She must concentrate. She was an angel, serving both the memory of her late aunt and – she tried to focus on the fact despite the urge to come – her own financial interests. She must not succumb to the immediacy of pleasure.

Mandy opened her eyes. To her dismay she realised that she was rhythmically thrusting her pantied pubis into the kneeling man's face. Bridling at her own weakness of resolve, she stepped back a pace and struggled to compose herself.

'Nanny will now teach you, and teach you most severely, never to steal her nylon stockings again. Down. Get down. On all fours.'

As he did so, she unbuckled her leather belt and slipped it from her waist. The coiled length of supple hide felt surprisingly light in her open palm.

'Bottom up.'

He crouched, the nylon stocking at his shaft still trailing through his thighs down to his heels. Mandy stooped and gathered up the slack. He grunted as she tightened it – tugging gently at his erection. Jerking the stretched nylon upward, she drew it between his cheeks, working the material deep into his cleft where it scalded the sensitive flesh. His groans melted into softer moans, as he wriggled in an attempt to escape her controlling domination. Mandy imperiously planted her left brogue down on his left buttock, quelling and subduing him completely. At the touch of the firm foot, he froze beneath her absolute authority over his nakedness.

'I am going to give you a very special treat,' she purred, yanking the nylon deeper into his cleft. 'Nanny's belt. Nanny's brown leather, golden-buckled belt. I'm going to punish your bottom with Nanny's lovely belt.'

He bowed his head. Down on all fours – captured and controlled by the nylon binding his shaft – he inched his buttocks up for the lash. Mandy shouldered her belt and tightened her grip on the nylon stocking, winding the bronzed tether four times around her left hand.

'Nanny's leather belt,' she whispered, dangling the length of hide down and teasing his naked cheeks with the buckle. 'Such a special treat for such a naughty boy.'

Flicking the belt up, she snapped it down instantly across the bare bottom. Grunting in his pleasure-pain, the crouching man spasmed in response. Mandy felt the straining erection tighten the stocking in her left hand. The belt whipped down again, and again, crack-snapping across his scalded cheeks. After the fifth lash, Mandy tugged the stocking, supremely controlling his engorged shaft. Whipping the belt down again, twice, she sensed the throbbing urgency of the captive flesh.

'Three more red stripes across your naughty bottom and then Nanny will give you another little treat.'

'Please, Nanny, please, do it, do it quickly. Now,' he implored.

'How dare you tell Nanny the correct way to punish you,' Mandy snapped, teasing the swollen erection with the nylon stocking and tormenting the whipped buttocks with the dangling strap.

'Please, Nanny, please –'

'Nanny knows best.'

'I beg you . . .'

She felt the taut stocking twitch as he trembled on the point of his explosive climax. She tantalisingly relaxed her firm grip, allowing the tight nylon to slacken a trifle. He squeezed his whipped cheeks together in an ecstasy of anguish.

'No. Not yet. You cannot have your pleasure until Nanny has completed her task of dispensing your pain.'

His forehead nuzzled the carpet as he arched his buttocks up, arched them up as if yearning for the fierce lash.

'No, wait until I've whipped you.'

Snap, crack. She brought the belt down. Then again, leaving another cruel red stripe across his cheeks. But before the leather had kissed his flesh for a third stroke, Mandy felt the stretched nylon straining as he came. She whipped the buckled belt down for the third stroke, savagely searing his buttocks, the swipe coinciding with his scream of dark pleasure. The final lash had established her absolute authority over him, rocketing him into a violent climax. Shivering and perspiring, he sprawled on the carpet. Mandy dragged the toe of her leather brogue down his spine, then squashed it into his whipped cheeks.

'Time you had your morning wash. Come along.'

He shuffled after Mandy as she paced across to the hand basin.

'Up. No, remain kneeling.'

As he steadied himself on his knees, the soaked nylon trailed from his spent shaft. He gazed up, his blue eyes swimming with devotion. Mandy unwound the stocking and wiped the tip of his twitching penis. Tossing the nylon aside, she ordered him to stand up.

He rose. She motioned him against the sink.

'Nanny is going to wash you, now. Up on tippy-toe.'

He did as she commanded, spilling his balls over the

edge of the white porcelain into the warm water. Scooping up a handful of creamy suds, Mandy washed his balls, palming them with deliberate firmness before squeezing them with a gentle severity that left him gasping aloud. A small cloud of sullen resentment darkened the sky of his blue eyes. Mandy squeezed harder; the clouds lifted immediately.

After rinsing the matted pubic nest, Mandy ordered him to turn round. 'Nanny wants to wash your bottom.'

He turned but kept his thighs clamped together.

'Legs apart.'

His reddening face became a stubborn mask.

'Do as Nanny says,' Mandy insisted, a stern note in her voice.

Still he refused to surrender and submit his bottom to her soaped fingers. A sudden, sharp spank made him blink. The spanked cheek – the left one – reddened but remained clenched. With waspish impatience, she spanked his bottom again.

'Give Nanny your bottom,' she commanded, a spank punctuating each terse word. Her voice was curdled with delicious dominance.

'Shan't,' he blurted out. 'Won't.'

'Silly little boy,' she murmured, fingering his cleft silkily. 'Don't you know that your bottom belongs to any female in authority who wishes it? It is theirs, always, to control as they will. At prep school, the nurse will own it. She can examine it, punish it, whenever she wishes. And then, at boarding school, your bare bottom will belong to Matron. In the privacy of the san, she will give you many merciless rubber-gloved examinations – and frequently use the strap and cane across your naked cheeks. Your bottom is doomed to an eternity of female control and ownership. So stop being silly and part your legs and bend over this instant.'

Submitting to her stern authority, he bent over and surrendered his punished buttocks to her strict control.

'Nanny does not like a sticky bottom. Let's see if we can't wash it nice and clean.'

Her soaped fingers explored between his cheeks, dwelling at the tightened sphincter.

'Relax,' she whispered venomously, sensing his continuing attempt at resistance.

Hesitating at first, he succumbed to her crisp command. Her index finger slid inwards.

'Now Nanny is going to make sure that your bottom is properly clean, isn't she?'

'Yes, Nanny,' he whimpered, thrilled to be enthralled.

Picking up a yellow nail brush, Mandy soaped the firm bristles before applying it vigorously to his sensitive cleft. Staggering forward, he crushed his swollen erection against the curve of the hand basin, smothering a scream of sweet suffering. The bristles skimmed his inner flesh with ruthless affection. He writhed, but Mandy pinned him firmly at the nape of his neck. All attempts to escape the burning flame at his cleft – and the even fiercer flames of shameful humiliation – proved useless. Nanny was strict and Nanny was stern and her little boy was helpless in her hands.

'Always do what Nanny tells you to, understand?'

'Yes, Nanny.' He had been broken, his will now subdued.

'Now touch your toes and give me your bottom completely.'

Slumping down abjectly, he proffered his buttocks. They were now hers, absolutely.

'And this is what you get for even thinking of being so wickedly disobedient.'

She savaged his cleft for a full three minutes. Crying out, he lurched across the sink, squirting his hot seed. Mandy continued to ply the stiff bristles even as his shaft pumped out the spurting orgasm. Down on the carpet, his naked feet twisted in ecstasy.

'There. Nanny promised you another little treat. Now

Nanny is going to wash you again, and towel you dry. Then, I think, a nap. Yes. Nanny will put you to bed and you will have a little nap.'

'Yes, Nanny.' He shuddered as the rough towel began to torment his balls.

Curled up in bed, hugging teddy, he listened enraptured as Mandy read to him from Biggles. It was a ripping chapter. High over France, in a clear blue sky, Sopwith Camels gave the Hun Fokkers a good hiding. Propellers glinted, machine guns chattered and black smoke plumed from downed planes. Good vanquished evil in a world of black and white. As Biggles nosed his limping bus down towards a makeshift 'drome behind enemy lines, the naked submissive, still hugging teddy, fell fast asleep.

Mandy closed the Biggles book quietly and contemplated her sleeping charge. He looked pale and exhausted, drained of the liquid lust she had drawn from him with spanking – or milking – hands. But on closer examination she noted with pride that he was drained too of the creased frown of care, the burdens of high office.

Politics – where half of your acquaintances were instant comrades but all who knew you were potential enemies. Biggles flew in a blue sky, his enemies clear to see in their brightly painted planes. The sleeping politician, she knew, patrolled a very different battle zone where everything was murky and the only colour was grey.

Smoothing down her crisp, striped uniform, Mandy felt pleased with her work. Here at Sternwood Grange, the movers and shakers in society, the people who really mattered, sought their solace. And it was granted to them: through leather, silk and supple bamboo cane. Remembering her late aunt with renewed admiration, Mandy turned her gaze down upon the sleeping face.

She gently caressed a stray lock of his dark, curled hair. He was a perfect example of Sternwood Grange at its best. Destined to command, he came here to obey: shrugging off for a time the relentless pressures that besieged him.

How much? The question flickered across her brain. How much, she wondered, had he paid? Sophie had let it slip that all the residents paid in cash, in advance. Rising softly, Mandy tiptoed around the bed and across the nursery floor. In the adjoining dressing room, furnished in a more adult fashion, she found the wardrobe – and, in it, his dark-blue suit. Fishing out his wallet was the work of a moment. The House of Commons pass, club membership cards to Whites and the Athenaeum, several gold credit cards and his Coutts chequebook were quickly examined. The chequebook. She thumbed through the stubs, coming to the most recent. Good. The dates corresponded with his sojourn at Sternwood Grange. A four-figure sum had been drawn out in cash. Now she knew.

Replacing everything exactly as she found it, Mandy paused to add a mischievous touch. Skipping silently back into the nursery, she plucked up the abandoned nylon stocking and returned to the dressing room. It was still sticky with his spurt of hot release. Grinning at the thought that he might accidentally pull it out during a visit to the Whip's office, she stuffed the memento amori into his inside pocket.

A soft sound brought her back into the nursery. Sonia had entered, bearing a large lunch tray.

'Vegetable soup and rhubarb crumble,' she whispered, pulling a gruesome face. 'Nursery food for baby over there.'

Mandy took the tray and set it down carefully.

'Asleep?' Sonia asked, nodding across at the bed.

Mandy smiled. 'Busy morning with Nanny.'

'Ooh,' the minx gurgled, bending down to inspect the

sleeping submissive. 'Don't I know him? Isn't he an MP?'

'Yep, only just, though. He's got a very small majority.'

'Not from where I'm standing, it isn't.'

They collapsed in smothered giggles. Mandy joined the pert little maid and hugged her, then spanked her bottom. Returning to the lunch tray, she started to pepper and salt the vegetable soup. Looking up, she saw Sonia playing gently with the flaccid penis.

'Put that down,' she hissed.

'Only looking,' Sonia said, pouting, returning the penis to its resting place between the darkly haired thighs. 'Bit touchy, this morning, aren't you?'

'I can't –' Mandy began.

'Mind you, everyone is this morning. It's this thunder brewing up. Makes people edgy.'

'Probably.'

'Or because the mistress is coming tomorrow. Another flying visit –'

'Celia Flaxstone is coming?' Mandy snapped.

'How do you know her name?' replied Sonia in amazement. 'Besides, Erica and Partridge have had a terrific row down in the kitchens and then Partridge went off in tears and then Erica punished all the maids without exception. Look.'

Pulling up the velvet skirt of her maid's uniform, Sonia exhibited the damage done to her naked cheeks by the cruel wooden spoon.

Mandy approached, knelt and kissed the sore, red bottom better. Although the hot bottom was delicious, her mind was on other things. So, she thought, the mistress of Sternwood Grange is due tomorrow. Why? Had Mandy's cover been blown? Preoccupied by this and equally disturbing possibilities, Mandy's tongue and lips neglected the eager cheeks.

'It hurt,' Sonia murmured. 'Kiss me better.'

Mandy smiled and, setting aside the rapid flood of speculations whirling in her brain, buried her face into the waiting cheeks. Soon her tongue was busy. Sonia inched up on tiptoe, thrusting her punished buttocks back into Mandy's face. Lapping gently at first, then rasping the reddened cheeks more fiercely, Mandy tongued the ravished flesh.

'Mmm,' purred the maid happily, wriggling free at length. 'I've got to get back. It's all upside down today. I'm only a maid and yet Erica's letting me serve lunches upstairs. Catch you later,' she whispered. At the door, she paused and turned.

Mandy raised her eyebrows questioningly.

'Tell sleeping beauty he gets my vote anytime.'

Mandy stamped her brogue silently; Sonia fled, giggling.

Trapped in the cage of polished pinewood that formed the struts and tray of the highchair, the naked man strained back from the spoon at his mouth.

'Open wide,' Mandy snarled.

He shook his head vehemently, refusing the soup.

'Very well. If you won't eat up, Nanny will take her belt to your bare bottom.'

He parted his lips and meekly swallowed the spoonful of soup.

'Nice pudding if you eat it all up. Nasty, sore bottom if you don't.'

The soup was finished in two minutes. Mandy brought the bowl of golden crumble before him. He eyed it greedily. The silver spoon winked above the delicious crust of caramelised brown sugar. Thick yellow custard anointed the fragrant pudding. Mandy plied the spoon deftly, heaping up a delicious mouthful. He strained forward, eager for the delicious crumble. At the last possible moment, Mandy withdrew the spoon.

'No. You have been a bad boy. No nice pudding for

you.' She placed the laden spoon down in the sticky custard.

One of the exquisite refinements of the adapted highchair was the feature which Mandy had put to full use: it pinned the occupant's arms straight down, imprisoning them completely. In his wooden cage of restricting bondage, the naked man rocked and writhed.

'Stop that at once,' she warned, quelling his tantrum with a stern gaze.

'Sorry, Nanny,' he wheedled. 'May I have some –'

'Nanny says no. No pudding for naughty boys.'

He hung his head down.

'Still hungry?'

'Yes, Nanny,' he mumbled.

'Nanny will see to that, never fear. Goodness, isn't it hot?'

At the window, the pewter sky seethed, sulphurous with the impending storm. Mandy removed the wooden tray, but kept her charge penned in his pinewood bondage.

'So hot,' she said gently, 'I think I'll just unbutton this tight uniform. Would you like Nanny to unbutton her tight, crisp uniform?'

He looked up excitedly, the sulky mouth that mourned the crumble now smiling. He nodded eagerly.

'Hmm?'

'Yes,' he whispered hoarsely.

She peeled down her bodice and exposed her brassiere-cupped bosom. The wooden chair rocked. She prised out her left breast, thumbing the nipple slowly. The highchair rocked violently.

'Nanny most certainly won't have her little chap getting down from his highchair still hungry, will she? No, of course not. Nanny will feed him herself.'

The soft breast, bunched up by the cup underneath, was swollen and ripe. The heavy mound of creamy flesh all but buried his nose as his lips worked busily at the hard pink nipple.

'Suck slowly,' she commanded, her slit quite wet from arousal as his hot mouth devoured her breast. 'Ouch.'

He had inadvertently nipped her nipple in his excitement.

'Sorry, Nanny,' he mumbled, the words of contrition muffled as his lips pressed into her warm softness.

'Nanny accepts your apology. Accidents will happen. Nanny will just have to train you more carefully, that's all.'

Cupping and controlling her breast, she guided the erect nipple along his parted lips. Using the peaked stub of sensitive flesh like a lipstick, she traced the outline of both lips.

'Please, Nanny, oh please . . .' he moaned.

'Be still and stay silent. Nanny will attend to you in her own good time.'

Dominating her captive nude, Mandy used her breast with wicked subtlety to humiliate and delight him in turn. Her stray fingertips casually brushed his penis, checking his mounting arousal. The shaft grew engorged, throbbing heavily as it hardened. Suddenly the highchair rattled and jerked – she sensed his imminent orgasm. Dropping down on her knees, she exposed her other breast, cupping it against the other so that her bunched bosoms bobbed a mere two inches in front of the twitching erection.

'Yes,' he hissed urgently.

'Silence. Nanny is in strict control.'

She thrust her breasts closer, then closer still, until both nipples grazed his shaft. Bending closer, Mandy captured and imprisoned the shaft between her cushioning breasts and squeezed, working her warm pillows of satin rhythmically until, groaning and writhing in his bondage, he came.

'Oh, dear,' Mandy tut-tutted in her most Nannylike tone of dismay. 'Just look at what you've done. You've made Nanny's breasts all wet and sticky, naughty boy.'

She examined and fingered slowly his splashes of hot delight which had spattered her rounded breasts. Pearls of semen gathered at, then slowly dripped from, both her erect nipples.

Outside, lightning flickered down from the blackberry clouds, etching their solid forms with silver. Seconds later, a peal of thunder ripped the sultry silence apart.

'Storm's breaking at last,' Mandy sighed. 'Are you frightened of the thunder, little man?'

He shook his head, contemptuous of the suggestion.

'Don't be insolent or Nanny will take the hairbrush to your bottom. Now answer me properly. Are you frightened of thunder?'

Before he could reply, the room, now in gathering darkness, was lit up by a terrific flash of bluish-gold lightning. The crackling roar followed almost immediately.

'Not scared.' He shrugged.

'Boasting is a very wicked offence. It is always punished most severely in every well-disciplined nursery,' Mandy cautioned, her voice crackling with more tension than the static in the room. 'Nanny does not like a coward, of course, but she will not tolerate rude and boastful little boys. Get down from your chair and go over to your bed at once.'

His eyes flashed sullenly as he clambered out of the wooden highchair. Mandy slapped his bare bottom twice, harshly, and ordered him not to dawdle. He turned, scowling, and rubbed his sore bottom.

'Well?' Mandy challenged.

'Bully,' he dared to whisper.

'How dare you,' she said softly. 'How dare you question Nanny's absolute authority over you. Get down on your knees this instant,' she commanded, in a voice louder than the rumbling elements overhead. 'Down on the carpet. Nanny promised you the hairbrush and the hairbrush you shall have.'

'No, Nanny, no. Please, I'm sorry –'

'Not so brave and boastful now, are we? Now that we are about to have our bare bottom hairbrushed, hmm?' Mandy taunted, sweeping up the hairbrush from the dressing table and returning to straddle the snivelling, crouching man. 'Bottom up,' she barked. 'Come along, get your bottom up, young man. Nanny's going to beat you.'

She knelt, her nylon-stockinged knees brushing against his naked thighs. Mandy lowered the cherry-wood hairbrush – bristle side up – across the expectant cheeks. The polished wood kissed the surface of the buttocks; Mandy saw them spasm.

The growling in the sky was almost continuous now. The heat became almost unbearable. Mandy stood up, leaving the inverted hairbrush balanced across the crown of the buttocks, and stripped off her Nanny's uniform dress. Now scantily clad in her brassiere, panties, suspender belt and shining nylon stockings – she had kicked off the brogues – she resumed her kneeling position. Picking up the hairbrush, after briefly but dominantly flattening the upturned cheeks with its polished wood, she placed her left hand down across the nape of his neck. Her wet slit pulsed as she felt his tamed nakedness squirm. In silence, she gazed supremely at the bottom she was about to set ablaze. Mandy's tummy fluttered, so delicious was her mounting expectation: she relished the knowledge of his thick shaft burning into the carpet, of the suppleness of her wrist for superb spanking action, of the sharp sound of polished wood punishing naked cheeks – this knowledge seared her mind, making her brain as hot as her slit.

She took a deep breath to calm her agitation. 'Nanny has a question for you,' she said in a controlled voice. 'Will this storm be a big one? Or is it going to fizzle out?'

'Don't care,' came the surly response – most of it lost in the carpet.

The hairbrush cracked down. 'Don't care was made to care,' Mandy whispered softly, raising the brush back up to shoulder height.

'Sorry, Nanny,' the naked man mumbled. 'It will not last. It will fizzle out.'

'Let's hope you're right, my little man. Why does Nanny say that? Because Nanny is going to use the hairbrush across your bare bottom every time the lightning flashes –'

Even as she spoke, the walls of the room around them seemed to lurch and dance as a blue and white veined fork bolted down outside the window. The blinding flash was followed by a huge, rolling crackle up above. The hairbrush swept down, swiping the defenceless cheeks pitilessly, leaving them reddened and ablaze. The buttocks bucked and jerked after the Judas kiss of the polished wood.

Then the storm broke: both in the Suffolk sky above and across his naked bottom beneath the cruel hairbrush. Seven times in rapid succession the dark sky spat out its dazzling fury – and seven times the rounded buttocks burned as the hairbrush cracked down savagely.

An eerie silence filled the brief lull. There was no flash of lightning – which meant a respite for the scalded cheeks – but a stuttering peal of thunder echoed across the darkened Suffolk landscape. The rain fell heavily now, hammering against the window panes. Both punisher and punished tensed expectantly. Nanny's fingers tightened at her victim's neck. A triple flash flickered, bringing the hairbrush down once, then again, and even yet again. The punished man cried out aloud, groaning his sweet suffering. Mandy clamped her thighs tightly together at his curdling moans, then parted them, peeling the damp nylons apart at the top of her thighs where the bronzed sheen soaked up her wet excitement.

Tossing the hairbrush down, Mandy mounted the

175

naked buttocks, splaying her thighs across the punished cheeks and plumping her silk-sheathed bottom down on to his hot flesh. Straddling his reddened cheeks, she rasped the wet silk of her panties against them, then squeezed her nyloned thighs together, her stocking-tops tormenting his nakedness. Gripping him firmly as she rode him, bareback, she slid deliberately from cheek to cheek, grinding the sticky plum at her pubis into him.

'Oh, yes, Nanny, yes, please . . .' he moaned, his voice thick with drunken ecstasy.

She taloned his shoulders, her knuckles whitened, then drew her legs almost primly together and lay down on top of him, every inch of her body pressed fiercely into his. Perched on top, her breasts crushed into him, she rode him fiercely, pumping the wet silk stretched across her pubic mound into his crimson buttocks.

Outside the nursery, the storm approached its climax, the furious elements spilling over in a molten crescendo. Inside the nursery, a shrill cry of delight filled the room as, gouging his erection into the carpet, the naked man ridden by the nanny tensed stiffly and shuddered on the brink of orgasm.

Mandy sensed the paroxysm about to explode. 'Not until Nanny says so,' she warned.

He grunted thickly as her left hand clutched and controlled his thick, dark hair.

Scissoring her nyloned legs rhythmically, Mandy totally dominated her human mount: legs together, then legs apart, she maddened and bewitched him – and always her wet slit rasped his hot cheeks. He cried out long and loud, his exquisite pleasure almost choking him as she rode harder and faster, burning his shaft into the carpet.

'Now,' she commanded, rising abruptly and spanking his right buttock with her flattened palm.

As the spanking hand echoed sharply across the ravished cheek, she dragged her labia across the left buttock.

Arching up in the powerful splendour of orgasm, he roared his delight and came like a bull, almost tossing her off in his writhing frenzy.

'You've been a good boy for Nanny,' Mandy murmured, now completely naked.

He rolled over in bed and gazed up adoringly with softened blue eyes. 'Thank you, Nanny. Thank you very much for a super day.'

'Nanny thinks you deserve a sweet. Give Nanny the Liquorice Allsorts. I know you've hidden them under teddy,' she said with mock severity.

He groped under the yellow bear, pulled out a box of Bassetts and surrendered them to her outstretched palm.

She placed the box on the bed, opened it, and then tapped his flaccid penis. 'Up,' she demanded.

It stirred but failed to rise. Gently, she thumbed his balls. Again, it flickered with interest but could not manage to stiffen to a full response.

'Dear me,' she whispered, 'my little man has had a busy day. Let's see if Nanny can help.'

The blue eyes widened anxiously.

'Tell me,' Mandy continued coaxingly, 'how has Nanny punished you today?'

The blue eyes closed. His litany was brief but breathless. In an urgent whisper, he recounted the spankings, the leather belt, the cane and all the discipline of the day. As she listened attentively, Mandy saw the erection rise. By the time he had excitedly whispered the word 'hairbrush', he was sporting a thick, strong shaft.

Mandy settled herself on the bed, her heavy buttocks dimpling the mattress. Dipping into the box of Allsorts, she selected a brown, white, black and orange cube in a delicate pincer of finger and thumb.

'Open wide,' she instructed.

He sank his dark curls on to the white pillow, lips parted greedily. Mandy, instead of placing the sweet on his tongue, gently lowered it down on to the tip of his glistening erection. He groaned, his wide eyes staring in fascination.

'Keep your mouth open,' she warned. 'Two strokes of the cane for every one you miss.'

His penis quivered, almost but not quite dislodging the perched sweet. Mandy eased herself down, squashing her naked breasts into his lower thighs, and positioned herself at the thickened shaft. Aiming carefully, she curled her second finger into her thumb tip. Judging the angle, she flicked. The Liquorice Allsort vanished into his mouth. His teeth worked busily at the sweet as, down at the base of his belly, his shaft twitched.

'Another.'

He shook his head, refusing more.

'It was not a question, it was a command,' she whispered.

He swallowed quickly and parted his lips.

There were eight sweets left in the box. Mandy took two for her own enjoyment and placed the remaining six on the sheet. One by one, they were positioned on his penis and flicked into his mouth. He had to strain to catch them and, fearful of the sweet severity of the cane, was careful not to miss. Each time Mandy flicked a sweet, she deliberately brushed his throbbing shaft with her fingertips.

'All the sweets have gone,' she observed. 'Nanny thinks it's time you went beddy-byes.'

As she tucked him in tightly, she spotted his right hand stealthily inching down beneath the coverlet to his erection. Inching down, she knew, to relieve his pent up, unexploded orgasm.

'No,' she chided, slapping his wrist. 'Nanny thinks that is a naughty habit so Nanny is going to make sure

178

that her little man doesn't play with himself during the night.'

The thunder had rolled away to the north. Norfolk was getting it by now, she mused. Through the rain-speckled window pane, she saw that the sky was washed out: the pale-blue air had been rinsed by the sudden summer storm. It was late afternoon. Teatime in London, though nobody she knew ever actually had tea there. In the House of Commons, sober-suited statesmen would be whispering their strategies over buttered scones, concealing their true intentions as they spread red jam with silver knives, smiling as they lied candidly over large wedges of date and walnut cake. Here – she smiled to herself as she bound both of his wrists to the bedposts with her nylon stockings – their future leader was wriggling in his sweet restraint.

'Not too tight?' she inquired. 'Nanny wants you to be comfortable.'

He strained at the bondage.

'Well?' she insisted.

'Mm,' he grunted, attempting – but failing – to kiss Mandy's naked breasts as they brushed his face momentarily.

Her task of binding his wrists to the bedposts completed, she took the pillow from beneath his head and, stepping down off the bed, wedged it between her parted thighs.

'Nanny is going soon. It is time for you to get some rest. But Nanny will return.'

He groaned aloud as she dragged her fingernail up along the length of his erection. He was swimming in ecstasy – an ecstasy she sternly denied him to spill.

'When Nanny returns, she will inspect you. If you have wet the glass, you will be whipped.'

'The glass?' he echoed, uncomprehendingly.

'The glass,' she repeated firmly, taking an empty tumbler from the bedside cabinet and inverting it over his erection.

'But, Nanny –'

'Silence. I will give you your pillow back when I have made good use of it.'

With one hand grasping the corner of the pillow that jutted out below her belly and the other hand grasping the corner emerging beneath her buttocks' swell, Mandy dragged the plump white softness back and forth between her thighs. It took less than two and a half minutes of concentrated fury to bring herself off – she came, sweetly and loudly and was quite wet.

'There,' she gasped softly, approaching the bed.

His blue eyes gazed up, hypnotised.

She positioned his pillow so that the wet patch greeted his lips. He swivelled his head, but the wet patch was broad enough to greet them again on the other side. He writhed.

Bending down, Mandy kissed his forehead tenderly. The tumbler danced on the twitching shaft.

'Goodnight, my little man, but be careful how you dream. And don't you dare dream about Nanny. No naughty dreams of Nanny getting dressed, or Nanny spanking you on the bare bottom.'

His erection jerked. The tumbler trembled.

'Remember,' she whispered darkly, stroking each of his stocking-bound wrists, 'Nanny will return. And if the glass is wet?'

'I will be whipped,' he murmured in tones of dread delight.

Seven

Through the large sash window, the panes still speckled
with raindrops, Mandy glimpsed the last of the sunset.
The sky over Suffolk was streaked with lemon, the night
clouds ominously dark with the promise of rain.

Mandy saw, but could not hear, a scattering of rooks
in ragged formation returning to roost in the distant
elms. As a maid, confined to the noise and the heat of
the busy kitchens, she had seen little of the world
outside. As an angel, more windows were open to her.
Of all the new perspectives revealed to her since
becoming an angel, two were of the greatest significance:
her appreciation of the scale and scope of the financial
potential of Sternwood Grange, and her growing
awareness of her appetite for discipline and punishment.

Mandy pushed these thoughts aside and fingered the
array of expensive clothes. As an angel, she was
expected – indeed instructed – to help herself and dress
from a gorgeous wardrobe. The only stipulation was
that she had to dress to please. Not herself, but any
residents she might encounter. All the clothes were cut
with erotic chic, and were designed to entice and
inflame. She fingered an ice-blue leather mini-skirt then
weighed the sheer silk of a scarlet blouse before
wriggling her left foot into the tight leather of a red
stiletto.

These were not the angels' working uniforms: the
crisp outfits, starched and laundered for the Games

Room. These were not the uniforms for Nanny or Nurse, donned to discipline and delight the submissive residents. The clothes Mandy was selecting were for informal wear when off-duty.

Deliberately, Mandy rejected several delicious items before selecting a beige polo-neck jumper, in clinging cashmere, a lightweight leather jacket, a ribbed and belted camel skirt and a pair of calf-length black leather boots to go over her chocolate-brown tights.

She dressed. The cashmere clung to her breasts, shaping and cupping their firm swell. She plucked at its softness, but on release it sprang back to hug her bosom amorously. The ribbed camel skirt felt good. It flattered her thighs and buttocks, managing to reveal more than conceal her superb curves. The boots perfumed her nostrils with the raw tang of virgin leather. She thrilled to the whiff of hide, instantly recalling warm belts she had pressed her dry lips on to after punishing a bare bottom. She eased her feet into the boots. The kiss of leather haunted her imagination.

There was no mirror in the room, to Mandy's surprise, so she had to dress by touch alone. Mandy palmed her jumper and skirt several times, smoothing her clothes intimately and firmly. Satisfied with her selection, she left the small room quite moist with arousal for her appointment with Erica.

Why had she, she wondered, been ordered to attend a debriefing? There had been no witness to her session as Nanny. Rowena and her Pentax had not been in attendance. Would Mandy have to give a full verbal report on her day, recounting every spank, stripe and stroke. What words would she find to describe the most intimate moments of dominance and punishment.

'Come in.'

Mandy entered, obeying the cropped blonde's command.

Erica glanced up from the flickering screen. Mandy caught the brief frown. My choice of clothes, probably,

Mandy reasoned. Too dull and dour for the residents. And what had Erica been watching on the video, Mandy wondered.

'You've had an interesting day, I see,' Erica remarked. 'One of mixed success, though.'

Mandy joined Erica in front of the screen, but remained standing. 'How do you –' she began.

Erica replied by jabbing the remote. Images of Mandy, dressed as a nanny and spanking a reddening bare bottom, filled the wide screen.

'Video. Three hidden cameras have recorded everything that happened in the nursery today. If he ever makes it to Number Ten, the Mistress will be in possession of a nice little extra source of income.'

Blackmail. Mandy grew hot with anger, and then burned with shame. Aunt Clare would never have approved. Besides, Mandy thought, her triumph in pleasuring him, and his memories of the pleasure, would be tainted by any future attempts at blackmail. She felt used and bitterly resented the ploy.

'I've seen this through twice,' Erica continued, fastforwarding to the end. Consulting a piece of paper, she knelt down and peered at the counter. 'We'll take a look at the three most successful sequences first.'

The video blinked and clicked. In a big close-up, held in freeze-frame, Mandy saw her own hand applying the soaped nail brush to her victim's cleft.

'Total dominance,' Erica murmured approvingly. 'You have rendered your subject into a helpless infant having his bottom cleaned. A brilliant piece of severe nannying. Well done, girl.'

Mandy gazed at the bare buttocks, frozen in a clench of anguished ecstasy. She saw how her knuckles dimpled the soft cheek as the nail brush skimmed along the exposed ribbon of the cleft. She could only imagine the sweet, delicious torment. Drinking in the image of her fierce dominance, her labia parted into a sticky pout.

Erica fingered the remote, her eyes monitoring the counter. The video whirred, clicking to another freeze-frame. Mandy saw her hand captured in the moment of wiping a stray dribble of soup from her baby-victim's chin. No bare buttocks, straps or canes were visible, but the image of power, dominance and supreme control proved to be highly charged. Mandy's slit grew juicy. Erica studied the picture for a full minute, again pronouncing her approval. She took up the remote once more.

'Your most accomplished moment was, I believe, this.'

Erica showed a three-and-a-half-minute sequence of Mandy punishing the bare buttocks with the hairbrush during the thunder storm. At least seventeen searing strokes were administered during the clip before Erica pressed the pause button, leaving the reddened bottom quivering on the screen.

'But there were mistakes, my girl. Errors of taste and judgement. Watch.'

The cropped blonde glanced down at her sheet of paper, pressed rewind and squinted at the backward flow of the numbers on the video counter. Click. Another short sequence flooded the screen: Mandy riding the punished buttocks, dragging her pantied pubis across the crimsoned crowns.

'Too intimate, girl. He can sense and feel your wet flesh. That is wrong. Flesh must not normally touch flesh – except for the punishing hand – between a dominatrix and her submissive. And look. There.'

In a big close-up, Mandy saw herself gripped by her own ecstasy. Eyes tightly closed, she rode the hot buttocks with gathering frenzy.

'Altogether wrong, girl. You should be cool, detached and seemingly indifferent. That is what fuels their dark delight and feeds their sweet despair. Understand? Never allow your own feelings to spill over.'

'Yes,' Mandy murmured dutifully, secretly resenting the presence of the prying camera in the nursery. Suddenly she blushed. Had she come? Had the camera recorded her orgasm? Had Erica already seen her jerking in the paroxysm of climax? She squirmed at the thought of the cropped blonde perusing the images, gazing steadily at intimate close-ups of Mandy in ecstasy.

'Second mistake,' Erica continued crisply, 'was this.'

Mandy looked at the screen and saw herself flicking the Liquorice Allsorts from the erect shaft into the submissive's mouth.

'No, no, no. All wrong. Deny your victim any such reward. You should have taken up each sweet in your teeth and enjoyed them yourself, understand? Never weaken and indulge your victim. The dominatrix must be cruel and ruthless.'

The video revealed Mandy's third mistake: using the pillow between her naked thighs until she came. This lapse was summarily criticised and dismissed. Mandy hung her head in shame – but her slit seethed, fired by the potent images on the flickering screen.

From the shadowed outbuildings came the thin chime of the stable clock. Midnight. Mandy, without a watch, had thought it was later. She sighed, resigning herself to at least another hour's wait. She had secreted herself in a ground-floor storeroom at the rear of the building, from where she hoped to make a bid to escape when the vans arrived. They were due tonight, three of them. Mandy planned to return to London in one of them as a stowaway.

An hour to go. She was still deliciously disturbed after the video debriefing with Erica. Outside, the moon broke through the rain clouds, filling her hiding place with silvery light. The storeroom revealed its contents to her gradually: she saw the glint of the canes, the curved

shapes of spanking paddles, the gleam of oiled whips
and the sinuous coils of leather straps. As her eyes
became accustomed to the half-light, she saw the
handcuffs; chains and restraints; hoods and masks;
harnesses and other instruments of punishment,
humiliation and bondage.

The heat at the base of her belly ignited and a slow
trickle of lava seared her slit. Mandy reached out and
carefully selected a cane. She held it reverently between
inquisitive fingers, thrilling to its supple touch.
Thrumming it softly through the silver moonbeams, she
relished the low note from the hymn to suffering as the
wood sliced down. Her fingers tightened around the
cane. She drew it up to her mouth and kissed it, then
licked its gleaming length. Replacing the cane, she
inspected a whip, feeling the full extent of the lash
between a trembling pincer of finger and thumb. Her
nipples burned as they peaked stiffly in response to the
oiled hide. She dared not risk snap-cracking it, but
closed her eyes and imagined it caressing a naked
bottom, kissing the creamy flesh with crimson.

Mandy was breathing heavily now, the cashmere at
her swollen bosom stretched and straining. Reaching
behind, she fingered the array of dangling belts, then
turned to thumb the soft rubber aprons, hoods and
basques pegged on the wall to her left.

A single red glove caught her eye. It had no partner,
not being one of a pair. It was a single, elbow-length
glove to be donned by a dominatrix: sheathing the hand
that wielded the whip, swished the bamboo cane and
fingered each burning stripe across the punished
buttocks. Mandy rubbed the red satin glove, then
clenched her fist and crushed it. It was for her a symbol
of Sternwood Grange: exotic, expensive and supremely
erotic. An enigmatic piece from a jigsaw puzzle which
when assembled represented domination, submission,
pleasure and pain.

She squeezed her fingers into the glove, dragging it slowly up to her elbow with her teeth. Tomorrow, in London, with the assistance of her own expensive but capable lawyers, Sternwood Grange would be no more than a few dry documents: xeroxed wills, title deeds and affidavits. After that, it would be no more than a delicious memory and a large sum of money in her bank account. Tonight, in the moonlight, the sense of the place was both urgent and powerful: the erotically charged atmosphere was intensified both by her memories and experiences, and by the canes, whips and instruments of bondage.

Mandy inched the ribbed skirt up over her thighs and let it ride up over her buttocks. Pushing her panties down to her knees, she parted her legs and surrendered her pubis to the satin-gloved fingers at her belly. Before the vans came, she would bid farewell to Sternwood Grange, and salute it in a manner most fitting. Her gloved finger sought out and found the wisp of her pubic fringe. Moving down gently, it traced the outline of her labial lips with delicate strokes. She brought the satin-sheathed fingertip up to the flesh-hood covering her clitoris: the love thorn stirred and stiffened beneath the probing satin.

The moon vanished behind a scudding bank of clouds, leaving the storeroom in complete darkness. Mandy did not notice: her eyes were already tightly closed. Crushing her bare bottom against the line of dangling leather belts behind her, she worked the satin glove down at her hot slit, thumbing her erect clitoris expertly as she prised her sticky flesh-lips wide apart. Mandy paused, pacing her approaching climax. She lowered her gloved arm to drag her wrist against her labia, rotating it slowly to tease and torment the wet flesh with the rasp of satin. A cane rattled as it settled in its pile. The sound brought her memories of bamboo punishments flooding back. Memories of harsh pleasures and sweet pain: the delicious dread of a supple cane hovering over naked peaches, the cruel thrum of the slicing wood, the crisp stroke across upturned buttocks, the red stripe as the bamboo caressed the buttocks savagely.

The dangling belts behind her pressed their leather tongues into her bottom, one strap forcing its hide into her splayed cleft. Mandy squeezed her cheeks to capture and contain it, her bottom jerking in fresh delight. The leather at her flesh brought more haunting memories – of both punishments received and punishments administered. Her gloved hand flew across her weeping fig; the muscles at the base of her belly tightened. She conjured up the snap-crack of belts and straps across her own – and others' – suffering cheeks. She was coming now, her inner muscles spasming in sweet paroxysms as the climax gathered within her and exploded.

The moon emerged from behind the clouds, filling the storeroom once more with silvery light. It outlined the lengths of bamboo stretched out in obedient repose, the whips, rubber-wear and restraints. Mandy opened her eyes, drank in the symbols of fierce delight and sweet torment, and orgasmed violently. Buckling under the ferocity of her climax, she sank back into the belts and straps dangling behind her. At her right thigh, the wet satin fingertips of her gloved hand hung inert. Only the thumping of her heart broke the absolute silence of the night.

She saw the approaching lights before she heard the engines of the Transits. Slipping out into the shadows of the neglected kitchen garden at the rear of Sternwood Grange, Mandy gasped. It was chilly and dank in the darkness. She had chosen her clothes for the escape well. Inside the back of the Transit van it would be cold, and London was at least two hours' drive away.

She crouched down between two dripping blackcurrant bushes, shrinking back from the sweep of the

188

approaching headlights. She counted three white Transits, nose to tail in a tight convoy. The yellow beams dazzled her as the three vans swept up to the entrance. Doors opened and slid shut softly after the engines had died; Mandy knew why: nothing must disturb the residents.

Dark shadowy figures moved silently between the opened back of each van and the open kitchen door in the rear-basement area. Boxes and crates were taken in, and heavy laundry bags brought out. Mandy had considered smuggling herself out in a laundry bag, but it would have left her helpless and with no chance of a quick getaway once in London.

The men moved quickly and, within minutes, their nocturnal operation was almost completed. For Mandy, shivering between the blackcurrant bushes, it was all happening too quickly. The rear doors of the leading Transit were already closed, and the driver aboard. Mandy felt a surge of panic well up within her as she heard the engine purr. The wheels turned slowly, crunching the wet gravel softly. The engine of the second Transit coughed into life; its rear doors closed against her. It had to be the third van, she realised. And it had to be now.

She sprinted across to the rear of the last Transit and jumped headlong into its wet belly, landing on two laundry bags which muffled her fall. Footsteps approached almost immediately. She cringed in the shadows as the measured tread grew louder. A shadow fell across her, then two soft, smelly, black bin bags were thrown in – one split, oozing a vegetable slime over her hair and face. Mandy crouched in a hedgehog-like ball, fearful of discovery. The double doors closed with a soft thud. Moments later, the Transit lurched into life and moved off slowly down the drive.

Mandy removed a Dover sole bone from her soiled skirt and a pulpy avocado skin from the inside of her boot. She sensed the Transit slowing down – but remembered the cow trap at the end of the drive. She waited for the thump of tyres over the grille of metal bars, knowing that, once across it, London would be within her grasp.

The Transit stopped. Waiting in queue for the leading vans to negotiate the narrow cattle grid, Mandy supposed. She heard doors being opened and closed. Her heart raced wildly. Soft footsteps trod alongside the Transit and paused at the rear doors. Mandy's heart hammered in the darkness – almost stopping as the doors were wrenched open. A strong torch beam stabbed the unlit interior, catching and dazzling Mandy like a rabbit in a headlight.

'Get out, you stupid little bitch,' Erica snarled. 'Quickly, girl.'

Trembling from the shock of being discovered just when she thought she was safe and free, Mandy scrambled over the stinking bin bags and clambered down into the cold night air.

'Got her,' Erica called out to the driver. She closed the doors firmly and slapped the side of the Transit. 'Take her away.'

As the van sped off, Erica raked the beam of her torch up and down Mandy's shivering body. 'I knew you were going to attempt an escape,' she said, a note of triumph in her voice.

Mandy blinked into the strong torch beam.

'The clothes you picked. Could only mean one thing. Gave yourself away completely, fool.'

Mandy remembered the frown that had greeted her as she had entered Erica's room for the debriefing earlier on. Now she understood. She bowed her head, fearful and defeated.

'Strip.'

'But –'

The cropped blonde swapped the torch in her right hand for the wicked little crop in her left. 'At once.'

190

Reluctantly, but fearful of the crop, Mandy peeled off all her clothing until only her boots remained.

'Tights and boots as well,' Erica snapped, tapping Mandy's thigh with the loop at the tip of the crop. 'I want you naked.'

Hopping as she struggled to remove the boots and tights, Mandy squealed as her pink feet trod the wet gravel. The crop flickered out twice across her bottom.

'Silence. I will not have the residents disturbed.'

Mandy stood penitently, shivering and clutching the soiled clothing to her naked bosom.

'Turn around and keep three paces and three paces only ahead of me,' Erica snarled. She pointed the torch down at Mandy's feet, illuminating the drive back to Sternwood Grange. 'Walk,' she barked, applying the crop across the naked buttocks before her. 'You'd better get a shower before . . .' She did not finish her sentence.

'Before?' Mandy asked timidly.

'Before punishment.'

After restoring her chilled nakedness under a stream of hot water, Mandy stopped shivering. Erica stood at the entrance to the shower, gazing at the bare bottom she was about to beat. Mandy closed her eyes and offered her breasts up to the warm sluice; the cropped blonde leant in and turned the tap over to cold. Mandy shrieked and huddled, arms across her breasts, beneath the icy cascade. She made a bid to leave the shower but Erica, crop at the ready, forced her back under the cruel deluge.

'Out,' ordered Erica, when she was satisfied that Mandy had suffered enough.

Mandy scampered out and pawed for a towel. Erica whisked it away.

'No towel. You'll be warm, soon enough. Very warm.'

At these words, Mandy shivered – not entirely from the cold.

'Follow me,' the cropped blonde commanded.

Conscious of her nakedness in contrast to Erica's fully clothed body, Mandy felt both vulnerable and humiliated. As if able to read her mind, Erica said that, from now on, Mandy was to remain naked at all times.

'I can't –' Mandy began to protest.

'Silence. You will remain naked at all times. You have broken the trust placed in you and going naked will be part of your punishment. And without clothes,' Erica laughed grimly, 'you won't get very far. This way.'

Part of your punishment. To remain naked was only part of her punishment. What else awaited her, Mandy wondered. Where was Erica taking her? They were not going upstairs to her bedroom.

'In,' came the curt command.

They entered the gym. Mandy saw Partridge standing over by the wall bars.

'Didn't believe me, did you?' Erica crowed. 'I told you she was dressed for an escape bid. Caught her in one of the Transits.'

The housekeeper turned her large, brown eyes upon Mandy in a sorrowful gaze.

'Up against the wall bars, girl,' Erica instructed, swiping Mandy's bare bottom with the crop. 'Partridge took you on here at Sternwood Grange and so she will administer the punishment.'

'The girl is tired,' Partridge reasoned. 'Cold and tired. Can we not see to her in the morning?' the gentle housekeeper remonstrated.

'If she's cold and tired then a taste of the cane should soon warm and wake her up. Twelve strokes, to begin with,' Erica laughed. 'Arms up and out against the wall bars.'

Mandy stretched up on tiptoe as she grasped the wooden bar above.

'Did you say strap or cane?' inquired Partridge.

'Cane her. Cane her bottom good and hard,' Erica

rasped, standing alongside Mandy to appreciate the punishment at close quarters.

Mandy's knuckles whitened on the wall bar as she heard Partridge pace across the wooden floor of the gym, a bamboo cane gripped in her right hand. The cane-tip addressed Mandy's wet bottom almost tenderly, tapping off the undried pearls of water clinging to the swell of her rounded cheeks.

'Commence,' barked the cropped blonde impatiently.

Partridge took up her position and raised the cane aloft. Mandy closed her eyes and eased her breasts away from the wood which cushioned them. The first stroke swept across her naked cheeks, lashing them intimately and striping them red. She grunted and jerked her nakedness into the wall bars, punishing her bosom on impact. The cane sliced once more, and then again: the two strokes coming unexpectedly in swift succession. Mandy squealed. Both strokes swiped her perfect peaches, leaving crimson kisses across their crowns.

'Harder. I want the bitch to suffer.' The voice of Erica curdled in the uncanny silence of the gym. 'She has caused me a lot of trouble tonight. She must learn her lesson. Learn, and suffer.'

Partridge planted her feet apart for the next six strokes. They were administered briskly and crisply, leaving Mandy's bare bottom ablaze. The housekeeper stepped forward, pressing the bottom with the length of the cane, and pretended to arrange Mandy's right arm at the wall bar.

'Nearly done,' she whispered. 'All over soon.'

Mandy nodded imperceptibly, acknowledging the whispered words of encouragement.

'Stand up straight. Bottom up,' Partridge barked, for Erica's benefit.

Mandy obeyed, presenting her striped cheeks for the remaining strokes.

'Wait,' Erica intervened. 'I'll finish the punishment.

You may go.' She dismissed the housekeeper with a curt nod.

Partridge reluctantly surrendered the cane and departed. As the door of the gym closed behind her, a sense of dread stole into Mandy's mind. She was naked and alone – with the cropped blonde.

She heard but could not see Erica placing the bamboo cane down on the polished floor. She sensed the cropped blonde approach, then felt cruel hands gripping each of her caned buttocks and squeezing them, then spreading them apart. The hands of her tormentress squeezed again, bunching the buttocks tightly. Mandy's cleft became a thin crease as her soft cheeks bulged. Then the cupping hands taloned, dragging the cheeks apart, causing the cleft to yawn. Mandy whimpered.

'When the mistress comes down from London tomorrow, my girl, she will want a full explanation. She will want to know every detail. Why you decided to go, where you were heading for, what you proposed to do. So you had better have some good answers ready. She will of course be very disappointed in you. There will be many further punishments.'

Mandy clamped her thighs together and bowed her head.

Erica thumbed the hot cheeks and spread their softness painfully apart, bringing Mandy up on her toes in anguish.

'I am going to cane you now, then leave you to contemplate how foolish you have been. If, on my return, you can convince me that you are truly sorry, I may omit to inform the mistress of your disloyalty and stupidity.'

The mistress: Mandy thought of the havoc the grey-eyed solicitor would wreak on her bare bottom with a flexed crop or bamboo cane.

'If you cooperate completely, I may decide to keep this unfortunate matter strictly between ourselves.'

Mandy twisted her head to see over her left shoulder. 'I'm sorry. I don't know what –'

'No,' Erica purred, sweeping her palm up across the naked, punished cheeks. 'Do not lie too hastily, girl. Let's have no sudden contrition. You planned the escape very carefully. The warm clothing, and the timing of the vans prove that much. I want to know the truth.' She cupped and squeezed the hot cheeks slowly. 'And only the truth. Now turn round and face the wall – and give me your bottom.'

Mandy stretched out her arms and, grasping the wall bars, braced herself for the concluding strokes of her prescribed punishment. Obediently up on tiptoe, she thrust her bare bottom up, her cheeks rounded and poised for their imminent stripes. They came in a sudden rush, swishing down across her bottom with a venom Partridge had not achieved. Mandy's toes curled up in anguish as she pressed her lips against a wall bar to smother her squeals. The concluding stroke sliced into her buttocks, searing them with a burning flame.

'Stay exactly where you are. I will return to hear your explanation within the hour,' Erica whispered, tapping the naked bottom with the tip of her cane.

Mandy unclenched her hands from the wall bars and soothed her ravished rump, skimming her palms across her reddened buttocks. Despite the caning, she felt relieved. Erica had caught her and had severely punished her, but no lasting harm to her ultimate plans had been done. Most importantly, her identity was intact – an identity which Celia Flaxstone would soon unmask on close inspection. But Erica was not going to inform the mistress, if Mandy proved wholly cooperative. She decided to play into Erica's hands, and renew her bid to escape in a few days' time.

The caning had left her hot and sticky. She ached to touch herself but dared not risk being discovered playing with herself by the cropped blonde. She hated Erica: hated being naked before her, hated being at her mercy. Mandy also hated the knowledge Erica seemed to have of her weaknesses, cravings and desires. The cropped blonde seemed to unerringly know all of Mandy's lustful yearnings and secret wants. Mandy hated this because she knew it gave Erica erotic power and dominance over her – a dominance Erica might choose to exploit.

Mandy risked another furtive rub at her caned cheeks. She thought of the punishment, and how Partridge had been sweet, caning her just within the bearable limits of pleasure-pain. Mandy had almost relished that part of the punishment, but Erica's stripes had been cruel. She had swished the bamboo with savage intent and withering accuracy. The concluding strokes had been almost unbearable, turning Mandy in a moment from trembling desire to shivering dread.

Time passed slowly, achingly slowly. Erica would return. What then? Would Mandy be interrogated in depth tonight? It was already two – later, perhaps – and she felt exhausted. Mandy knew that she must remain alert and keep her mind razor-sharp. Her story must be sound, with no discrepancies or inconsistencies – easy enough perhaps in an ordinary grilling but, when naked, beneath the shadow of a cane, it would be all too easy to make a fatal slip. Above all, Mandy realised, even when being kiss-whipped by a crop, her identity and true purpose here at Sternwood Grange must remain her secret.

The door to the gym opened and Erica entered.

'I have decided not to bother the mistress with this matter, girl. You have much to thank me for. I hope you show your full appreciation.'

Saved from the close scrutiny of Celia Flaxstone, Mandy was prepared to be very appreciative. 'Thank you . . .' she started to gush warmly, then stopped. Out of the corner of her eye she saw that Erica was naked.

196

'And how grateful are you going to be, tonight. Mmm?'

Mandy remained silent, her mouth dry, her hands prickling with a sudden sweat.

'I worked out your escape route. I know you hid in the storeroom. I found the glove.'

Mandy burned with shame, bitterly resenting Erica's discovery.

'That storeroom is full of interesting items, isn't it? I don't blame you for succumbing. I have selected –' her voice dropped to a thick whisper '– a few of the pieces stored there. I think you might find them interesting.'

Canes? Whips? Paddles? Mandy's bare bottom tightened.

'I don't –' Mandy stammered.

'I find them very interesting,' Erica said softly. 'I am sure you are going to agree. After all, the mistress need never know about your naughtiness, need she?'

It was not a question. It was a veiled threat. Mandy knew that she was now completely at the mercy of the cropped blonde. Though they were both naked under the neon lights of the gym, Mandy felt vulnerable and afraid. She hung her head. She was Erica's now, utterly and entirely – and they both knew it.

'Put this on,' Erica murmured, approaching Mandy and whipping her bottom playfully with a black rubber brassiere.

The soft rubber weighed heavily in Mandy's open palm. Her nipples thickened as she gazed down at the moulded cups. Slowly, she eased her bosom into it and fingered the stretchy straps. The cups had been talcumed, allowing Mandy to fit and fill the soft rubber with her swollen bosom. To her surprise, her nipples peered out and then emerged through the peek-a-boo holes: forced out through the rubber slits by the weight of her breasts settling into the brassiere. The rubber gripped, feeling strangely tight and undeniably sensual.

Mandy's nipples stiffened into firm peaks, becoming pink stubs against the black of the rubber cups.

Erica lowered her face to Mandy's left breast. Closing her lips around the exposed nipple, she sucked hard. Mandy squeezed her buttocks tightly together in an attempt to deny her delight. Gazing down, she saw the cropped blonde, naked and bending, sucking fiercely at her nipple. Erica buried her face in the warmth of the rubbered breast, then applied her rasping tongue, and finally her nipping teeth, to the nipple. Mandy felt the wetness at her slit oozing forth. She closed her eyes and shuddered.

Erica withdrew her mouth and murmured, 'Now try this.'

It was a rubber mask. Mandy felt her belly tightening. She hesitated.

'I want you to put it on.'

Mandy held it in her right hand, her fingers sinking into the black softness.

'You know of course how severely the mistress deals with failed runaways. Most severely,' Erica remarked in a conversational tone. 'They're often whipped three times a day for at least a week.'

Mandy donned the mask. It fitted tightly, pinching her face and flattening her cheeks. Tiny holes allowed her to breathe at the nose and mouth – but speech, like sight and hearing, was denied to her. Surrendering to the overwhelming sensation of the rubber, she tasted its harsh tang and, with that tang, the bittersweet taste of submission. Deprived of her essential faculties, she felt mute, blind and utterly helpless.

Erica led her captive across the polished floor of the gym to a vaulting horse. Mandy came to an abrupt halt as her belly collided with the solid flank. She felt a dominant hand at her bare bottom, urging her to mount. She climbed up, and then lay face down across the horse. Mandy's rubber brassiere kissed the scuffed hide: her nipples tightened exquisitely. Mandy felt Erica pulling her arms behind her back, then drawing her passive wrists together and positioning them at the point where her spine tapered into the swelling curve of her bottom. Handcuffs snapped silently into place, pinioning her into helpless submission. Mandy sensed that Erica had donned a single rubber gauntlet; she felt the softness of it as a palm caressed her bottom firmly, then the severity of it as the spanking began.

The sensation was as eerie as it was deliciously dire. The soundless spanks from the rubber-gloved hand exploded as if out of thin air across her upturned cheeks, flattening their curved crowns and burning them with a slow, spreading fire which licked at her cleft and labia, flickering down to ignite her pulsing slit.

The splayed fingers of the dominant hand pressed her rubber-encased head down into the horse. Mandy's tongue and lips tasted the tight rubber of the mask, finding it just as disturbingly delicious as her bare buttocks found the rubber gloved spanking. Soon she was coming, her wrists in their handcuffs intensifying her sense of utter helplessness and total submission.

Unable to see or hear – or even touch herself – the unique experience of orgasming in restraining bondage was shattering. Her belly imploded as hot waves rippled down to her spasming flesh below. Did Erica know? Was she scrutinising and savouring Mandy's helplessness? These thoughts and half-formed fears fuelled another – and then another – climax. Dizzy with the dark delights of discipline and total domination, Mandy squirmed and writhed across the leather of the vaulting horse.

A rubber-sheathed finger probing at her wet slit presented Mandy with an unpleasant truth: Erica was not only aware of her orgasm, she was clearly examining – indeed coaxing and controlling – the sequence of climax upon climax. The spanking had ceased after the second of the orgasmic paroxysms, but the rubbered fingers returned to caress her cleft and tease her oozing slit.

The rubber fingertip tapped her anal whorl inquiringly, as if testing the rosebud for the heat of its stickiness. Mandy squeezed her buttocks together as another climax gripped her in its implacable violence – but the probing finger would not be denied its desire. Mandy stiffened, gasping into the moist heat of her rubber mask. The finger worried her tight sphincter determinedly, forcing it to open up like a rosebud. It accepted the intrusion unwillingly, the spasming muscle making entry difficult rather than a smooth glide. Threshing in her bondage, Mandy inched her breasts and belly along the back of the leather horse in a desperate bid to evade the firm finger at her secret flesh. Three severe spanks exploded silently across her hot cheeks, stilling her and staying her tortuous progress. She sank down on the leather, crushed under the cropped blonde's supreme authority and absolute domination.

Then nothing. What was happening? Where was Erica? What was the cruel dominatrix planning, doing? Gone to collect a wooden spanking paddle or a length of bamboo cane? Was Mandy's bare bottom to suffer, suffer until Erica herself came? Was the lustful tormentress seeking to achieve her own hot orgasm with a crop in her rubber-gloved hand?

Mandy wriggled, feeling the wetness of her own climax on the leather horse beneath her. The silence, the helplessness, the darkness at her eyes – suddenly these tortures became unbearable. She screamed a silent scream, giving mute tongue to her delicious dread, hearing only a mournful echo of her anguish in her spinning brain. Where was the cropped blonde? What was she doing? Gazing down upon and relishing Mandy's utter helplessness? Would Mandy shortly be doomed to feel Erica's tongue, lips and teeth at her spanked cheeks?

Suddenly, before she fully understood what was happening, the handcuffs were removed. Mandy was so startled that she kept her hands and palms together in unholy prayer, at the swell of her punished buttocks. She felt Erica taking her arms and arranging them so that they now stretched out before her. She felt, but could not see or hear, the handcuffs being snapped back at her wrists. Erica withdrew, leaving Mandy helpless and immobile again. In her renewed bondage, Mandy lay still, her mind feverish with dark anticipation and dread imaginings.

Then she remembered the picture. When she was just seventeen, Mandy had stayed at a friend's flat after catching a Bruce Springsteen gig. Fingering between the paperbacks on a shelf while ice cream, cake and coffee was being rustled up by her old school chum, Mandy had discovered the folio of lascivious French prints. One had made a lasting impression on her curious, pubescent mind.

It was one of a set of naughty-nineties prints from Lille, which the Bishop of Paris had ordered to be publicly destroyed, and Freud had consulted in his essay on female sexuality: it depicted three Belgian firemen surrounding a naked Frenchwoman in her bedroom. The legend at the bottom of the print briefly explained that, while visiting her sister in Ghent, she had overturned her night table, causing her lamp to spill and set fire to the carpet. In the print, the young naked beauty shrank back, cowering in shame from the three uniformed officers, who were each trailing nozzled hoses up between their parted legs. Two of the shining nozzles were dribbling against the woman's belly and thighs; the third was still squirting a jet from its stiff hose upon her naked bosom.

It was a picture that haunted Mandy's imagination: a

powerful study of shame, humiliation and erotic power. Mandy had often summoned up the image when playing with herself at bathtime or in bed: it was her favourite fantasy. Sometimes she was in the room, as voyeur; sometimes she was the naked beauty penned in by the uniformed firemen; always, when enjoying the potent image, she came.

It had been her first glimpse of female masochism, and it had fuelled many a pussy-rubbing climax. But now, masked and handcuffed across the leather horse, she was experiencing the velvet violence of total domination and discipline. The burning image in her brain of Erica, naked and predatory at the side of the vaulting horse, was infinitely more disturbing than firemen with their splashing hoses.

She felt a hand at her left shoulder, then one gripping her right forearm. Erica was mounting the horse – and then mounting Mandy, easing her pubic curls down on to the hot cheeks of the spanked bottom. Pinning Mandy's shoulders down as her thighs straddled the buttocks between them, the cropped blonde rode the cheeks she had just chastised. Mandy felt the rasp of the pubic curls against the swell of her buttocks, and jerked and bucked violently to topple the unbidden rider. Erica's hands slid between the rubber brassiere's cups and the scuffed hide of the horse. Squeezing dominantly, she instantly asserted her supremacy over her victim. Frozen in her fearfulness, Mandy lay prone and still, unwillingly accepting and all the time hating the outrage visiting her naked bottom. She shuddered as the cropped blonde's labia splayed apart, smearing her hot ooze on Mandy's cheeks.

The hands at Mandy's rubbered bosom taloned the flesh mounds savagely. Mandy squealed a mute protest. Erica's open flesh-lips grew hotter and wetter against the passive buttocks – soon she was hammering herself into Mandy's soft bottom. The rhythm broke: the rider stiffened, her thighs taut. Mandy could not smell the feral juices, could not hear the primal scream of ecstasy – but despite being deaf, dumb and blind to Erica's orgasm, Mandy knew that the cropped blonde had come.

Eight

She had been brought, blindfold and naked, to the room an hour after sunrise. Erica had made no mention of Mandy's escape attempt – or the sequel of punishment and domination – as she led her stumbling captive down the carpeted stretch of the Long Gallery. They had turned abruptly to their left: Mandy knew at once that she was being shepherded into the lair of a dominant resident. Inside, having forced Mandy to kneel, Erica withdrew.

The sounds of sucking filled the air: of lips devouring juicy flesh. Grapefruit, Mandy decided, decoding the noise. She would have to remain kneeling patiently while the dominant devoured her late breakfast. Mandy strained to catch the sounds of the breakfast table, the chink of a coffee cup, the scrape of a buttered knife across golden toast. Only the sound of the fierce sucking greeted her efforts. Mandy felt uneasy, hating the blindfold at her eyes.

She decided to risk a quick peep. If detected, it would only earn her a stripe or two across her bare buttocks. Clenching her cheeks expectantly against the sudden lash, she pretended to draw her hand back through her hair, surreptitiously lifting the blindfold a fraction as she did so.

Two naked beauties, locked into a *soixante-neuf*, lay curled up on the carpet before her. The sucking intensified as both mouths worked hungrily: not at the moist pulp of breakfast grapefruit as Mandy had supposed, but at the more succulent flesh of wet labia. The blindfold had only been inched up for a split second, but Mandy had captured the scene before her in its entirety. It remained etched vividly on her retina: the curled, naked women; the embracing, sinuous limbs; the hot eyes drowning in lust; the delicious blonde curls tossed in abandon and, above all, the fact that the two naked women were identical twins.

The sucking became more frenzied. Gasps and smothered moans filled the air. Mandy felt her own slit prickle with interest as the carnal feasting came to a climax. From the sounds that followed, she sensed that the couple were now stretched out on the carpet, momentarily spent and sated.

'Take off your blindfold.'

The voice was Nordic. Finnish, Mandy thought. It had a peculiar sing-song lilt, the tone sinewed with a metallic crispness. Whatever its origin, Mandy knew that it was the voice of an accomplished disciplinarian and dominatrix.

'Quickly.'

Mandy obeyed, her bosom rising as she raised her hands to untie the blindfold, then bouncing softly as her fingers fumbled at the knot. The scene that greeted her gaze was unsettling. Two naked thirty-year-olds, severe and unsmiling, were standing hip to hip, thigh to soft thigh. They stared down at Mandy, devouring her kneeling body with hungry eyes. Mandy gazed up shyly, secretly astounded at how similar they were. Never before had she seen twins so utterly identical: and their nakedness emphasised the likeness. She marvelled at the untamed, tumbling blonde curls, the ice-blue eyes, the slender shoulders, the heavy breasts and tapered hips. It was exactly as if there were one deliciously dominant nude standing next to a long mirror – but then Mandy spotted the difference: one nude was shaven at the pubis, the other sported a bush of golden fuzz.

Mandy raised her left hand up to her ear lobe and tugged at it nervously. The twins advanced, their thighs brushing gently, their heavy bosoms bobbing. They trod the carpet with naked feet, their silent footfalls loud with exquisite menace. Mandy, kneeling, suddenly found her lips three inches from the shaven pubis. Her mouth went dry. The pulse at her throat gathered momentum, becoming deep and rapid.

'Lick me. I want you to lick me,' came the lilting command.

Mandy pressed her warm lips against the delta, parted them and flickered her tongue out. The flesh was soft and sweet, like probing a ripe damson. Working her tongue cautiously, she teased the pink clitoris.

'Harder. You can do better than that. Or be made to do better.'

Redoubling her efforts, Mandy lapped feverishly, knowing that, if she failed to please, the cane or crop would surely fall down across her bare bottom.

'Faster,' came the stern injunction.

Mandy closed her eyes and tongued the sweet flesh furiously. To her alarm, the other twin stalked around behind her and straddled Mandy's shoulders with warm, wide buttocks. Mandy flinched from the graze of pubic fuzz at the nape of her bowed neck, but the delta kissed her skin firmly as, above, the twins embraced and kissed. Opening her eyes and looking up, she saw the delicious swell of the breasts, nipples peaked, of the shaven twin. The naked blondes kissed passionately, and the rounded bosoms bounced, as Mandy's wet, muscled tongue probed deeper and deeper.

The dominant being tongued gave Mandy crisp commands. When doing so, the shaven nude spoke distinctly in almost perfect English. Between themselves, they chattered rapidly, their clicking consonants and terse vowels alien to Mandy's ear. Icelandic, she decided eventually.

They spanked her next. It was, at the beginning, a playful bout of erotic dominance in which they imprinted their authority with smooth palms across Mandy's quivering cheeks. She was arranged across the thighs of the shaven twin and trapped into the punishment position: one slender hand at her neck, one slender leg trapping and controlling her thighs. Before the slaps rained down, a flattened palm had circled her naked cheeks firmly, exploring every inch of the helpless, supple flesh. Mandy tightened her buttocks as the palm curved, expertly moulding itself to the swell of her cheeks. A dominant finger – whose, she did not know – traced the outline of each peach-cheek before settling halfway down the crease of her cleft at her anal whorl.

Mandy inched her bottom up, unashamedly relishing the imperious fingertip. Deep in her cleft, her rosebud grew warm and sticky. Aroused, she was now impatient for the stinging caress of the spanking hand across her upturned cheeks. The dominant twins were in no hurry. They inspected Mandy's vulnerable nakedness intimately, dimpling the crowns of her creamy flesh-mounds with squeezed fingertips while working their thumbs at her sphincter.

The suspense made Mandy's belly coil up like a tightened spring. She wriggled across the naked thighs, wobbling her cheeks invitingly, but they did not succumb, choosing instead to maintain their absolute dominance and total control. Mandy writhed under their reign of supremacy, and struggled to provoke the punishment she had dreaded, but now desired.

The shaven blonde swept her hand across the soft curve of both cheeks. Palm upward, she dragged her knuckles across each heavy buttock, then knuckled the cleft, spreading the cheeks apart. The second twin lowered her face down. Mandy could feel the warm breath at her sphincter, and the controlling hand at her

207

neck tightening. Mandy clenched her buttocks in self-protection, but the tongue dipped down to taste the flesh splayed apart by the knuckled hand.

Mandy threshed, squealing and protesting, as the unshaven twin knelt firmly against her, burying her entire face into the softness of her bottom. Soon the lapping, then the probing, became unbearable. Mandy felt her inner muscles spasm as the thick tongue explored the length of her velvety cleft.

The spanking followed immediately. Across the thighs of the more dominant twin, Mandy sweetly suffered three and a half minutes of severe, intimate punishment. The sharp staccato of spanks echoed around the room as the chastised cheeks bounced and slowly turned pink, then crimson, then scarlet.

Mandy ground her wet slit across the supporting thighs over which she was spread and pinioned. Delighting in the discipline, she surrendered her bare bottom to the blonde. The spanking ceased, for the moment. With maddening politeness, the dominatrix relinquished her ownership of the hot cheeks and offered Mandy's buttocks to her twin to chastise. The kneeling blonde, who had tongued Mandy so expertly, accepted the offer and spanked Mandy harshly. Mandy bucked and squirmed, the climax welling up within her now imminent – only a few sharp spanks away.

The spanks did not come. Suddenly, Mandy felt the heavy bosom of the shaven nude, over whose lap she was stretched, crush down and pin the other twin's hand to the cheeks she had just punished with her palm. The trapped hand slowly slid out from beneath the breasts, leaving the deliciously warm weight nestling dominantly on the spanked cheeks. Mandy cried out with raw pleasure as the fiercely peaked nipples burned into the satin skin of her buttocks – then whimpered as her orgasm spilled out in spasms of gentle violence.

With the bare breasts dominating her spanked

bottom, Mandy came. As she paroxysmed, the kneeling twin fingered two slits: Mandy's and her own wet crease, probing each tightened flesh in rhythmic unison. Rocketing into a fresh orgasm, Mandy moaned long and loud. The nude twins remained cool, silent and seemingly aloof, their very indifference fuelling Mandy's renewed climax.

Iceland: the home of volcanic steam, boiling lava and frosted ice. They came from the land of glacial fire, embodying the eternally frozen inferno. This knowledge, and the knowledge of their self-control, burned with a sweet heat in Mandy's brain, torching a third, then a fourth orgasm. Control and domination, she had discovered, were sweet, but to be so hot, punished and naked, to be so stickily aroused and so urgently kindled by the lips, tongues and hands of these identical ice-maidens was sweeter still – the sweetest surrender and submission she had ever known or imagined.

Leaving her curled up on the carpet, they withdrew, pausing to sip vodka and champagne cocktails from a single, fluted glass. The shaven twin took the ice cube from the cocktail and plied her labia with it, rubbing the smiling flesh-lips with firm, downward strokes. Taking the red cherry out, she sucked on it hard then thumbed it into her flesh just below the clitoris. Kneeling, her twin plucked out the glistening cherry between her teeth. Mandy shuddered as she watched the teeth slice the cherry in half, and shuddered again as the two pieces of cherry disappeared into the naked blonde's mouth.

Mandy, now kneeling on the carpet, was studiously ignored. She ached with resentment, eager for their acknowledgement and chaffing at their indifference. Momentarily exiled from their erotic realm, she desired to be readmitted – on almost any terms imaginable.

Abandoning the cocktail, the twins returned to where Mandy knelt, encircling her with soundless footsteps. The dominant twin stood, legs astride, in front of

Mandy, while her twin knelt down behind: Mandy shivered at the rasp of the pubic curls against her recently spanked, and still sore, bottom. Cupping Mandy's breasts, the kneeling twin held them in a squeezing, vice-like grip. Mandy thrilled to the sensation of her nipples thickening into the controlling palms. Pulling her captive backwards, the twin pulled Mandy down on to the carpet. Swiftly mounting, the unshaven twin lowered her fleshy buttocks down on to Mandy's upturned face. The soft warmth of the descending bottom squashed and smothered Mandy for a brief moment, a brief moment in which sight and breathing were denied, a brief moment of exquisite torment and delight. Shuffling slightly, the twin eased her buttocks slightly, allowing her victim to breathe.

Mandy gulped for air, her hands pawing at the carpet as the scissoring thighs tightened their grip, trapping and controlling her torso and rendering her immobile. The heavy cheeks pressing into her face rose a fraction as her tormentress leant forward and threaded her arms beneath Mandy's knees. Then the plump rump settled firmly down again as the arms gathered up Mandy's legs and dragged them up from the carpet. Once her legs were raised up, strong hands parted them at the thighs, exposing her wet fig. Mandy could not see, but could both sense and then feel, the presence of the other twin, the shaven vixen, kneeling down at her exposed delta. The unseen mouth closed on her, lips and tongue busy at her slit. Mandy struggled, but to no avail. The devilish twins were determined in their enjoyment of her: one pinning her down contemptuously with her bare bottom, the other mouthing her splayed labia with absolute impunity.

The tongue at her slit lapped slowly, luxuriously, at first. Then the rasping became more urgent. Soon the thick muscle was probing. Mandy felt its firmness inside her, the angle of approach affording deep penetration.

Her squeals were muffled by the soft flesh of the buttocks on her face. As the tongue explored her inner, most secret flesh, the buttocks above commenced a rhythmic joggling. Cruel hands grasped and squeezed her breasts once more, punishing and pleasuring the helpless flesh-mounds and tormenting her nipples up into peaks of fire. Above her face, the swollen cheeks were riding her ruthlessly, the heavy flesh raking her mouth so that Mandy could taste the bitterness of the hot cleft. With a cunning dexterity, the rider managed to drag her slit across Mandy's mouth with each thrusting sweep and backward jerk of the hips.

'Tongue her.'

The command came from the twin mouthing Mandy's labial flesh, not the naked twin who was to be tongued.

Mandy's tongue protruded, thrusting up into the acrid cleft, the tip just touching the rosebud sphincter.

'No, not there,' the twin cried, wriggling her bottom. 'There,' she hissed, lowering her gaping flesh-folds down on to Mandy's mouth. 'There.'

Perched above her victim, the unshaven nude planted her hot slit over Mandy's tongue just as the other twin's tongue at Mandy's own slit started to trigger a climax.

The three naked women were briefly frozen in their frenzied lust. Fusing hot flesh to hotter flesh, they quivered as violent orgasms raked their nakedness. Mandy screamed into the buttocks above, biting them in her passionate paroxysms, as the tongue at her opened furnace stoked fresh flames. Driven into the fury of her climax, Mandy tongued the sweet flesh above with renewed vigour and violence. The naked rider gripped her mount and ground her slit down, coming furiously on to Mandy's shining, slippery face. Mandy sensed the weight of the buttocks above shifting as her tormentress knelt up, and felt the tongue at her slit withdraw as the shaven dominatrix also knelt. In mute

211

understanding, the blonde twins were now locked in a deep French kiss above her pinioned, helpless nakedness.

The dildo, they informed her, both fingering its length in harmony, was carved from an Icelandic walrus tusk. It was over two hundred years old, the cherished relic of initiation rites performed in the long, dark nights before spring came to melt the ice that bound the iron land. Mandy saw that the gleaming curve of ivory was etched with runic inscriptions: an unholy pagan prayer dedicated to the goddess of ice-fire. Mandy quailed at its sinuous, wicked length, clamping her thighs and clenching her buttocks at the very thought of its penetration. The twins perceived her token resistance and exchanged slow, knowing smiles.

Tied to the bed, her arms and legs splayed and secured at the wrists and ankles to the wooden posts, Mandy gazed up fearfully. Kneeling in silence at either side of her bed of bondage, the nudes played with their ivory shaft, probing one another's mouth with its blunt tip. Mandy had been gagged tightly with a cruel band of crimson serge. Above it, her eyes were wide with fearful apprehension. She shook her head from side to side vigorously, signalling her unwillingness. To her relief, both twins gazed down at her, nodding their understanding.

'Not until you plead with us,' the shaven dominatrix murmured. 'Not until you beg us,' she added in a curdling whisper.

Mandy heaved a sigh of relief, certain in the knowledge that she would never want – or whimper for – the dildo.

'But you will,' the whispering voice continued, as if the naked blonde had been reading Mandy's troubled mind.

They removed the tight gag and, hands entwined

tenderly around the ivory shaft, fingers interlocking in carnal unison, the twins guided the phallus to Mandy's mouth, using it on her lips like a lipstick. Denying what seemed to be self-betrayal, Mandy found herself opening her lips wide as if eager for the blunt tip inside her mouth. It slid in, probing her wet warmth. She tightened her lips around its cool length, sucking gently at first, then with a fierce desire to possess. Inside her, it teased the roof of her mouth, then dominantly flattened and tamed her tongue. It was intimately erotic, and Mandy juiced down at her hot slit. The twins, eyes darting down to note her involuntary response and reaction, played with the dildo for several more minutes, plying it into her mouth until the patches of sheet beneath Mandy's parted thighs was stained dark with her wet ooze. Then, hands still wrapped around the dildo, they guided it slowly, teasingly, down over her chin, against the arch of her straining neck to her breasts below.

The hard tip of the ivory shaft traced the soft contours of her naked bosom with exquisite delicacy, delighting her silken flesh as it faithfully fingered its passive swell. The tip addressed each nipple in turn, tapping each tiny pink bud up into pale-purple peaks of fierce pleasure. Mandy writhed, the bondage at her wrists and ankles burning into her bound flesh. At her pouting labia, the sparkling ooze of her arousal widened the spreading stain. The gag was firmly replaced, the crimson serge biting into her mute mouth, renewing her sense of utter helplessness – a helplessness as absolute as her capitulation and desire for the dildo.

Mandy struggled to resist her innermost yearnings, stunned at the possibility of her submitting eagerly to the shaft. Taking her breasts, one in a left hand, the second in the other kneeling twin's right hand, they nosed the dildo down along the swell of her hip, across her flattened, tense belly and across to her upper, outer thigh. Mandy jerked as the blunt tip dimpled her soft flesh. Riding her dominantly, it descended into, then against, her ultra-sensitive inner thigh. Mandy squealed as the solid weight of the phallus scored her satin flesh just above her right knee. Slowly, with maddeningly tantalising circular sweeps, it inched back up towards the hot pulse of her open slit. She jerked her hips and pounded her buttocks as her splayed thighs were ruthlessly teased, her mind no longer certain that it would be able to deny what her aching body desired: the thrust of the dildo inside her tight warmth.

It inched up a fraction closer, and then a fraction more, the clasped hands nudging the tip up to kiss-tease her tiny, erect clitoris.

With a supreme effort, Mandy shook her head. No. No. She mouthed her protest into the wet gag, still denying her desire for the dildo. Ignoring her totally, the guiding hands at the ivory shaft directed it to finger her wet labia with firm, downward strokes. At each stroke, the cunning hands swiftly speared the shaft up along the crease of her cleft, briefly forcing the firm length between her tightly clenched cheeks.

The delicious torture lasted for a full eight minutes. Mandy's aching body burned with the effort of her denial but burned more fiercely with the seething flame of desire. Suddenly, the spasms inside her told her – and told the predatory eyes of the watching twins – that she was rapidly approaching the point of no return. Her orgasm would be soon; her climax was imminent.

Gasping audibly, she nodded, signalling her readiness for the cruel shaft. Further denial and resistance was useless: they had smashed her resolve completely and broken her spirit. They had crushed her rebellion, and bent her mind and body to their lustful will using the dark skills of erotic prowess and the spells of sexual witchcraft. Shuddering, she submitted and surrendered, closing her eyes and expecting the blunt thrust.

It did not occur. Opening her eyes, she stared up in bewildered frustration to see the bottom of the unshaven twin hovering above the bed, the plump cheeks held apart to receive the probing dildo. Pumping the phallus deep into her twin's anus, the shaven nude guided the shaft into the tight sphincter. Mandy threshed in her fury and confusion, and threshed with renewed violence as she felt the drip, drip of the hot juices splashing down on to her breasts from the weeping slit of the speared twin.

She heard their harsh laughter and then the taunting words of the dominatrix.

'We made you want it, no? But you cannot have it. Not even if you beg. It is sweet, is it not, to light the flames of desire and then douse them with denial. Yes,' the alien voice from the land of fire and ice reflected aloud, 'it is sweet.'

For Mandy, her capitulation tasted as sour as her subsequent humiliation: sour and bitter.

Mandy stirred fretfully in her sleep. Exhausted after her ordeal at the cruel hands of the sadistic twins, she had showered, and then slumped on to her bed. Her dreams had been troubling, forcing her to relive her earlier humiliations and erotic torments. In her dreams, she heard again the alien accents of the Icelandic blondes, giggling at her distress and plotting further humiliations as they examined her bare body for further dark pleasure. Mandy moaned softly and turned over in her sleep.

Into her sleeping brain came other remembered voices, murmuring softly. Mandy tossed and turned, tormented by the sound of Erica and Celia. Then she awoke abruptly, and sat up. At the foot of her bed, the phantoms from her dreams were solidly fleshed: Erica and Celia stood gazing down at her. Mandy rubbed the sleep from her eyes, then shrank back, pulling the sheet up to cover her naked breasts.

'The mistress has been informed of your escape attempt, girl. She is, as I warned you, most displeased. You are to be whipped soundly.'

Betrayed. Mandy burned with resentment, hating Erica for tricking her into compliance and submission – and hating herself for being so easily duped.

'Get up,' Erica rasped, snatching the sheet away.

Mandy rose and stood by her bed, shivering and angry. The solicitor narrowed her grey eyes as she inspected Mandy's naked body. Mandy shielded her breasts protectively against the stern gaze.

'Turn around,' Erica commanded.

Mandy reluctantly turned, presenting her bare bottom for their examination.

'It's a superb bottom, isn't it?' Erica simpered. 'Are you sure you won't whip it?'

Mandy blushed furiously as they bantered over her impending stripes. She heard them discussing the merits of both the strap and the cane.

'As long as she suffers, I will be satisfied,' Celia Flaxstone remarked. 'I have more important fish to fry.'

'They are coming tonight, your buyers?'

Mandy did not hear the reply: the solicitor must have merely nodded. Buyers. Mandy tugged her ear pensively. Who could they be and what were they hoping to buy?

'Turn around, girl,' Celia said softly.

Mandy obeyed. The solicitor stared at her intently, then gasped as she spotted Mandy's blonde pubic tuft.

'Mandy?' the solicitor mused. 'Amanda. You are Amanda Silk, aren't you?' she demanded in a tone that needed no reply. 'You are, aren't you, you little bitch.' The tone was one of anger, though still tinged with the amazement of its own discovery.

Mandy gazed back steadily into the grey eyes.

'Who is Amanda Silk?' Erica demanded, puzzled.

Heads together, they stood at the foot of the bed in a

huddled whispering. Twice, Erica looked up, flashing Mandy ominous glances. Mandy felt the tension mounting at her chest and throat. Although she had every right to be here – she owned Sternwood Grange – she felt vulnerable and apprehensive. There were two of them, fully dressed: she was naked and alone.

'Partridge brought her in, gave her shelter and work,' Erica whispered fiercely.

'Partridge will pay dearly for her final mistake in my employ,' Mandy overheard the solicitor reply vehemently.

They turned from their whispered conference and approached Mandy. 'What do you think you are doing?' the solicitor snapped.

'Getting dressed,' Mandy replied, hoping that her attempt at nonchalance disguised her hammering heartbeats.

'Have you been given permission to do so?'

'Don't need it. I've seen all I need to see here. I'm getting dressed and going back –'

'You're going nowhere, Miss Silk, until I say so.'

'You can't –'

'Take those panties off at once. Erica,' Celia rasped.

Erica pounced obediently at her employer's sharp command, wrestling Mandy expertly down on to the bed and jerking down the panties in one swift wrench. With a dominant flourish, her panties were tossed aside, leaving Mandy naked and helpless.

'You have caused me a great deal of trouble, Miss Silk, vanishing from London with so much to sort out and resolve. How did you learn of Sternwood Grange and what did you hope to achieve by coming here?'

Mandy played safe and remained silent.

'I am selling Sternwood Grange tonight. You will remain –'

'That's not possible. I've seen the will. I inherited it. It's mine, all mine. You –' Mandy stopped, instantly regretting her foolish outburst: the pain she had just incautiously secured for that bare-bottomed receptionist in the Bird Cage Walk offices would be as nothing to the pain her own bottom might now suffer.

'So,' Celia purred. 'You've seen the will, hmm? Inquisitive little bitch, aren't you? Tie her to the bed, Erica. Tie her tightly, mind. We can't have our little heiress wandering around at large tonight of all nights, can we?'

Mandy struggled but was soon overpowered, arranged across the bed and bound securely at the wrists to each bedpost.

'You will assign your rights to Sternwood Grange to me.'

'Never.'

'Then you will have to be persuaded,' the grey-eyed solicitor murmured, her tone cool and unruffled. 'I will enter into brief negotiations with you, Miss Silk, of course, but please bear in mind that it is I who have the upper, dare I say, the whip hand?'

Erica giggled.

'Cane her,' Celia instructed. 'Cane her slowly. I am going down to the office. On my laptop, I will draft a contract which you will sign, assigning all title deeds and outright claims to Sternwood Grange to me. Do you understand?'

'Never,' Mandy vowed. 'I'll fight you all the way. You'll see –'

'A very sore bottom when I return. A bottom which will suffer even more should you prove stupidly stubborn.'

'How many strokes?' Erica inquired eagerly. 'A dozen?'

'Do not bother counting. Punishment as persuasion must not be meanly measured. Cane her hard. And,' Celia continued suavely, fingering Mandy's passive cheeks dominantly, 'I want you to try out the

218

Indonesian bamboo I brought down with me from London. It should achieve the desired results. Twenty, thirty strokes, who cares? I want this little untidiness cleared up before my important visitors arrive this evening. There must be no impediment to the successful sale of Sternwood Grange.'

Celia Flaxstone watched as Erica slipped out to collect the cane. Bending down, she stretched her hand out and took a painful pincer of Mandy's bare bottom between her finger and thumb. Twisting the captive flesh, she chuckled darkly. Mandy squealed aloud.

'You make a worthy adversary, my dear Miss Silk. I rather think I underestimated you. First point to you, undoubtedly. Coming down here was a big risk. But a risk you have taken and lost. Game, set and match to me, I think. Ah, here is Erica with the cane. After a taste of this little persuader all the way from the rain-soaked forests of Indonesia, you will not only be willing to sign but eager to do so. Commence.'

The door closed on the retreating solicitor just as the first stroke of the cane whistled down to slice across Mandy's upturned cheeks. A second withering stroke brought a torrent of abuse from Mandy's lips. The tip of the cane came to rest, passive but potent, across the left buttock.

'Silence,' Erica demanded.

Mandy ignored this instruction and, wriggling in her tight bondage, shouted abusive scorn at her chastiser. Erica placed the cane reverently on the bed and clasped Mandy's hair in both hands.

'Silence, you stupid bitch,' she hissed. Mandy twisted her head and snapped at Erica's wrist, almost but not quite nipping at the flesh with her bared teeth.

'So, the bitch bites?' Erica laughed, then fished up a nylon stocking from the back of a bedside chair and bound it around Mandy's mouth, gagging her victim tightly. 'Now let's hear you squeal.'

Picking up the cane, she took a half-pace back, judged the distance to the naked buttocks expertly and delivered three searing lashes in rapid succession. Mandy jerked and writhed, mouthing mute obscenities into the nylon gag.

'My mistress has important clients coming. You must give your consent to the assignment of title deeds. This is only a taste of what you will suffer if you choose to refuse.'

The cane sparkled in the evening sunset as it swept down across the soft cheeks below, lashing into their satin swell to leave thin, reddening stripes. Mandy grunted into her gag. The nylon stocking at her lips was already dark with a wet stain where she mouthed it furiously. At the bedposts, above the bound wrists, her fingers splayed out in anguished response to every searing stroke.

Erica paused after nine swishing swipes, tapping the crimsoned cheeks warningly. 'Give up whatever spurious claim you may think you have on Sternwood Grange and your suffering will cease. Don't be a fool, Miss Silk.' She dragged the tip of the wood across the curve of each punished buttock. Mandy jerked her hips and tossed her cheeks up in an effort to rid her scorched cheeks of the tormenting cane. It was a futile gesture, invoking swift retribution for her token rebellion: Erica responded immediately with two searching, scalding strokes after which she depressed the crowns of both cheeks with the levelled cane in a gesture of supreme control and total dominance.

'You will sign,' Erica snarled, raising the cane aloft. 'No matter how long it takes to persuade you.'

Never, Mandy resolved. Never. She was determined to cling on to her rightful inheritance, no matter what the immediate pain might be. Resigning her bottom to its inevitable suffering, Mandy consoled herself with the fragile comfort that Sternwood Grange was legally hers.

The cane flashed down twice, striping her buttocks severely. Her buttocks seethed where the thin wood had bitten into her naked flesh, spreading a flame of fire across the quivering globes. Again, and then again, the choice Indonesian bamboo cracked down, visiting the defence-less cheeks with blistering kisses of exquisite agony. Erica paused once more, pacing the punishment with strict supremacy over the suffering buttocks. Pressing the cane sternly down into the striped cheeks, she counted the reddening lines across the creamy flesh aloud.

'And that is only a fraction of what you will suffer,' she whispered, dimpling the hot curves with the tip of her cane. 'We'd better have a few more, hmm?'

Swish. Mandy jerked in writhing anguish as Erica plied the wood across an already existing stripe, turning the deep pink to a painful red. Swish. The next cut was equally severe and slicing. Swish. Again, the cruel wood lashed down, licking the bare bottom with a fiery tongue of flame.

The door opened and Sonia and Sophie, propelled by Celia Flaxstone behind them, stumbled into the bedroom. Erica promptly shouldered her cane in a salute to the mistress of Sternwood Grange.

'I think she is ready to sign,' Erica gushed. 'The bamboo has spoken.'

'It has a very persuasive voice, but Miss Silk may prove to be stubborn. Will you sign?'

Mandy shook her head. Sophie and the minx stared in fear at the stripes across her bottom.

'Very well, then the cane must speak again.'

Levelling her cane, and flexing her supple wrist, Erica took a pace towards the bed.

'But across different cheeks,' Celia purred. 'Sophie and little Sonia have come to relieve you of any personal discomfort, Miss Silk. They will bare their bottoms and your stripes until you decide to change your mind and sign.'

Despite her bondage, Mandy managed to twist her head around. She saw the two naked girls being ordered to touch their toes.

'They will suffer twenty strokes between them, and then another dozen each, leaving you perfectly free to make up your mind. I shan't hurry you, Miss Silk. It is entirely for you to decide. Cane them,' she instructed. 'Cane them hard.'

Erica swished the cane down across Sophie's bottom. Mandy heard the bamboo slice into the upturned cheeks. The next stroke swept across Sonia's pert buttocks. Mandy heard the minx squeal and stagger forward.

'No. Stop. No,' Mandy shouted into her strict gag. They must not suffer, they must not be punished. But her pleading went unheard. Mandy strained again to peer over her shoulder. She glimpsed Sophie, a reddening weal across her rump, shivering as she tensed herself for the next stripe. Beside her, her naked bottom poised for punishment, the minx trembled under the shadow of the hovering bamboo.

'Excellent. Give them six apiece,' Celia instructed. Folding the draft agreements – there were two copies – across her heavy bosom, the solicitor sat down on the bed alongside Mandy's ravished cheeks. Settling down comfortably, her thigh grazing Mandy's with unexpected intimacy, she started to palm Mandy's bottom soothingly as the cane swished down across Sophie's poised cheeks.

Sophie grunted twice under the bamboo, but Sonia squealed aloud. Mandy flinched at each sorrowful sob – and flinched again at the dominant hand caressing her own scalded cheeks. Erica sliced the Indonesian cane down across Sonia's upturned buttocks again, and again, until the first six strokes prescribed by Celia had been ruthlessly administered.

'Another dozen, each?' Erica asked, expectantly.

'Yes,' Celia consented. 'Wait,' she added softly, as the cane was raised above the whipped cheeks. 'Will you sign now, or must they suffer more?' she asked, fingering Mandy's bottom firmly.

Sophie was silent but Mandy heard Sonia's sniffling half-sobs and knew in her heart that she could not put the wretched little minx through any more sorrow. It was not fair, and it was not worth it. Sophie had a generous spirit despite her jealous streak and the minx had been loyal – and a loving little playmate. Whatever she was in danger of losing, Mandy was not prepared to sacrifice such affection.

Mistaking Mandy's silence for a possible refusal, the grey-eyed solicitor played her trump card. 'Read it carefully,' she urged, turning to page three of one copy of the closely typed agreement and holding it out in front of Mandy's face. Intuitively realising Mandy's concern for Sonia, she ordered Sophie out of the room. The minx remained, trembling as she strained to touch her toes, her striped buttocks perfectly presented for punishment.

'You get a one-off, non-repeatable payment of twenty thousand pounds. Sign, and the money is yours. You will be free to go tomorrow.'

'Don't,' Sonia blurted out. 'Whatever it is, don't do it –' Her words were silenced, cut short by a brutal slice of the cane.

'Sign,' hissed the solicitor. 'Sign, and we will consider the matter settled once and for all.'

Mandy nodded.

Gagged still, but with her right hand untied and given a pen, Mandy signed and dated both copies. Satisfied, Celia gathered up her copy of the agreement and tossed Mandy's down on to the bed.

'My visitors are due shortly. I must be there to receive them. Tie the other one to the bed, Erica. We'll see to them later. And there is Partridge to punish, don't forget. We shall put on a bit of a show for the prospective purchasers. Let them see Sternwood Grange at its best.'

Sonia joined Mandy, face down, on the bed, and was tightly bound. Celia and Erica departed, closing and locking the door behind them. In the silence, Mandy heard Sonia weeping gently. She inched her soft nakedness closer to the little minx to comfort and console her.

Sonia gulped and twisted her face sideways. 'What did they force you to sign?'

Startled, Mandy turned to find that Sonia was not gagged as she had supposed. Her blue eyes widened hopefully. The sight of Sonia's wide mouth, and white teeth, filled her mind with a riot of possibilities.

'Was it to do with this place? Sternwood Grange?'

Mandy nodded vigorously, wishing Sonia would use her teeth to undo the gag around her own mouth.

'A sort of secrecy clause?'

Maddened by the questions, Mandy shook her head. Her blue eyes implored Sonia to work on the gag.

'But the money,' Sonia chattered on imperviously. 'You've been given a lot of money, Mandy. Would it have been more if they hadn't been caning me? You wouldn't have signed,' she added in a guilty rush. 'It's my fault, isn't it?'

Exasperated by her gag – and the minx's endless questioning – Mandy writhed fruitlessly in her bondage. She ceased her struggling as Sonia twisted across and planted deep, devotional kisses on her shoulder. Relishing the velvety brush of lips against her aching flesh, Mandy suddenly laughed into her gag. If only Sonia was a bit brighter, she giggled to herself, they could be free.

'Oh, look,' Sonia gasped, reading the contract. 'It says that you, blah blah on this day blah blah, Amanda Silk . . .' She muttered the next three lines.

Mandy screamed silently, letting go of her pent-up frustration. The means to freedom were only inches away, but the minx was now using her mouth to turn over the first page of the agreement.

'You own Sternwood Grange?' Sonia suddenly squeaked, her voice thrilling with excitement.

Not any more, Mandy sighed silently. There was another pause.

'Mandy,' Sonia whispered urgently.

Mandy grunted into her gag.

'It doesn't actually say anything anywhere here about giving you any money.'

Mandy stiffened in alarm. No, it was a mistake. The little fool was reading the wrong page. Mandy had seen it in black and white.

'I hereby grant unreservedly and absolutely blah blah . . .' Sonia rattled on breathlessly. 'Look. See for yourself. Was it on page one?'

Mandy shook her head.

'Page two?'

Again, Mandy tossed her head impatiently.

'Then read page three,' the minx grunted, squashing her breasts into the bed as she turned the page with her tongue and then, picking up the agreement between her teeth, placed it down where Mandy could just manage to read it.

Mandy's eyes burned into the paragraph which had promised the one-off payment. The original, now with Celia Flaxstone, had expressed the terms clearly in both words and figures. No such agreement to pay was contained in her copy. Mandy closed her eyes. She had been duped by the clever solicitor, duped into signing over her inheritance. Her rightful legacy was about to be sold. And Mandy, naked, bound and helpless, could do nothing.

Nine

There was a rustling in the ivy at the window. Mandy twisted and strained, expecting to see an owl. It was Sophie, balanced precariously on a ledge. Mandy remembered how high up above the ground they were.

The window opened with a squeak which woke Sonia.

'What?' Sonia murmured sleepily, then whispered Sophie's name excitedly as she saw the girl climbing down into the bedroom.

Mandy relished her freedom from the gag and sighed with relief as Sophie's fingers loosened the knots of her irksome bondage. Untied, Mandy wriggled off the bed and rubbed her wrists as Sophie undid Sonia's restraining ropes.

'The door's locked,' Sophie warned.

Mandy nodded.

'We'll have to go out through the window.'

Sonia and Mandy hugged and kissed their rescuer.

'Partridge is down in the kitchens. Erica is punishing her. I must go down –'

'We'll come with you. We'll help any way we can,' Mandy whispered.

'I just want to be there, afterwards . . .'

'I know,' Mandy said sympathetically.

Sonia whimpered, admitting to her fear of heights. Naked and afraid, her eyes filled with tears and her breasts trembled.

'Stay here, we'll come back for you later.'

'No, don't leave me, Mandy, oh please don't leave me,' the little minx pleaded. 'I'm more scared of Erica.' She rubbed her striped buttocks, remembering the cruel slice of the cropped blonde's cane.

'I must get to Partridge,' Sophie said impatiently.

'Yes. You must be with her.' They exchanged glances, then smiled. 'We must all go,' Mandy added gently, putting her arm around the little minx. 'Sonia. Do you trust me?'

Sonia nodded vigorously.

'Then listen. We'll put a blindfold on you and get you out of here, OK?'

The minx was silent but eventually agreed. They found a strip of linen and, with her soft bosom brushing Sonia's breasts, nipple to nipple, Mandy tied it tightly around the trusting eyes that gazed lovingly into her own. Sophie took one hand, Mandy the other, as they guided Sonia to the window.

'I'll go first,' Sophie volunteered. 'I'll take the same route that got me in.'

Mandy nodded, holding Sonia gently to her breast as she watched their rescuer clamber out on to the ledge.

'Now you,' she whispered encouragingly. 'I'll be with you all the time. Just feel your way. Don't think about anything.'

Sonia's cleft widened as she straddled the window sill and pawed her way out on to the ledge. Mandy's controlling hand guided the shivering girl's thigh, remaining at the left buttock as the minx stood up and clung to the ivy. Mandy gave the captive cheek a reassuring squeeze.

'Get closer in towards the ivy,' Sophie urged.

The minx shuffled closer in to the wall, her bosom rustling the dry leaves. Mandy checked the hand and foot holds.

'We're going to go sideways, like crabs. It's only twelve feet then there's another open window,' Sophie explained.

227

Their progress was slow. Sonia, wedged between the supporting thighs on either side, gripped tightly as she inched her way along the ivy-clad wall. She suffered the most: with her breasts squashed into the ancient brickwork, her nipples were ravished up into peaks of fierce pain. Then she froze, refusing to go any further. Mandy caressed the nape of the minx's neck, then drew her fingertip slowly down along the dimpled spine.

'In a moment, you will feel me. I will be inside you. As long as I am connected to you, you have nothing to fear.'

The minx nodded, brushing the ivy with her fringe, then gasped aloud as Mandy slid her straightened finger inbetween her cheeks, directly into her tight warmth.

Guiding and gently propelling Sonia, Mandy kept her finger tightly in place. She felt Sonia's sphincter grip. Connected so intimately, and feeling more secure, the little minx inched gingerly towards the waiting window.

Inside, Mandy cuddled and comforted Sonia, examining and then kissing the bruised breasts. Holding the shivering minx tenderly, she undid the blindfold and praised her for her bravery. Cupping her naked buttocks, she squeezed the cheeks gently as she sucked on each nipple to soothe and ease their soreness.

Sophie had been rummaging for clothes but could only unearth a pair of white cotton panties and a pair of black sheer tights. She handed them over to the naked girls with a rueful grin.

'That's all, folks,' she said, doing the Bugs Bunny voice.

Mandy grinned, took the white panties and coaxed Sonia into them. Easing the stretched cotton up over the minx's buttocks, she fingered the elastic and let it snap into the slender waist. Sonia knelt to help Mandy into the sheer black tights but there was no more time for amorous play – Partridge was being punished downstairs. Even as Sonia's inquisitive fingertips were dappling against Mandy's meshed bottom, the brown-eyed housekeeper was being severely lashed.

'Let's go,' Sophie urged.

They followed her down through the silence of the sleeping house. Sternwood Grange was in darkness as they crept, floor by floor, down to the kitchens in the basement. The glow of yellow light greeted them as they approached along the final passageway – as did the ominous sound, the swish-crack, of a slicing leather strap. They froze. Against the yellow wall ahead they saw, silhouetted on the peeling plaster, the dark shadow of a naked woman. The line of the ripe breasts, wide hips and rounded buttocks was unmistakeably that of a voluptuous woman. Sophie moaned softly as her eyes traced the familiar curves of Partridge. Mandy reached out and held Sophie's hand, giving it a reassuring squeeze.

The shadow showed the nude's arms stretched up and drawn together at the wrists. Above the bound wrists, they could just discern the faint shadow of the links of a taut chain. Partridge was naked and strung up in the Gibbet for her punishment.

A harsh snapping sound accompanied the flickering shadow of a leather belt: the curve straightening out as it savaged the swell of the naked cheeks. Sophie gasped and bounded down the passageway towards the light. Mandy followed swiftly, her nyloned footfalls silent upon the flagstones. Reaching out, she caught and restrained the girl in front. Folding Sophie in a comforting embrace, she drew her back away from the danger of discovery.

'No. We can only wait. Wait and watch. When it is over, then you shall comfort her. We all will comfort her.'

Sophie pressed her tear-stained face down into Mandy's shoulder. Mandy felt her wince as another crack-snap of the belt signalled the kiss of leather across defenceless cheeks.

Sophie looked up and nodded tearfully. They kissed, all jealousies and misunderstandings forgotten. Mandy felt once more the softness of the other's body pressing into her as Sophie flinched in response to the sound of the strap across the naked buttocks in the kitchen. The punishment was out of sight, but it haunted their imaginations, forcing them to visualise the cruel hide licking the reddening cheeks. Sonia joined them, her eyes wide with fear as she gazed at the shadow of suffering etched upon the flaking plaster of the wall.

Eight more times the strap was raised, out of sight, in the kitchen. Eight more times, they saw its shadow crack down across the silhouetted buttocks. Eight more times, the huddled girls shivered at the sharp snap of leather across quivering flesh – and renewed their shivering as they heard the grunts and moans of Partridge in her suffering.

They scattered, scampering into the shadows like mice before the paws of a patrolling cat, as Erica emerged from the kitchens. Her cropped head down as she trod the flagstones, she rolled up the leather strap into a tight curl. Halfway down the dim passageway she stopped, thrusting her buttocks up against the plaster wall. Dragging up her skirt and yanking down her panties, Mandy watched as Erica brought the leather strap – curled around her right fist – against her exposed slit. Signalling Sonia and Sophie to remain absolutely silent, Mandy crouched and gazed as, further down in the shadows, the punisher pleasured herself with the instrument of punishment with increasing ferocity.

Mandy closed her eyes and tried to extinguish the flame of erotic curiosity, the flickering tongues of dancing lust, that burned in her brain. She shuddered with delicious dread at the thought of the warm hide, soft and supple and fresh from the buttocks it had just blistered, rasping against the wet, silky flesh of Erica's labia. The cruel lash which had planted hot kisses upon soft creamy cheeks was now being plied against the punisher's splayed, wet slit.

Opening her eyes and peeping into the shadows, Mandy's tongue grew thick in her dry mouth as she watched the cropped blonde ruthlessly leather her clitoris. Arched up on her toes, her thighs wide, her panties stretched between her knees, Erica was punishing herself against her open flesh-lips with the tip of the strap.

The black mesh of the tights grew warm and damp at Mandy's pubis as she watched the sadistic punisher use the strap to a different purpose. Mandy tried to deny her excitement and wet arousal but succumbed to the overwhelming thrill of pleasure coupled to pain, of delight bound tightly to dread. Sad as she felt for Partridge, she relished the sight of the cropped blonde punishing her slit sweetly into orgasm.

Erica came silently, pounding and grinding her naked buttocks into the rough plaster wall as her knees buckled under the powerful spasms of her climax. The leather strap slowly unfurled to dangle, limp and lifeless, down from Erica's open right hand. Mandy saw, under the light bulb, the glint of wetness spangle the dark hide, saw the sweat glisten on the cropped blonde's face – and sensed the wet heat at her own slit behind the taut mesh of the sheer tights that clung to her pubis.

Silently, Mandy wiped her moist palms on the sheen of her black-nyloned buttocks. Erica staggered away from the wall and adjusted her panties and skirt. Shouldering her strap, she strode off into the darkness. The three girls regrouped. They had, from their respective hiding places, all witnessed Erica's display of self-pleasuring. Mandy sniffed at the heady pungent tang of their mixed scent of arousal.

They hurried into the kitchen to find Partridge stretched in the Gibbet, her heavily fleshed buttocks an angry shade of red where Erica's strap had lashed the naked cheeks. Sophie kissed and comforted the housekeeper, whispering soothing words as their lips fused. Sonia's palms sought out and found the ripe breasts of the whipped woman. The minx squeezed the captive bosom tenderly. Mandy's lips, and tongue, worked busily across the swell of the punished bottom, licking and lapping, kissing and healing the ravished cheeks.

The three comforters crushed the comforted between their urgent bodies. Mandy's arms encircled Partridge, pulling Sonia's face into the punished housekeeper's bosom. The minx's pantied pubis kissed the bound woman's sticky labia, the cotton clinging to the pouting flesh-lips. Mandy's sheer black tights grazed the whipped buttocks as she pressed her hips into the rounded cheeks. Up above, the chain rattled as Partridge bucked in response.

Exchanging tongues, Sophie and the housekeeper kissed deeply, lingeringly. Sonia ground her panties firmly into the warm delta as she sucked fiercely on the nipple in her mouth. Mandy felt the first spasm of the housekeeper's orgasm as the hot cheeks quivered against her cool belly.

Sonia's hands slipped down over Partridge's hips to capture, cup and squeeze the heavy cheeks. Her fingertips scraped against the sheen of Mandy's black tights. Peeling the waistband down, the minx scrabbled at Mandy's pubic fuzz. Mandy blindly sought out Sonia's mouth. Prising the minx's lips from Partridge's breast, she slid her first and second fingers deep inside the open mouth.

Up above, below the dry rattle of the Gibbet's chain, Partridge and Sophie were tonguing each other furiously, both fused into an inevitable, rapidly approaching climax. Below, Mandy and the minx fingered each other frantically. The chain jerked and danced as all four came: slit to slit, flesh to flesh, in a welded paroxysm of liquid lust.

'My honey trap has caught quite an interesting little haul,' the voice of Erica snarled, her low voice breaking the silence of their exquisite joy.

Mandy turned, her eyes clouded by orgasm, her face slack and pale. Sonia squealed with fear.

'Take them to the gym. Yes, all four of them,' Erica instructed.

Mandy shrank back from the three sallow-skinned, dark-suited men who stepped forward. They did not obey the cropped blonde immediately, but stood, mouths open, drinking in the last ripples of orgasm convulsing the nude in the Gibbet.

'Quickly, your master will be waiting,' Erica snapped. 'You can enjoy these bitches at your leisure later.'

Mandy, obeying the strict instructions for silence, followed Erica and one of the three dark-suited thugs along the corridor towards the gym. The others followed behind, shepherded by the remaining two heavies. They must be the muscles, not the brains, of Erica's party, Mandy calculated. Iraqi or Syrian, she could not tell. Probably cruel and definitely dangerous, she decided. The henchmen of the buyer of Sternwood Grange. But why were they being brought to the gym? She had waived the rights to the deeds. Why would the shrewd solicitor risk complicating matters? Risk Mandy fouling up the sale?

They were led into the gym. Celia ignored them, other than instructing Erica and the heavies to gag and then tie the four captives to the wall bars. As Mandy, Sonia, Sophie and Partridge were stripped of whatever scant clothing they wore and bound face inwards to the gym wall, Celia continued her discussions with a hawk-nosed man of Arabic appearance. Mandy only managed a fleeting glimpse before rough hands peeled down her tights, palmed and pinched her buttocks dominantly, then yanked her arms up and bound them tightly by the wrists to the wood.

'So glad you could join us,' the solicitor began drily, sauntering across the polished floor of the gym to address the four bare bottoms. 'May I present Mr Ozzam,' she continued, 'he is from –'

'Many countries,' a silky voice intervened. 'Details do not matter, nor do border controls. One has so many passports.'

Turkish? Or did Mandy catch the flat vowels of Eastern Europe there. Albanian, perhaps. Latvian possibly. Celia's careful laughter broke into Mandy's thoughts. 'But of course. Details do not matter. Mr Ozzam is here to purchase Sternwood Grange.'

'It is agreed,' Mr Ozzam replied in the cosmopolitan accent Mandy found so difficult to place. He clapped his hands delightedly, adding, 'It is everything you said it would be.'

'There's more,' Celia added teasingly.

More? Mandy froze, fear forming in her brain.

'Three million,' Ozzam enthused.

'Three million, sterling,' the solicitor echoed, clearly proud of her coup.

He's being ripped off, Mandy calculated. She knew the valuation and potential. How had she hoodwinked him?

'And when you refurbish, build and extend, your investment will be doubled in a year.'

Mandy frowned. So that was it. She knew now how Celia had managed to rip Ozzam off by several hundred thousand. Sterling.

'Mr Ozzam runs a very similar establishment in Beirut. He is, he assures me, always looking for fresh faces.'

'Flesh, certainly,' Ozzam whispered excitedly. 'Faces, they do not matter so much. But new flesh is highly prized in my humble house of pleasures.'

The half-formed fear in Mandy's brain took shape. Suddenly, she knew what Celia had in mind.

234

'Sternwood Grange comes, as the contract will specify, with fixtures and fittings. These four beauties are an option, Mr Ozzam. Would you care to inspect them more closely?'

The heavies stood aside smartly, their leather shoes squeaking on the polished floor, as their boss strode across to join the solicitor beside the four bare bottoms.

'Your ancestors probably enjoyed the delights of examining naked females before the slave sale, Mr Ozzam,' Celia observed suavely. 'I hope you have inherited their skill and judgement.'

Ozzam thumbed Sophie's soft rump, and traced the swell of her outer thigh.

'Young and tender, Mr Ozzam. To be served up, like pink, juicy lamb, to the discriminating appetite. The flesh of both are sweet and tight. An older man's meal.'

Ozzam fingered the stripes across Partridge's whipped cheeks. Mandy heard his breath coming in excited gasps.

'Mellow fruit for you, Mr Ozzam. Sweet, succulent and darkly fleshed. Think of a seasoned fig, split and oozing after many summers.'

Ozzam grunted excitedly, knuckling the house-keeper's cheeks fiercely then palming them expertly as if weighing her swollen buttocks. As he turned to Sonia beside her, Mandy heard his curse of approval.

'A filly, Mr Ozzam, who has yet to taste the bridle or the bit. A spirited filly yet to bear the weight of a rider across her flesh. An interesting acquisition.'

'Worth her weight in gold,' Ozzam muttered, fondling Sonia's apple breasts. 'I know a prince who would drown me in diamonds for one so young, so untried.'

Turning to Mandy, he paused.

'An English rose, Mr Ozzam. A rare bloom in the desert.'

Mandy shrank from the cruel hands at her bosom, the thick fingertips rubbing her nipples, judging her flesh expertly. The hands caressed her belly and thighs, then spread around to her bottom. She felt both thumbs at her cleft, then sensed his face close to her skin. He sniffed deeply.

'An English rose,' he grunted. 'With an intoxicating perfume.'

She felt the thick thumbs splay her cheeks wide apart, and burned with shame as he bent down to inspect her intimately.

'This one, like the others, has been whipped recently, no?'

Mandy felt the stubby fingertip tracing the red lines of Erica's cane strokes.

'All of them have been punished since sunset,' Celia conceded. 'That one especially needs the kiss of the cane. Be sure to remember that. Stripe her regularly, Mr Ozzam, and she will perform exactly to your pleasing.'

'I will remember,' Ozzam promised.

'They will all respond well to discipline,' Celia continued. 'They are like flowers in the desert, my dear Mr Ozzam.'

'How?' he queried. 'Flowers in my desert suffer and thirst before they blossom.'

'Exactly,' she whispered. 'These four thirst for punishment. Be sure that they suffer before they blossom. Especially our sweet English rose.'

'Excellent,' Ozzam grunted. 'I will remember that when they are in my humble house of pleasures.'

'Why not reserve them for those clients who prefer fiercer pleasures: the delights of the whip and cane?'

'It is as you say. These four will serve my very discerning gentlemen.'

Mandy shivered. Beside her, she heard Sonia whimper anxiously into her gag.

'We will exchange contracts tomorrow,' Celia concluded, guiding Ozzam to the door.

'And those?' Mandy heard him say. 'Are they included in the price?'

'Of course. I promised you a little extra, didn't I?'

'But, my dear lady, they are worth –'

'They are a token of my good will. I will have them marked as sold for you,' the solicitor said reassuringly. 'Erica.'

Erica stepped forward and, opening a red lipstick, drew a thick red circle on each of the four naked bottoms. Mandy clenched her buttocks but Erica's spank softened them into submission: loathing the cool kiss of the lipstick, Mandy felt the large O branded on her left buttock.

'See? They are now yours. But come. Let us take some supper together. And, tomorrow, we shall have a whipping party in honour of the sale of Sternwood Grange. A fitting memento, I think.'

'But how delightful. I may have the very whip for just such an occasion,' he replied, his voice fading as he passed through the gym doors.

When Ozzam had stroked his thumb down the length of the minx's cleft, he had caused her to jerk violently in her bondage. The sudden jolt had slightly loosened the cords at her slender left wrist. Straining and struggling like a rabbit in a snare, she wriggled and writhed in the darkness until her aching left arm was free.

They were startled by her soft voice when she had untied her gag. 'I'll just undo the other arm if I can and then I'll undo your knots.'

Moments later, the freed hands were unpicking the cords of those still bound until all four women sank their bottoms down on to the polished wooden floor, easing the burning ache at their wrists. Partridge, overwhelmed by the evening's events, sought information and explanations.

'So much is happening that I don't understand,' she sighed.

They told her, each whispering excitedly as they fitted in another piece of the picture which puzzled her.

'I remember,' the brown-eyed housekeeper said. 'It was your eighteenth birthday. Your aunt was very cross with you –'

'And you came upstairs and –'

'Whipped your bottom. Amanda Silk, why of course.'

They hugged in the darkness, delighted at their reunion.

'But Celia tricked Mandy out of her legacy,' Sonia chipped in breathlessly, quickly completing the story.

'Then we'd better all get out of Sternwood Grange tonight,' Partridge decided, her tone emphatic. 'I will look after you, girls. I'll get you safely back to London. Trust me.'

'Dear Partridge, always so loyal. But I'm staying,' Mandy whispered. 'You three go. And look after each other. I've got things to do here.'

'But you can't,' Sonia protested, kneeling closer to Mandy in the darkness. Their breasts brushed. Mandy felt the minx's pink slit press her belly and shivered with delight. 'You know what she's planned for tomorrow. A whipping party. And then it'll be off to Beirut and I'll never see you again,' she wailed.

'I'll be OK,' Mandy promised. She gave them her London address. 'We'll meet up there in a day or two.'

'You're not going to try to take on that solicitor woman,' Sophie gasped, appalled. 'She's dangerous. And Erica, she's –'

Mandy kept her plans secret, but consoled them. 'No, I'm not going to deal with those two just yet. They will have to wait.'

Tearfully – little Sonia sobbed and clung on hard – they whispered their farewells in the darkness of the gym, promising to reunite in Notting Hill before the week was over.

'Be sure you all get right away,' Mandy made them promise. 'It's your only chance.'

Reluctantly, they promised.

'You must get away. But I must take my own chances.'

Mandy had worked out, by a process of elimination, that Ozzam would be in the gilded bedroom in the East Wing. As Celia's guest of honour, he would have been given the stateroom once graced by the presence of the Cavalier king.

Stealing through the moonbeams that fingered the darkness up on the second floor, she was within ten feet of the massive double doors when a strong hand closed around her mouth, and its partner grasped her wrist and twisted her arm up behind her back. An ever watchful heavy had pounced silently out of the shadows and intercepted her.

'What you want? What you do?' snarled the man, the garlic on his breath overpowering her as much as his skilful strength.

'Mr Ozzam,' she mumbled meekly into the hard palm at her lips. 'I have been sent to pleasure him.'

'He sleeps,' the heavy grunted, pinning her to the wall, squashing her bosom painfully as he lodged his knee in her buttocks.

'Then wake him,' Mandy gasped. 'Or,' she added with a brazen bluff, 'face his anger in the morning.'

The knee left her cleft; she peeled her breasts from the wall. She felt the grip on her arm loosen – a fraction – as the bodyguard considered this.

'You come,' he decided, dragging her naked body up to the double doors as if it were a bin bag. Dropping her on to the carpet, and pinioning her down with his foot, he tapped on the aged oak. Three short raps and one long. The left-hand-side door opened immediately. Mandy saw another heavy loom into the moonlight.

'She has come for the boss.'

'He sleeps.'

'Then wake him.' Pause. 'Or,' Mandy's goon said, stealing her line, 'face his anger in the morning.'

239

It worked. Minutes later, both heavies were sent into the exile of the corridor beyond the closed double doors as Mandy stood, nakedly demure, at the foot of the once royal bed.

'So, English rose, you have come to pleasure me?' Ozzam purred, staring at her with hot, narrowed eyes.

She gazed back at him, wondering when and how to begin. 'I was worried,' she whispered.

'You were worried? On what account?'

She took a deep breath, feigning an effort. 'That in your humble house of pleasures, the other girls already there would be more accomplished, more versatile, more experienced than me. I do not want to disappoint.'

'Do not have such fears, girl. The whip and the cane await you. One will teach and the other will train you so that you will learn to give complete satisfaction. But I do not understand. Why come to me tonight?'

'I thought – it was a foolish thought – that I would learn from you. When you touched my nakedness earlier I felt your skill and strength. Your touch was sure and certain, my body told me so.'

'So?' The tone could not disguise his evident pleasure of her flattering tribute. Between his thighs, the silk sheet bulged.

'Who would buy a sports car without a test drive? Try me now, tonight,' Mandy added quickly. 'Teach me what I must know.'

Ozzam's interest intensified. Mandy palmed her breasts, bunching them deliciously, then dropped her fingers to pluck at her pubic fuzz. She was vulnerable, naked and delicious in her guise of reluctant willingness. His eyes flickered slowly like those of a lizard stirring in the sun. Under the taut silk, Mandy saw his keener interest thicken and rise proudly.

'Come into my bed, English rose. Let us see if we can open your soft petals tonight while the dew is still on them. Let us sip your nectar and judge its sweetness –'

'And if I am ready to be plucked,' Mandy murmured, slipping in alongside his naked body.

Ozzam was in his late forties, his body firm and lean. Mandy saw the scars on his shoulders and thigh. Not the scars of bar-room brawls, but of AK-47 fire and shrapnel. Ozzam had lived in the very teeth of death. Such men were without mercy. His eventful life had aged his face, adding cruel lines to his dark eyes and sensual mouth. Mandy peered shyly at his mouth. This was a man who had tasted all the dishes, all the delights of the flesh, she calculated. Now she was his titbit for the hour, naked as a shorn lamb. How could she hope to satisfy this greedy epicure, to whet and sate his jaded appetite?

Already his hands, then his mouth, were feasting at her bosom. His thick shaft raked her upper thigh and pierced her belly as he lurched over in the bed of silk, poised to crudely mount and penetrate her as she lay wide-thighed below.

Closing her eyes, she tried desperately to remember any and every trick she had picked up while serving the clients here at Sternwood Grange. Her brain became a kaleidoscope of fragmented images as she felt his hard flesh nudging at her labia. One idea burned brighter and deeper than all: taunt and tease.

Yes. That is what she should – must – do. Not strive to please him in passive surrender but plan her assault on his quivering senses with subtle skill. Taunt and tease. She would kindle in him a raging desire – then deny him satisfaction.

She wriggled herself free from beneath his nakedness, and nimbly straddled him, splaying her buttocks on to his thighs and pinning him down with her hands on his sinewy shoulders. She felt his steel muscles ripple beneath her soft naked warmth, and knew that he could pitch her off and ravish her in a split second.

'I am here to please and pleasure you, master,' she

murmured, bending to lick his nipples teasingly. 'Grant your servant, this English rose, a chance to blossom.'

To her delight, she felt the coiled tension in his shoulders slacken. He was surrendering – but the jerking twitch of his shaft up against her bottom was a stern reminder of his savage potency. It was going to be dangerous.

Shuffling her satin-smooth buttocks slowly and sensually up along his body, she nudged her breasts into his face. Dangling the luscious globes an inch before his eyes, she nipple-teased him, skimming his cheeks and then his lips with the pert peaks before crushing her bosoms down to bury him in their soft warmth. Jerking back her hips, she swept her cheeks down against his shaft: the rod of pulsing iron speared her cleft as she jiggled her breasts and drowned him. Suddenly, skimming her wet slit down his flesh, she sat back between his knees and captured his erection between her bouncing breasts. She bunched her satin cushions between her trembling palms so that her nipples kissed his glistening spear. He gasped and swore softly, pumping his hips violently to enjoy the warmth and depth of her tight cleavage. She crushed her breasts together until they ached, capturing and trapping his thrusting shaft. Slipping her right hand in front of her bosom to keep him ensnared within her flesh, she searched for his balls with her left hand. She found the sac and squeezed.

Ozzam's belly tensed; his eyes became fierce slits. Mandy knew that he was coming, was about to explode in her bosom. Swinging her breasts free, she released him. Denied what he chokingly desired, his left hand taloned the silk sheet in a paroxysm of fury, ripping it as a tiger claws its prey. The twitching shaft beat the empty air, pulsing and throbbing in vain. Mandy just managed to hide her smile of triumph as he cursed and begged for release.

'Daughter of a witch, finish me,' he grunted, 'finish me.'

'As you command, master,' she whispered softly.

He eased himself back into the pillows, surrendering his erection with a mixture of pride and submission. Lowering her face, she pursed her lips and blew softly on the angry head of his shaft.

'Feel the sweet zephyr as it blows upon the burning sands at sunset. Feel how good it is, my master, prince of the desert, to have the cool wind caress your burning flesh.'

He moaned drunkenly, threshing beneath the weight of her thighs and buttocks. Her cleft was hot and sticky; she pressed it down into him firmly, branding him with her heat. He screamed a curdled scream of violent delight. She slipped her left hand up between his thighs, fingernailing him deliberately before capturing his balls once more between her thumb and fingertips. Twisting and turning his sac, she owned and controlled him completely.

'You'll taste the whip, bitch. I'll lash you –'

'This –' she spoke serenely, ignoring his blustering '– is the healing balm of the cool oasis.' Her voice was now a carnal sigh. She spilled her spittle along his throbbing shaft. 'How sweet are the waters at the oasis, my prince of the desert, feel how they cool your heat.'

'Now,' he roared, pawing desperately at her head to force her mouth over the erection an inch below. 'Now, bitch. Take me. I, Ozzam, command it.'

'Patience, my master. Not yet. Not yet,' she murmured softly, 'for my prince should know that there is an even softer place for his aching flesh to rest. Truly, in all the desert, he will not find a tighter sheath for his sword.'

Turning deftly, she released his balls and swivelled her buttocks towards him. Quickly gathering his straining shaft in her hand, she eased her bottom towards its engorged head. Wedging the tip into her cleft, she slowly, tantalisingly, dragged it along the velvet flesh between her parted cheeks. Three times, in maddeningly slow succession, she forced the pulsing flesh between her heavy buttocks before nuzzling it against her wet sphincter.

This time, his scream was a silent scream. Grappling drunkenly, he tried to clutch her soft cheeks between veined, taloned hands. She brushed them away imperiously and, perched above his thighs, clenched her anal whorl's rosebud muscle rhythmically – drawing his length in a quarter of an inch at each delicious spasm. Groaning in his ecstasy, he begged her openly and loudly for completion. Unable to thrust and penetrate, he was at the mercy of her cunning buttocks. She toyed with his anguish and protracted his sweet suffering.

He cursed her violently once more, but Mandy continued to deny him. His harsh words became sweet pleading, choking with suffocating torment. With a twisting lunge, he bucked and jerked, toppling her from her throne of dominance. She fell from the bed and lay sprawled, face down and bosom crushed on the carpet.

He pounced, straddling her, his spear once more at her gaping cleft. Greedy hands prised her helpless cheeks apart, forcing the cleft to yawn deeply. Her sphincter sparkled, a red rosebud on the tremulous verge of opening. He swallowed, and grabbed a fistful of her sweat-drenched hair.

'My English rose, the moment has come for you to be –'

'Take me, my master, for I am but a sugared sweetmeat upon your silver dish. I am as the honeycomb between your bared teeth: the passing pleasure of but a moment. But I know where,' she whispered fiercely, 'there is darker meat for your appetite. Meat more toothsome. Wild, untamed game, providing meat more fitting for my master's table.'

The words arrested his lust, confusing and tormenting him. 'Where?' he choked in his fury. 'Where?'

Before she could reply, she felt him shoot his load. The squirting stream of hot silver splattered her hair, neck, shoulders and dimpled spine. Pitter pat. Pitter pat. It rained down like a sudden summer shower kissing the hot asphalt of a blistering road. She squirmed, causing the spillage to course down her spine and collect in a puddle at the swell of her buttocks. She felt it swimming, then flow down into her cleft. He rose and staggered across to the empty bed. Mandy wriggled over and wiped her buttocks dry on the carpet.

'Take me to this –'

'Rare fruit? Come,' she whispered. 'I will show you.'

They stole out of the gilded bedchamber. Had Charles Stuart been so royally entertained? Mandy wondered, glimpsing the torn sheet as she left through the huge oak doors. Out in the moonlit corridor, Ozzam silenced the heavies. His authority at once quelled the surprise and concern.

'Leave me be. I will go with this girl. I trust her.'

Mandy took Ozzam by the hand and led him down the corridor, turning out through French windows on to an octagonal balcony. They paused in the moonlight. She shivered, naked in the night chill.

'Sit a moment. I have something important to tell you.'

'You?' he sounded amazed. 'Something to tell me, Ozzam?'

'Yes,' she replied with quiet confidence.

Something about her serious tone of voice calmed him.

'Buying Sternwood Grange is a very big mistake.'

'Why do you say this?' he barked.

'Many reasons. To start with, you are paying too much. Several hundred thousand too much.'

He protested vehemently, but she was well rehearsed

and armed with a flood of facts and figures. She presented her facts coldly and clearly – unit costs, overheads, depreciation – with all the professionalism her days at Millbank had taught her. Although she knew she had convinced him, he wavered.

'Then there's Special Branch. Always sniffing around.'

In the moonlight, his sallow skin paled. She explained that many of Sternwood Grange's clientele were very important people. Important enough to have Special Branch interested in their welfare. She whispered several names. His eyes widened like a child's with wonder.

'And you can't build, refurbish or extend. This is a Grade II listed building.'

She hit him with all her meticulous research carried out in London: land searches, preservation orders and severe planning restrictions. 'You can't even paint the back door without a full public inquiry. Anything historical, and the press descend like vultures.'

Three minutes' silence followed.

He broke it with an angry, bewildered voice. 'How do you know these things? What is your interest in Sternwood Grange?'

Should she? Dare she? She decided to risk it: telling him, briefly, her true identity and how Sternwood Grange was hers, not Celia's to sell. And, she added, she was not selling.

'If you buy, it will mean protracted court cases. And publicity,' she warned.

That clinched it. The man with five passports and no nationality cursed softly into the night. Turning, he shrugged. 'But where is this forbidden fruit you promised me?'

'Come, let us pay them a visit. They are in bed by now, but not sleeping.'

Ten

Through the one-way mirror, Mandy and Ozzam watched as Erica pleasured her grey-eyed mistress. Celia lay back in the pillows of the sumptuous bed, her naked thighs apart. Kneeling, her weight dimpling the satin sheet, her head bowed submissively, Erica was tonguing Celia's pink slit.

'There,' Mandy whispered. 'These two have yet to know the sovereignty of a man. They have yet to taste firm male flesh. A challenge fit for the loins of a desert prince, no? And to capture and tame both – such a princely prize,' she suggested, fingering his vanity with her honeyed tongue. 'But beware, Ozzam. Any man who dares to tame and train them in order to ride their rebellious thighs must bring a brutal tenderness to the bed. Even if he be a prince, he must approach such tigresses masterfully, whip in hand.'

He grunted softly and nodded. She saw him peering as if hypnotised through the thick glass, his face a mask of stern pleasure as Celia shrieked and came: writhing and twisting. Turning her gaze back to the one-way mirror, Mandy saw the solicitor clawing at and squeezing her breasts as she ground her wide buttocks into the satin beneath.

'There are many reasons guiding your decision,' Mandy said softly, insinuating the idea in his brain. 'Many.'

'Why should I trouble to take these bitches back to Beirut?'

'If you return empty-handed, your trip will have been an expensive waste of time. And,' she added, calculating the effect carefully, 'you will lose face. You must return to your house of pleasure with a worthwhile prize. Take them back to Beirut. When you have savoured their flesh, put them to work for you.'

'They would make an interesting addition,' he agreed, as if adding two thoroughbreds to his stable.

'And the cropped blonde would make a splendid disciplinarian. She would keep your seraglio in strict order.'

'That is good. Sometimes the girls become difficult. They require firm handling. Discipline would be good,' he conceded.

'And Celia –'

'Ah,' he whispered, 'you speak of the bitch who proposed to cheat me over Sternwood Grange.'

'You are entitled to your fill of revenge. Satisfy yourself with her, then put her to work for you. She is a skilled lawyer with a sound commercial brain. Put her under the whip, and your books under her, and watch your profits grow.'

Mandy saw what she had looked for: his eyes narrowed, a glint of greed sparkling deep in their depths. She was winning his mind. Now it was time to capture his body.

'Excellent advice, English rose. But how do I get –'

'Leave it to me. Trust me, and I will not disappoint you. I do not seek to cheat you of your money. Sternwood Grange is mine, and is not for sale.'

'Not for sale,' he echoed, clenching his fist. 'I have been made a fool of in my people's eyes. She will pay a keen price for that.'

'You, and you alone, must exact that price, Ozzam. But you will not leave completely disappointed. Sternwood Grange prides itself on its hospitality. Kneel.'

His eyes flickered expectantly.

'Kneel,' she urged. 'It is my wish that you enjoy these two. I will guide you through their weaknesses and expose you to their desires. Armed with such knowledge of them, you will be able to penetrate their resistance and bend them to both your flesh and your will.'

Breathing hard, he knelt closer to the glass panel, returning his fierce gaze to the room beyond. There, on the bed, he saw Celia's hair flounce as she mercilessly spanked Erica. The cropped blonde's reddening bottom faced the one-way mirror. Ozzam's tongue licked his dry lips as he watched the solicitor's firm, slim hand sweep down harshly across the upturned cheeks. Erica squealed and threshed her legs. Celia dominantly trapped the punished blonde's feet and continued the harsh spanking.

'Watch,' Mandy whispered in his ear, fishing out his penis to palm its hot length in her cool hand.

Steadying himself against the glass with outstretched arms, Ozzam shuffled his knees and spread his thighs apart. She started to pump him slowly, curling her fingers tightly around his swollen flesh and jerking her wrist sinuously in strict time with the spanking hand ravishing Erica's bare bottom. He stiffened to a shaft of steel; his belly and shoulders tensed. Celia brought the erotic chastisement to a painful conclusion with a staccato flourish of eight searing spanks; Mandy pumped vigorously eight delicious times. As Erica slithered, hot bottomed and squealing, down from Celia's thighs, Ozzam came, clouding the glass of the one-way mirror with his spurting release. He groaned sweetly and sank back, spent. Mandy caught the pungent whiff of his sweat, his excitement and his hot, male lust.

In the room beyond the glass, Mandy saw the solicitor selecting a black and gold dildo. Palming the phallus, she weighed its nine curved inches then traced its wicked snout with her fingertip. Erica got on all fours and crawled to the feet of her dominant mistress. Kneeling up, she crushed her breasts into the straddling thighs, gazing unblinkingly into the dark pubic curls.

'You must watch and learn,' Mandy encouraged. 'It is essential that you discover all their secrets.'

Ozzam obeyed, kneeling up once more against the one-way mirror and surrendering his semi-erect shaft to Mandy's controlling hand.

'Observe. Learn their appetites and discover their lustful yearnings. With each new revelation, they deliver themselves into your power,' Mandy purred, gripping his engorged shaft tightly in her left hand and palm-polishing the hot, slippery head with her right.

Beyond the lust-smeared glass, Celia was probing Erica's open mouth with the gold-tipped length of ebony.

'See? The cropped blonde takes her pleasure there, in the mouth. Note it well, Ozzam,' Mandy urged, her supple wrist now pumping him gently. She sensed his buttocks tighten and felt his veined thickness swell within her encircling grasp.

'See how eagerly she tongues it, sucks on it. This is your sure and certain knowledge, Ozzam. Now she must take you, even if you have to bind her hands behind her back the first few times.'

He remained silent, but his twitching erection spoke eloquently of the plans he had for Erica in the humble Beirut house of pleasures. Mandy pumped harder. Faster. Through the glass, they watched Erica turn and crouch, face and breasts crushed into the carpet, offering up her buttocks.

'Look. The cropped blonde accepts it there. Look, and remember, Ozzam. She will, when naked in your bed, deny you nothing.'

The grey-eyed solicitor stroked the cleft between the eager cheeks before probing the tight anal whorl. In the

250

darkness of their hiding place, Ozzam grunted and steadied himself against the glass. Mandy increased the tempo of her pleasuring hand as she jerked him towards his third climax. Their view of Erica, now squealing her orgasm into the carpet, was blurred by the sudden splatter of Ozzam's hot release.

'You will have much pleasure training these two in your bed,' she murmured, milking him expertly. He shuddered as she thumbed his hot, wet helmet. 'But be firm with them,' Mandy continued, 'such women are strong willed.'

'They will find how persuasive I can be,' he replied softly.

'Spare your words and use the whip. Leather speaks a tongue all women understand.'

'I have seen enough,' Ozzam said huskily, his eyes bleary with exhaustion. 'I am convinced, English rose.' He struggled to rise.

'No, not yet. Wait,' Mandy urged. 'They have not finished. Wait a little while and watch them at their forbidden sport. You will learn much more, I promise you. It is a rare privilege for a man, even one such as you, Ozzam, to witness the crimson rites of Lesbos.'

'Such things are not so rare to behold. I have witnessed these female games many times, my little English rose. Why, every night in Beirut, we put on a live floor show –'

'Perhaps. But then, the players know there is an audience. Tonight, Ozzam, they know not of your prying eyes. You are a witness to that which is forbidden to the sight of all men.'

He nodded, and she saw a smile of satisfaction spread across his sensual mouth. Mandy smiled her own secret smile as she felt his erection rise up once more within her curled fist.

'You have advised me well, English rose. Your words are true. It is as if I were invisible, right there in the room with them –'

'Watch,' Mandy hissed. 'Take note. The kneeling blonde is about to pay full homage. Thus it will be when she is naked at your feet.'

She gripped his erection and coaxed it into a fierce spear of angry flesh once more as they peered together, their faces almost touching, through the lust-smeared one-way mirror.

They saw Celia standing and squeezing her breasts almost viciously, her thighs wide apart, as the blonde kneeling before her wedged the base of the black dildo in between her teeth and guided it up towards the hot slit above. Ozzam gasped as Erica's face inched closer, then closer still, driving the black wand deeper inside the flesh of her dominatrix.

Mandy pumped. Celia arched up on tiptoe, a soft scream torn from her parted lips. The solicitor buried her taloned hands in the cropped blonde's hair as Erica thrust her face repeatedly into the pubis. Mandy saw the pale face of the kneeling nude grow wet and glisten as Erica rammed the cruel phallus home, bringing her lips repeatedly against Celia's labia in a frenzy of carnal kissing.

Ozzam's heavy hands became fists at the glass. Mandy quickly synchronised her pumping hand to Erica's thrusts into Celia's slit; Ozzam growled and tensed, exploding seconds later up against the glass with such ferocity that both pairs of eyes in the room beyond turned briefly and stared vacantly.

Mandy froze, squeezing Ozzam's flesh fiercely. The eyes beyond the glass returned to gaze upon one another, thinking the faint sound at the glass no more than a fluttering moth, Mandy supposed.

Ozzam dropped to the floor, his head cradled on Mandy's naked thighs. She fingered his damp, sweat-soaked hair tenderly. At the glass of the one-way mirror, the hot smear spread slowly down.

'Come,' she whispered. 'You need a little wine to revive you. You must be thirsty, no?'

He assented, nodding his face into her belly. She felt his chin grazing her blonde pubic curls.

'But first, I must wash you. Wash and refresh your tired flesh.'

He whispered his approval. They rose and crept away towards the hot, scented bath she planned for him. He slipped his hand into hers, willing to be led.

Down in the kitchens, in the cosy darkness, she served him with moist sponge-cake fingers and chilled Vouvray. He ate and drank greedily. Mandy padded back to the fridge to retrieve a second bottle. Out of the corner of her eye, in the bar of sudden light cast by the open fridge door, she saw ten tiny toes crinkle up anxiously. Smiling, she took the bottle out and closed the door. The toes vanished.

Back at the table, she sat down and picked up the corkscrew.

'Why don't you join us, Sonia?'

Ozzam spluttered, startled as the minx, still naked, stepped out from her hiding place and scampered across to join them at the table.

'Why didn't you go as you promised?' Mandy asked, attempting a stern tone which was instantly belied by the hug and the kiss, the cake and the wine she showered on the little naked minx.

'Go?' Ozzam queried.

'My friends in the gym. You bought us all in the slave sale, remember?' Mandy teased.

He raised his glass of Vouvray in mock salute.

'They're free. And supposed to get away tonight.'

He nodded. 'Very wise. So?' Ozzam asked, turning to Sonia. 'Why did you not go?'

'Couldn't,' she said simply, swallowing a huge mouthful of cake.

'Could not?' he pressed, his smiling eyes teasing her seriousness.

'Couldn't leave Mandy. Ever.' She licked her fingers one by one and scanned the table for more cake.

'Such loyalty you inspire, English rose. It is more than loyalty, perhaps. It speaks to me of devotion.'

'What about poor Partridge and Sophie?' Mandy inquired.

'They stayed, too,' Sonia said a little defensively, as if diminishing her sin by their actions. 'Partridge said she just couldn't leave you. Out of loyalty to your aunt. And then Sophie decided to stay out of loyalty –'

'To Partridge,' Mandy said.

'With such staff as these, Sternwood Grange will surely thrive and prosper,' Ozzam observed. 'I, sadly, can only get obedience through fear.' He drained his glass. 'What of tomorrow?'

'Just come down to the gym as planned,' Mandy replied softly.

'But you? And your friends?'

'Do not be alarmed at what you see. Let's keep the surprise for Celia.'

'So be it. I am in your hands.' He shrugged.

'You certainly have been tonight,' she grinned.

He bowed, conceding the quip. 'I will go and rest.' He turned to go, pausing at the Gibbet. 'What is this? Some domestic device? Such a thing is not to be found in Beirut.'

'Not in the kitchens, possibly,' Mandy answered enigmatically.

'It's for hanging meat up. Until it is high,' Sonia explained. 'Game meat.'

'High?' Ozzam said, puzzled.

'Ripe,' Mandy explained. 'Toothsome and pliant.'

'Ah, the rabbit, the hare and the pheasant when he is shot, no?'

'Amongst other prey.'

In their bed, Mandy cradled Sonia's sleeping body, from time to time caressing the shoulders, hips and curved buttocks of the sleeping minx. Dawn was an hour away and, with the sunrise, Mandy knew, came stern duties to be done. But, for the moment, in the silence of these remaining dark hours, there was sweet pleasure to persue.

Mandy thrilled to the loyalty – and bravery – of the little minx. She bent down and kissed the sleeping girl's hair. Sonia murmured and stirred, rustling softly in her sleep as she twisted on the cotton sheet. Mandy risked another kiss, not wanting but half wishing to disturb and awake the minx. Planting her lips lightly against the sleeping eyes, she licked them tenderly with the tip of her tongue. Sonia moaned sweetly and wriggled, her trapped breasts bulging within Mandy's encircling arm. The minx opened her eyes with delight as Mandy succumbed to temptation and kissed her firmly, lingeringly, on the mouth. Sonia opened her lips, accepting Mandy's gently probing tongue.

The minx snuggled down into the bed, still relishing the squeeze of Mandy's encircling arm. At the window, an owl hooted softly. Soon the larks would be soaring into the violet of the breaking dawn. Spreading her thighs, Sonia inched her bottom up from the sheet, willing her pubis up to Mandy's impatient fingers. Stroking the soft curls, Mandy slipped her forefinger between the moist labia. The minx wriggled, jerking her hips up higher. Turning her hand slowly, Mandy positioned her wrist at the wet warmth, dragging it up and down against the minx's slit. Sonia squeezed her thighs together, trapping the slender wrist at her heat with a shrill squeal of glee.

Perched on her left elbow above the wriggling nude, Mandy smiled down gently at the happy face on the pillow. Kissing the tip of Sonia's nose, she twisted her wrist, rotating it cunningly. It was a tender pleasuring. Not for them the rabid carnality and frantic thrusting of Celia and Erica.

At the window, the dawn chorus broke with lyrical birdsong. The little minx came just as sweetly, burbling her contented satisfaction just as gently as the soaring linnet. Wriggling down in the bed, she mouthed Mandy's breasts and then her belly, until she brought her mouth against her pubic mound. Pressing her lips to the sweet flesh, she sucked and licked, her tongue-tip finding the erect clitoris. Mandy's belly fluttered and imploded as, minutes later, she crushed her spasming climax down into Sonia's shining face. The sun climbed up through the pink and silver clouds, its golden fingers stroking their nakedness as they lay, limbs interlocked, lips to lips, bosom to bosom, slit to slit.

'Time to go,' Mandy said, her voice breaking the silence. 'We'd better get down to the gym.'

Kissing her, Sonia slipped out of bed and scrambled for a bra and panties.

'Don't bother. They'll expect to find us naked. We won't disappoint them.'

The double doors slapped together as they entered the gym.

'We knew you'd come down here,' Sophie squeaked, bounding out of the shadows and hugging Mandy. 'Partridge and I will stand by you, whatever happens. We're all in this together.'

'Yes,' the brown-eyed housekeeper echoed, joining them. 'It is what your aunt would have wished, Mandy.'

Mandy blinked the tears of emotion and affection from her eyes. For all they knew, these two could be aboard a private jet before dusk, Beirut bound for a vile servitude in bondage, yet they had chosen to remain.

'What now?' Sophie whispered. 'There's still time. Flight or fight?'

'Fight,' Mandy hissed. 'Trust me, the odds are not as bad as they seem.'

'Then we should get back to the wall bars and let

them find us as they left us. At least we'll have the element of surprise,' Partridge suggested.

They each assumed the position Erica had left them in after last night's slave sale, contriving to wear loosened gags and cords that to the superficial glance appeared tightly secure.

Mandy closed her eyes. Who was boiling the early-morning kettles? she wondered. Were the other maids making melba toast to the exacting requirements of the residents? Were the flowers cut and arranged in their crystal vases? Were the quails' eggs softly boiled and peeled?

The greed of Celia and the blind obedience of Erica had caused standards of service to slip of late at Sternwood Grange. Mandy felt the blood of her aunt flowing through her. Like Aunt Clare, she took a fierce pride in the comfort of her residents. In the face of impending danger, all she could think of was clean linen, fresh bamboo canes and the other luxuries demanded by her guests. The residents came first – in every respect. Only one mind could focus on that absolute maxim, she realised with a sudden glow of pride: the mind of the mistress of Sternwood Grange.

The double doors slapped together as Celia Flaxstone, followed by Erica, Ozzam and his entourage, entered the gym. Flicking on the harsh neon lights, they formed a semi-circle facing the display of naked bottoms at the wall bars.

'What have you there?' Celia asked brightly after greetings had been exchanged between the new arrivals.

'This?' Mandy heard Ozzam's smooth voice reply. 'This is the whip I promised you.'

'You have bought a whip for me?' she said delightedly.

'Yes,' he countered evenly, 'I have bought a whip for you.'

'Excellent. After the sale is concluded, we shall have a whipping party to seal the exchange of contracts.'

'There will certainly be a whipping,' Ozzam said softly, 'but there will be no sale.'

'No sale?' the solicitor gasped, her voice rising a shrill octave. 'But we agreed –'

'Ah, greed. Now there is an interesting word.'

'I said agreed. It was agreed –'

'Nothing was agreed except that I would bring a whip. For you.'

Erica suddenly paled, sensing the threat in his ominous tone. She backed away several paces. An alert heavy blocked her retreat, propelling her back under the glare of the neon.

'Those who cheat Ozzam pay a heavy price. More than the bloated price you tried to extort from me.'

Celia quavered, sensing danger, but her professional training loosened her brain and tongue. 'If you wish to negotiate a lower price, we will do so. I only asked –'

'For something you were not entitled to,' he thundered. 'You are not the mistress of Sternwood Grange.'

Fear turned the solicitor's face pale. She clutched at her throat nervously.

'I was only doing what she told me to do,' Erica suddenly snivelled. 'None of this has anything to do with me –'

'Such disloyalty.' Ozzam smiled sadly, uncurling the whip slowly. With a vicious snap-crack, he lashed the polished wooden floor. 'And yet,' he continued, coiling the whip around his left hand, 'I have seen true loyalty here at Sternwood Grange.'

'Take these four and go,' Celia stammered. 'Just go, now. They are yours –'

'These four are neither yours to give nor mine to take,' Ozzam whispered.

Erica made a desperate dash for the door. Springing from their pretence of bondage, Sophie and Partridge intercepted her. Celia Flaxstone shrieked her astonishment.

'Come here, my little English rose,' Ozzam boomed lustily, signalling to Mandy. 'Are you sure you will not sell me Sternwood Grange?'

Mandy smiled and kissed him but shook her head. 'No. I have fallen in love with my inheritance. I propose to stay here. Partridge, you are in charge once more. Will you take Sophie as your assistant?'

The housekeeper, overwhelmed by the speed of the unfolding drama, nodded vigorously.

'I know you will treat the maids fairly, and pay them well. Though,' she added softly, running her finger over the coiled whip in Ozzam's clenched fist, 'I trust you will be firm when it is necessary for you to be so.'

'You have chosen wisely, English rose. They have proven their loyalty to you and will continue to do so. Your enterprise will prosper, of that I have no doubt. But there is one small purchase I wish to make.'

'Name it,' Mandy murmured. 'If I can grant it, it will be yours, Ozzam.'

He pointed the levelled whip at Celia and Erica. They struggled and cursed but were easily overpowered by the attendant heavies.

'There is a place for both of them in my humble house of pleasures.'

'No,' Erica screamed. 'You can't –'

A huge paw at her lips smothered her anguished protests.

'You cannot buy them,' Mandy said.

A ray of hope gleamed in Celia's grey eyes.

'No?' he queried, his sensual lips pursing in disappointment.

'But you can take them freely. I want no payment. It is purely a private matter between yourselves.' She grinned.

Ozzam laughed, a delighted, braying bark. He cracked the whip with evident relish.

Celia paled to an ashen white, slumping in the grip of

259

the heavies. She trembled with fear and rage, cursing Mandy and Ozzam.

'Gag them both,' Ozzam ordered. Gags were brutally applied.

'You are taking them back to Beirut?' Mandy asked.

'Yes. But first, I was promised a whipping party. Let us see if Miss Flaxstone can honour at least one promise.'

'May I see your whip? It is something of a speciality, I believe.'

'Take it, English rose. I know you will put it to good use.' He handed her the four and a half feet of supple hide. 'It is the stretched penis of a bull camel. I store it in virgin olive oil to keep the lash pliant.'

Mandy weighed the six ounces of potent pain in her open palm. The oiled hide gleamed, causing her slit to pulse and moisten.

'It is surprisingly light,' she whispered.

'And surprisingly lethal,' he chuckled darkly. 'Only to be used by a skilled hand. Are you an adept in the arts of discipline?'

'Practice makes perfect, I am told. What time do you plan to depart?'

'A little after noon.'

'Then we must lunch together before you go.'

'We have so little, yet so much, in common. I would like to invest in Sternwood Grange, against a percentage of your profit. And you must come to visit me in Beirut.'

'Splendid. We will drink a toast to both ideas.' Turning to Erica, she pointed the whip at the wretched cropped blonde. 'Take her to the Gibbet. Punish her thoroughly, each of you.'

Partridge and Sophie, hand in hand, led the procession out of the gym, with the bodyguards bringing up the rear. Mandy crushed the coiled whip to her naked bosom, thrilling to the glistening hide at her nipples. Soon, Mandy knew, her loyal friends would have the cropped blonde stripped and suspended in the Gibbet. Soon, Mandy thought, eager hands would be grasping canes to stripe-slice Erica's naked buttocks.

'And see to it that every resident is served with chilled champagne with their breakfast,' she called out after them. 'Today is a day for celebrations.'

Celia, gagged but unbound, inched towards the double doors.

'You cannot escape,' Mandy warned. 'There is nowhere for you to go, except Beirut.'

Grappling at her gag and loosening it, the desperate solicitor tried to bargain. Vast sums were mumbled.

'You may remove the gag,' Mandy conceded coldly, ignoring all the urgent pleading. 'I have no objection to hearing your sobs of torment when I whip you. Take your clothes off. Strip,' she barked sternly. 'I want you naked for the lash.'

Ozzam strode across the polished floor and grasped Celia's blouse. 'May I?' he asked Mandy.

'She is yours, Ozzam. Do what you will. All I crave is one session with the whip.'

'That I grant you freely,' he grunted, ripping the blouse savagely from his captive. The dark skirt was dragged down, leaving Celia shivering in fear and dread, clad only in a white brassiere and sheer black tights.

'I want her naked,' Mandy whispered, 'with her hands bound.'

Ozzam used his mouth, biting the brassiere away and spilling the solicitor's heavy breasts. Standing behind her, he ground his pelvis into the sheen of the tights across her swollen buttocks and cupped her bosoms, squeezing masterfully.

'The fruit is ripe – the harvest will be heavy,' he grunted, closing his eyes in an ecstasy of lustful anticipation.

'Bare bottomed and bound,' Mandy prompted, cracking her whip.

261

Ozzam opened his eyes and smiled. 'As you command, my little English rose.'

He thumbed the black tights down over the swell of the quivering cheeks and dragged them away from the wriggling feet below. Binding the tights around Celia's wrists at her belly, he presented the naked solicitor to Mandy for inspection.

'I'll punish her across the vaulting horse,' Mandy announced, pacing softly across the floor to stand before Celia.

The whip rose and addressed each swollen breast, teasing each painfully peaked nipple up into purple buds of exquisite torment. Mandy traced the oiled leather down across the flat belly and stroked the pubic curls below.

'To the horse,' she commanded.

Ozzam lifted the wriggling solicitor in his fierce grip and carried her across to the scuffed hide of the vaulting horse. Arranging Celia face down along its leather back, he stood aside, his eyes hot coals of eager expectation.

Amanda Silk drew herself up to her proud height. Flicking the whip back, she judged the distance, so that each of the twenty lashes would sear and stripe the bare buttocks accurately, pitilessly and ruthlessly. She snapped the whip – a practice crack to test its suppleness. Across the hide of the horse, the naked cheeks clenched in a spasm of dread. The whipper smiled, knowing that the next time the harsh leather snapped, the bare bottom would jerk in earnest.

NEW BOOKS

Nexus

There are three Nexus titles published in May

The Correction of an Essex Maid by Yolanda Celbridge
May 1998   Price £5.99   ISBN: 0 352 33255 7
Rescued from degradation, naive young orphan Sophia joins the
House of Rodings, a training school dedicated to the worship and
correction of the naked female rear. She meets a cast of submissive
and dominant females, all adoring or envious of Sophia's voluptuous
bottom. Becoming mistress of the school's flagellant society, she
thrives in the complex ranks, rules, and punishments of the House's
hierarchy. By the author of the popular *Governess* and *Maldona*
series, also available from Nexus.

Rites of Obedience by Lindsay Gordon
May 1998   Price £5.99   ISBN: 0 352 33256 5
When shy journalist Penny Chambers is sent by her boss to investigate the cause of Whitehead Academy's unusual success, she is not
prepared for the dark new sexuality that the strange academy, its
lascivious students and stern staff awaken in her. The student's education consists of a wide spectrum of specialist erotic training – in
both submission and domination – under a strict regime of discipline.

Annie by Evelyn Culber
May 1998   Price £5.99   ISBN: 0 352 32881 9
Taken into service in a Victorian stately house on the outskirts of
London, the young Annie swiftly learns her duties as a special kind
of maid. Under the watchful eye and the corrective hand of her
female guardians, she is set to perform a variety of indelicate enter-
tainments for special guests whose pleasures are found by indulging
their affections for the unique loving and chastisement of such pretty
young posteriors. This is a new edition of one of Nexus's most
popular tales of correction.

Amazon Slave by Lisette Ashton
June 1998   Price £5.99   ISBN: 0 352 33260 3
Stranded, alone and penniless in the Amazon basin, Emily thinks things can't get any worse. It is only when she boards the *Amazon Maiden*, however, that her dark journey truly begins. The captain expects only one thing from his crew: absolute obedience. Insubordination is not tolerated; punishment is delivered swiftly and mercilessly. Captivated by the beautiful Emily and her arrogant defiance, the captain is determined to enjoy her submission. By the author of *The Black Room*.

A Master of Discipline by Zoe Templeton
June 1998   Price £5.99   ISBN: 0 352 33261 1
When naive young schoolteacher Ruth is sent by her employers to Damocles Priory to learn how to administer punishment, she has no idea that the emphasis will be on practical experience. After her initial reluctance, she allows the masterful clergyman Reverend Mould to help her live out her submissive fantasies and to explore her most perverse desires. Damocles Priory is not all it seems to be, however, and the lewd reverend is taking an unusually personal interest in Ruth's education. Will she learn to take the upper hand before it is too late? By the author of *A Degree of Discipline*.

Nexus

NEXUS BACKLIST

All books are priced £4.99 unless another price is given. If a date is supplied, the book in question will not be available until that month in 1998.

CONTEMPORARY EROTICA

THE ACADEMY	Arabella Knight		
AGONY AUNT	G. C. Scott		
ALLISON'S AWAKENING	Lauren King		
AMAZON SLAVE	Lisette Ashton	£5.99	June
THE BLACK ROOM	Lisette Ashton		Mar
BOUND TO SUBMIT	Amanda Ware		
CANDIDA IN PARIS	Virginia Lasalle		
A CHAMBER OF DELIGHTS	Katrina Young		
THE CHASTE LEGACY	Susanna Hughes		
A DEGREE OF DISCIPLINE	Zoe Templeton		Feb
THE DOMINO TATTOO	Cyrian Amberlake		
THE DOMINO QUEEN	Cyrian Amberlake		
EDUCATING ELLA	Stephen Ferris		
EMMA'S SUBMISSION	Hilary James		
EMMA'S SECRET DOMINATION	Hilary James		Jan
FALLEN ANGELS	Kendal Grahame		
THE TRAINING OF FALLEN ANGELS	Kendal Grahame		
HEART OF DESIRE	Maria del Rey		
HOUSE OF TEMPTATIONS	Yvonne Strickland		
THE ISLAND OF MALDONA	Yolanda Celbridge		
THE CASTLE OF MALDONA	Yolanda Celbridge		
THE ICE QUEEN	Stephen Ferris		
JENNIFER'S INSTRUCTION	Cyrian Amberlake		
JOURNEY FROM INNOCENCE	Jean-Philippe Aubourg		

JULIE AT THE REFORMATORY	Angela Elgar		Feb
A MASTER OF DISCIPLINE	Zoe Templeton	£5.99	Jun
A MATTER OF POSSESSION	G. C. Scott		
MELINDA AND THE COUNTESS	Susanna Hughes		
MELINDA AND SOPHIA	Susanna Hughes		
MELINDA AND ESMERELDA	Susanna Hughes		
THE MISTRESS OF STERNWOOD GRANGE	Arabella Knight		Apr
THE NEW STORY OF O	Anonymous		
ONE WEEK IN THE PRIVATE HOUSE	Esme Ombreux		Mar
AMANDA IN THE PRIVATE HOUSE	Esme Ombreux		
PARADISE BAY	Maria del Rey		
THE REWARD OF FAITH	Elizabeth Bruce		
RITES OF OBEDIENCE	Lindsay Gordon	£5.99	May
THE SCHOOLING OF STELLA	Yolanda Celbridge		
SECRETS OF THE WHIPCORD	Michaela Wallace		
SHERRIE AND THE INITIATION OF PENNY	Evelyn Culber		
STEPHANIE'S CASTLE	Susanna Hughes		
STEPHANIE'S PLEASURE	Susanna Hughes		
VIRGINIA'S QUEST	Katrina Young		
WEB OF DOMINATION	Yvonne Strickland		

ANCIENT & FANTASY SETTINGS

CAPTIVES OF ARGAN	Stephen Ferris	
THE CLOAK OF APHRODITE	Kendal Grahame	
DEMONIA	Kendal Grahame	
THE DUNGEONS OF LIDIR	Aran Ashe	
THE FOREST OF BONDAGE	Aran Ashe	
NYMPHS OF DIONYSUS	Susan Tinoff	
PYRAMID OF DELIGHTS	Kendal Grahame	

EDWARDIAN, VICTORIAN & OLDER EROTICA

ANNIE	Evelyn Culber	£5.99	May
ANNIE AND THE COUNTESS	Evelyn Culber		Apr
BEATRICE	Anonymous		
CHOOSING LOVERS FOR JUSTINE	Aran Ashe		
THE CORRECTION OF AN ESSEX MAID	Yolanda Celbridge	£5.99	May
DEAR FANNY	Michelle Clare		
LYDIA IN THE BORDELLO	Philippa Masters		
LYDIA IN THE HAREM	Philippa Masters		
LURE OF THE MANOR	Barbra Baron		
MAN WITH A MAID 3	Anonymous		
MEMOIRS OF A CORNISH GOVERNESS	Yolanda Celbridge		
THE GOVERNESS AT ST AGATHA'S	Yolanda Celbridge		
PRIVATE MEMOIRS OF A KENTISH HEADMISTRESS	Yolanda Celbridge		Feb
SISTERS OF SEVERCY	Jean Aveline		Mar

SAMPLERS & COLLECTIONS

EROTICON 3	Various	
THE FIESTA LETTERS	ed. Chris Lloyd	
NEW EROTICA 2	ed. Esme Ombreux	
NEW EROTICA 3	ed. Esme Ombreux	

NON-FICTION

HOW TO DRIVE YOUR WOMAN WILD IN BED	Graham Masterton	
HOW TO DRIVE YOUR MAN WILD IN BED	Graham Masterton	
LETTERS TO LINZI	Linzi Drew	

Please send me the books I have ticked above.

Name   ....

Address   ....

               ....

               ....

               .... Post code ....

Send to: **Cash Sales, Nexus Books, 332 Ladbroke Grove, London W10 5AH**

Please enclose a cheque or postal order, made payable to **Nexus Books**, to the value of the books you have ordered plus postage and packing costs as follows:

UK and BFPO – £1.00 for the first book, 50p for the second book, and 30p for each subsequent book to a maximum of £3.00;

Overseas (including Republic of Ireland) – £2.00 for the first book, £1.00 for the second book, and 50p for each subsequent book.

If you would prefer to pay by VISA or ACCESS/MASTERCARD, please write your card number and expiry date here:

....

Please allow up to 28 days for delivery.

Signature ....